The Butterfly PROJECT

Emma Scott

Author of the Full Tilt duet

The Butterfly Project

Cover art by Melissa Panio-Petersen

Interior Formatting by That Formatting Lady,
https://thatformattinglady.com/

Mother, May I? graphic novel concept by Emma Scott

Mother, May I? graphic novel original art by Christopher Stewart,
http://redacesmedia.com/

Mother, May I? graphic novel lettering by Nic J. Shaw,
http://www.ironbarkdesignshop.com/blog/

Other Titles by Emma Scott

The Full Tilt Duet
I'd love you forever, if I only had the chance.

How to Save a Life
Let's do something really crazy and trust each other.

RUSH
Maybe was a sunrise on a new day. Maybe was hope.

Acknowledgments

This book exists because of the love, help, and support of Melissa Panio-Petersen, Robin Renee Hill, Joy Kriebel-Sadowski, Angela Bonnie Shockley, Sarah Torpey, Hilaria Alexander, K. Larsen, Emma Adams, Noemie Heloin, Bill Hairston, Christopher Stewart, Kathleen Ripley, and Jennifer Balogh, as well as with every last member of Emma's Entourage. You never cease to amaze me; your support has been so incredible, so constant, so warm and enthusiastic, I'm just overwhelmed every day.

Bloggers and readers…Where on earth would I be without you? Every time I release a book I'm reminded all over again of the generosity of the blogging community; a volunteer army that reads and reviews or promotes simply for the love of books. I'm so grateful to all of you for what you do, for me and every other author seeking to have their voice heard.

Melissa Panio-Petersen, you are so much more than my right-hand gal. You are an amazing artist, graphic designer, and one of the most thoughtful and kind-hearted people I've ever known (with a wicked sense of humor to boot). I want to be you when I grow up. Thank you, and with love.

Suanne Laqueur…this is my fourth book to have benefitted from your editorial genius, and for four books I've been promising that there won't be a crazy-ass deadline. And in all four instances, the deadline has been crazy and yet you come through for me with humor, love, and sex jokes to spare. Let's always be us.

Playlist

Heathens, 21 Pilots
Don't Stop Believing, Journey
My Way, Frank Sinatra
Purple Rain, Prince
One Way or Another, Blondie
You're the Inspiration, Chicago
I'll Be Home for Christmas, Frank Sinatra
Oasis, Wonderwall
HandClap, Fitz and The Tantrums
Human, Rag'n'Bone Man
Man To Build a Home, the Cinematic Orchestra

Dedication

For Robin, my searchlight in the fog.

I may have strayed off the path and wandered aimlessly from time to time, but thanks to you I was never lost.

The Butterfly PROJECT

Part I

"My vengeance is my guilt."
--Ovid, *Metamorphoses*

ASK.
MOTHER
MAY I ...?
By Zelda Robi
CHACK
MOTHER... M-MAY I... LIVE?
NO.
BLAM
BLAM

1

Zelda
November 29th

"No heart," I whispered into my coat collar.

Icy wind howled down the crowded New York City street, whipping my long black hair behind me, and ripping the words from my mouth. My eyes stung but it was just the wind. I never cried. Never. Not even after being rejected by three of the biggest graphic novel publishers in Manhattan. My eyes were watering from the wind.

Three rejections in two days. The managing editors at each publishing house bled together in my memory to form one composite bastard, his smug, indifferent eyebrows raised over my work. Mildly impressed, but not impressed enough.

"Interesting concept and excellent art. But…pass."

The third pass from BlackStar Publishing came with a tiny glimmer of hope, though. The managing editor wasn't interested, but as the meeting ended, his assistant pulled me aside. Iris Hannover looked hardly older than my twenty-four years, with dark hair, red lipstick and a hard look from behind her stylish glasses. A hard look, but not a mean one. As if she were sizing me up.

"It's not even December and everyone's in vacation mode," Iris had said. "If you can make some revisions and get me the storyboards within the next few weeks, I'll make sure my editor takes a second look."

"What kind of revisions?" I said.

"You have something here." Iris tapped my portfolio. "Your art is fantastic, but the story has no guts. It's all premise, no pulse. No heart. Find the heart."

"No heart," I whispered again.

I blinked hard, glancing at 6th Avenue where a slow train of cars and cabs made its way uptown. Everything was gray. The sky, the pavement, the buildings. A drab cityscape sketched in charcoal and black ink, where the only thing the colorist remembered was the yellow of the cabs. Pedestrians jostled me, bundled against the chill in hats and scarves. Their stride was brisk. Unlike me, they knew where they were going, and what came next.

I clutched my portfolio tighter. My soul was inside it. The mock-ups for my graphic novel, *Mother, May I?*

And it has no heart.

I could admit it wasn't sentimental or emotional. No romance or tears. It was pure violence and action. A dystopian time-travel story of blood and vengeance. My heroine's quest was to murder pedophiles and kidnappers before they could act. To save her soul from the guilt and regret she'd lived with since the murder of her own child. There was no knight in shining armor swooping in to do it for her.

Isn't that what audiences wanted? A *Jessica Jones* or a *Black Widow*? A tough heroine who kicked ass and didn't need a man to save her?

No, they wanted heart. Good fucking luck with that. My heart had been ripped away from me when my nine-year-old sister, Rosemary, was snatched in a Philadelphia grocery story on a summer afternoon ten years ago. A horrorshow that unfolded between the aisles of breakfast cereals and soups. I'd watched it happen and I couldn't stop it. I failed her, and the guilt for that failure had been eating away at me from the inside out like a cancer ever since. *Mother, May I?* was born of that howling pain.

It was either draw or lose my fucking mind.

Iris, the assistant at BlackStar, wanted revised storyboards in a couple of weeks. But I had no clue how to find the heart of the story, and no good place to work on it. Over the last three days, my food, cab fare, and rent at the shithole youth hostel where I was staying had eaten through my savings like a plague of locusts. I could go back to Vegas, but it felt like utter defeat.

I needed a quiet place to think and sort this out. This corner of 6th Avenue wasn't the place to do it. I wiped my stinging eyes on the back of my sleeve—*stupid wind*—and stepped to the curb, hand raised to hail a cab before I remembered my dwindling funds.

No more cabs, Miss Money Bags, I scolded myself. I'd have to brave the subway system or figure out the bus.

I crossed the street to the subway station and took the staircase down. It was a short ride from Midtown to the hostel near the Port Authority. I emerged from the subway and walked along a busy sidewalk fronting adult stores, smoke shops and bail bonds outlets.

The Parkside Hostel wasn't anywhere near a park, but sat above a tiny shop that sold NYC touristy kitsch: sweatshirts and snow globes, key chains and Statue of Liberty piggy banks.

When I first got out of the cab three days ago, all the touristy junk made me smile. Like the naïve dumbshit I was, I'd bought a tacky postcard that screamed "Makin' it in the Big Apple!" across the top. It was cheesy as hell, and after one of the publishers wrote up a contract for *Mother, May I?* I was going to send the postcard to Theo, my friend and boss at the tattoo shop where I'd worked in Vegas. He'd get a laugh out of it.

Two steps inside the hostel's grungy foyer with its dirty tile and flickering fluorescents, and I could already hear loud talk, shouting, and blaring music coming from the upstairs hallways. I could hardly sleep here, never mind work.

My first night at the Parkside had been roommate-free. I spent the long hours like Tom Hanks in *Big*: rickety dresser pushed up against the door and me curled in a ball on the bed. I tried to make myself as small as possible while watching a roach scuttle along the floorboard against the wall. Scared shitless.

But I didn't cry.

I unlocked the door to my room. The bright red and yellow of the postcard I bought for Theo was the first thing that caught my eye. The second thing was that every item of clothing I'd brought to New York, minus what I was wearing, were strewn all over the floor, along with travel-sized bottles of shampoo, soap and lotion; even my little box of birth control pills. The room had a bank of four lockers. My assigned locker's door was bent and hanging off one hinge. The second night of my stay, a roommate had stormed in, grunted her name—Jane—and dumped a ratty-looking sleeping bag onto her bed. She stuffed a blue duffel into one of the room's two lockers and took off. I hadn't seen her since.

Now, all of her stuff was gone.

"The hell…?"

My heart began to pound, and I backed straight out of the room, heading downstairs to the front desk, which resembled more of a subway tollbooth. I rapped on the plexiglass with a shaking hand to get the attention of the manager. He was a bored-looking guy with a balding head and potbelly. He rifled through a nudie magazine and puffed a miniature cigar, the smoke of which filled the box and seeped out of the round hole cut at the bottom of the glass.

"My room," I said. "Someone broke into my room. They went through my bag. My roommate is gone and so is her stuff. Maybe it was her?"

I don't know what I expected—the same level of outrage maybe. Or at least mild concern. Instead the guy heaved a sigh and tossed his magazine down. "Christ. Did you remember to lock the fucking door on your locker?"

I stared. "What…? Yes. Of course," I said, anger burning up some of my fear. "Yeah, I locked the damn door but someone tore it off."

"Shit," the guy said. "Did they steal anything?"

"I don't know," I said. "I kind of freaked out. I didn't stick around to look."

Of all the stupid things I'd done since getting here, leaving my money in that hostel room was not one of them. I kept my stash tucked into a wallet that attached to my belt loop and fit under my black pants. I carried my laptop with my art portfolio. The only other items of value were my art supplies…

Oh my God.

I felt the blood drain from my face, like a sketch leeched of color. "Oh no. Oh shit, no."

Panic drove me back upstairs, vaguely aware of the manager's heavy tread on the stairs behind me. I rifled through my stuff, feeling ill that someone else—some stranger—had had their hands on my clothes. My *underwear*. But they'd left it all. The only clothing items of value were my pea coat and boots, both of which I was wearing. But my art supplies were gone. My fold-up, portable desk, my pens and pencils, my Canson drawing pad…

Why? Why would anyone steal pens and paper?

Because they were the best kind. My prized possessions. The tools by which I created my art. I felt as though I were missing fingers from my hand.

"Anything taken?" the manager asked.

"Everything," I said, my stomach clenching so hard I could

barely breathe. "They took everything."

The manager made a disbelieving hmmph. "Doesn't look like it to me. You got stuff all over."

It's over. It's all over.

I swallowed down tears and began throwing my clothes into a pile.

"Are you going to call the police," I muttered, as I gathered my stuff. "Or do all of your guests get free access to other guests' personal belongings?" I stopped, glanced around. "Wait. My suitcase. Where the fuck is my suitcase?"

My black, brand-new rolling suitcase—a gift from one of my roommates when I left Vegas—was nowhere to be seen.

"They took that too," I said. "They took my suitcase and they took my art." I spun around to glare at the manager. "Not *they. She.* The girl you put in here with me. It had to be her, right?"

"I suppose so." The manager sighed and pulled a smartphone from his pocket.

Two police officers arrived thirty minutes later. I waited in the lobby, the rest of my clothes and toiletries in a black trash bag on my lap. The cops took my statement and said they'd searched the rest of the rooms but didn't find anything.

"Roommate checked-in under the name Jane Doe," the manager said. "As in D-O-U-G-H."

"Jane Dough?" I pinned the manager with a hard look. "Are you fucking kidding me?"

The guy shrugged. "She paid cash. She could call herself Mother Theresa for all I care."

Mother Theresa had checked-out sometime this morning and was now long-fucking-gone.

"We'll let you know if anything turns up," one of the policemen said. His smile was kind, but I could hear the subtext. *Don't hold your breath.*

The manager held up his hands as if to show how empty they were of responsibility. The liability waiver I'd signed upon check-in covered his ass, and he knew it. But after the cops left, he looked at me sitting alone with a goddamn trash bag on my lap, and his face softened a little.

"Hey kid," he said. "How about a free night? Least I can do, right?"

I nearly told him where he could put his free night but the sun was sinking fast. Where was I going to go?

Philadelphia's only a two-hour train ride.

"Fine," I snapped at the manager, cutting off the thought. "I'll take the free night, but I want a *single* room."

He scrubbed the bristle on his chin with fat, stubby fingers, then nodded. "Yeah, yeah, okay."

In my new room, I threw the garbage bag on the full-sized bed and took stock. A tiny desk and chair were in one corner, but no pen or paper in the drawer.

I have no pen or paper.

Blinking hard, I used my phone to calculate my options. I had $700 to my name. If I went back to Vegas—*Don't even think about crying, Rossi*—$300 would get swallowed by the bus ticket. Then another $300 would have to go toward the room I was renting.

If I stayed in New York, my $700 wouldn't last twenty-four hours. A deposit on an apartment would wipe me out and I wouldn't survive the rest of the month. And there was no way I could stay at this hostel instead and try to rework my graphic novel.

"And rework it with what?" I reminded myself with a bitter pang. My art supplies were gone. The thought struck me in the chest every time, followed by the more practical ache that it would cost at least $50 to buy pens and paper that didn't totally suck.

I tossed my phone onto the stiff orange bedcover, calculations done. The upshot: I was fucked. Failed. I'd have to go back to Vegas, to my old room in the over-crowded apartment, with a rotating door of roommates. I was sure Theo would give me my job back at the tattoo place, but I didn't want it. I was tired of tattooing. I hated watching my art get up and walk out the door, never to be seen again. I wanted something to hold in my hands. Something the entire world could see…

Your stupidity is matched only by your pride.

Tears threatened and I hurled myself off the bed before they could take hold. I stuffed the trash bag of my belongings into the locker and slammed it shut. It was dinnertime.

I had to admit defeat, but I decided the city owed me one decent meal before I left for Vegas. I grabbed my portfolio and headed out.

2

Zelda
November 29th

Rupert—one of my Vegas roommates—told me the East Village was the place to get an artsy feel for the city. The last thing I felt was artsy but having a general direction was better than feeling completely fucking clueless and lost. I went back to the subway and jumped on a train heading in a south-easterly direction. I got out at the Astor Place Station, and walked along St. Marks to 2nd Avenue.

I was trying to keep note of my surroundings—bohemian-looking bars and shops—while I searched for a place to eat that wasn't total crap without breaking my puny bank either.

I stopped in front of a small Italian bistro. A red and white-striped awning read Giovanni's. *How cliché*, I thought while letting myself be enveloped by the warm scent seeping into the street. Tomato sauce and garlic, basil and rosemary…

Rosemary.

A wave of homesickness swamped me so hard, I was dizzy. My mom's kitchen had smelled like this, once upon a time.

I clutched my portfolio to my chest like a shield and pushed open Giovanni's front door. The bistro was tiny—fifteen tables, each with a glass cup burning a lone candle. Plastic red and white-checkered tablecloths, plastic bunches of grapes on the wall, and poorly painted Italian landscapes.

Cliché central, and yet the food smelled just as good as my mom's. The scent wrapped around me and carried me to memories of her kitchen, to a time when I had a sister. When the two of us bickered and pulled each other's hair, then dodged the light swat of Mom's wooden spoon for rough housing like animals near the hot stove.

Go home, a voice whispered in my mind. *Get on a train and go home.*

But home wasn't what it had been. Rosemary's abduction had dropped my family from a great height of warmth and love, to shatter like glass at the bottom of a cold black pit. We were all broken—my parents, grandparents, aunts and uncles… My big, loud, Italian family muted by the unthinkable.

Was my mother cooking again? I didn't know the household routines anymore; I'd been away for six years. A self-imposed outcast. The guilt of my unimaginable failure to Rosemary had made me an exile. My mother's gentle urging lured me back, and once or twice a year I gave in and visited, hoping this time I could believe them when they said it hadn't been my fault. And every time I was left panic-stricken and shattered by memories that screamed otherwise. Those memories had driven me from the urban sprawl of Philadelphia to the deserts of Nevada, where nothing looked familiar.

Giovanni's was familiar.

The grief and homesickness was a tidal wave now, and I nearly bolted back outside. The bartender called at me from behind the long curl of mahogany running the length of the restaurant.

"How many, miss?"

I knew being this close to Philly was a risk when I came out east, but the onslaught of memories was almost too much. I wasn't a coward. I was tough. A tough cookie, my dad used to tell me. *A tough cookie who didn't back down from anything.* I wasn't about to let memories bully me back into the cold New York night.

"Table for one," I told the rotund man who wore shirtsleeves, a vest, and a tie that also had grapes on it.

He jerked his head at a tiny two-top near the back. I took the seat, the shakiness wearing off as I realized how hungry I was.

I can do this. Be normal. Eat something.

I set my portfolio at my feet. The candle flickered in its cup on the table. A busboy wordlessly dropped off a hard plastic cup with water and two slivers of ice floating in it while I perused the menu.

A waitress—a friendly young woman with dark hair piled on her head and gold hoop earrings—took my order: ziti and a glass of house red wine. I was doing a pretty good job of managing the utter shittiness of the situation until she came back and plunked the steaming food in front of me. It was just like Mom's, I thought, except that my mother would've added too much basil to hers, and my grandmother would've complained and they'd spend the rest of the night bickering…

My vision blurred. My chest felt tight and I couldn't get the air past my throat. I pushed from the table toward the tiny hallway that led to the bathrooms. The women's restroom door was locked.

"Shit."

Without thinking, I hurried through the too-bright kitchen, past the steam and cleanser-smelling dishwasher, and out the back door to a tiny alley lined with a rickety wooden fence. A dumpster faced the restaurant, its lids bulging with plastic bags. My breath plumed in shaky little bursts, and I hugged myself in the bracing cold.

Get a grip, I thought. *Jesus, it's just food. It's just… this city. You failed, so what? You're not the first naïve twit New York chewed up and spit out, and you definitely won't be the last.*

Tough talk but meaningless. It wasn't my graphic novel being rejected that hurt; I could take it if the art wasn't up to par. But being told it had no heart…

No heart. It wasn't my *heart*; it was my lungs gasping for air as I'd chased after the van. It was my voice screaming for help, *someone please fucking help* because I couldn't run fast enough. I hadn't screamed loud enough. I'd failed Rosie then, and I'd failed her now. Failed to tell the story. The book was an apology spread out over a hundred black and white pages, colored with tears and inked with regret; everything I didn't do that day was embedded in the drawings, and my heroine's rage—her merciless thirst for vengeance—was my only relief.

And it was rejected.

"Now what the fuck do I do?" I whispered.

"I don't know," a low, gravelly male voice said from behind. "Maybe not freeze to death in this stinking alley?"

I nearly jumped out of my damn skin and spun around. A tall, lean guy around my twenty-four years was at the backdoor of the restaurant, garbage bag in hand. Blond hair and a scruff of beard, wearing a white dress shirt, black pants, and white apron. The busboy.

"You okay?" he asked.

"You scared the shit out of me."

"Sorry." He chucked the garbage into the dumpster, then fished in his back pocket and produced a pack of cigarettes. "Why are you hanging around back here?"

I shrugged and stood as tall as my five-foot, three-inch height would allow. “Seems as good a place as any,” I said.

The guy lit a smoke. “Are you lost?”

Yes, in every way possible.

“No, I just needed some air.”

He gave me a dry look. “Some fresh, garbage-smelling air?”

A smartass. One of my people. But not what I needed at the moment. I started for the back door. “Whatever. Sorry to bother you.”

“You’re not bothering me.” He exhaled twin plumes of smoke from his nose. The smoke mixed with the vapor of his breath in the chill air. He didn’t say anything more but watched me with dark blue eyes under furrowed brows, nonchalant but observant.

“Aren’t you supposed to be working?” I asked.

“Smoke break.” He held up his cigarette. “I thought that was fairly self-evident.”

“Touché.”

“Want one?”

“I don’t smoke.”

“Probably for the best. Your food’s going to get cold.”

“And then I won’t get any dessert?”

The corner of his lip turned up, and he settled himself on one of three stairs leading to the back door of the restaurant. “What’s the matter?”

“I just needed a moment alone,” I said. “But I guess that’s not going to happen.”

“Guess not.”

My eyes widened. “God, you’re annoying.” I shivered in my coat, my stomach still growling. Cigarettes, I remembered, were great appetite suppressants. “Okay, yes, I’ll take a smoke.”

He produced the pack again and scooted over to make room for me on the stairs. I sat beside him, and pulled my long hair out of the way. I took the cigarette and watched him as he lit it for me. His eyes in the lighter flame were a dark crystalline blue, like a sapphire with a hundred facets…

My chest constricted and my body bent in half as I coughed out a cloud of smoke.

“You okay?”

I nodded vigorously. “It’s been a while,” I said between coughs, my eyes watering. I remembered why I didn’t smoke in the first place. “This tastes like ass.”

The guy smirked. "Put it out carefully and I'll take it back."

"No, I'm good. I think I need it." I inhaled again, let out a long exhale that took some of my anxiety out with it. My rumbling stomach settled down.

For a minute the busboy and I sat on the stoop and smoked in silence. I glanced at him from the corner of my eye. Beneath his long-sleeved shirt, muscles were nicely defined. His jaw was cut at a fine angle and the straight line of his nose was interrupted by a small break. His blond hair was longish on top but short around the sides and his face. God, his face…

He's ridiculously good-looking. Too perfect. Like a hero in a comic.

"You got a name?" he asked, his eyes still on the alley.

"Zelda," I said.

His glanced flickered to me. "Zelda? Like—?"

"Like the game, *The Legend of Zelda?*" I snorted smoke out my nose. "I haven't heard that a hundred million times."

The guy shrugged. "I was going to say like F. Scott Fitzgerald's wife."

"Oh," I said. "Actually…yeah. My mother had a thing for Fitzgerald. I'm named after his wife. My sister—" I coughed, pretended it was the cigarette smoke. "Rosemary. She's named for a character in one of his books."

"*Tender is the Night,*" he said. He took in my widened eyes and looked away. "I had a lot of time to read the last couple of years."

I nodded. I didn't ask why and he didn't ask me about my sister. A good trade.

"And your name is?" I asked.

"Link," he said, and then leaned away from my death glare with a small laugh. "Beckett. It's Beckett."

It suits him perfectly, I thought, and then scolded myself. *How would you know? Don't get stupid over a pretty face.*

"So what's your story, Zelda?" Beckett asked

"Not much to tell," I said. "I came, I saw, I got my ass kicked. New York City is an unforgiving place."

"You're an actress?"

"Artist."

Beckett nodded, exhaling smoke.

"Are you an actor?" I asked. He was good-looking enough, that was for damn sure.

He shook his head. “Bike messenger.”

“Oh. Cool. Bike messenger and busboy.” Beckett shot me a look and I held up my hands. “Nothing wrong with either one. It’s an honest living.”

He snorted. “Yeah. Honest,” he said, spitting the word, and then was silent for a minute. “Anyway, I only bus tables twice a week. For extra cash.”

“I heard rent’s a bitch here.”

“You heard right.”

A short silence fell that wasn’t altogether uncomfortable. I glanced at Beckett sideways again, at the cut of his jaw and the dark blue of his eyes. Even under the shabby lone light over the door, his eyes were brilliant. He was taller than my short frame, and his body exuded safety. It was like being in the lee of a stone sheltering me from the cold wind of the city. For the length of a cigarette anyway.

“Do you live in Manhattan?” I asked.

“Nope. Brooklyn.” He gave me another look. “There’s actually more to New York City than Times Square and the Empire State Building.”

I rolled my eyes. “No kidding? I was going to ask if they were renting apartments in the Statue of Liberty.”

He almost smiled. “You’re looking for a place?”

“Nope, I’m done,” I said. “I’m in over my head already.”

Beckett nodded. “I hear you. I work two jobs and I’m short this month by eighty bucks. I’m going to have to give blood.”

My eyes widened. “You give blood to make rent?”

“Once or twice. It’s no big deal. Clinic on 17th gives $35.”

“You’d still be short $45.”

“I’ll go to another clinic.” Beckett sniffed a laugh at my dismayed expression. “I’m kidding. I’ll sell something. One of my albums, maybe, which would suck.”

“Albums? Like, vinyl?”

He nodded. “I have a few classics, mostly from my grandfather. I inherited his collection when he died. Others are from sidewalk sales. People don’t know what they have and sell cheap.”

I took a shallow drag off my cigarette. It was making me nauseous. Or maybe it was the idea of this guy selling prized possessions—not to mention his *blood*—to make rent.

He must've seen my horrified expression, and he waved his hand, dispersing both the smoke and my worry. "It's no big deal."

"Why don't you get a roommate?" I asked.

"I live in a four hundred square-foot studio. I have yet to meet anyone I'd share that amount of space with without wanting to kill them inside of a week."

I nodded. "Back in Vegas I have my own room in a house with about ten roommates. I can tolerate only two of them and then only half the time." I turned my gaze upward, to the night sky that was hazy with the city lights, and felt impossibly deep and empty. "Why do you stay if it's so hard to live here?"

Beckett took a drag from his cigarette, as if he were buying time before answering.

"Brooklyn, born and raised," he said finally, still not looking at me. "Where else would I go anyway? Different city, same struggle." He finally brought his gaze to mine. "So you're getting out?"

"On the bus, tomorrow," I said. "I can't stay. I was here for a job interview—sort of—and it fell through."

"What was the job?"

"You'll think it's stupid."

"Yeah, I probably will." His smile was dry.

I laughed a little. "Smartass. I draw graphic novels."

He stared at me blankly.

"Long-form comic books that tell one continuous story," I said.

"Like *The Walking Dead*?"

"Exactly. I have one mocked up and I came here to pitch it to a few publishers. They all rejected me. Well, one *half*-rejected me, but it doesn't matter. I can't stay in the city long enough to make any changes, and I wouldn't know what changes to make if I could."

Beckett studied the cigarette between his fingers. "Why can't you stay?"

"Where do I start?" I ground out my cigarette under my boot heel. "My poor planning? My dwindling funds? The fact I was robbed today? Or that I was naively hopeful the publishers would adore my work and sign me on the spot? Take your pick."

Beckett shook his head, his mouth turned down in his grimace. "Wait, go back. You were robbed?"

I nodded and waved away the last of the smoke, wishing my failure could be as easily dissipated. "I came here like a wide-eyed twit with a dream, and I crashed and burned."

"You tried. That's more than most people do."

"Tried and failed."

"So try again."

"I wish," I said, letting my gaze roam over the dingy back alley. "I feel like I'm so close to breaking through. That last publisher gave me some hope. If I could pull a few weeks out of my ass, I'd have a chance. But it's impossible. I have to go back to Nevada."

"You don't have friends or family nearby?"

Yes, and only two hours by train.

"No," I said, and decided I'd said enough to a total stranger. The last thing I needed was the terrible homesickness to well up again. I stood and brushed off the ass of my pants. "Anyway, it is what it is. Thanks for the smoke."

"Were you hurt?"

I turned, glanced down at Beckett. "What?"

"You said you were robbed," he said, his voice low, his eyes holding mine as if he were forcing himself to hear this. "Did they hurt you?"

"No, I… No. I wasn't there. It was a break-in."

He leaned against the wall and his sigh plumed out in front of him in the cold air. It sounded relieved. "I'm sorry, Zelda."

I frowned. "Not your fault. Like I said, the city kicked my ass. The sooner I get the hell out of here, the better for all involved."

Beckett ground out his smoke and got to his feet. He was at least six-two, yet it didn't feel imposing to stand in his shadow. It felt…

Safe. I feel safe with him.

"Do you know how to get back to wherever you're staying?" he asked.

"The same way I got here, only in reverse," I said, covering my unsettling thoughts with sarcasm. Because that was safe for me.

Beckett stared at me a moment more, studying me, and finally seemed to come to some sort of conclusion. "Okay." He walked with me through the kitchen and held the swinging door that led back to the bistro floor open for me. For a moment, I was cloaked in his masculine scent: cold air, cigarette smoke, and cologne.

"Good luck, Zelda."

"Thanks…" I said, inhaling deeply. I came to my senses a second later, called, "You too," just as the swinging kitchen doors closed between us.

The restaurant was cozy-warm compared to outdoors, and nearly empty. The manager was tallying up receipts at the register, while the bartender emptied his dishwasher on the other side. Someone had bagged up my food, and my portfolio—thank God—was still where I had carelessly left it under the table.

I'm on a goddamn roll.

I paid my bill and stepped out into the winter chill. My breath was as thick as the smoke I'd had with Beckett, and I hunched deeper into my pea coat.

Now what?

Back to that shitty hostel for my complimentary free night. I envisioned myself at the bus station the next day, heading back to Las Vegas with my stuff in a trash bag and my tail between my legs. The hostel room wasn't really free. I'd paid for it with my brand new suitcase, my art supplies, and my dignity.

Shame burning my cheeks, I turned right and started walking. I'd told Beckett I was going to take the same subway back, but I had a shit sense of direction. Nothing looked familiar and the buildings rose all around me, making me feel small. And lost.

At the corner, I pulled out my phone to find one of those city transit apps my friends told me about. While I waited for it to load, I heard voices in front of Giovanni's. Beckett was saying goodnight to the bartender and the waitress with a bicycle hauled up on his shoulder. He set it down on the sidewalk as I watched, then took up the helmet slung on the handlebars. He turned my way as he fastened the strap under his chin.

I quickly looked back to my phone.

Out of the corner of my eye, Beckett walked his bike down the twenty feet or so to my corner. He'd changed out of his busboy attire, and now wore black weather-proof pants and a deep blue, well-worn Gor-Tex jacket. His small backpack had a wide strap that ran diagonal across his chest instead of over his shoulders. What looked liked a small CB radio was clipped to it.

"You good?" he asked.

"Peachy."

I tapped an icon of a small bus in white against a lime green backdrop. The app loaded a bunch of buses, subway lines, stations and stops, and a bunch of times next to each.

“Calling a cab?” Beckett asked.

“No, I’m…” I bit off a curse. I didn’t know how to make heads or fucking tails of the app. “I just need to get to the Astor metro station.”

“That’s my station,” he said. “I’ll walk you.”

I looked up. “You’ll walk me?”

“That’s what I said.”

“Thanks, no. I can manage.”

Beckett shrugged. “Suit yourself.”

But instead of climbing on his bike, he began to walk—slowly—and in the opposite direction I’d intended to take. With a huff, I followed behind.

“You don’t have to do that,” I called, keeping a good ten yards between us.

“Do what?” He shot a glance over his shoulder. “Why are you following me, Zelda? Is it because my station happens to be your station?”

I rolled my eyes, and clutched my portfolio tighter. A red light unhelpfully allowed me to catch up to him.

“Just to the station,” I said.

Beckett nodded, a small grin flitting over his lips. “Just to the station.”

We walked the next block in silence. My leftovers bag banged against my thigh one too many times and I went to chuck it into the next trashcan. I couldn’t stand to eat it fresh off the stove, and I sure as hell wasn’t going to eat it cold in my shitty hostel room.

“Wait,” Beckett said. “You don’t want it?”

“No.”

He held out his hand. “I’ll take it.”

I handed it over, feeling like an ass for wasting food.

“It’s not for me,” Beckett said, not looking at me as he zipped up his backpack and slung it back over his shoulder. We resumed our trek.

Three blocks later, we came to the station entrance that looked vaguely familiar to me as the one I’d taken earlier. Beckett lifted his bike onto his shoulder to take the stairs down. The bike’s yellow paint was chipped and the rear reflector cracked. Light but sturdy, it looked like a cross between a racing bike and a mountain bike, with straight handlebars instead of curved. Though the frame looked a little dinged-up, the chain and gears were free of rust. Beckett obviously took good care of the important things.

"You always take your bike on the train?" I asked as he set it down inside the station.

"Have to. It's a bitch in the morning, but until they make a better way from here to Brooklyn…." He shrugged.

"You live in Brooklyn but work in Manhattan?"

"Six days a week." He jerked his head at a transit map on one cement wall of the station next to a token dispenser. "Where are you staying?"

I pursed my lips. "At the Hotel None of Your Business."

"Are you always this difficult with people who offer to help?" Beckett asked, his blue eyes glinting in the station's yellow light.

"I'm not difficult," I said. "I'm cautious. Big difference."

"That's smart," he said. "But you obviously don't know the city. At least give me a neighborhood and I'll point you to the right train."

"8th Ave, near the Port Authority," I said, refusing to be touched by his offer.

Beckett frowned. "Lots of people coming and going from there. Maybe not the safest at night. At this hour."

He walked his bike toward a cement bench and sat, keeping his bike balanced against his knees. He pulled a cell phone from his pocket. "What's the name of the hotel?"

"It's not a hotel, it's a hostel. The Parkside. But you don't have to—"

"Cool. I'll go with you."

I blinked. "You'll go *with* me?"

"My bad. I meant, I happen to be walking to the Parkside Hostel tonight." He studied his phone, scrolling with his thumb. "You're free to walk with me, if you want."

"You don't have to do this," I said. "I don't know New York that well, but I do know where I'm going is the exact opposite direction of Brooklyn."

"Different borough, even," he said, not looking up.

I frowned, at a loss. Finally, I sat beside him on the cold cement bench. "I can't tell if you're being chivalrous or stalkerish."

"Neither," he said. "If I wake up tomorrow and read on the blotter that you were mugged on the way back to the hostel, I'll feel like shit. I'm doing this for me. Not you."

"Okaaay… Thanks?"

"Don't mention it."

A hundred different smart-ass retorts came to mind but I found myself tongue-tied into silence. This guy—Beckett—wasn't like anyone I'd ever met before.

"Are all New Yorkers like you?" I asked.

"How am I?" Beckett replied, still not looking up.

"If I were drawing you, you'd be Enigma Man. Taking damsels in distress to their shitty hostels in crappy neighborhoods, miles out of your way, and asking for nothing in return."

"Should I demand a reward?" Before I could answer Beckett turned to me, his dark blue eyes boring into mine. "And it's not for nothing. I told you, I'm doing this for me."

I pursed my lips. *There's a story here.*

A train screeched into the station.

"Do I get on?" I asked.

Beckett's gaze flickered up then back to his phone. "Next one."

Another silence fell. He didn't look at me, and only our elbows brushed now and then. But for all his aloofness, I still felt that sense of being sheltered in his presence.

Another train screeched in on a current of warm, aluminum-smelling wind.

"That's yours," Beckett said, and tucked his phone in an inside pocket of his jacket.

He walked his bike onto the train, forcing the few commuters who stood near the door to move over. No one gave Beckett a hard time for it, and he didn't look like he'd give a shit anyway.

I stepped in after him and he jerked his head to a free seat a couple rows down. I took it, again perplexed by his strange brand of chivalry. The train lurched off and I held my portfolio tight to my chest. Beckett held onto a rail, his bike easily resting against his thighs. He hardly moved with the train's turns, like a sailor on a ship. He didn't obsessively study the transit map near the door like I did, either, but when the train slowed for the third time, he turned to me.

"Your stop."

Our stop, I amended. But I followed him off, and followed him through the station and up the stairs to the street. Back into the cold of the night.

"Address?" he asked.

"If I don't tell, you'll just Google it from the name I stupidly gave you, right?"

"Much faster if you tell me," he said, a glint of humor in his eyes.

I huffed a sigh and told him the address. Beckett immediately started off, as if he'd been to the Parkside Hostel a hundred times before. It was so uncanny, I had to ask.

"Have you stayed there before?"

"No."

"How do you—?"

"I don't know the hostel, I know intersections." He tapped the handle of his bicycle. "It's my job."

"Oh. Right. That makes sense."

I decided to keep my mouth shut before something even dumber popped out. Truth was, I was grateful Beckett was with me. The streets were dark and full of shadows. I clutched my portfolio and walked as close to him as I dared without *looking* like I was sticking close to him.

Beckett walked easily but his eyes looked ahead and side to side, alert and aware. It was as if his body was on auto-pilot with familiarity for the city, but his mind stayed sharp. Ahead, a homeless man was keeping warm on a subway grate. As we approached, he suddenly barked at us for some spare change. I jumped back. Beckett stopped too, but only to pull a few dollars out of his pants pocket.

"Have a good one, man," he said, pressing the bills into the man's hand and continuing on.

The homeless man muttered something in return, and shuffled off in the opposite direction.

My mouth opened and then shut. *He's short on rent and giving his tips away?* Maybe he hadn't been telling the truth about his rent situation, but I didn't think so. He'd given the man money the same way he was taking me to my hostel—like he didn't have a choice.

We arrived at the Parkside Hostel. No one sat behind the glass enclosure of the lobby, but I had a twenty-four hour key.

"Okay, so this is it," I said. "Thanks for getting me here, especially since it's so far out of your way."

"No problem," Beckett said, his gaze roving up the street, to the door behind me, down to his shoes, and finally back to me. The silence grew thick between us. It was dim under the wan yellow light of the hostel's entry, turning Beckett's dark blue eyes almost purple. His mouth opened, as if he would break that silence, then snapped shut again.

He climbed onto his bike. "Good night, Zelda."

"'Night."

He pedaled away with a speed that seemed unsafe on the dark city streets. He rode with perfect competence, like a Tour de France athlete: leaning into a turn, smooth as silk and lightning fast. Within seconds, he was gone.

I stared a long time at the dark space where I'd seen him last. I wasn't going to see him ever again, and I couldn't decide how I felt about it. It wasn't regret sighing in my chest. More like a strange sort of…nostalgia? As if I missed him.

The feeling of safety was gone. I missed that too.

I trudged up to my room and flopped onto the bed's thin mattress; the springs squeaked and groaned under my weight. I called up Rupert's number on my phone. He was my most trustworthy roommate (which wasn't saying much) and I needed him to pick me up from the North Vegas bus depot in a few days.

"Oh, hey, Zel," Rupert said. In the background, I could hear music and loud voices. "What's up? How's the Big Apple treatin' ya?"

I frowned. He sounded like a guy whose girlfriend just came home and he's got another girl hiding in the closet.

"Not as well as I hoped," I said. "I'm coming back in a few days and wanted to lock in a ride back."

"You're coming back?" The noise behind Rupert became muffled and I knew that meant he'd closed himself into the tiny pantry off the kitchen. "Shit, Zel, that's rough."

"Tell me about it," I muttered, then sat up. "Wait. Rough for me or you?"

"Um, well…"

"Rupert, what's going on?"

"I sort of rented your room."

I nearly dropped the phone. "You did *what?*"

"You told me staying in New York was a sure thing."

"I said it was *probably* a sure thing." I stopped, realizing how that didn't make any sense and shook my head in impatience. "Anyway, I also said to wait until you got the call from me before you did anything with my room. *This is that call.*"

"Calm down. You can find another place. You can—"

"Not without a deposit *and* first month's rent," I said. "Goddammit, this is not what I needed to hear right now."

"It's my bad, Zel. The couch is yours," Rupert said. "For as long as you want. Or you can bunk up with Cheryl until something better comes up."

"How magnanimous of you," I said, rubbing my eyes.

"Huh?"

"Nothing."

"You know how it is around here, Zel. People coming and going…" I could hear the shrug in Rupert's voice. "We thought you were going."

"Yeah, well, I wasn't." I bit the inside of my cheek until the tears in my throat subsided. "Get your ass to the bus station in three days. I'll call you with the time."

Rupert's relief was a gust over the phone. "You got it. Tell me when. I'll be there." A short silence. "And hey, Zel? Sorry it didn't pan out for you over there. Those publishers don't know what they're missing."

I tried to say thanks but it came out a croaky whisper. I hung up and let the phone drop to the dingy bedspread.

I moved to the window and stared at the brick wall of the adjacent building. I had to crane my neck up to see the night sky, and there were no stars. Nothing but a dull, dark blue swath, cold and indifferent.

3

Beckett
November 29th

The train to Brooklyn was pretty empty for a Friday night. The streets on my block in an unsavory corner of Williamsburg were quiet too, but for a guy shouting into his cell phone as he passed me, and a siren wailing in the distance. New York always had at least one siren wailing in the distance.

My walk-up was wedged between ten other walk-up tenements, some brick, some cement. Most with graffiti. I climbed the two flights to my floor with my bike on my shoulder. Fluorescent lights flickered and buzzed along the narrow hallway. Stopping in front of 2C, I whipped my messenger bag off my shoulder, unzipped it, and pulled out the bag of Zelda's leftovers. Thankfully the box inside the plastic bag was intact. The food even felt a tiny bit warm.

I knocked.

Thirty seconds later, I heard floorboards creak and a lock being thrown. The door cracked open the width of its chain and sharp brown eyes peered out from a nest of wrinkles.

"Hey, Mrs. Santino," I said. "Got something for you. Hope you're in the mood for Italian." I glanced at my watch. "At twenty after midnight."

She sniffed, shut the door. The chain rattled and the door opened again, this time wide enough to snatch the bag out of my hand. Her eyes raked me up and down, her lips pursed. She sniffed again and shut the door.

I shook my head with a chuckle. "Goodnight, Mrs. Santino."

At 2E, I unlocked the door and flipped a switch. My tiny place was bathed in ugly light from a single overhead fluorescent. I rolled the bike over the thin, industrial carpet to its corner near the bathroom.

Ten steps and I was in the kitchen. I took a swig of bottled water from the half-size fridge, and moved to the window. My Brooklyn neighborhood was groggy under the deepening night that would never go fully dark against the city lights.

Zelda was out there, across the river in Manhattan, hopefully safe in the hostel she dubbed a shithole. I sucked in a deep breath and let it out slowly. I did my part. I got her there safe.

Be safe, Zelda.

I sat at the little table under the window, flooded with a sudden urge to talk. To *express*, as my English teacher, Mrs. Browning, in high school was always urging me.

Express how you feel, Beckett. Unlock your heart. Your words are beautiful. And they have power.

It sounded like a bunch of flowery bullshit at the time, but my teacher's advice never left me. I wanted to believe words had power. The power to change the past. To fix what was broken. To heal. By writing them down on paper, they could work some kind of magic on the reader.

I had one reader. Mrs. J. It was the end of the month, and I hadn't written her a letter yet. I hadn't known what to write about until tonight.

I pulled pen and paper out of a drawer.

November 29th
Dear Mrs. J,

In high school, there was this girl named Hannah Walters. Hannah wanted to be an actress and if her asshole father hadn't pressured her toward law school, she'd be killing it in Hollywood right now. Or maybe Broadway. She got the lead in every school play. Other kids would always be pissed at her getting all the glory, but only until opening night. Then it was obvious she'd earned it.

Senior year, the spring play at PS 241 was Rashomon. Have you ever seen it? They made a movie out of it too. Anyway, it's a Japanese story about a samurai, his wife, and a bandit. The bandit kills the samurai and rapes the samurai's wife. That's one version, anyway. In another version, the wife seduces the bandit and she helps kill the samurai. In another, the samurai kills himself. Each person—the bandit, the wife and the dead samurai (through a spirit medium)—tells a different story and the audience is left to wonder which one is true.

My buddies and I decided to get drunk and crash opening night. Just to make fun of it, not to actually watch. But the play was too good. We had nothing to make fun of. My friends saved face by saying it was boring and left after the second act. I stayed to the curtain call.

Hannah Walters played the medium. She came on stage as this crazed, almost ghostly creature, writhing and beseeching the spirits until the dead samurai speaks through her, telling his story. She was dressed in white rags that glowed under the lights and her face was pale, with eyes like dark, black pits that could see into the spirit world. Her voice was a keening wail, as if it physically hurt to let the dead speak through her. I felt like I was under a spell, helpless to tear my eyes away.

After the show I told Hannah that she was the only thing worth watching on that stage. Her response was to kiss me. I think she was drunk on the success of the show or maybe high on her performance. I didn't care. I kissed her back, and tasted the chalky whiteness of the greasepaint on her lips. It was like tasting a part of that magic she'd created.

We dated for a grand total of three months, until her dad threatened to cut off my dick with a hedge clipper if he caught me near her again. I wasn't good enough for his daughter. Too poor. Too rough. A tall kid with shabby clothes who lived with an ailing grandfather who lacked the strength to discipline him.

Losing Hannah wasn't a high point of my life but did I love her? Not sure. Her performance in Rashomon has stuck with me almost as much as she has. But Hannah had magic in her. I think I loved that.

I've been with a bunch of women since. Had sex with, I should clarify. Nothing lasting. Nothing I wanted to pursue. No one who seemed like they had magic in them too. Does that sound cheesy? Probably, but there's so much that's shitty in this world, when you find something that shines against all that dirt and darkness, you gravitate toward it.

I met a girl tonight.

Her first impression wasn't magical, not by a long shot. In fact, she was a pain in the ass. But smart. All of five-foot-nothing and beautiful, with large green eyes that looked miles deep. Long black hair like silk. I had to fight the urge to touch it.

She's leaving the city tomorrow. A job interview fell through, which sucks. But hell, she took a chance. A swing and a miss, but at least she stepped up to the plate. She's an artist. Draws comic books. I had a million questions for her. I wanted to ask and ask, because I was sure that I could talk to Zelda for days and never run out of things to know.

Yeah, her name is Zelda. I didn't get her last name. Because I didn't ask that or any of those hundreds of other questions. She's leaving town, but that's not why I kept my mouth shut. It was because of you, Mrs. J.

See, our story is sort of like Rashomon. It has three players: you, your husband and me. The wife, the dead samurai, and the bandit who killed him. Unlike the play, our story only has one interpretation. You came home to find thieves in your house, your husband's heart gave out, and he died. There is no other version.

I didn't ask this girl, Zelda, to grab a coffee with me. I didn't ask for her number. I walked her to her hostel and I let her go. After all, one question too many and she'd learn I'm a felon who did two years for armed robbery. Not the stuff of great first impressions. No magic there.

Anyway, who the hell am I to even try to start something real with a girl? You were married to Mr. J for twenty-seven years. I remember that from the DA's report. But my friends and I—my fellow bandits—we ended it, didn't we? I helped to end it.

The dead samurai is always dead and that doesn't change no matter who tells the story.

I'm sorry. I'm so sorry. That will never change either.

Beckett Copeland

I read the letter over, then put it in an envelope and wrote *Mrs. J* on the front in my tiny, precise handwriting. Gramps used to say my lettering was a perfect imitation of a typewriter. We didn't actually have a typewriter and couldn't afford a computer, so I had to hand-write everything for school.

I tossed the envelope on the desk and glanced around my place, trying to see it through my parole officer's eyes. Roy was coming over tomorrow for our monthly pow-wow. I had a few chores yet to do, so I crouched down by my album collection, stacked upright against the wall next to my desk. I used to have more but the winter had been rough for the bike messenger business, and for my employer, Apollo

Courier, in particular.

I plucked out Journey's *Greatest Hits* and set it on my Crosley C10 two-speed record player. Ebay said I could get $400 for it. I'd sell a kidney first.

I set the needle on the vinyl. After a crackle, "Don't Stop Believing" filled the studio. I straightened up a few things, did some dishes and collected some dirty clothes into my laundry bag. I was done before the song ended. With a place this small, having clutter would drive me fucking nuts.

I cracked the window and smoked a cigarette while I listened to the music. It was a good album. Kind of cheesy, but I sometimes think what's considered cheesy is actually just something put in the simplest terms.

Don't stop believing.

That's it. No metaphor. No poetry. Straightforward advice worth about $35 at any pawn shop. I might have to hock it, but I'd miss it.

"You'd miss having a roof over your head more," I said, squashing my smoke out on the sill.

Roy didn't like the smell of smoke in the apartment, so I kept the window open another few minutes. The radiator was acting up again, and soon my breath began to plume with every exhale. I shut the window and gave the radiator under it a kick. It groaned and a gust of warm air huffed out. Enough to warm my hands by for a minute, then it settled back to a trickle of heat that would be just enough to keep me from freezing my nuts off all night.

I reluctantly took off my weatherproof jacket and pants and quickly exchanged them for sweatpants and two t-shirts. I pulled on another sweatshirt, then climbed into bed and wrapped myself in the covers, waiting to feel warm. The old, cold ache shivered across my skin and settled into my gut.

I wanted a woman in bed with me.

I wondered if I should try to hook up with someone tomorrow night but brushed off the idea. The complications weren't worth it, and like I'd told Mrs. J, pursuing something more than sex was out of the question.

But I still wanted it. I wanted to listen to the sound of someone else's breathing beside my own. I wanted to hold a woman and have her body pressed against mine, her arms and legs wrapped around me tight, our bodies shielding each other from the cold. One person alone against winter was rough. But two people, together…

Together. A word I never used.

"Get over it," I muttered into my cold pillow. Mrs. J's pillow was cold too. Her bed empty. Thanks to me, she couldn't use the word *together* either.

I dropped into sleep and dreamt about Hannah Walters' wailing medium, only it wasn't the dead samurai she channeled. It was Mr. J.

Hannah swooped across the stage, pantomiming a middle-aged-man surprised by four thieves looting his brownstone. Hannah's hand clutched her chest as the heart attack expanded in Mr. J's. Hannah screamed. Or maybe it was Mrs. J as she watched as her husband crumpled to the floor, the life leaving his eyes before his head touched the hardwood.

I stared at the unfolding drama, just as transfixed as I'd been watching *Rashomon* in high school. Unable to look away. Forced to bear witness to what I'd done.

Look and see, Hannah wailed.

Watch a man die…

…and know it happened because of you.

BLAM!

The door buzzed at precisely eight a.m. the next morning. I was already up and dressed, coffee brewing. A smile split Roy Goodwin's face when I opened the door for him. He sported a big Tom Selleck mustache and dressed like a social studies teacher—lots of polyester pants and button-down shirts. Sometimes he even wore a sweater vest.

No vest this morning. He shook out of his windbreaker, snagging the Department of Corrections ID badge clipped to his shirt pocket.

I was sure some of his other parolees thought Roy was soft. Maybe the desperate ones even tried to fuck with him. That would be a mistake. Under his rounding bulk, Roy was trained and quick. A former FBI agent, he'd asked for reassignment as a PO five years ago. Said he wanted to stop chasing down criminals and start helping them. From where I was standing, he was good at his job.

"How you been, Beckett?" Roy asked, tucking his clipboard under an arm and rubbing his hands together.

"Can't complain," I said. "How's Mary?"

"She's wonderful. Sends her regards."

"Tell her hi for me," I said. "Coffee?"

"Please," Roy said. "Winter's going to be a bitch, I can tell already." He glanced around my tiny, barebones apartment. "I'm going to get started while you whip me up a mug, yeah? One cream, no sugar."

"Got it."

I fixed his coffee while he went through the bathroom, checking the shower, the hamper, the drawers under the sink and the medicine cabinet. He was thorough, but respectful, which I appreciated. My first PO had been an asshole who used to tear my place apart like he was doing a search and seizure for a cop show on TV. I had him only a month and then got transferred to Roy. I never knew why, but I sure as hell didn't complain about it.

Roy came out of the bathroom making notes on his clipboard. He tucked it back under his arm and went down on hands and knees to check under my bed. He searched the two cushions on the couch, under the coffee table and inside its one drawer. Then, like a reward, his fingers walked through my album collection. He sat back on his heels, Chicago's *Chicago 17* in his hands.

"Wow. Now that's a find." He glanced up at me. "Don't tell me someone dumped this beauty at a sidewalk sale?"

"That one was actually part of Gramps' collection," I said. "No idea how or why he got it. Frank Sinatra was more his jam. You want me to play it?"

"Does a bear shit in the woods?"

Roy handed me the album, and I set the needle while he made a few more notes on his clipboard. "I'll take that coffee now," he said, smiling at me through his mustache while "You're The Inspiration" filled my apartment.

I felt, for one strange second, like I was in one of those '80s family sitcoms where the dad is always understanding no matter how bad the son fucks up, and there's always a happy ending.

You're losing it, Copeland, I thought. *It's the song and Roy's Tom Selleck mustache.*

The thought made me smile. Roy had gone easy on me with his search, as usual, although I made it pretty easy on *him*. I had no pictures on the wall to hide baggies of drugs behind, no vases to stash a weapon in, no decorative shit of any kind.

Ray sat on the tiny couch facing the small, on-its-last-legs flat-screen TV perched on two milk crates. I took the ratty chair to his left. The place was so small I could reach behind me and almost touch the bed. Roy set his coffee on the scratched wooden coffee table, still smiling. But behind his eyes I could see he was studying me.

"You clean?" he asked, almost apologetically.

"Does a bear shit in the woods?" I said, and that made him laugh.

Drug testing wasn't part of my parole deal unless Roy suspected something, but he could do a spot check whenever he wanted. He asked every month if I was clean and I told the truth. Roy could sniff a lie the way most people could wake up and smell the coffee.

And besides, drugs were never my problem. Being desperate for a life other than the one Gramps and I had been stuck with was my problem. Seeking that different life at the expense of someone else had also been my problem. Mr. J dying in front of me and two years at Otisville Correctional had cured me of seeking.

"How's work at Apollo?" Roy asked, setting his clipboard on his knee.

"Slow," I said. His face crumpled in concern and I added quickly, "But December usually picks up. There's a ton of last minute crosstown deliveries around the holidays. And lots of takeout. People don't want to brave the cold on their lunch breaks."

"I heard Uber was cutting into the messenger business."

"I'm doing okay, Roy."

Roy made a note on his clipboard. "And Giovanni's?"

"Fine."

"Rent is due in two days." He took a slow sip of his coffee, his eyes on me over the mug. "You good?"

He was psychic, this guy, I swear. But no point in lying to him. "I'm a little short, but I've got it covered."

"How?" he asked, his voice soft.

My throat tightened. Roy was as old as my father…if my father was still alive and hadn't drunk himself into an early grave already. He and my mother had taken off when I was eight. They could both be dead for all I knew. Or cared.

"Same *legal* way I always do," I said.

Roy leaned back on the couch.

"I still have one more shift at Giovanni's tonight," I said. "I can pull it out."

I didn't add that the chances of making eighty dollars bussing tables for one night was a long shot of epic proportions. But because it was Roy, I didn't have to.

"It's against regulations," he said slowly. "I'm not supposed to even offer—"

"So don't," I said and forced a smile to blunt the edge off my voice. "I'm fine, Roy. I'll survive. I always do."

Selling my *Journey* album would get me halfway there. Giving blood would make up the rest. Weird how the two felt almost the same.

Roy looked like he was going to argue, then let it slide. "All right, so back to business. Have you had any contact with Mr. Carlyle, Mr. Lorens, or Mr. Nash?"

"No," I said. Also the truth. None of the other guys who were there for the robbery had tried to contact me and I sure as shit wasn't going to seek them out.

"Good."

"I thought Nash was sent back to Rikers," I said.

Roy's brows came together. "And how did you hear that?"

"Darlene," I said. "She's better than a gossip rag when it comes to this shit."

"Be careful with her," Roy said. "Junkies are like black holes. They suck everyone into their darkness sooner or later. I'd hate to see you get mixed up with her or her dealer."

"She doesn't have a dealer," I said. "She's been clean for months." I didn't add that Darlene Montgomery, for all her fucked up-ness, was a friend. A good friend. I didn't make a habit of kicking friends to the curb because they'd made some mistakes. I'd made a mistake. A huge one. And Darlene and our small gang of friends didn't judge me for it. The least I could do was return the favor.

Roy made a note and asked me a few more standard parole check-in questions, and then set his clipboard down for good.

"So what's new, Beckett? Tell me something good."

I met a girl…

"Not much to report," I said.

"Are you seeing anyone?"

Fuck, how does he do that? I turned my gaze away from Roy's man-to-man-we're-chums-shooting-the-shit smile.

"Nah, no one special. And besides, convicts are usually swipe left material in most dating scenarios."

"Swipe left…?"

"It's a dating app thing." I waved my hand. "Never mind. Stupid joke."

Roy nodded and asked his next question with a mix of hope and reluctance. "Doing anything fun for the holidays?"

"Yeah, Roy. I'm flying to Jamaica," I said. "Going to lie on a beach and drink rum and not come back until spring." I shot him a crooked smile. "Is it too late to put in my request?"

His chuckle sounded heavy. "A tad too late."

I'd completed one year of parole with two to go. Until then, I couldn't so much as leave New York state without the Board's approval and then only with a thirty-day lead-time and recommendation from Roy. Leaving the country wasn't even an option.

"So I was thinking…" Roy began slowly, leaning over his knees, fingers steepled. "My sainted wife makes a mean Christmas ham. She does it up with pineapple slices. You know, the kind with maraschino cherries in the middle? And she decorates with those little spikes of cloves in the most exact pattern you've ever seen." He knocked my knee with his hand. "I'd almost have to take it as an insult to her if you refuse to give it a try this year."

He said it lightly enough. Same as he did last year. My grandfather died a month before my foray into the criminal underworld, and now the Copeland family tree consisted of me, myself, and I. I hated Roy knowing that. Hated my life was an open file for him to read. But it was a consequence of being charged with a Class C felony. My past was available to anyone who wanted to know. I was a convict. Even after I was done with parole in two more years, it would follow me forever.

That's the price you pay…

I smiled wanly at Roy. "Maybe I'll stop by."

I may as well have said, "Not on your life," and we both knew it. Since my parents bailed on me, I didn't make a habit out of getting too close to people. Roy was my parole officer. Once I finished probation, he'd vanish out of my life too. No sense in complicating things.

Roy held my gaze for a moment, and I didn't blink. Ten seconds of heavy silence, and he gave in, slapped his hands on his knees. "Okay, Beckett. But it'll break Mary's heart."

He smiled gently and we stood up together. He headed for the door while I took the three steps to my little desk under the window. I grabbed the envelope marked *Mrs. J* and handed it to Roy.

"See that she gets this, yeah?"

Roy's smile was soft. "Of course." He knew the drill. I'd been writing Mrs. J letters, one a month, since prison. Thirty-seven so far. The one in Roy's hand was thirty-eight.

"Any, uh…?" I cleared my throat, dragged my gaze over the floor. "Anything from Mrs. J? Any word?"

"No," Roy said quietly.

I nodded. "She probably just throws them in the trash without reading. I don't blame her, but…"

My words trailed as Roy opened the letter and read what I'd written. He had to. He couldn't give the wife of the man we killed anything without checking it first. The lack of privacy—again—cut me like a knife.

Roy looked up at me, a strange smile on his face. "Zelda. Like Fitzgerald's wife."

"That's exactly what I said," I replied brightly before I remembered not to give it away.

Our eyes met again with the moment growing thick with all Roy wanted to tell me: about guilt's poisonous erosion of everything I'd worked to build after prison. I could hear his unspoken plea that I forgive myself, and I could taste the denial I would shoot him down with. I wasn't charged with murder or manslaughter when Mr. J died because he'd had a bad ticker to begin with. But that was a technicality in my book. His poor health didn't mean shit to me.

I didn't say that to Roy. We'd said it all before. In another life, I could've loved Roy Goodwin. I could have spent holidays with him and his sainted wife, eating pineapple-and-maraschino studded ham. But he was wrong about forgiveness. Mr. J was dead and the only person who could forgive me was his wife.

At the door Roy drew on his jacket and wagged his finger in my face. "Tell that landlord of yours to fix that damn radiator already, capisce? It's cold in here."

"Fix it?" I said with a dry grin to make him feel better. "I set it low on purpose. Keeps me sharp."

"Ha! Sure you do."

Roy reached up with the hand not holding my letter to Mrs. J and patted my cheek. Exactly the way Gramps used to do. It was too personal an action for a PO to take with his parolee, but he did it and I let him. His hand was warm. Fatherly.

I pulled away.

"You take care, Beckett. Call if you need anything, and I'll see you next month."

I nodded, grateful he didn't say—or offer—anything more, and shut the door behind him.

I took off the Chicago and put on Frank Sinatra. I set the needle to the third track. "My Way" filled my studio.

It was Gramps' favorite.

4

Zelda
November 30th

The dream came as it always did, in slices of memory. Shifting visions that jumped through time quickly, dragging me toward one moment.

Where's your sister?

The yellow tile of the supermarket floor. Shelves of soup, rows of cans with blue, red and brown labels.

My mother's voice again, the question that would haunt us for six months until the police told us exactly where she was...

Where's your sister?

My fourteen-year-old eyes saw Rosemary at the end of the next aisle over.

The man leading my little sister away by the hand.

Her look back over her shoulder.

Her little face, uncertain and nervous.

And my helpless stare back.

Always in the dream, I was helpless.

I tried to call out but my voice was gone. I tried to move, but my legs were lead. It wasn't until they were outside, rounding a corner, out of sight, that I was freed from the invisible, paralyzing bonds.

I tore after them, as I had in real life.

Screams ripped out of my throat, like they had ten years ago.

And in the dream, like then, I was too late.

The van screeched away and I was too slow or scared (*or young,* everyone tried to tell me*)*_to stop it.

Rosemary was gone.

I woke with a cry tearing out of my throat, my body drenched in sweat. I blinked at my surroundings, gasping for breath, my eyes wide.

The hostel! My mind was screaming, as if to preserve itself.

You're in the hostel in New York, not there! Not in that day!

A great sob strangled my gasps until I swallowed it down and gulped air. And as I always did when this nightmare gripped me, I calmed myself by reimagining the outcome. I sketched it out in my mind's eye, in jagged black and white.

I was strong, not a small fourteen-year old girl. I had a baseball bat. Or a knife. Or a gun. My sister looked over her shoulder. Uncertain at first, then her face morphed to relief. Because I was there. I tapped her abductor's shoulder, the asshole who'd conned a little girl to come with him. When he turned, it was *his* face that twisted with uncertainty. And then fear.

And then pain.

Ten years' worth of pain. Mine. My father's. And especially my mother's.

I closed my eyes and breathed through it, like how they tell women who are in labor to do. Breathe through the pain. Wait until it unclenches its claws and lets go. Relax into the relief. Try not to dwell on the next wave coming. Knowing it's coming.

I closed my eyes and breathed that hot fire of my rage away. When the memories subsided, I tossed off the covers and moved to the window. I filled my gaze with the city. Grey hard edges, stark vertical lines even the sun couldn't soften. New York was mean. Cold and indifferent. It didn't have the familiarity of Philadelphia, or the remote security of Vegas. This city rising up outside my window didn't care if I lived or died, stayed or went, succeeded or failed.

Come at me, it whispered. *Or go back. It's all the same to me.*

But not to me. My graphic novel was for my mother. I wanted—I *needed* the world to witness my mother's rage. I hadn't saved my sister. My art was the only thing I could do for her.

"I'm not leaving," I said quietly, the words floating in a bubble above my head, precisely inked in black and white.

Something inside me clicked into place, and I turned my focus to how to make this impossible situation a reality.

If I used my Vegas rent money and the bus fare I'd planned to get back, I had $400 to put toward a place to live, and $300 to live off until I got a job. I opened my laptop and searched for rental listings for people needing a roommate.

I called a few places that sounded halfway decent and was told my $400 deposit wasn't going to cut it. Not even close. The not-so-decent places were eager to take my money but set off every instinctual alarm I had. Others weren't so bad but the apartments were at the far edges of Queens or the Bronx. They may as well have been on the moon. The day's hours slid away as I searched.

At around one p.m. it occurred to me I hadn't eaten anything and regretted giving last night's leftovers away.

To Beckett.

The only person I knew in the city.

You don't know him, I told myself. *You know nothing about him.*

But that wasn't exactly true, I realized. I knew a lot of things about him. He was okay to talk to. He was a smartass and kind of cold-shoulder-y, but so was I. I didn't feel itchy or uncomfortable in his presence. He didn't ring my instinctual alarms. He gave money to homeless people when he was short himself. He worked two jobs, one of which required him to get up at the crack of dawn five days a week to bike around Manhattan. He kept leftover Italian food for a friend, and took strange women a borough away from where he lived, to make sure they got home safely.

He's a decent guy, I thought. And he was short on rent.

I grabbed the garbage bag full of my stuff, my portfolio and laptop, and headed downstairs. The manager was there, behind his glass wall. I returned the key and checked out, praying I wouldn't be back that night.

I had some time to kill, so I bought a gyro and a lemonade off of a street vendor, and spent the rest of the afternoon wandering the city, trying to familiarize myself with the subway, the buses, the different landmarks. But if this crazy-ass plan worked, Manhattan wouldn't be the borough I'd need to know.

I shivered in my pea coat as the sun began to drop and thick gray clouds settled over the city. A cold wind whistled and rain—almost sleet—began to fall. I ducked into a Starbucks, stretching a cup of coffee over the hours and wondering if I were crazy. Wondering if my plan, like my graphic novel, was doomed for rejection.

At twenty to seven, I stepped back onto the street. I turned into the cold wind that sliced my face like little knives, and started making my way back to Giovanni's.

The little bistro was dead. The storm must be keeping people at home. Last night, Beckett told me he needed good tips from this shift to make his rent. I'd done enough waitressing in high school to know it wasn't going to happen. The wait staff wasn't going to make eighty bucks, never mind the busser.

But I can fix that.

I scanned the dimness for him, a tangle of nerves twisting in my gut. At the bar, the manager was talking to the bartender. They both smiled politely as I approached.

"Hi," I said, hurriedly tucking the garbage bag between my legs and the bar. "Is Beckett working tonight?"

Please say yes. Please say yes. Please—

"He sure is," the manager said. "He comes on at seven. Normally it's five but I had a feeling it was going to be quiet tonight. You a friend of his?"

"Sort of," I said, easing a sigh of relief. "I don't want to get him in trouble or anything. Just wanted to talk when he had a break."

The manager smiled brightly. "Beckett's never been late to work. I can give him a few minutes with a *sort of* friend."

I smiled faintly and the manager went to greet a couple who had braved the storm to come inside.

The bartender, a middle aged man with graying hair, and a tie and vest over his white shirt jerked his chin at me. He looked like an extra in a Sinatra film. All old world grace and charm. "Get you something, miss?"

"Just a Coke, please."

The same waitress who'd waited on me the night before—big hair, big hoop earrings—sidled up to the bar.

"Christ, it's dead as a tomb in here," she said. "Three vodka martinis, Vince. Two for my customers and one for me to make this shift worthwhile." She shot me a wink.

"Nice try, Darlene," Vince muttered, setting the soda in front of me. While he poured vodka—for two—into a shaker, I turned to the waitress.

"Can I ask you a question?"

"Of course," she said. "I got nothing but time."

"Have you worked with Beckett long?"

A smile broke over her face instantly. "About a year, every

Friday and Saturday night. It's torture."

"Torture?"

She cocked a fist on her hip and leaned on the bar. "Have you *seen* him? He's a beautiful specimen of masculine hotness, and I've been trying to take him home with me forever. I have to settle for him being my best friend."

I smiled into my Coke. "I was wondering more about his character."

Darlene stared at me blankly.

"I mean, what's he *like*?" I said.

"Girl, he's the best. A truly good guy, and God knows there's not enough of those. At least not in my vicinity."

Vince set two perfect martinis on Darlene's tray. "You're breaking my heart, Dar."

She snorted. "You've been married since before I was born, old man." She jerked her thumb at me. "She's asking about our Becks. Tell her, Vince."

"He'd give you the shirt off his back even if it was the only one he had."

Encouraging, I thought, trying not to let my hopes fly too high.

"What's with all the questions, anyway?" Darlene asked, her friendly demeanor turning suspicious. "He's not in trouble, is he?"

"No, no, nothing like that." No plausible white lies came to me, so I shrugged and said with a grin, "I guess I'm trying to go home with him too."

"Ha! Thatta girl," Darlene said with a salacious wink. She hefted her tray, and leaned in to me. "Good luck, honey. I'll be cheering for you. Or being really freakin' jealous, one of the two."

I sipped my soda and stuffed my face with the free bread Vince set before me, and waited for Beckett. He showed up at exactly six-fifty and hit the floor at seven on the dot. He went right to work, tub in hand, bending his tall form over a table to clear away the remnants of someone's dinner.

I steeled myself and slipped off my stool to approach him.

"Hey," I said.

Beckett glanced over his shoulder once. Then twice. The dark blue of his eyes lit up for a moment. Then he frowned and went back to work.

"What are you doing here? Is the ziti that hard to resist?"

"I need to talk to you."

"I just came on. I won't have a break until nine."

"Yeah, but it's dead in here," I said. "And it's important."

Beckett finished the table and straightened up. He hesitated, glancing at the manager, who was chatting with Vince behind the bar.

"Give me a sec," Beckett said. He jerked his chin toward a table for two in the back corner. "I'll meet you there."

I nodded and took a seat. The candle flickered in its cup. Darlene came by and removed the second place-setting. She was recommending the pasta fagioli soup when Beckett slid into the chair opposite.

"Hey, Dar," he said, his smile and tone both casual and affectionate.

"Hello, dar-*ling*," she cooed at him before sidling off and shooting me a knowing smile.

"I only have five minutes," he said.

"I ordered soup," I blurted.

Beckett's dark brows—darker than his blonde hair—furrowed. "Congratulations?"

I shook my head, the heat rising in my face. "I meant, I didn't know if you wanted anything too. I could order you something?"

His frown deepened. "I'm working. In theory. Why are you still in the city? I thought you had to go back to Vegas."

"I did. I was going to. But I don't want to."

I took a sip from my soda as my mouth had gone dry. Beckett was looking at me like I was an alien life form, and a hostile one at that. *This is never going to work,* I thought and then wondered if I wanted it to. Maybe he was an asshole. Maybe Darlene and Vince were wrong. Maybe my own first impressions of him were off. I had a pretty good track record following my gut instincts when it came to people, but maybe this time they'd failed me like every other part of this disastrous trip.

But louder than any impression of Beckett, instincts told me that I needed to stay in NYC. There was nothing left for me in Vegas and Philly was too painful. My graphic novel was good. It could sell. I just needed the time to fix it. The surety of that conviction calmed my nerves.

I folded my hands on the table and leaned in. "I have a proposition for you."

Beckett leaned back. "Okay."

"I want to be your roommate."

His eyes flared wide, and I saw his Adam's apple bob above the collar of his dress shirt.

"You want to be roommates," he said, his voice strangely low.

"Nothing permanent or long-term," I said. "You won't be stuck with me for a year or anything. A month or two at the most, until I get settled. Then I'm out of your hair forever."

He stared at me for a long minute, blinked and then gave a short, disbelieving snort of laughter. "You want to be my roommate," he said again.

"Yes."

"In my four-hundred square foot studio."

"Well, yes..."

"You won't have any privacy. *I* won't have any privacy."

"I'll do my best to stay out of your way."

Beckett was silent for a moment, his eyes full of thoughts. Then he said, "Sorry to disappoint but I don't want or need a roommate."

"But you need the money, right?"

He crossed his arms over his chest "Well, shit, I'm so thrilled I told you that personal stuff last night so you could use it against me tonight."

"I'm more desperate than you are, trust me," I said. "My shitty situation got a hell of a lot worse since last we spoke. My idiotic roommates in Vegas rented my room out from under me." I reached under the table for the trash bag. "Behold. The sum-total of my worldly belongings."

Beckett's eyes darted to the bag and I saw the softening again, for half a second, and then gone. I tucked the bag back between my feet.

"I'm not saying this to pressure you," I continued. "I'm saying we're both screwed, right? We can help each other out. This is how."

Beckett drummed his fingers on the table, then he shook his head as if shaking off an unwanted thought.

"You don't know me," he said in a quiet voice. "At all."

"I know some. I asked about you—"

"You *asked* about me?" His voice raised as he leaned over the table. "Who?"

I leaned back. "Vince. And Darlene."

Right on cue, Darlene came back with my soup. "Here you are, hon."

"She ask you about me?" Beckett said to her.

"She sure did." Darlene reached to pinch his cheek. "I told her you were the perfect specimen of masculine hotness."

I inwardly groaned as Beckett's face went red. "No," I said, heat rising to my own cheeks in embarrassment. "Tell him the *other* thing you said."

Darlene heaved a sigh. "Oh. Right. I said you were one of the truly good men left in the world. One of the best." She leaned toward me conspiratorially. "He tries to keep it a secret but he's super bad at it."

She winked at Beckett, who stared at her as she retreated.

I tried to hide a smile behind a sip of soda. "It's not the same as a background check, but Vince said the same thing. More or less."

"Uh huh." Beckett leaned back in his chair, arms crossed, his expression flat. "And what else did your background check turn up? Please, enlighten me."

I sighed and pushed my drink away. "I'm sorry. I didn't mean to pry into your life. But I'm a girl, you're a guy…" I shrugged. "The stakes are higher for girls in strange cities, okay?"

"And what about the stakes for me? Who do I call for references before I let a total stranger live in my space? Maybe your idiotic roommates in Vegas?"

"You're right," I said. "No, you're totally right. Do you have a pen?"

He blinked and then huffed a short laugh. "A pen? Sure, why not?" He fished around in his busser half-apron and fished out a ballpoint.

I dragged a cocktail napkin toward me and wrote down a name and number, slid it back across the table.

Beckett picked up the napkin. "Theo Fletcher."

"My old boss at the tattoo shop I worked at in Vegas. He can vouch for me."

Beckett watched me for a minute then tossed the napkin down and rubbed his eyes. "Look, Zelda, I'm sorry shit fell apart for you here, but living with me… It's not the solution."

I clenched my hands into fists under the table. "It's the only solution I have, and it helps both of us. You told me to try again, remember?"

"When?"

"Last night. I said I'd tried and failed, and you said, *try again*. So here I am, trying again." I leaned forward. "I can't stay at that hostel. It's loud and unsafe, and I need to be able to work on my novel. I need to fix it so I can *try again*. I know if I leave this city, I won't come back. Not for a long time. I'm on the verge of something, I can feel it. I just need a little bit of time and you need the money." I bit my lip. "Don't you?"

"Forget what Darlene said, Zelda." Beckett's voice was heavy now. "It's my parole officer you should've talked to."

I sat back in my chair. "Your parole officer?"

Beckett took in my shock with his lips pressed together in a tight smile of resigned bitterness. He rose from the table. "Nice talking to you. I gotta get back—"

"Wait," I cried. "Just…wait. Please."

Beckett hesitated, then sank back down. I didn't know what to say or how to ask the next question. He tapped his fingers on the table as my soup grew cold between us.

Finally, he said, "Armed robbery."

"Armed robbery," I say. "So…you had a gun."

"Yes," he said, his stare cold. "I had a gun. And a mask. Like the bad guy in a movie."

I didn't know what to say, afraid any more questions would just make this story worse, and send me back to Vegas.

"Okay."

"Is it?" Beckett shifted in his seat, his words dripping with sarcasm. "Is it *okay* that I robbed a brownstone in the Upper East Side with three other guys? And that the owners—a married couple—came home early and surprised us? And we sure as shit surprised them right back. In fact, we surprised them so badly with our guns and our masks, that the man dropped dead of a heart attack."

My stomach dropped and I felt all the bread I'd eaten sit in my gut like a lump of cement. "He died?"

"Sure did," Beckett said. "We weren't charged with murder or manslaughter, though the DA certainly tried. Mr. Johannsen had a history of high cholesterol, a previous episode of angina, yadda yadda, so we got lucky in that respect."

The bitterness was thick and it was obvious to me that Beckett didn't consider himself lucky by any stretch.

"So I helped rob a place, accidentally killed a man, and served two years in prison. How does that sound? Am I still ideal roommate material?"

I laughed weakly. "I've seen worse on Craigslist."

Beckett stared.

"Sorry," I said. "I make bad jokes at the worst times."

"A joke," Beckett said. "So nothing of what I said bothers you? My criminal record? The fact I killed a man?"

"You didn't," I said. "The man died, but you didn't kill him. Not like premeditated murder. It was bad timing. You didn't intend—"

"It doesn't matter what I *intended,*" Beckett said. "It's what *happened.* The man is dead and if we hadn't been there to steal from him, he wouldn't be. End of story."

"But you feel bad about it," I said, like a person scrabbling over the edge of a cliff. "It's not like—"

Beckett's stare turned icy. "I feel *bad* about it? I feel…" His words were lost in a tangle of disbelief, and I knew I'd blown it even before he said, "This conversation is over."

He got to his feet, and this time I didn't call him back. I sat at the table alone, my soup untouched. Defeated.

Maybe this is for the best, I thought. *Armed robbery is bad. Two years in prison is bad. He's a total stranger; I was stupid to think this would work.*

Except that Beckett didn't seem any more or less dangerous than any stranger I'd tried to rent a room from that day. And it was obvious he regretted his crime. The pain in his eyes when he'd spoken about it was bright and glassy. I'd see that look before, in every mirror I'd ever looked into. I recognized the weight of guilt hanging around his neck, because I wore it too.

Maybe that's why I felt safe around him instead of fearful for what he'd done.

Or maybe you're so desperate to stay in the city, you'd throw caution down the toilet to shack up with a felon.

Maybes didn't matter. Beckett wasn't interested and clearly this was the universe warning me away from making yet another terrible decision.

Darlene came back with a to-go container for my soup, her mouth turned down into a pout. "No luck, either huh?" She clucked her tongue. “Such a shame. But good on you for trying.”

“Yeah, I tried,” I muttered.

Tried again. Failed again.

I glanced up at her. “Do you know about…his past?”

“You mean that he did time? Of course. He’s my best friend. And it’s sort of how we met. The boss here works with the DOC. He likes to hire parolees. Give them a fresh start.” She tucked a lock of brown hair behind her ear, shrugged while her gaze fell to her shoes. “Like me.”

“Oh?”

“Yeah.” Darlene slipped into the chair across from me. “I got some stuff to work out with drugs, okay? But Becks… He’s not messed up. He has a heart of gold, I promise.” She lowered her voice. “He had a bad situation, you know? Desperate. So he did something stupid but he regrets it. Every minute.”

She looked over my shoulder.

“I think we’re closing up now. The boss mentioned he might, since the storm is so bad. His wife gets nervous about the power going out.” Darlene stood and waved a hand. “Anyway. Come around again, yeah? Don’t let that big dummy push you away too.”

I wanted to tell her it was too late, but there was no point. I wasn’t going to see her again. I grabbed my portfolio, my to-go bag with the soup, and headed for the front door.

I slipped out of the bistro, head down, ready to get the last of this hopeless trip over with.

Outside, the rain was coming down in silver sheets, the drops exploding on the street. I fished in my trash bag-style luggage for my red and white fold-up umbrella.

The bistro door opened behind me, and some of the staff of Giovanni’s crowded out, hunching under hoods and opening umbrellas.

“The boss is closing early, just like I said,” Darlene shouted, holding the collar of her coat over her head. “Not like we had customers anyway.” She smiled brightly at me in the rain, and now that I was looking for it, I could see the toll drugs had taken on her. It was written across her brown eyes and seeping out, to ring them in shadows.

I wasn’t a spontaneous hugger, but I found myself throwing my arms around Darlene and giving her a squeeze.

"Oh," she said. "Okay." And she hugged me back.

"You take care," I said, letting go.

"I will, thanks. You too!"

She hurried off, and it was sort of heartbreaking how happy she was that a strange girl had hugged her.

I busied myself with opening my umbrella just as Beckett emerged, his bike on his shoulder. He shot me a glance as he set it down between us, and pulled the hood of his jacket over his head.

"You're going to get drenched," I said dully.

"I'm good," he replied, though I noticed he eyed the street with a sigh of resignation.

"Your station is my station, right?" I said.

"Yeah, I guess it is."

I opened my umbrella and moved closer to him. I struggled to put the umbrella over both of us. He was so damn tall, I could hardly reach.

"What are you doing?" he asked.

"God, you're a beanstalk," I muttered. "I'm giving my arm a cramp trying to reach you from all the way down here. Here." I handed him the umbrella. "I'll take the bike, you cover us."

Beckett took the umbrella I shoved in his hands, and I didn't miss the small smile on his lips as I took the handlebars and started walking, keeping the bike between us. He held the umbrella high, shielding us from the worst of the storm.

While the rain was driving down hard, the wind had abated. We weren't blasted from all sides, but the sound of the water pelting my umbrella was loud and relentless. We speed-walked through the dark and empty streets to the Astor Station. Beckett handed me back my umbrella and carried his bike down the stairs.

A handful of sodden people waited for trains on two sides, their umbrellas or coats making puddles all around them.

"Thanks for the cover," Beckett said.

"No problem," I said. "So…see you. Or not, I guess."

"Yeah," he said heavily. "See you."

We parted at the bottom of the stairs, me to the inbound platform, him to the outbound on the other side of the tracks. I watched from my side as Beckett walked his bike to wait for his train that was just now screeching into the station. The train stopped, obscuring him from view. Cutting him off from me.

So that's it then.

My legs felt strangely hollow and I started toward a round cement bench on my side to sit and wait for the train that would take me back to the hostel, to Vegas, to the life I had instead of the life I wanted.

The Brooklyn-bound train on the other side pulled out of the station.

Beckett was still there.

My breath jumped in my throat and I froze, unable to do anything but watch him take his bike and come around to my platform. He sat down beside me on the circular bench, bicycle resting against his knees, sort of half-turned away from me.

After a moment, he said, "The gun wasn't loaded."

"Okay," I said.

"My buddy gave it me before the break-in. I told him I didn't need or want it, but he said it was for insurance. To scare anyone off who tried to stop us." His eyes grew heavy with memories. "It worked."

"Okay."

"Loaded or not, it's considered armed robbery," he continued, and then met my eye unflinching. "I never wanted to hurt anyone. I never would."

I didn't know what to say so I said the truth. "I believe you."

Beckett's expression lightened a little. "What I did… It was a stupid fucking thing to do."

I nodded. "Yeah, well, I dropped everything and came twenty-five hundred miles to a strange city with no back-up plan."

Beckett smirked. "Not quite the same league."

I couldn't save my sister.

"No," I said. "But we've all made mistakes, right?"

For a long moment his deep blue eyes searched mine. Finally, he nodded, but I felt as though he could see straight into my heart and agreed with what he saw there.

"They were supposed to love it," I said, to give my pain a different source. "My graphic novel. I was so sure they would love it but they didn't. How fucking stupid is that?"

Beckett dropped his gaze to the bike balanced against his leg. He ran a hand along the frame, and a scene sketched itself in my mind: a young boy with messy blond hair petting a beloved dog. A companion who leaned on his leg and barked with joy when he came home from school. Until Beckett was sent away.

The scene faded out of my mind, erased and replaced by the young man sitting next to me. Did anyone miss him while he was in jail? I wondered. Was anyone waiting for him when he got out? Did he have a family somewhere that he couldn't bear to face either?

"I don't want to sell any more of my records," he said, pulling me from my thoughts.

"I don't want to go back to Vegas."

The silence between us lasted through another train's arrival and departure.

"My place is a studio," he said. "No walls, no bedroom. No privacy. My couch is tiny and it's not a fold out."

A sudden heat flooded my chest. The warmth of hope.

I kept my voice cool and casual. "I was thinking I could get an air mattress, you know? One that I could keep out of the way during the day so it wouldn't take up space."

"That could work."

"And I know $400 isn't exactly paying my fair share, but I'd get a job right away to make up the rest."

"You won't even have a real bed," he said. "$400 is fair."

"Is that half the rent? I want to pay half—"

"It's close enough."

I waited for him to say something more and when he didn't, I said, "I'm quiet. I don't play loud music unless it's in my earphones. I'll work at my job, work at my graphic novel and try not to bother you."

He nodded. "The radiator hardly works no matter how many times I tell the landlord," he said. "You'll be cold. A lot."

"I can handle cold."

"Monday through Friday, I messenger for ten hours a day," Beckett said. His fingers trailed over a stretch of yellow metal frame on his bike. "Friday and Saturday night I bus at Giovanni's but Sunday—tomorrow—is my day off. I do whatever the hell I want on Sunday, even if that's nothing at all. I watch football, I listen to music—on my record player, not earphones—or I sleep."

I nodded. "I'll keep out of your way."

"You'll have to meet my parole officer, Roy," he said, meeting my eye.

I met his right back. “Okay.”

“I have to tell him my situation has changed. It’s fine so long as you don’t bring anyone over with warrants or drug problems.”

“I don’t know anyone here,” I said. “And I’m not exactly a social butterfly. Any and all stereotypes about comic book geeks you may have heard apply to me.”

Beckett gave me a dry smile. “You seem pretty ballsy for a geek.”

“Anything for the art.” I stuck out my hand. “Rossi. Zelda Rossi.”

He took my hand in his large one. It felt rough. Warm. Strong.

“Beckett Copeland.”

“Nice to meet you, Beckett Copeland.”

As we let go hands, the blinking sign on the Brooklyn-bound side announced a train about to pull in.

“I must be crazy,” he muttered. “Or you are.” He nodded at the tracks. “This is me. Or…us?”

This is us.

I went with Beckett Copeland to Brooklyn.

5

Beckett
Nov 30th

We came out of the Clinton-Washington Avenue station to find the rain had stopped. It was a short walk down Washington to my place and we were quiet for most of it. My eyes did plenty of talking, though, straining sideways to look at Zelda Rossi.

She only came up to my shoulder, and was hunched in her coat but I could tell that was from the cold, not from fear or nerves. A small smile played over her lips and the same relief I felt was mirrored in her brilliant green eyes when the streetlights hit them.

I led her up the two flights to my floor, and stopped at 2C.

"You sure you don't want to save this for tomorrow's lunch?" I asked, holding up the bag with the container of soup from Giovanni's she'd said she regretted ordering.

She eyed the bag then looked away. "No, I think I need to lay off the Italian food for a while."

A shadow crossed her eyes. I'd seen the same flicker of sadness last night, when she told me she had no family nearby.

Mrs. Santino must've heard us talking because my knuckles hardly grazed the door of 2C when it opened.

"Hey, Mrs. Santino," I said. "You in the mood for some soup tonight?"

She ignored me, and her squinty eyes narrowed in on Zelda. "Hmmph," she snorted, snatched the plastic bag out of my hand and shut the door.

I glanced down at Zelda. "Deep down, I know she's grateful."

She laughed a little. "Is that where last night's leftovers went too?" she asked as I rolled my bike down to 2E.

"I try to bring her food whenever I can," I said, fishing out my keys. "I don't know when or why that started, but I've never seen her leave her place. Never see anyone go in or out. Granted, I work ten hours most days but..." I shrugged. "She's always up at all hours, and she always takes it when I offer, so I figure she must need it."

"That's mighty nice of you, Copeland."

I glanced down as I unlocked the door. The shadow was gone from Zelda's eyes. A softness replaced it. An almost dreamy expression that made me bang my knee on my bike as I wheeled it over the threshold.

"So this is it?" she said, following.

"This is it," I said. No going back now. Letting Zelda move in was either going to save my ass from rent hell, or it was a colossal mistake.

Or it might be really good.

I tossed that thought into the hallway and closed the door. I meant what I wrote to Mrs. J the night before. I didn't go beyond casual sex with women. Zelda wasn't going to be anything but a roommate. A few weeks here, and then she was gone.

She was looking around the place, not saying anything.

It's all I got, I thought. *Take it or leave it.* I crossed my arms, prepared for a sarcastic remark, or even a flat-out, *This isn't going to work.*

"Well, we're going to be cozy, aren't we?" she said, a small laugh bursting of out of her.

"Something funny?" I asked, trying not to sound like a defensive asshole.

"No, not funny," she said, "I'm relieved. I'm so relieved you have no idea. Yeah, this place is small but it's *clean*. It's *tidy*." She poked her head into the bathroom just to the right of the front door. "Oh my God, it's a fucking *miracle*."

She reemerged from the bathroom, her smile brighter than ever. "The guy I shared a bathroom with in Vegas? Flushing the toilet was against his religion."

"So that's...disgusting," I said, a chuckle breaking past my cold front.

"Tell me about it. Another gal straight-up admitted she didn't do dishes. Oh, she cooked and she ate and she *used* dishes, but she didn't *do* dishes." Zelda was in the kitchen now, her fingers trailing over the crappy, but clean formica countertop. "This is heaven..."

"I don't like clutter," I said with a shrug.

"Me neither. I'm kind of a neat freak, actually," Zelda said. She gave me two thumbs up. "This bodes well, Copeland."

"So far so good," I admitted. "Except I don't know where you're going to sleep tonight. It's too late to get an air mattress."

She took the six steps to the couch. "I'm small. I can squish up on this for one night."

"You sure?" I rubbed the back of my neck. It ached just thinking about sleeping on that ratty old couch.

"I'm a good adapter," Zelda said, her glance landing and lingering on the table under the window.

"Yeah, you can work there," I said, moving to gather up some loose papers and my ancient-on-the-verge-of-dying laptop. "I hardly ever use it."

Zelda's eyes filled with a strange sort of happiness, and she went to the small table and set her portfolio on its scratched surface. "Perfect." She looked at me. "This is really perfect."

"I'm glad," I said.

It was the truth. After I'd served two years of a five-year sentence, the judge let me out for good behavior. He told me I'd paid my debt to society, but I disagreed. I still had a lot to make up for.

The silence between us thickened and Zelda's eyes fell to my album collection stacked vertically against the wall between the table and TV. She knelt in front of them. "Can I?"

"Sure."

"This stuff is older than anything I usually listen to," she said as she pored through my collection. "I'm basically musically illiterate. If it's not currently playing on an alternative station, chances are I don't know it."

She stopped and drew an album from the stacks resting against the wall. "Hold the phone… This one, I know." She flipped the album around. *Parallel Lines* by Blondie. "'One Way or Another' is the unofficial theme song to my graphic novel."

"Oh yeah?"

"Yeah. It's set in the future so this is classical music to my heroine. 'One Way or Another' is the song she uses to psych herself up."

"For what?"

"To go back in time to waste the bad guys."

"Of course."

She flipped the album back around to read the liner notes. "*'I'm gonna getcha, getcha, getcha,*" she sang, softly and horribly off-key, and then laughed lightly at herself. "Anyway."

She gave the album one last fond look before returning it to the exact place she found it and sat back on her heels. "Yep, this is pretty perfect, Copeland. Probably more for me than for you."

"It's a good arrangement for both of us," I said.

"Yeah, well, I still think I'm getting the better deal. And I'm stealing your privacy."

"I shared a six-by-eight foot cell with another guy for two years. I can handle this situation for a month or two."

Smooth, I thought. *Ease her mind by reminding her you're a felon.*

She hugged herself in her thick coat. "Okay, well. I guess I should call my old roommate. Let him know the deal."

"I should call Roy. My PO. He'll need to meet you."

She smiled faintly. "Okay."

Happy, asshole? You scared her. Or at least I'd stolen whatever small amount of equilibrium she'd felt upon first arrival. But maybe that was okay. I didn't want her to live in fear but maybe it was better if she never forgot what I was.

Or moreover, it's better you *never forget what you are.*

Zelda sat on the couch to call her people and I called Roy from the kitchen. I got his voicemail and left a quick message, speaking in a low voice.

"Hey, Roy, it's Beckett. Turns out you were right about rent being rough this month so I took in a roommate. Just for a few weeks at most. I know you need to meet her so call me whenever. Thanks."

I started to hang-up but a strange feeling—a warmth—swept through me.

"It's Zelda," I added to the end of my message and then hung up.

I stared at my phone then turned to see Zelda had finished her call too. Our eyes met and I offered her a smile. She smiled back.

"I told my Vegas roommate to send me some stuff," she said. "Don't worry, I don't have much. Just the rest of my clothes, and my tattoo machine and inks, though I don't know if I want to tattoo anymore."

"I could ask the boss about getting you a job at Giovanni's," I said.

"It's nice of you to offer, but I don't want to serve Italian food either. I'll start looking for something tomorrow."

"Sounds good."

The air between us had downgraded from tense to merely awkward. Two strangers figuring out their situation. I wanted to do more to set her at ease but what could I say? *I promise I won't hurt you while you sleep?*

"I'm beat," Zelda said. "You mind if I wash up and call it a night?" Her expression turned uncertain. "Or are you a night owl? Did you want to stay up and watch some TV?"

"Nah, no TV. Just accordion practice."

She arched a brow.

"Didn't I mention it?" I said. "I play the accordion between midnight and four a.m." I cocked my head in mock concern. "That's not going to be a problem, is it?"

"Gee, I can't imagine how," she said.

"I hope you like polkas."

"Who doesn't?"

Zelda laughed and slipped out of her pea coat. I took both as good signs. The tension loosened. She was settling in. Laughing at my dumb jokes.

She hung her coat on the hook by the door and took her trash bag to the bathroom. I kept an ear on the sound of running water as I stripped out of my work clothes as fast as I could. The bathroom door was the only partition in this joint. The potential to be caught half-naked had gone from non-existent to probable. I pulled on sleep pants and a sweatshirt. The water kept running. Good. Then I realized the couch wasn't sleep-ready.

"Shit."

I rummaged in the tiny closet next to my bed, I pulled down an old blue comforter that smelled musty but clean, and a small throw pillow I'd had since-God-knew-when. I laid them over the couch just as Zelda came out of the bathroom wearing leggings, socks, and a slouchy sweatshirt. Her hair was piled up on her head and square, black-framed glasses were perched on her small nose.

Great, I thought sarcastically. *So glad she's not totally fucking cute or anything.*

"I stashed my stuff in the cabinet under the sink," she said.

"Hope that was okay."

"More than okay. You live here now."

The words hung in the air between us.

"Yeah, I guess I do," she said after a moment. "I haven't paid you yet…"

"Tomorrow is the first," I said. "You can pay me then." I indicated the blanket. "The couch really isn't great for sleeping. I hope the blanket's enough."

"It's perfect," Zelda said. She set her glasses and phone on the coffee table, then laid down and burrowed under the blanket.

I went to the light switch by the door. "You good?"

"Yes. Thanks."

I flipped the switch and crossed in the darkness to my bed and climbed in. Across the short distance between us, I saw Zelda's faint smile, her chin just above the covers, her eyes already starting to close.

"I'm so tired," she said softly. "I didn't realize until just now how tiring it all was."

"I know what you mean," I said, thinking of the stress that had wrapped around my guts for so long, squeezing and tying me into knots. Come tomorrow, I'd no longer short of rent. In fact, with Zelda's $400, I'd have more breathing room than I'd had in a long time. I could hold on to my albums—not to mention my blood. No longer struggling to keep my chin above water. I could relax. For a little while, at least.

Already the air moved easier in and out of my lungs. And I wanted to thank her. I wanted to say something—anything—to let her know she could relax, too. That she could catch her breath and think, without worrying about getting robbed or rejected.

"Goodnight, Copeland," Zelda said, her voice heavy. "Thanks for agreeing to this crazy arrangement."

"It's good for both of us."

"Yeah."

"And Zelda?"

"Hm?"

She was already slipping toward sleep. Unafraid. She was brave, this girl. And tough. I smiled to myself.

"Nothing. Goodnight," I said, and fell under too, listening to someone else's breathing besides my own.

6

Zelda
December 1st

I woke with heavy arms and legs, and drowsy thoughts. I was balled up on Beckett Copeland's small couch savoring what I called the World's Most Comfortable Position—on my side, hugging the pillow, bundled and warm with no alarm clock driving me out of it. I snuggled deeper, and glanced across the tiny living space to where my new roommate slept.

Beckett was on his stomach, his face half-buried in his pillow. The unburied part was smoothed of tension, his brows unfurrowed. More at peace than when he was awake.

"Enigma Man," I whispered to myself. A hero who feeds his neighbors, gives rent money to the homeless, and opens his apartment to total strangers. No special powers, other than simple generosity.

And who did two years in federal prison for armed robbery.

The feeling of safety faltered a bit, but returned easily and wrapped around me, like his comforter. I burrowed deeper and went back to sleep.

The smell of coffee found me some time later and pulled me back up. I blinked and sat up. Beckett was in the kitchen, at the coffee maker.

"Sorry if I woke you," he said.

"No, no, it's fine. Do your thing. Pretend like I'm not even here."

"That's not going to happen," he said softly, then coughed. "Yeah, so can I offer you some pretend coffee?"

I grinned. "Black, please." I tossed off the cover and shivered as I crossed the five steps to the kitchen counter.

"It's that useless bastard," Beckett said, and handed me a mug. He leveled a stink-eye at the old-school radiator under the window, with its chipped white paint. "It works just enough to keep us from freezing to death."

"The landlord know about it?"

"I may have mentioned it to him once or twice," Beckett said with a small smile.

"Does he need to know about me?"

"Better that he doesn't," he said. "He'd probably try to jack up the rent."

"Which is?"

Beckett a long sip of coffee.

I set my mug down. "I want to pay half. Whatever it is, it's fair that I pay half."

"We already negotiated your rent, given that you don't have a *bed,*" Beckett said. "Four hundred bucks. Final offer."

I thought about arguing but Beckett's expression told me it was useless. "Fine." I rummaged in my trash bag by the couch for my belt wallet, and fished out four of my remaining seven hundred dollar bills. I laid them on the formica, where Beckett eyed them as if I'd just put a soiled diaper on his kitchen counter.

"Thanks," he muttered, and swept up the bills and pocketed them. "So. You need an air mattress, right?"

"If you could point me toward a good place to get one, that'd be great."

"Sure thing."

We opened up my laptop on the table under the window. After locating a sporting goods store, Beckett showed me how to navigate the Brooklyn bus system. His head was bent close to mine. He smelled of coffee and warmth and all things masculine.

Knock it off, Rossi, I told myself. The celibacy of the past year had been lying dormant. Being in close proximity to an ungodly good-looking male like Beckett woke it up like a fire alarm in the middle of the night. I gave myself a mental shake and focused on the bus lines and streets.

"Great, thanks," I said, gnawing my lip. "Got it."

"You don't look like you got it," Beckett said.

I made a face. "I walk up Atlantic to Vanderbilt, take the B69 towards downtown, get off at the corner of Vanderbilt and Dekalb. I got it. I'm not completely helpless."

Beckett frowned at the rain that had begun to hit the window over the desk in slanted silver droplets.

"Maybe I should go with you."

I snapped my laptop shut. "It's your day off, remember?"

"I remember," he said. "But you're going to need a bunch of shit to get settled in, right? Food, the mattress, whatever else you need. After today, I'm at work all week until seven at night at the earliest."

"So?"

"So you need to get to know the city. Today's your day to learn the ropes. Or at least this neighborhood."

I bit my lip. "It's raining. It's your day off."

"And I get to decide how to spend it." He shook his head. "God, you're stubborn."

"I thought I was being considerate," I replied, hands on my hips.

He laughed at my pinched stare. "Oh, I get it. You're one of those girls."

My eyes widened. "Sorry? I'm *which* kind of girl?"

"The kind who insists on doing everything for themselves and doesn't let anyone help."

I crossed my arms over my chest. "I seem to recall asking for your help last night in a rather epic, pride-sacrificing kind of way."

"Yeah, but that was different. I'd bet a million bucks if offered, you'd have said thanks but no thanks."

"You underestimate my desperation," I said. "Also, since when is being independent a bad thing?"

"It's not. Turning down an offer of help is stupid." He did a double-take of my unrelenting stare. "Wow. It's been a long time since a girl looked at me like that."

"It's been awhile since you called a girl stupid?" I asked.

"I didn't mean that *you're* stupid. I just mean…" He ran a hand through is hair. "Look, will you just let me help you to the damn store? The mattress is going to be heavy as fuck, it's pouring rain, and the buses around here don't always attract the most savory of characters, okay? I don't know if you noticed last night, but this neighborhood isn't exactly Central Park West."

I kept my arms crossed, my lips pursed. "It's not *pouring* rain."

Outside, lightning lit up the window and thunder bellowed a split second later. The rain morphed from a light drizzle to a heavy deluge, pattering against the window as if it were trying to get in. Beckett's smug smile was maddening.

I threw up my hands. "Oh, have it your way."

Twenty minutes later, we were dressed in coats and weatherproof jackets, huddled together under my umbrella at the bus stop as the rain came down in sheets.

I glanced up at Beckett, that annoying feeling of being safe came over me again, coupled with a strange tangle of emotions.

Like possibly, maybe, perhaps guilt for giving him a hard time about helping you?

My mother had always told me that gratitude comes first. *"No matter what happens, even on your worst day, find something to be grateful about. It'll make you feel better."*

I glanced up at Beckett again, then along the street with its row upon row of tenements under a gray sky.

"I've been on my own for a long time," I said in a low voice.

Beckett was standing so close to me, I felt it when he shifted. "Yeah, I get that," he said. "I have too."

"You get used to doing things a certain way," I said. An old sedan, low to the ground, with rusted hood, passed us. "For survival."

I glanced up at him. He glanced down at me, then looked away, nodded. "I hear you."

"So what I'm trying to say is—"

"You don't have to," he said, cutting me off. "It's cool."

I frowned. "My mother used to tell me that gratitude—"

"Bus is here," Beckett said.

The B69 lumbered up and lurched to a stop. The doors opened with a hiss. Beckett led me to the door, and closed the umbrella. "After you."

I stopped to fix him a look.

He sighed. "You're welcome, Rossi, now get on the damn bus before we're drenched."

I got on the damn bus.

At the sporting goods store, I picked out a twin-sized air mattress. The thick rubbery thing was packed in a box that was exactly as Beckett had said—heavy as fuck. My arms started to scream after about ten minutes. Wordlessly, he took it out of my aching arms, hefted it onto his shoulder and shot me a look that said, *Don't even think about it.*

I hid my smile in my coat collar.

I bought a small storage box for my clothes, then we hit a small Halal grocery store on the way home for a few items I couldn't live without—lettuce, bread, cheese, a few vegetables, and salad dressing. I made a note of the bus and streets so I could come back and properly shop without Beckett needing to supervise.

The rain had let up, leaving the bus stop in a puddle. Beckett glanced at the grocery bag I was shifting from one hand to the other. "You do much cooking?" he asked.

"I like to. In Vegas, the kitchen was usually too disgusting to contemplate, but now that I'm here, I thought I'd take it up again." I glanced up at him. "You?"

He shook his head. "I get back from work around seven most nights after riding for ten hours. I'm too tired."

"I can cook for us," I said. "I'm not Julia Child or anything, but I have a few recipes up my sleeve. My mom taught me." Those last words slipped out before I could catch them back, and I barreled on before Beckett thought to ask about my family. "It's something I like doing when I get the chance."

"You don't have to cook for me," Beckett said.

"I'm going to feel like a mighty big asshole if I cook dinner for myself and none for you. You don't want to make your new roommate feel like an asshole do you?"

He smirked but said nothing.

"Oh, I get it," I said. "You're one of those kind of guys."

He glanced down at me. "What kind of guy am I?"

"The kind who is ridiculously full of man-pride and doesn't let anyone do anything for him." My lips twisted in a smirk. "I'll bet if you got lost, you'd cut your arm off before you asked for directions."

"That's right," he said, his look smug. "Because I don't get lost."

"But you do eat, right? So how about this? I'll cook enough for two and whatever you don't eat I'll be forced to give to Mrs. Santino."

He didn't look at me but I saw a smile before he caught it. "I can live with that."

Back at the apartment, Beckett got to work pumping up the mattress while I unloaded my groceries into the kitchen. When the mattress was inflated we both stood over it. I was satisfied but Beckett frowned.

"It doesn't look too comfortable," he said.

"Are you kidding?" I sat down on it and bounced up and down a couple of times. "It's like sleeping on a trampoline."

I was joking but Beckett didn't smile.

"The radiator is terrible. You're going to be cold on the floor."

"I'm going to be fine," I said. "It's just for a month or two. And anyway, I signed up for this remember?"

He looked as if he were about to protest when his cell phone rang. Still wearing a sour look on his face he answered. "Oh, hey, Roy." He listened for a few moments, his brows furrowing deeper. "Yeah, I guess that would be okay. Let me check with her." He dropped the phone to his side. "Roy, my PO, wants to take us to dinner tonight. Him and his wife."

"Is that normal parole officer protocol?"

"It's normal Roy Goodwin protocol."

"Sounds great." I hauled myself off the air mattress and chucked him on the shoulder. "Don't look so grouchy, Copeland. Someone wants to buy us dinner? Tell him I'm in. Just nothing fancy okay? My ball gown hasn't arrived yet from Vegas."

Beckett put the phone back to his ear. "Yeah, that sounds fine Roy. See you at seven." He hung up and slipped the phone back in his pocket. "Okay. Dinner at seven."

"Why do you look like we're going out for dental surgery instead?"

He shrugged. "Nothing. It's fine."

"Is there anything I should know before? Anything he's going want to know about me?"

"Do you have a criminal record?"

"I once jumped a subway turnstile without paying. Does that count?"

He started to smile, then a thought crossed is eyes. "Where?"

"Where what?"

"Where did you jump a subway stile? Here?"

I tucked a lock of hair behind my ear. "In Philly. Once. Long time ago."

"Oh. I was under the impression you'd never been to a big city before," he said. "Aren't you from Vegas?"

"Not originally," I said. I struggled to lift the mattress. "So where should we stash this sucker during the day?"

Beckett took the other end and together we leaned the mattress along the wall between his closet and the front door.

"It's not the prettiest of décor," I said.

"It's fine," he said.

I moved my meager belongings out of the garbage bag and into the little storage container I'd bought. Beckett fiddled with his bike. We were both quiet, but any minute I expected him to ask me about Philadelphia, or about my family. Then he'd know they were a two-hour train ride away, and the next obvious question being why I wasn't staying with them instead of crowding into his tiny place?

But he didn't ask anything; he put on one of his albums—Prince—and I didn't have to answer.

Around six o'clock, I rummaged through my small stash of clothes, searching for the most presentable and the least wrinkled. I'd never heard of a PO who took his parolees out with family members, as if it were a Sunday dinner instead of an inspection of me.

I found a pair of black leggings and a black blouse that wasn't too disheveled after its stay in the trash bag. I gathered my clothes up. "I'm going to take a shower, if that's cool," I said. "Unless, you wanted to go first…?

Beckett looked up from the sofa, where he was watching a local news channel. "You go ahead," he said. "I'll jump in after."

I nodded and locked myself in the small bathroom that hardly had room for a shower stall, toilet, and single sink. It was like walking into a den of masculinity: The usual scents of cologne, deodorant, soap and shampoo, were all there but with none of the fruity flavors that I liked. Instead, they were simple and unfussy. Clean and sharp. Before I could stop myself I inhaled deeply.

This is him. This is Beckett.

I didn't know where that thought came from or what to do with it. I looked around, taking in his most intimate space—a space he was now sharing with me. A single toothbrush on the sink with a tube of toothpaste rolled up neatly from the bottom. A single bar of soap in the dish. One lonely bottle of shampoo in the shower stall.

I put my shampoo next to his, and my bodywash next to his soap. *Better.*

The shower here was tiled in pale green ceramic squares, and the fixtures were older than me. But it was clean. Almost cozy. I didn't feel as weird as I thought I would, in some strange guy's shower.

It's your shower now too, I thought, as I let the water drench my hair and run down my back. Working conditioner through with my fingers, I found myself humming "Purple Rain" under the showerfall.

I dried off and turbaned my hair tight in a towel, then got dressed and did my makeup, going easy on the black eyeliner. I emerged from the bathroom, leaving the scents of my perfume and shampoo to mingle with Beckett's.

"All yours," I said.

He turned and looked over the back of the couch from where he sat. His eyes dropped down my body, then up, then looked away. "Thanks."

I took his spot on the couch, still warm from where he'd been sitting and he took a turn in the shower where I'd been. Naked. Ten minutes ago.

Day Two, Rossi, and you're already having impure thoughts about your roommate.

I grabbed the TV remote and flipped channels, and left it on a loud, obnoxious, unsexy commercial.

Beckett came out of the bathroom.

He looked sharp, but not expensive. His dark jeans were neat and his blue dress shirt untucked. Under the ugly fluorescent lights, his damp hair gleamed a little like gold. *Brassier than gold,* I thought, the artist in me running fingers along colored pencils to pick the right shade. I'd use a chrome-tint ink for his hair and stubble. Cobalt or sapphire blue for his eyes…

Beckett waved a hand up and down. "Hello?"

I blinked. "Sorry. You look…" *Devastating.* "Nice. You look nice."

His eyes softened while his expression didn't. It was something I noticed happening often. How his face sent one message while his eyes sent another.

"Thanks," he said. "You look really nice, too."

We both look nice, I thought. *The most impotent word in the English language. So why does the room feel electric?*

I rose off the couch. "Am I presentable to a parole officer and his wife?"

A small smile escaped to flit over Beckett's lips. "Perfect. Fine, I mean. You look fine."

Fine. Nice's first cousin.

I liked 'perfect' better.

The silence between us was thick, and it abruptly shattered with the buzzing of the doorbell. Beckett went to the intercom.

"Roy?"

"In the flesh," came a man's cheerful voice. "We have a cab."

"Be right down."

Beckett pulled my coat off the hook by the door. I started to take it from him but he was holding it open, ready to help me into it.

"And they say chivalry is dead," I said, as I turned my back to him as he slipped my coat over my shoulders.

"My grandfather was big on manners," Beckett said.

"He taught you well," I said gently.

Beckett said nothing as he zipped his weather-proof jacket and pulled a knit beanie over his head. I grabbed my umbrella and we went down.

7

Zelda
December 1st

"I have to say, Copeland," I said as we descended the two flights of stairs down, our footsteps echoing in the dingy corridors. "This feels like I'm going to meet your parents."

"They're not my parents," he said. The cold tinge to his voice gave me a shiver, but he looked apologetic when we arrived at the door to the street. "Roy and Mary are good people. I'm sure you'll love them."

I nodded and kept my smartass remarks to myself. He obviously didn't want to talk about parents or family either. I could appreciate that. Holy hell, could I ever.

Roy and Mary Goodwin stood outside, next to the cab. All beaming smiles, like proud, emotional parents on prom night, despite Beckett's words to the contrary. Mary, a somewhat plump woman with brown hair that brushed her shoulders, greeted Beckett with a hug, then held his face in her gloved hands to look at him.

"How are you, sweetheart? It's been too long." She kissed him on the cheek, then turned to me. "And you must be Zelda? I'm Mary. So happy to meet you, darling."

"Thanks. You too," I said.

"Roy Goodwin, young lady," Roy said, giving my hand a fatherly squeeze. "Pleasure to meet you."

"You too, Mr. Goodwin," I said. "Or is it Officer?"

"No formalities here," he said. "Just Roy. I hope you're hungry. I thought we'd head to a joint on 3rd Avenue. You build your own hamburgers. Ain't that something? Sound good?"

"Sounds great," I said.

Roy Goodwin had to be the most cheerful human I'd met in a

long time. Apparently the ills of society he dealt with every day in his occupation were unimportant when compared to building one's own burger. I couldn't help smiling, but Beckett looked stoic, as if hardening himself against some ordeal.

I elbowed him in the side as we shuffled around the cab to determine who would sit where. "He's your *parole officer*?" I whispered. "He's great. They both are."

He nodded and made a noncommittal sound.

There's a story here, I thought, realizing how little I actually knew of Beckett Copeland. Things were happening so fast—moving in, then going to dinner with the Goodwins. I had a sense of being dropped straight into the middle of a book without having read the early chapters.

But not bad, I thought. *I'd read more.*

Beckett sat in the front seat of the cab and because I was small, I sat wedged between the Goodwins in the back. They chatted and bickered, both with each other and with Beckett. Their manner was so casual and familiar, so unconscious, I couldn't shake the impression they *were* family.

Maybe they are. Or as close to it as he has. I could ask him—later, privately. But then again, questions about his family would only beget questions in return.

Forget it, I thought, enjoying Beckett's irritated grimace when Mary reached over the seat to smooth down the collar of his jacket and pestered him about getting a haircut.

The Burger Bistro had polished wood floors and brick walls. A huge serving bar ran down its middle, where patrons could choose their own burger fixings and fries. The place was packed, loud with conversation. After loading up our plates, we spied people vacating a table for four and grabbed it.

"Isn't this *great?"* Roy said. "It's always this packed, because it's just that good."

"How do you like it, Zelda?" Mary asked, just as I took a monster bite out of my Jack cheeseburger with extra pickles.

I nodded and tried to smile through cheeks full of food. I'd hardly eaten in the last few days—having given up two meals to Mrs. Santino. I was ravenous, and burning with embarrassment for pigging out. I swallowed my half-chewed bite and washed it down with soda. "Really good," I finally managed.

"I'm so glad."

She released me from her spotlight smile but before I could sink my teeth again, Roy asked, "So tell us, Zelda, where did you and Beckett meet?"

"At Giovanni's, two nights ago," I said. "I needed a place to live, kind of on the fly. Beckett took pity on me."

"We worked out a mutually-beneficial agreement," Beckett said. "Just for a month or two."

A look passed between him and Roy, then Roy turned a smile on me. "Well, I think it's wonderfully smart to combine forces like that. Teaming up with someone else makes things like rent and utilities that much easier to tackle, right?"

Beckett concentrated on his food, swirling a French fry in a little paper cup of ketchup. "It's a good arrangement."

His voice wasn't hard, just indifferent, but I didn't miss the glance he shot me. As usual, his face and voice were holding the table at arm's length, but his eyes… The vulnerable softness there he couldn't conceal.

Under Mary's direction, the conversation roamed all over easily. Eventually Beckett's nonchalance loosened up and he laughed at Roy's bad jokes. I almost made it out of the dinner un-interrogated, but as we sat back to let our food settle, Mary put her hand on mine.

"Zelda, sweetheart, tell us about yourself. Are you from New York originally?"

"No," I said, avoiding Beckett's eyes. "I'm from Las Vegas."

"And do you have family there?"

I took a sip of soda to buy some time but there was no sense in lying. "No, they're here on the East Coast. Philadelphia, actually."

"Oh, that's close," Mary exclaimed. "How nice for you. Will you be visiting them during the holidays?" She leaned over and gave a nod of her head Beckett's way. "We'd love to have this one over but he always plays hard to get."

"Mary," Roy said in a mildly warning tone.

"I know, I know, but a gal can hope, can't she?" Mary smiled at me. "But what were we saying? Do you have plans for the holidays?"

I shifted in my seat. "I'm not sure yet."

That was a version of the truth. My parents understood how hard it was for me to visit them. I'd only seen them a handful of times in the six years since I'd moved out. I wanted to go. I missed them horribly, but it was physically torturous. My body always protested a trip home in a variety of terrible ways…

Panic began to edge its way under my skin.

Oh shit, no…Not now. Why now?

I hadn't had a full-blown attack in a year, but I recognized the symptoms. Usually the anxiety was a slow build; a thermostat's red mercury climbing to the top. This felt like it was starting at the top and straining to explode out. My heart began to pound and my brow broke out in a sweat as everyone at the table watched me.

"I…" I swallowed. "I don't…"

Roy and Mary exchanged looks and Beckett's brows furrowed.

I struggled to inhale as the scene around me started to morph slowly, a photograph emerging in a dark room, to Handy's Grocery, with rows and rows of colorful cans, and my sister at the end of the aisle.

Mary's voice came from far away. "Are you alright, dear?"

Where's your sister?

Beckett shoved his chair back, and the scraping sound jolted me a little. But not enough. My throat was closing and it felt as if every nerve ending had been set on fire. A hand closed around my arm and Beckett gently pulled me to my feet.

"She told me she has…um…a phobia," he said, his voice muffled against the thrashing of my pulse in my ears. "Busy, enclosed spaces. Isn't that right?"

I stared up at him through a terrible, fuzzy haze of memory that tried to swamp me, and nodded.

Roy started to rise from his chair. "Should I call someone…?"

"No, no, she needs some air," Beckett said, grabbing my jacket off the back of my chair. "Meet us outside in five, okay?"

He didn't wait for an answer, but helped me through the small maze of tables and chairs, to the sidewalk outside and around the corner. The cold, night air was like a slap to the face—one that I desperately needed—and I sucked in air, leaning heavily on Beckett who had me securely by the arm and back.

"You okay?" he asked, studying me intently. "Or should I call someone after all?"

I shook my head, remembering what a therapist told me when I was sixteen. *Deep breath in…deep breath out,* I thought, envisioning the air—tinted blue for the cold—pass smoothly into my lungs and back out again. The memory of the grocery store aisle retreated, like a movie fading to black, then fading in on a new scene—a burger joint parking lot and Beckett holding my hand. My pulse slowed and quieted.

"I'm okay," I said, exhaling.

"You sure?"

I nodded again. "I'm good. Thanks."

Beckett let me go slowly, then helped me into my coat. "Panic attack, right?" he asked.

"How did you know?"

His coat was still in the restaurant. He jammed his hands into the front pockets of his jeans, his breath pluming in the air. "Buddy of mine had them in high school," he said. "Does this happen a lot?"

"Not a lot," I said. *Too much. Even once is too much.*

"But there's a trigger?"

"Yeah," I said, and huddled into my coat. "Family stuff. This one took me by surprise."

Beckett nodded. "Maybe talk about it later?" he asked in a low voice. His gaze followed a car leaving the parking lot. "In case it happens again so I know what to do."

"You knew exactly what to do," I said, humiliation turning my cheeks ruddy faster than the cold air. "I'm sorry I made a scene."

"You didn't," Beckett said with a small grin. "But Mary might just take you home with her now. I'll have to find a new roommate."

Somehow, a smile spread over my lips when minutes ago I felt like I was being strangled by memories.

Roy and Mary came out of the restaurant wearing identical expressions of concern.

"Zelda, are you alright, dear?" Mary asked.

I noticed Roy's glance danced between Beckett and me.

"She's fine," Beckett said.

"She can also speak for herself," I said lightly.

Beckett shook his head with a small smile and held up his hands in surrender.

I turned to Mary. "I'm really sorry about that. It came on me so fast, I got a little…overwhelmed. It hasn't happened in awhile so I wasn't prepared. Although I guess I never am."

"You have nothing to be sorry about," she said, looking at Beckett fondly. "And I'm so happy that Beckett knew exactly what to do for you."

I glanced up at him. *Yeah, he did.* I'd never had a panic attack come on so quickly, so strongly and then fade away almost as fast.

Roy handed Beckett his coat. "I've called a taxi. Should be here any minute."

"You don't have to wait out here in the cold with me," I said.

"We're happy to," Roy said.

Together, we huddled under the bright yellow fluorescents of the Burger Bistro until the cab arrived, my shoulder touching Beckett's the whole time.

The taxi pulled to the curb.

"I'll take the front," Roy said when Beckett moved for that door. "How do you young people say? I'm calling shotgun?"

His smile was bright but I sensed a sharp intelligence under all the joviality. Roy didn't miss a thing. Beckett didn't argue, just opened the back door. I slid to the middle, next to Mary, and Beckett folded himself in beside me. His legs were so long, his thigh rested against my knee.

"Sorry," he muttered.

"No worries," I replied.

Mary filled the cab with pleasant chatter the whole way back to Beckett's place. "Thanks so much for dinner," I said as I got out. "It was nice to meet you."

"A pleasure, sweetheart," Mary said. "I hope I see you again soon."

"Most assuredly," Roy said. He exited the car to join his wife in the back. He stopped to briefly touch my shoulder. "Take care," he said, with an undertone of *thank you.*

We went upstairs, an evening's worth of mysteries and unspoken personal history lagging behind. Beckett said nothing, but his deep blue eyes were full of concern.

Goddamn panic attacks. Each time I had one, another piece of myself broke away, leaving me less whole and weaker than before.

I'm not weak. I'm fine. I'm doing just fine.

"Uh, so it's hard to imagine Roy as a parole officer," I said.

"Try imagining him as an FBI agent," he said.

"What? No way."

"I know. Can you picture Roy, armed with his service weapon and wearing a bullet-proof vest, busting some perp's door down?"

"Does not compute," I said.

We reached the door and Beckett pulled a set of keys from his jacket pocket.

"I don't think he was in the field much, but even so. He looks more like a social studies teacher than a parole officer."

"He's great," I said. "He and Mary both. And they obviously like you a lot. Do they treat all of his parolees the same way?"

"I'm sure they do," Beckett said, though he didn't sound sure at all. He unlocked the door and held it open for me. "We're going to need to get a key made for you," he said.

"I can do it tomorrow," I said, shrugging out of my jacket. "I have to go out and pick up a few things, namely new art supplies. Oh, and a job."

Beckett took my jacket and hung it for me. Utterly casual, as if he'd been doing it every day for years. "Okay, I'll leave it with you."

"Thanks."

We took turns in the bathroom, changing, washing up and brushing teeth. I laid the air mattress on the floor and settled Beckett's big blue comforter over it.

"Sheets," I said, making a burrito out of the blanket rather than sleep directly on cold rubber. "My shopping list for tomorrow: sheets, art supplies, a job."

Beckett frowned, eyed the air mattress with a sour curve to his lip. "You sure you're okay on that thing?"

"Snug as a bug." I glanced at my phone beside me on the floor. "It's only nine o'clock," I said. "Please don't call it a night on my account. I get tired after…an episode. But you go ahead. Watch TV or whatever."

Beckett rubbed his stubble, the dark look still on his face. "I have to be up at five to catch the train. I'll just make sure the radiator doesn't quit. I don't want you to be cold."

"I'm fine. Really."

Beckett banged on the radiator, and cursed under his breath. It gave a small whine and a hiss that seemed to satisfy him. He hit the lights and climbed into bed.

"Goodnight, Zelda," he said.

"Goodnight, Beckett." I'd almost said 'Copeland' but after he'd helped me through the panic attack, it didn't feel right in that moment. Despite my best effort, my almost-breakdown had pulled us a tiny bit closer together.

Focus, Rossi, I thought. Tomorrow I would buy new art supplies and get to work on my graphic novel. That's what I was there for, and nothing more.

The air mattress was cold and smelled like a tire, but I fell asleep quickly. I dreamt of standing on a storm-swept island. A monsoon tore across the sky and ripped the water into monstrous waves that roared and tried to devour me. Beckett was there, standing between me and the white-foamed water that churned and boiled, his back to the danger. In his hands was my pea coat, of all things.

I don't want you to be cold, he said, helping me slip it on. He smiled a sad, wistful kind of smile as the tidal wave crashed around us, around *him.*

I stood in the shelter of his tall, strong body and the water never touched me at all.

8

Zelda
December 2nd

I woke the next morning to Beckett softly closing the bathroom door. I blinked sleepily at my phone. 5:02 a.m.

God, how does he do it?

The sound of the shower running came on a few seconds later, and I sat up, looking to the window over the desk for signs of rain, but it was too dark to tell. I grabbed my phone again and checked the temp.

"Thirty-one degrees?" I whistled low in my teeth. "Holy shit."

The thought of Beckett riding around Manhattan in that cold for ten hours gave me a shiver. I tossed off the big blue blanket and padded into the kitchen.

"Curse you," I muttered at the radiator, and made coffee in the small pot, then hurried back to the relative warmth of my air mattress.

I was dozing when I heard the bathroom door open and footsteps go past me on the floor to the kitchen.

"What's this?" Beckett asked from the other side of the counter.

"The coffee fairy came while you showered," I mumbled.

"Oh, really?"

"Sshhh. I'm sleeping."

I felt Beckett's gaze on me and I pushed up to sitting, brushed the hair out of my eyes. "What's that look for?"

"You good for today? You know where to go to get what you need?"

"I'm good, I promise," I said. "And you're going to be late for work."

"We should probably exchange cell phone numbers." He sipped his coffee. "In case of emergencies."

"Right." I grabbed my phone and we exchanged digits.

"702 area code?" he said with a dry smile. "Better change it. You're a New Yorker now."

"That remains to be seen. If I crash and burn—again—it's back to Vegas for me."

Beckett nodded, but said nothing. He drained his mug. "Thanks again for this."

"Yep."

From back under my blanket, I watched him pull on his weather-proof jacket, and his messenger bag that crossed his chest. He wore tight-fitting pants too that accentuated the lean muscle of his body, but didn't look nearly warm enough.

He does this for a living. He's used to it.

This was followed by another thought,

Who asks him if he's going to be okay?

"Are you going to be okay?" I blurted, my words bypassing the checkpoint I usually had in place between thoughts and words. He gave me a strange look, somewhere between perplexed and touched. "I mean, it's really cold out there," I added. "Does all that gear keep you warm?"

Beckett smiled softly. "I'm fine, thanks. I'm used to it."

"Oh sure. I figured as much…"

An awkward silence fell. I retreated back into the blanket; Beckett's expression closed up like shutters.

"Key's on the kitchen counter," he said, walking his bike through the door.

"Thanks. I'll make a copy."

"Right. See you tonight."

"Have a good one."

"You too."

The door closed, mercifully ending the stilted, roommate chit-chat.

Hey, this is what you want, right? No distractions. No sweet smiles from beautiful men.

Still, there was no harm in Beckett and me becoming friends, especially since we were living together. I didn't make friends easily. There was too much I didn't want to talk about. I kept people at arm's length with sarcasm and stupid jokes. My relationships with guys were casually friendly or casually sexual. No digging beneath the surface.

It was how I survived the ten years since Rosemary disappeared.

But you're here to work, so get to it.

I vowed then and there to get a night job. I worked best on my graphic novel at night, but I could stay out of Beckett's way better if I worked the night shift as a server. Maybe drawing during the day would give me the perspective I needed to see the changes BlackStar Publishing wanted.

But you offered to make him dinner.

"I still can, we just won't eat it together," I said into the empty apartment, then rubbed my eyes. "I'm losing it. *Focus,* Rossi."

I showered and changed into my last clean pair of black leggings, an oversized white pullover and my boots. I was putting my makeup on in the bathroom, when I heard a key turn in the front door's lock.

"You forget something?" I called.

No answer, but footsteps crossed the apartment, and a second later I heard the refrigerator opening. I cracked the bathroom door.

"Beckett? Hello?"

Still no answer, but the rummaging in the kitchen continued. A cabinet door squeaked. The tinny rattle of the utensil drawer being opened and shut.

I peeked out of the bathroom and into the kitchen area. A skinny woman stood at the counter with her back to me. Brown hair, tight jeans and a black sweater, earbuds in her ears. She sang under her breath and danced—and not badly—while spooning cottage cheese—*my* cottage cheese—straight out of the container. When she turned sideways, I recognized her as the waitress from Giovanni's. Darlene.

I crossed my arms and cleared my throat. "Hi."

The woman's eyes widened, and she nearly choked on her food. "Jesus!"

The spoon went flying and white curds erupted out of the container as she slammed it down to brace herself on the counter with both hands.

"Oh my God, you scared the crap out of me," Darlene cried loudly, her earbuds still in. Breathing heavily, she pulled them out, recognition slowly dawning in her eyes. "You're the chick from Giovanni's..."

"Zelda."

"Zelda..." She studied me, confused. "Why are you here?"

"Why am *I* here?"

"Wait." Darlene's kohl-rimmed eyes widened and a smile spread over her wide mouth. "Wait, oh my God, you didn't. You did *not!"*

I blinked. "I didn't what?"

"You? And Beckett?" She held up her hands and rotated them in circles in the air. "You know…?"

"No," I said. "God no, nothing like that."

I moved around the counter to join her in the kitchen. It was too small for two people, so I gave her a gentle shove out of my way so I could get a sponge. I started cleaning the cottage cheese that had splattered on the counter and the wall.

"So what is it then?" Darlene said, picking up the container and spoon to resume her snack on the other side of the counter. "What else could it *be*?"

"We're just roommates for a few months. I need to work and splitting rent makes sense."

"Ohhh," Darlene said. "Is that why you were at Gio's, asking about him?"

"Yeah, pretty much," I said. I took the container away from Darlene and fixed her with a look. "It's to make rent bearable. It makes sense."

She sucked on the spoon, eyebrows waggling. "You said that already. And rent, *schment.* You're shacking up. Sexy times are sure to follow."

I turned to put the cottage cheese back in the fridge and let the cool air waft over my cheeks for a moment.

"There will be no sexy times," I said, shutting the door. Firmly. "He works all day and I'm going to find an evening job. Right now, actually. So if you don't mind…"

Darlene didn't get the hint. "I'll go with you. Oh my God, I thought today was going to be super boring, but we can go to the city and do girl stuff. You want to work in Manhattan, right?" She clutched my arm with a sudden thought, and her eyes widened. "Oh my god, Zel, I just had an idea. You could—"

"No way," I said before she could finish her sentence. "I'm not working at Giovanni's. Or any other Italian place."

Her face fell. "Bummer. Why not? Aren't you Italian?"

"Yeah, I am. But…"

"Oh, I get it," Darlene said. "Once I could only afford Ramen noodles for an entire month. Couldn't look at them afterward. You must get sick of Italian food, right?"

No, the opposite. I miss it.

"Something like that," I said.

Darlene bounced along next to me as I gathered my bag and coat. "Whatever you want to do, do it in Manhattan. Much better money there. By the way, what *do* you want to do?"

I blinked at Darlene's energy and wondered if it was natural or synthetic. I searched her eyes for signs of drugs but they looked clear, near as I could tell.

Don't be a judgmental bitch. She's just happy. You should try it sometime.

"I'm a tattoo artist," I said. "But I'd rather wait tables. The money is more immediate."

Darlene linked her bracelet-clad arm in mine. "Girl, I will hook you *up*."

"I need to buy some art supplies too. And get a key made." I raised my eyebrows at her as I locked the door. "Maybe you have a recommendation for a key-making place?"

She laughed. "You're so funny, Zel. Becks gave me a key six months ago when I was in a bad way. To help me get away from some bad elements, you know? But that was a long time ago." Her expression drew down as if pulled by heavy memories. "I'm clean, I swear. I don't bring that shit around Becks. It could get him in big trouble with his PO, and I would never do anything to hurt him. Not one thing. Ever."

She was practically on the verge of tears now and I slung my arm around her, even though she was a good six inches taller than me in her ankle boots.

"I believe you, Dar," I said, giving her my warmest smile, one that hadn't seen the light of day in a while. "I notice Beckett has a strong humanitarian streak running through him."

Darlene's own smile returned, chasing the clouds of guilt off her face in an instant. I envied her for that.

"His grandfather raised him," she said, and we started down the hallway. "Always taught him to do right."

"What about the robbery?"

She sighed. "A bad mistake that he'll never forgive himself for." She shook her head. "He only had his Gramps. No other family. And they didn't have a lot of money. Desperation makes you do crazy things."

I nodded, and swallowed a heavy lump that suddenly rose in my throat. "Yeah, I get that."

"He writes letters to Mrs. J. The wife?" She waved her hand. "But I should let him tell you the story. If you can ever get him talking." She wagged a finger in my face. "But no matter what he tells you, he's a good man. It's in his blood, and one stupid mistake can't change that."

I smiled. It felt nice to hear Beckett spoken of that way.

Because he's a virtual stranger I have to sleep three feet from every night. That's all.

Outside, there was no rain, but the sky was slate gray and the sidewalks silvery with puddles. The city sprawled around and above me. I was suddenly glad to have Darlene at my side. Not just a guide but a new friend. I liked her. We clicked immediately; despite the fact she seemed to be the polar opposite of me. She also seemed the type who wouldn't take it personally if I didn't want to talk about things. Back in Vegas, my female roommates acted as if I withheld personal shit just to spite them. Darlene, I imagined, would give me a shrug and a smile, and keep going.

I linked my arm in hers. "Shall we?"

"Yes," she said, beaming ear to ear. "Let's."

I told her about my graphic novel on the train into Manhattan. We swayed side by side, holding onto the rail above us. It was an hour past the heavier commuter traffic of weekday mornings, still the car was full, its passengers huddled into dark winter coats. Graffiti, like inky tattoos, marked much of the walls.

"So first stop is art supplies?" she asked. "I know a store in SoHo you'll love."

"Job first," I said. "I won't feel good about dropping a bunch of money on art supplies until I have an income."

"Can't eat pens and paper," Darlene agreed.

"I need a job, but I almost need the pen and paper more," I said. "If I don't get to work on my book tonight, I'm going to get… I don't know. Restless. Itchy."

"Like a junkie needing a fix?" She laughed at my awkward expression. "Oh my God, Zel, it's all good. I just meant that I know what *you* meant."

She faced forward, rested her cheek on her arm that held the rail above.

"Before I fell to the Dark Side, I was a dancer," she said. "Not a bad one either, I might add. And on the days I couldn't dance, I felt like I wanted to jump out of my skin. But in a good way. A clean way."

The train surged underground toward Manhattan. Darlene's large brown eyes darkened as she watched the blackness on the other side of the window. "When I started to get hooked on shit, I felt a whole different kind of restless. That addiction is dirty and gross. I miss the craving to make art. It's exactly like a drug, isn't it? If you go too long without doing it, it starts to eat at you."

I nodded. "That's exactly what it feels like." I let a few moments pass, to separate the drug talk from her art, then gently asked, "What kind of dancing did you do?"

"All kinds—jazz, modern, ballroom and tap. But my favorites were the Brazilian dances. Samba. Carimbo. Capoeira was my favorite. Have you ever seen Capoeira? It has a martial arts aspect to it, so it's kind of like fighting *and* dancing." Her voice faded a little. "It made me feel powerful."

"Do you ever think about getting back to it?" I asked, then shook my head. "Sorry, that's way too personal."

Darlene made a face. "Is it? Nah. Becks like to tease me that my life is an open book, left open to the naughty bits."

I smiled, noticing she didn't answer the question about returning to dance. With practiced ease, I changed the subject. "You and he are pretty close?"

"Best friends," she said automatically, then gave me a look. "Don't worry though. We're not like *that*. I'm totally rooting for you to bone him. I just want a full report if you do."

I coughed on nothing. "I'm not going to bone him, trust me."

"Yeah, right." She laughed. "You live together. It's a cold winter. He has that shitty radiator. I give you two weeks, tops."

"That's a losing bet, my friend."

"You have the most incredible eyes," she said suddenly, peering at me intently. "Like, huge and gorgeous, and pure green."

I moved back a little. "Thanks?"

"It hit me while we were talking earlier, and that's how I know."

"Know what?"

"That you and Becks are going to bone down."

I felt heat surge to my cheeks and I swatted her arm. "Will you stop saying that?"

She shrugged as if our destiny was out of her hands. "It's true. Your eyes are spectacular and Becks is a mushy romantic, no matter how standoffish he pretends to be."

I smirked, refusing to let her words sink any deeper than silly gossip. "*Bone down* and *mushy romantic* aren't exactly copacetic."

"I know, but I'm not a writer like he is."

"He writes?" I asked.

"Sort of. Best let him explain it." She studied my eyes a final time, then shook her head with a laugh. "Yep. He's a goner."

I looked away from her scrutiny and ignored the way my stupid heart tripped over itself. "Are we there yet?"

The subway screeched to a halt, and Darlene watched out the window for the station name. "Yep. This is us. Let's get you a jobby-job."

Darlene guided us to the 79th Street station on the Upper West Side. We walked along Amsterdam toward 81st, where casually elegant people in casually elegant winter wear strolled. We passed an elderly lady swathed in a fur wrap, walking two little Pomeranian dogs. Darlene knelt to pet one, chatting easily with its owner. The dog leaned its ear into Darlene's touch, but snapped at me with a yip when I tried to pet it.

"They're so cute!" Darlene cooed as we continued on.

I snorted. "They remind me of Fizzgigg. All teeth and fur."

She started at me blankly.

"From *The Dark Crystal*?" I said.

"Is that some comic book thing?"

I laughed. "No, it's a movie. Never mind."

"Here we are."

She'd brought us to a small, quaint-looking place with a yellow and white striped awning. On the window, in elegant white cursive, was the name Annabelle's.

I looked at the menu hanging in a neat frame on the door and frowned. "This is a breakfast and lunch place. I want to work nights."

Darlene huffed. "*Now* you tell me."

"I did tell you. I said I wanted an evening job."

She bit her lip. "Oh. I missed that part. But here's the deal; waiter jobs in Manhattan aren't easy to come by because the tips are good, right? So unless you have a stellar resume, you're going to need me. Do you have a stellar resume?"

"It might be a few stars short of a constellation."

Darlene snorted. "And you've been working at a tattoo place. Not a restaurant." She tugged my hand and opened the door. "Come on. The manager, Maxine, is a real bitch but the owner's nephew is in my rehab group. She owes me one."

Forty minutes later I came out with a job. I'd work Monday through Friday, eight a.m. to two p.m.

"You won't be working any of the more lucrative weekend brunch shifts," Maxine had said, peering hard at me through eyelids that labored under fake lashes and painted brows. "I have far more qualified personnel to work those shifts. However, you're fortunate I'm shorthanded as of this morning. You will be here precisely at 7:30 am tomorrow morning to shadow Anthony. You may go now. I have customers."

Darlene had kicked me—too hard—under the table in triumph. I had to admit I'd lucked out. The menu prices at Annabelle's meant I could make some decent money. More than a hundred dollars per shift, easily.

"I did good, right?" Darlene said as we left the restaurant. "Maxine is going to be the boss from hell, but you can take her."

"I've seen worse." A laugh bubbled out of me, along with relief that I could buy my art supplies with a clear conscience. I hugged Darlene hard. "Thank you."

"You're welcome," she said, beaming and walking as if she were ten feet tall.

At the art supply store in SoHo, I went a little crazy and bought fifty dollars' worth of Sakura pens, pencils, and a pad of Corson drawing paper. I prayed the quality of my supplies would somehow translate to higher quality of work. I still had no idea what I needed to change about *Mother, May I?* but at least I had decent inks with which to try.

"So, can you draw people?" Darlene asked as the guy behind the register bagged up my purchases. "Like portraits?"

"I did my share as a tattoo artist," I said.

"I always wanted to have my portrait done," she said as we headed back into the afternoon cold. "Once, when I was a kid, my dad took me to Coney Island and a street artist drew me. I was so excited, I could hardly sit still, waiting to see what I looked like through an artist's eye, you know?" Her smile tightened, her eyes kept straight ahead. "But when he was done, I cried and cried."

"Why? What happened?"

"It wasn't a real portrait. He'd done a caricature, you know? All goofy, exaggerated features, and a huge head. My freckles, which I was *totally* self-conscious about, were the size of quarters. It was supposed to be funny but it was kind of awful. He felt really bad and my dad got mad that I cried, but that's not what I thought I looked like. It stuck with me for a long time."

She glanced at me, and gave herself a shake. "God, tell me to shut up when I go off like that," she said with a sheepish laugh.

"Never." I gave her hand a squeeze. "I'll draw you some time, Darlene. If you want."

"You will? Thank you, Zel," she said. "You're a good friend."

I almost made a joke that we'd only known each other for a handful of hours, but it died on my tongue.

"So are you," I said.

Back in Brooklyn, we had a key made for me, did some more grocery shopping, then grabbed coffee at a donut shop. Around three, Darlene had to go get ready for her shift at Giovanni's.

"I work every night but Sunday," she said on the walk back to my place. "Marcello, the owner? He's a lifesaver. Literally. Not many employers would hire people with a record like me and Becks."

At my front door, she stopped and gave me a hug. "I'll replace your cottage cheese," she said.

"No way," I said. "Come over any time."

Her smile was warm as she walked backward down the street, then it turned sly. "I'll be sure to knock next time. I'd hate to catch you and Becks *in the act.*"

"You won't, trust me."

She put her hand to her ear, mouthing *What?* and miming that she couldn't hear me.

I laughed and waved her away, grateful she couldn't see the pink in my cheeks.

Ridiculous, I thought, taking the stairs up. Sleeping with Beckett, for any reason, would only wreck our arrangement. I was better off concentrating on my work, and I excitedly set up my new art supplies. I laid out the pens in a row, turned a fresh sheet of blank paper, and opened my portfolio to look at the panels I'd already drawn.

I wasn't arrogant enough to think it couldn't use improving, I just had no idea where or how to start. With a critical eye, I searched for flaws, for holes in the plot, places where *heart* was missing.

The days' shadows grew long over the desk as night crawled over the sky, smothering the light. It dampened all my good spirits as well. All the hopeful optimism from finding a new friend, a new job and a fresh start. I started dinner, paced the apartment, listened to music…nothing helped. When Beckett came back from work at 7:00, my sheet of paper was still completely untouched.

9

Beckett
December 2nd

For the first time in over a year, I came back to an apartment that wasn't dark and cold. The lights were on, Zelda was bustling around in the kitchen and an incredible smell wafted from the oven.

"Hey," I called, unstrapping my helmet and setting my bike against the door.

"Hey, yourself," she called back. "Dinner's almost ready."

Tugging off my thick, weather resistant gloves, I noticed the small coffee table was set for two. "Can I help?" I asked.

"Yeah, can I borrow those?" Zelda asked, indicating my gloves. "You have no potholders. How can you not have any potholders?"

"Lack of pot-holding," I said. I put my gloves back on and moved into the kitchen. "I'll do it. Wait, what am I doing?"

"Taking the casserole out of the oven. Careful." She winced as I took hold of the hot dish. "Watch your fingers."

The gloves worked fine as potholders. The heat of the oven made my cold face tingle, and the scent of the casserole made me dizzy with hunger.

"What is this?" I asked.

"Broccoli-cheddar noodle pie," Zelda said. "You're in charge of drinks. Beers are in the fridge."

I popped two IPAs while she spooned out a huge portion of casserole for me, a smaller for her. We huddled around the coffee table, her on the floor and me on the couch.

"What do I owe you for groceries?" I asked after we'd eaten enough to satisfy the hunger first.

"Nothing," she said. "And don't ruin the celebration with tacky money talk."

I grinned. "And what are we celebrating?"

"I got a job," she said. "It's not exactly what I wanted…" She glanced down at her food. "I was going for a night job to stay out of your way, but Darlene hooked me up with this place—"

"Darlene?"

"Yeah, she popped in rather unexpectedly. It's okay," she added quickly when I frowned. "I like her. A lot, actually. And she knew someone at a fancy brunch place on the Upper West Side, and got me a job. It looks like it'll be good money, but like I said, it didn't have evening hours." She glanced at me with those incredible green eyes of hers. A gaze that radiated both beauty and a sharp intelligence. "I hope that's okay."

"What? Yeah, of course." I blinked out of my mini-trance. "Why wouldn't it be?"

She shrugged, tucked a lock of long black hair behind her ear. "I don't want to get in your way."

"You're not in my way," I said. "You live here. Stop apologizing for it."

"I'm not *apologizing*," she snapped with sudden fire. "I'm trying to be considerate. You were the one who told me you didn't know anyone you could stand to live with in this small space."

I shrugged. "I do now."

She stared for a moment, the hard edges of her expression melting a little. "Okay," she said. "Good. But don't expect a casserole every night. This bastard took a long time to make and I've got a graphic novel that isn't drawing itself."

I bit back a smile. "It's the best dinner I've had in a while, Zelda. Thank you."

She opened her mouth, snapped it shut, then looked away. "You're welcome."

I cleaned up the kitchen then settled down with a movie on my laptop. Zelda sat down to work on her comic book. She bent over her sketchpad, her hair falling to form a wall between it and the rest of the world. She seemed to be having a hard time. Balls of paper littered the floor around the table by the window.

After an hour, she tore yet another sheet off the pad. I caught a glimpse of an inked sketch of a young woman with severe hair and a black body suit, before Zelda crumpled it up and added it to the pile.

"Not going well?" I ventured.

I expected—and sort of looked forward to—one of her sarcastic retorts. Zelda rested her chin on her hand, facing me. She was wearing her square, black-rimmed glasses that made her look smartly sexy as all hell.

"Not remotely well," she said. She kicked at the snowballs of paper at her feet. "And yet this is an improvement on the *absolute nothing* I did all afternoon."

"What's the problem?" I asked.

"The one publishing house that threw me a bone said they wanted to see revisions." She shook her head, her fingers trailing over pages of finished drawings. "I don't know what they want. It's not a romance or melodrama. It's action-adventure. Life or death, with a bit of chaos theory to boot."

"Chaos theory?" I set my laptop on the coffee table. "Now I have to check it out. Do you mind?"

"No, go for it," she said, vacating the chair at the desk so that I could sit. "Behold my graphic novel in all its heartless glory."

I pulled the first page to me. The same heroine in black leveled a gun at a pudgy guy on the floor.

"*Mother, May I?*" I said, reading the title header. "So what's it about?"

Zelda stood behind me and I could smell her perfume as she leaned in.

"It's set in the future, about one hundred years from now. It's a dystopian earth, but not because of nuclear holocaust, or pollution—although the planet's been pretty fucked up by that too. But what makes it dystopian isn't one cataclysmic event, but thousands and thousands of small ones. Murders, rapes, shootings…" She cleared her throat. "Child abductions, human trafficking. It all compounds and brings humanity to a collective low. No empathy, no consideration anymore for the planet or others. Everyone is out for themselves, like this terrible, gray cloud of anger and fear that hangs over everything."

"Sounds cheery," I said, "but kind of plausible too. So what's the cure?"

"Time travel. There's an agency called the Butterfly Project that culls news articles from the past about terrible crimes. They store the information in a database, then send special agents back in time to stop the crimes before they happen. The science isn't exact; there are a lot of bugs, but still they try. They hope the lessening of the misery in the past will lead to a brighter future."

My fingers clutched the edge of the table as those words dragged me back in time too. To the misery of my own past. The shitty, roach-infested apartment I'd grown up in with Gramps. The ratty furniture, the stained carpet. Gramps sitting in his favorite chair with the torn green vinyl. I smelled the smoke from the pipe he always clenched in his teeth. The way his narrow chest rose and fell in spasms when he coughed. His watery eyes and the smoky rasp of his voice.

"You deserve better than this, Beck."

I swallowed the jagged lump in my throat, pushing the memory down with it.

Lessening the misery of the past will lead to a brighter future.

Zelda had nailed the exact reason I agreed to the stupid fucking robbery in the first place. To lessen not only my misery, but Gramps', too. He deserved better. Except that it went horribly wrong…

I cleared my throat. "And so this chick in black is one of those agents who goes back in time?"

"Right. This is Kira. Her codename at the Butterfly Project is Mother."

Zelda's long black hair fell over my shoulder as she bent to tap on the drawing of her heroine. I glanced up at her.

Goddamn, she's beautiful.

Against the memory of my desperate life with Gramps, and the squalor we lived in, Zelda was a balm for my eyes. A beautiful sunrise after a week of gray skies. Just the touch of her clean, silky hair brushing my skin was a luxury.

"Okay," I blinked and tore my eyes from the pale, delicate curve of Zelda's neck. "What's…uh, so what's Mother's story?"

"Her child was murdered," Zelda said. "Now she's driven by vengeance. She goes back in time specifically to stop child murderers and pedophiles. She doesn't apprehend them. She kills them. Always. Without mercy."

Her finger pointed toward the drawing of a pudgy guy—a pedophile—begging Mother for his life.

"You ever hear that child's rhyme, Mother, May I?" Zelda asked.

"Sounds familiar."

"It's what Kira demands of all her pervs. She makes them ask, 'Mother, may I live?'" Zelda's jaw clenched. "And the answer is always no."

All at once, I felt like I was too close to her work. She wanted it back. I rose to give her the chair.

"Sounds intense," I said. "So what didn't the publishers like about it?"

"No heart," Zelda said with a snort, plopping back down. "I mean, I get that it's dark but it's *supposed* to be."

I moved to the kitchen to grab another beer. "Well, what else is the story about?"

"What do you mean?"

"What does she *do*? Who does she talk to?"

Zelda frowned. "Other agents. The scientists at the Butterfly Project."

"How come the Butterfly Project doesn't send someone back in time to get the guy who killed her daughter?"

"Not much of a story then." Zelda said with a small smile. "The science is buggy, like I said. Random. The database chooses the time and place, and the jumper jumps. Kira hopes to one day jump to her daughter's killer but the odds are astronomically low."

"Is she married? Does she have some poor schlub of a husband at home waiting for her while she goes back in time to kick pervert ass?"

Zelda smirked. "No, she's a loner. And *do not* tell me the heart this story needs is a love interest. Kira does not need to be *saved* by a man." Her voice grew low. "She's saving herself the only way she knows how."

"Okay." I sipped my beer and leaned on the counter. "Who tries to stop her?"

"Sometimes the pervs give her a hard time. Sometimes, she gets in trouble with local law enforcement, but she always outsmarts them."

I nodded. "But who *stops* her? Not physically, I mean. Mentally. Or, morally, rather."

"Morally?"

I shrugged, trying mightily to keep this conversation casual. "Is there a moral conflict about putting a bullet in some guy's head before he's actually done anything?"

"Not *some guy*," Zelda snapped. "A pervert. A disgusting, child-molesting animal."

"Yeah, but has she ever tried locking them up instead of murdering them? I can't imagine killing people is good for her soul, no matter how badly the guy deserves it."

Zelda stared at me as if I had grown a second head. "But that's just it. The guy *deserves* to die. Badly."

I held up my hands. "Hey, no argument from me there. I'm just saying, for the sake of your *story,* where's the conflict?"

Zelda's brows came together and I knew I was treading on thin ice. Criticism of anyone's art, no matter how good the intentions, could be risky business. Given the way her voice hardened over her next words, I guessed I was right.

"She has tons of conflict," Zelda said. "Her entire life is conflict. The guilt of letting her child…" She shook her head, her small hands clenching into fists. "Her daughter is *gone.* And she couldn't stop it. She lives with that every day, and the only relief she *ever* has is killing those who try to spread that endless pain to other mothers. Other families. Other sisters…" Her voice cracked on the word.

Holy shit, what is happening here?

I set my beer carefully on the counter. "Zelda…"

"So there's your conflict," she said, her voice trembling. She snapped her portfolio shut and I didn't miss the tears she blinked away behind her glasses. "You need the bathroom? I'm going to take a shower so I don't have to… So in the morning we don't…get in each other's way."

"Hey, I'm sorry if I—"

"You weren't. It's *fine.*"

She slammed the bathroom door, cutting me off before I could tell her I was sorry for butting in when her graphic novel was clearly more than the 'action-adventure' she described it. Her reaction wasn't defensiveness against criticism. Not even close.

The water started up, and I was too late.

There is heart in this, I thought, my fingers trailing over the pages of her work. *It's just buried under so much pain.*

Later that night, I turned off the lights. Zelda was on the damn air mattress that I already hated, and I climbed into bed. We exchanged stiff 'goodnights' and then a heavy silence fell. Time slipped by and sleep eluded me. I felt as if things between us were off-kilter; that if I didn't say something, we'd spend the next few days feeling as if she were walking around naked and vulnerable while I was fully dressed.

A restless rustle came from the air mattress and I took a chance.

"Hey," I said into the dark. "You awake?"

"Yeah," she said. "Can't sleep."

"That's my fault."

"No, it's not. I'm sorry I got a little crazy before. I appreciate you trying to help, but the graphic novel…" She sighed. "I don't know how to fix it because it's exactly what I need it to be, just as it is."

"I get that. I like your story, Zelda."

"You do?"

"Yeah, and I liked what you said about lessening the misery of the past to lead to a brighter future. That's kind of my story too. It's why I got in on the robbery that got me thrown in prison for two years."

"What do you mean?" Her large eyes glittered across the dim space between our beds.

"My grandfather took me in when I was eight years old. My junkie mom and alcoholic dad took off and Gramps took care of me. He did his best, made sure I got to school. He had no money, no great job, but he had integrity. It's all he had to pass down to me, and I failed him."

I rolled to my back, laced my fingers behind my head.

"Robbing that house went against everything he stood for, but by then I was twenty-one, working two jobs and he was in hospice. Liver cirrhosis. I knew he was running out of time and I wanted to give him a better life too. To take him somewhere nice before he died. A warm beach, maybe, where he could sit on the sand, turn his face into the sun and smoke his pipe."

"But that didn't happen," Zelda said softly.

"Nope. I got caught. Gramps died three days after I began my sentence. The hospice nurses said he wasn't mentally there. He didn't know what I'd done. Didn't know I tried to take what wasn't mine and that a man had died. He never knew any of it." I turned my head to look at her. "That's the only reason I can still get out of bed in the morning."

I imagined my story hanging in the air above us, like printed words for Zelda to read that I couldn't take back.

"Your grandfather did a really good job raising you, Beckett."

"He did his best and I fucked it up. I made a huge fucking mistake. It's not easy to come back from that."

"And you wish you could do anything to go back and change it."

"Yeah," I said. "Anything. I could use an agency like the Butterfly Project."

"Me too," Zelda said. "More than anything."

I rolled to face her, listening if she wanted to talk, silent if she wanted to sleep. She talked. From the nest of the comforter, her voice rose up laden with a deep, swampy pain. The words coming from some lonely place deep inside her. Rusty with disuse, buried so long in that dark well, even this dim light of the apartment suddenly seemed to bright.

"My sister was abducted," Zelda said. "She was nine. I was fourteen. I saw it happen."

Every muscle in my body constricted. "You saw…?

"Yeah. I saw and I couldn't stop it. I tried. I ran as fast as I could but the van was faster. I screamed so loud…"

Her voice failed and I squeezed my eyes shut in the dark as if I could block out the image of a young girl, black hair streaming behind her, chasing after something precious she would never catch.

"Jesus, Zelda…"

"But I… I failed. I failed my sister. My mom and dad." She inhaled raggedly. "So that's why I have panic attacks in burger joints when someone talks about my family. I can't visit them without falling apart and I don't want to anyway. The guilt is like a firestorm, burning me up inside."

"They don't *blame* you, do they?"

"No," she said. "But they don't need to. I know what happened. I was there."

I realized I'd unconsciously balled my hands into tight fists.

"Did they ever catch the guy? I mean…?"

"Yeah, they caught him," Zelda said, her voice calm with only a faint tremor at the edges. "Gordon James confessed to kidnapping and murder. He's been rotting on death row for ten years in Pennsylvania, and we—my family and I—have been waiting all that time for the call.

And when it comes, I'm going to sit in a small room and watch that bastard die. For closure, I guess. Some relief. I can't pull the trigger like Mother can, but I can witness it, you know?"

You don't want to see a man die, Zelda... I thought automatically, but kept it to myself. It wasn't my place to tell her what would bring her relief or peace, or spare her from the mountain of guilt she was carrying on her small shoulders.

Zelda heaved a steady sigh. "So that's what *Mother, May I?* is about. I can't go back in time to stop that asshole from taking my sister, but Kira can. Mother can, and I… I need that."

Go to her, I thought. *Go over there. You don't tell a story like that without someone at least giving you a fucking hug after. Some tiny piece of comfort...*

I couldn't move. The enormity of her story pinned me down. "I'm sorry, Zelda. I'm so sorry."

"I'm sorry I told you," she said. "I don't mean I regret it, I mean that it's an ugly story. I'm sorry you had to hear it, but do you want to hear something strange? I've never told that story out loud. Ever. Just thinking about it too hard without filtering it through *Mother, May I?* can bring on a panic attack of epic proportions."

"Yeah?"

"But I told you and I feel…relieved almost, which seems impossible." She smiled at me in the dark, beautiful and soft, and far away from terrible memories. "You missed your calling, Copeland. You should have been a therapist. Mine never got more than 'I'm okay' out of me."

"I'm glad if I could help."

"It's your voice," she said sleepily. "You have a nice voice."

I felt sleep settle over us both, as if we'd exorcised some of the ghosts that haunted us and now could get a little bit of rest.

A thought crossed my mind before I fell too deep.

"Zelda? Why did you call the time travel agency the Butterfly Project?"

"It's a little bit of chaos theory. A butterfly flutters its wings in Malaysia and the changes in air currents cause a hurricane in Florida. I love that idea. That even one tiny action can create an enormous effect. The agents who work for the Butterfly Project want to erase the tragedies that spread misery and pain in the hopes that better things will ripple out instead. Goodness, kindness, happiness." She smiled tiredly. "All the 'nesses."

"I like that," I said. "I like that a lot."

"Me too," she said. "Goodnight, Beckett."

"Goodnight, Zelda."

In the dark, I waited for her to fall asleep. I watched the shape of her in the dark, listened to the sound of her breath. When she was deep under, I fell too.

10

Beckett
December 3rd

I stepped out of the steamy bathroom the next morning to find coffee made again. It was only twenty minutes after five, but Zelda was at the desk scribbling away, bundled in a sweatshirt and scarf.

"Does your new job start early?" I asked, pouring myself a cup of coffee.

"No, but I couldn't sleep any more. I had one strange dream after another, and woke up full of ideas. Not sure what to do with them, but it's a start."

She smiled at me briefly and went back to her sketches. I felt the weight of our talk last night hanging between us, like a strange, combined energy that didn't know whether to stay or go. Divulging personal pain in the dark had drawn us closer, and the light of day now wanted to push us away.

I drank my coffee, grabbed a protein bar, and headed out. "Thank the coffee fairy for me," I said from the door. "And have a good first day at your job."

She turned on the chair, her knees pulled up to her chin. "You too," she said with a faint smile. She looked small and fragile from across the apartment, and the regret for not having been more comforting to her last night swamped me again.

But I must've stared a moment too long. Slowly, Zelda's hand rose to lower her glasses and her eyes crossed until they were perfectly, frighteningly, pointing straight at each other.

I laughed. "That's disturbing."

"Shoo," she said, turning back to her work. "You'll be late."

I smiled to myself, kept smiling down the stairs and out the door. For the first, and possibly last time, I was grateful for the cold, bracing air of New York City at 5:30 a.m. I didn't have someone to slap me in the face so it was the next best thing.

You're getting too close and you know it.

I rode my bike in the morning gray to the Clinton-Washington Avenue station. The whole ride on the packed train, my thoughts kept straying back to Zelda. To our conversation. Her pain and mine. And her smile right before she'd fallen asleep…

I almost missed my stop.

Apollo Courier operated out of a small, cluttered office in Two Bridges, Manhattan; with industrial carpet streaked with the mud and grime of hundreds of bicycle treads. Wes Young and Nigel Brooks were already there, their bikes resting against their hips as they plugged their first assignments into the their phones' GPS. Wes was a shorter guy than Nigel, dark where Nigel was light. Both were dressed in the warmest and most flexible biking gear they could afford.

"Copeland," Wes said, bumping fists with me. "Supposed to rain today, and then sleet off and on over the next week. You ready for this shit?"

"Can't wait," I said, and clasped hands with Nigel.

Nigel, an Australian, gave me a look through narrow eyes. "You got laid last night."

"I…what?" I half-stammered, half-laughed. "Not even close, but thanks for playing."

Wes, my best friend, was now scrutinizing me too. "You do look…different."

"I'm putting more fiber in my diet."

"No, no, no," Nigel said, tugging on his gloves. "Wesley is right. You look different in a freshly fucked kind of way."

Our receptionist, Ramona, rolled her eyes as she handed me my first assignment. She was sixty-two and had long learned to tune most of the messengers out.

"That's definitely it," Wes said with a laugh. "Spill. Who is she? Any chance it's someone we know?"

"Any chance you bozos will get to work some time today?" Ramona inquired without looking up from her computer.

We took our rides outside and saddled up. We each wore small CB devices attached to our messenger bag's cross-strap, and we all tuned to Apollo's frequency for jobs that came in on the fly.

"Lunch time, mate," Nigel said, heading out. "I want to hear details. Porno-level details."

"Fuck off," I said.

Nigel coasted away, scratching his back with his middle finger in farewell.

I snorted a laugh and caught Wes's knowing look.

"I didn't get laid," I said, "Sorry to disappoint."

"I believe you," Wes said. "Nigel's the gutterbrain, not me. But you do look different. Like all the heavy shit you carry around got a little lighter."

"That's deep, man."

He laughed. "I'm serious. You got some good news or what?"

"I got a roommate."

"Oh yeah? In your dinky-ass place?" Wes said and held up his hands as if it ward off my dark look. "Hey, I live in an art commune. Against my will."

"You live there for Heidi," I corrected. "Because you're whipped like a dog."

"Don't change the subject," he said. "We're freezing our nuts off talking about *your* situation. Not mine. And I'll bet cash money, your new roommate is of the feminine persuasion."

"Yeah, she is. Don't get all excited, Wes. You had a fifty-fifty chance of guessing right."

He ignored my sarcasm. "And her name is?"

"Her name is Zelda. She draws comic books."

"No shit?" Wes pursed his lips and nodded approval. "So she's already too cool for you."

I burst out laughing, a white plume in the chill air.

"Yeah, that's the truth. She's pretty fucking cool."

"Okay, she's cool but is she hot? Cool *and* hot?"

"And smart," I said. "She's got a great sense of humor, which helps to survive in my *dinky-ass* place."

"Uh huh, you dig her," my best friend said, just as his CB chirped a caller. He paused to listen, his eyes on me, then leaned his chin into the device and hit the outgoing button. "That's a ten-four, good buddy, over and out," he said in an exaggerated Southern drawl. He adjusted the chin strap on his helmet. "Welp, I give you my blessing for this arrangement. And everything that might come out of it."

"Nothing's going to come out of it," I said. "She's only staying with me for a few months to work on a project. It means a lot to her. I'm not going to risk messing that up. My place is too fucking small to have anything go bad."

"Yep, this all sounds like your typical Beckett bullshit," Wes said airily. "When I said you looked different before? I meant you looked happy. Whoever this Zelda chick is…maybe she's worth taking a chance on." He chucked me on the shoulder. "You're not in prison anymore, bro."

Wes rode out to his first delivery and I realized I was three minutes behind schedule to get to mine. I spent the next nine hours of my shift fighting bracing winds, watching the road for black ice patches and idiotic drivers making right turns without checking their blind spot.

By the time I got off the train in Brooklyn, my resolve to keep my distance from Zelda Rossi was frozen into my bones…

…and began to melt the instant I opened the apartment door.

She was cooking again—meatloaf by the scent of it—and hunched over her work at the desk.

"Hey," I said.

"Hey, yourself," she said brightly, and swiveled in the chair. Her hair was piled on her head and she wore those damn glasses that made it hard for me to think. "Meatloaf should be done in twenty." Her smile slipped a little. "God, you look like an icicle." She kicked the radiator at her feet. "Curse you."

"Sounds like you had a good day," I said. "How was your first shift?"

"The manager reminds me of Cruella DeVille but one of my co-workers, Anthony, more than made up for it. I laughed all day, and the money looks like it's going to be good. Win-win."

"Awesome."

I wanted to ask her about the graphic novel but thought I'd done enough damage yesterday, thanks very much. But Zelda's green eyes were bright behind her glasses, and she was electric with restlessness.

She bit her lip, touched her fingers to her chin. "So. After work, on the subway back, I had this flash of an image. For *Mother, May I?* And it wouldn't leave me so I drew it the second I got back."

"Oh yeah?"

"Yeah." She twisted a lock of hair around her finger. "You want to see it?"

"Sure."

I joined her at the desk. The sketch was of Mother with one of her victims on the ground at her feet, begging for his life. But a dark-haired guy in a trench coat was there in a halo of electric light, staying her hand from blowing the perv's brains out.

"See this guy?" Zelda said, tapping the sketch. "I don't know who he is, but he's jumping out of a rip in the space/time continuum, from the future, to stop Mother. He's going to stop her from killing that guy."

"I see."

"Stopping her from taking vengeance isn't something I ever wanted for her. But yet here this guy is. I think his name is Ryder. And he won't leave my brain."

"Okay."

"He's *not* a love interest, I can tell you that right now."

I forced a smile. "No?"

"No." Zelda looked up at me, her eyes searching mine. "Kira has too much shit going on to be any good to a guy anyway."

"Gotcha." I rubbed a sore spot on my chest where my messenger bag must've been pressing too hard all day.

"I don't know what he is yet," Zelda said, "but I think…" She glanced back at her work. "I think this is the right direction. And I wondered… If maybe you…?"

I blinked at her. "What are you asking me, Zelda?"

She huffed irritably through a hint of a smile. "Do I have to spell it out? Clearly you're some sort of muse because I hadn't had the first clue on how to fix this damn book until our little revelatory discussion last night. So maybe you've got something, Copeland. And Darlene says you're a writer. That true?"

"Not even close." I rubbed the back of my neck. "I write letters sometimes and that's it."

Zelda picked up the utility bill I was going to mail off the desk. "Is this tiny, perfectly precise penmanship yours?"

"Yes."

She tossed it down. "Okay, so here's how it works: a comic book is drawn and inked. Sometimes by one person, but there's also a person called the letterer. She—or *he*—does all the dialogue, any written text, et cetera. And often times, both artists collaborate on the story itself."

My eyes widened. "You want me to work on your graphic novel with you?"

She bit her lip. "Yes. Maybe. I don't know. I'm not a sharing-is-caring kind of gal, especially when it comes to my art. But what you said last night about the story…" She spun a colored pencil on the desktop. "It makes sense for Kira to have a foil. Because I think, maybe, the way people learn about themselves is to have someone challenge their beliefs, right? I'm not saying she's going to turn into a pacifist and stop wasting sick fucks who prey on little children. But maybe having someone asking hard questions will help reveal more of who she is. And that will help me find what the publishing houses want. The heart of the story. Her heart."

I couldn't believe what she was entrusting me with. It was overwhelmingly flattering. And exactly contradictory to my plans for keeping my distance.

"Zelda…"

"And on a practical level, this might—if it turns out well—make some money. If the assistant editor at BlackStar Publishing likes it. I think if I—if *we*—can deliver the revisions she wants, we can get a contract out of this."

"It's your book, Zelda. I don't want to take money out of your hands for scratching a few letters on the page."

She snorted. "You have no idea the care it takes to letter properly. I hate it, which is why I'm thrilled your handwriting looks like goddamn typeset. But more than that, Beckett, you'd be helping to craft the story. *And* splitting whatever money it happens to eke out, fifty-fifty, because getting this book out in the world means more to me than hoarding the payday."

I rubbed the stubble on my chin. "I used to write pretty good stories in high school. My teachers always seemed to lose their shit over them."

Zelda's face lit up like a flare of green and gold. "And did you *like* writing stories that made teachers lose their shit?"

I grinned. "Yeah, I kind of did." I shook my head a the weirdness of it all and heard myself say, "Yeah. Sure. I'm on board."

Zelda narrowed her eyes at me. "Now hold on, Copeland. Don't do it because I'm asking for help. Don't do it because you feel sorry for me or because you think you need to fulfill some sort of cosmic obligation. Do it only if you want to. Otherwise I'll be super pissed off at you."

I laughed. "No, I want to. Really. I'm honored you'd invite me into your work like this."

She gave me another sharp look but I could see the light in her eyes and it was beautiful.

"You're sure?"

"I'm sure." And that was the truth. I was surprised to find I wanted the job. To create something instead of delivering someone else's messages or cleaning up after their meals.

"And no quibbling about money shit," Zelda said. "We split anything this sucker makes, even if it's only enough for one meal off Micky-D's dollar menu. Then we split that too."

I laughed harder. *God, this girl.* "Yes, for God's sake. Yes."

Zelda's smile unfolded until it matched the brilliance of her eyes. She stuck out her hand and I shook it. "Welcome aboard, Copeland," she said. "And now, before my meatloaf burns, this is your first assignment."

She tapped the empty space above the guy—Ryder—as he burst out of the ether to stop Kira.

"What does he say?" Zelda asked, her voice turning soft. "What could he possibly tell her that might lead her to a different path? One that's not just vengeance and hurt and pain?"

I looked at this beautiful, smart woman sitting beside me. I didn't deserve a shot at happiness, but she did. I couldn't imagine what it must've felt like to have seen her little sister snatched before her eyes, and the guilt of not being able to stop it. I could tell her a thousand times it wasn't her fault, and I knew she'd never believe me. It would never sink in.

But maybe I can help her move past the rage and pain to something else. Some peace.

I set my fingertip by hers, in the empty space above Ryder. "He tells her, 'There's another way.'"

THERE IS ANOTHER WAY.

Part II

Love will enter cloaked in friendship's name. --Ovid

11

Zelda
December 15th

"You sure about this?" Darlene asked, as we perused the Christmas section in the Target at Atlantic Terminal Mall. "You really want a big ole tree?"

"God, no," I said. "We have no room. But a little mini-tree that can sit on our desk would work. And I want some lights too. I feel like I'm withering under that one ugly fluorescent."

Darlene beamed as we strolled the busy section, me trying to maneuver the big red cart among bins of gift bows and wrapping paper.

"I love it," she said. "And I love that you and Becks are working on your comic book together. He said it's really good."

I stopped the cart. "He did?"

She nodded. "At Giovanni's. He said once he started really looking at your work, he got excited about the potential."

"He did?"

"He did? He did?" Darlene parroted, and I gave her a shove, my cheeks burning. "Yeah, *he did,*" she said. "I believe his exact word was brilliant."

I quickly looked away as a flood of warmth spread to my chest.

"Do graphic novels make a lot of money?" Darlene asked suddenly.

"It's possible," I replied. I was still getting used to her ping-pong method of communication. "If they hit it big there's potential for some good money. But I'm not in it for that. I mean, I'm not stupid, I would love for it to be successful, but that's not why I'm doing it. And I think Beckett knows that the chances of striking it rich aren't that great."

Darlene's face folded in. "I hope you do make it big. Because

Becks has no health insurance and no savings. None of those messenger guys do. I'm thankful he hasn't been whacked by a cab yet, but how long is that going to last?"

"Jesus, don't say that." A sliver of ice slipped into my heart at the thought of him being hit.

"No, you're right, you're right. I shouldn't put it out there. I just worry."

Great. Now I will too...

"His job's pretty dangerous, isn't it?" I asked.

Darlene nodded. "Whizzing in and out of traffic for ten hours a day, in shitty weather. Or any weather, really."

"I never really thought about it before." I bit my lip, and Darlene leaned into me, a sly smile on her face replacing her worried frown.

"What's this I see? Tough chick Zelda, are you going soft on me? Over Becks?"

I sniffed. "For being worried about his safety? That's me being human, not..."

I fumbled for a word that wasn't going to get me in trouble, but Darlene was quicker.

"Not being smitten?" Her eyes widened with a sudden thought. "Speaking of shitty weather..."

I blinked. "Were we?"

"It hit twenty-three degrees last night." She batted her eyelashes innocently. "How is that air mattress working out? Or have you and Becks made some *alternate* sleeping arrangements?"

I rolled my eyes. "Not in the slightest."

I didn't add that the air mattress had long since worn out its welcome. I loathed crawling onto the cold, rubbery thing. But I didn't tell Darlene that, nor did I tell her Beckett gave it the stink eye every night when we took it down from the wall.

I definitely wouldn't tell her I lived within a tangled nest of emotions when it came to Beckett. He was, as Darlene had said, a perfect specimen of male hotness. I thoroughly enjoyed looking at him, especially when he was leaving for work and I was afforded a glimpse of his muscular legs in this biking gear. That flutter in my stomach was easy to explain: I was a warm-blooded female living in close quarters with a beautiful man.

Harder to explain, and getting more difficult to rationalize every day, was how I looked forward to him coming home. To his "Hey," in his deep voice. Or the way his deep blue eyes filled with thoughts and ideas as we worked on *Mother, May I?*

Together.

"Is that why you're not sleeping together? Because you like him?"

Darlene's words were like a slap to the face, and I wondered with a pang of fear if she'd somehow read my damn mind. "How do you figure that?"

She sighed dreamily. "I wish I could do that. Hold off, you know? Make it special? But I usually end up just doing it for fear the guy's going to run away." Her sly smile returned. "But you have Becks trapped."

"*Becks* and I are just friends. And now collaborators. It would be a colossal mistake to fool around and then have things go south."

"You assume they'd go south?"

"I'm terrible at relationships. Even if I wanted one with him—which I don't—there's too much at stake with my living arrangements and now the graphic novel. I'd be sure to fuck it up and ruin all of it."

"I don't get it," Darlene said, as we pushed the cart into an aisle that was stacked with boxes of Christmas lights. "You seem to have your shit together. More than I do."

I smirked at that. *Oh Darlene, I sit on a throne of lies...*

"The sex part is easy," I told her. "Being a good girlfriend? Not so much. The closest I came to having a boyfriend was a guy I dated more than a year ago. He complained I wouldn't know romance if it whacked me over the head. I was too distant and unfeeling."

I'm all premise, no pulse.

"So you're not all warm fuzzies, big deal," Darlene said. "Neither is Becks. Hard on the outside, soft on the inside."

I glanced at her. She'd sworn up and down that she and Beckett were only friends. Her insistence on playing matchmaker seemed sincere. But what if it were a cover to mask her real feelings for a guy she considered, in her own words, the best person ever?

The thought made my stomach twist. By now, Darlene wasn't just a valued friend, but someone I felt like I wanted to protect. She'd been knocked around by life and I got the impression it had made her dizzy; her hands and heart reaching for something solid to grab on to.

Another reason for me to keep it friendly with Beckett.

I reached out gave her hand a squeeze. "We need to focus on the shopping now, Dar, or else we'll succumb to the Curse of Target."

"What's that?"

"Where you walk in with a plan to spend twenty bucks, and you walk out having spent a hundred on a dozen things you didn't need."

She grinned broadly, and held up a Santa Claus toilet seat cover. "I need this in my life."

"Gah! We're too late."

Despite our best efforts to resist, the Curse got me too. I spent sixty dollars on a little tree decorated in tiny green and red lights, two strings of white Christmas lights, and a throw rug I didn't know I wanted until I saw it. But the floor in our apartment was a terrible, industrial gray. The rug was a geometric pattern with interlocking squares in jewel-toned colors. Masculine enough for Beckett, artsy enough for me.

Darlene and I were on the train back when she asked the inevitable holiday question.

"Are you going to be around for Christmas?"

My grip on the rail tightened. "I'm not sure yet. I need to call my parents, I suppose. Figure it out…"

I let my words trail off, hoping the topic would too.

Darlene sighed. "Becks is probably staying home, even though I bet Roy invited him over like he did last year."

"What's up with them, anyway?" I asked. "Roy and his wife took us out a couple of weeks ago, supposedly as part of Beckett's parole requirements. Instead, it was like Sunday dinner with family."

"I'm not surprised. Roy took a shine to Becks right away, way beyond what most parole officers would do. I wish my PO were half as nice. Mine's an asshole." She shrugged. "Anyway, Roy and his wife never had kids so maybe they're being extra nice to Becks for that. Or maybe they're just extra-nice in general."

"You think Beckett will spend Christmas with them?"

Darlene sighed again. "Probably not. He's all bent out of shape about the robbery. He told you about that, right? How the husband and wife came home, and the husband died?"

"Yeah, he told me."

"It eats him up even though it's totally not his fault. Not really. So he punishes himself, the big dummy."

This conversation was getting too personal, too fast, and I felt bad about talking about Beckett behind his back. Fortunately for me,

Darlene changed topics of conversation on a dime, and dropped it.

"I hate this time of year," she said. "I get so lonely, you know?"

"Do you have family to visit for Christmas?" I asked.

"Oh sure. They're just up in Queens. But my sister isn't a gigantic fuck-up like me. I'll spend the whole time listening to her talk about her great job and her great husband and her great 401k, blah, blah, blah."

"You're not a gigantic fuck-up."

"Says you," she said. "Maybe I just need to get laid. There's no better mood-lifter than an earth-shattering orgasm."

The little old lady on the subway seat in front of us nodded her scarf-covered head. "You got that right, honey."

Darlene and I exchanged looks, then we burst into laughter. Loud, belly-deep laughter that brought the best kind of tears to our eyes. And in those few seconds, Darlene lived in a genuine moment of unchecked happiness. The old lady chuckled with us and I wanted to kiss her for driving off the shadows that hovered over my friend.

I took a mental snap shot of Darlene in that moment, committed it to memory, hoping I could recapture it in pen and ink later.

I got home at four, staggering under my purchases. Beckett had already left for his Saturday shift at Giovanni's, but the scent of his cologne hung in the air.

I set up the Christmas tree against the window on the desk, arranging it behind some of my scattered drawings, and Beckett's practice lettering.

Next, I strung up the white Christmas lights so they ran all along the wall facing the front door, starting at Beckett's bed, and ending at the corner next to the kitchen.

The sun was already stealing the day's light. I shut off the crappy fluorescent bar that ran along the center of the ceiling and turned the little lights on. Their muted glow was beautiful in the twilight, like fireflies dancing along the wall.

I remembered when my parents had taken Rosemary and me to a firefly festival in Pennsylvania one summer. The look on Rosie's face when she caught one in her hand…

I sucked in a deep breath, pushing the air down into my lungs and the memory down with it. But it was the fifteenth of December. I couldn't put it off any longer. It wasn't fair to my Mom and Dad.

I drew out my cell phone and sat at the desk, my graphic novel spread before me. Our graphic novel now. Mine and Beckett's.

"And yours too, Rosie," I whispered into the dim, firefly light. The lights were coming on in the windows in the building across the way. Warm, yellow rectangles, with families within, cooking dinner or watching TV. Being alive and together and whole.

I scrolled through my contacts. My thumb wavered and then hit the green button.

My mother answered after two rings, and I imagined her in her modern kitchen on the old olive green rotary wall phone. A dinosaur she couldn't bear to get rid of, its cord like a tether, not letting her wander too far, but keeping her tied to whomever she spoke.

"Hello, Rossi's."

"Hey, Mom," I said.

A pause. An intake of breath.

"Hi, honey," she said, her voice rich and layered with relief, and love, and the quiet, gentle caution she always used when speaking to me. As if we could avoid one of my panic attacks if we were quiet and didn't wake it up. "How are you?"

"I'm good. I'm in New York City."

"Are you?" Her voice rose an octave. "What's happening there?"

I explained to her about the graphic novel, and Beckett, and how we were going to take it to a big publisher after the holidays.

"They're going to love it, sweetie," she said. "I'm so proud of you."

I blinked hard. "Thanks, Mom. How's Dad?"

"He's great, though I know he'll be sad to have missed your call. Bowling night."

"Oh, right. I'll call again soon to talk to him."

My mother's voice grew hesitant. "Do you think you're up for a visit this year? You're so close now."

I closed my eyes against the ache that clenched my heart. "I want to, Mom. You know I do. But…"

My eyes fell on the panel I'd drawn with Ryder bursting out of the sky to tell Kira there was another way.

"I'd like to bring a friend, if I could."

"Of course, honey," she said, practically shouting. "Bring anyone you want."

I smiled, and the tightness in my chest loosened. "It's not definite, I have to ask him—"

"Him? So this friend is a *him*?"

"Yeah, he's a him, but he's just a friend. And I don't know for sure if he'd even want to but…"

"But you'll ask," she said.

I smiled against the phone. "Yeah. I'll ask. I think it might help me not to freak out. To have him there."

Because I feel safe with him, always.

"If it's too hard for you, honey, I'll understand. We all will."

"I know, Mom," I said. "But I want to try."

"Because you're strong. You've always been strong."

Not always, I wanted to say. *Not when it counted the most.*

I got off the phone with my mother knowing I left her full of hope while I was riddled with draining doubts. The last time I'd tried to visit was my Dad's birthday last June. The second my cab from the airport pulled into my Rittenhouse neighborhood, I felt as if an unseen hand were squeezing my throat, and my skin tingled as if I'd been doused in ice water.

PTSD, the doctors had said. It was diagnosed ten years ago, the first time I fell into a hysterical fit—when I'd gone into Rosemary's bedroom and she wasn't in it. When I understood she'd never be in it again.

Panic attacks or PTSD or whatever they called it, forced me to take a bunch of meds to get through a visit home, and those made me sleepy as hell. A zombie, lurching along the outskirts of a terrible pain.

Still, I tried. For my family's sake, I tried once or twice a year. And once or twice a year, I came away with a giant reminder of how I was anything but strong.

But maybe if I had Beckett with me… If I had that sense of safety to lean on. If I had him at my back…

Maybe I could make it through.

Beckett didn't get back from work at Giovanni's until after eleven. I was still awake, poking at *Mother, May I?* and working up the nerve to ask him about Christmas. After my phone call with my mother, I was locked in. I couldn't back out now.

"Hey," Beckett said.

"Hey, yourself," I replied, and turned in my seat. Beckett stood in the apartment, the cold radiating off of him and ice crystals melting on his jacket. But his deep blue eyes were warm as they traced the string of lights along the wall to the little tree on the desk in front of me.

"What's all this?" he asked.

"Is it okay?" I asked. "I was seriously over that fluorescent monstrosity," I said, flapping a hand at the ugly bar above us that was off. The only illumination was the small desk lamp I worked under, and the garland of lights.

"It's… I like it," Beckett said. "I like it a lot."

"Great," I said, suddenly undone by the soft smile on his lips. "'Tis the season, and all."

I inwardly groaned at the sheer amount of cheese in those five words, but Beckett didn't seem to notice. He stripped out of his work gear, his eyes still on the lights. And me.

"And what about the rug?" I asked. "If you hate it, we can exchange it for something better, but…" I deepened my voice and made it smoky, like a stoner dude. "I think it really ties the room together."

Beckett blinked at me.

"It's a line from *The Big Lebowski*," I said, my cheeks on fire. "Never seen it? No? Never mind."

"It looks great," Beckett said, his eyes far away and thoughtful.

"Okay, great. I'm glad."

"I'm going to take a shower to warm up," he said, still sounding distracted.

"Knock yourself out."

I'm going to stop being a ridiculous dork quoting movies at you…

I vowed to ask him about Christmas when he got out, and settled myself on the air mattress to wait.

But Beckett emerged from the shower in a cloud of steam, wearing his sleep pants and a long-sleeved henley. Tension came with him like a cloud, as he stood over me, near the edge of his bed.

"This isn't going to work any more," he said after a moment.

"What's not going to work?" I said, a shard of fear piercing my heart.

"You on the floor. Me in the bed. It doesn't seem right."

A sigh of relief gusted out of me. "Jesus, I thought you were kicking me out."

He grimaced as if he'd eaten something rotten. "God, no. I would never…"

"I'm fine on the floor," I said.

"No, you're not," Beckett said. "It's all kinds of wrong. It's cold. Uncomfortable. And you just… You shouldn't be sleeping on the goddamn floor, Zelda."

Here it is. Here's the conversation. Darlene called it…

"It's not the floor, it's an air mattress," I said, my heart pounding against my ribs. "What's the alternative?"

"You sleep in the bed. I sleep on the air mattress."

I stared at him and he at me, like a contest of wills. It didn't feel like a battle, though. It felt like we were both resisting a pull instead of pushing away.

"That's nuts," I said after a moment, crossing my arms over my chest. "You'd be even more uncomfortable because you're so damn tall. I'm short. I can fit. It's no big deal."

"I don't like it," Beckett said. "I can't keep sleeping in a bed while you're on the floor. I don't give a shit how small you are, or how tall I am. You take the bed."

"No."

"*Yes*. I'll sleep on the air mattress. And that's final."

"Aren't we bossy tonight?"

He jabbed a finger. "Would you *get* in my fucking *bed,* Zelda."

We both froze as his words hung in the air above us. Heat flooded my cheeks as a speech bubble rose above my head. Utterly empty.

Beckett carved a hand through his hair. "Goddammit, I meant…You know what I meant."

I hugged myself, thrust my chin out. "Yeah, I know what you meant, and I don't need your pity."

"It's not pity. It's… *Goddamn.*" He made a frustrated sound, then put his hands on his hips, exhaling heavily. "Please, Zelda," he said. "Just do it. For me? For my peace of mind?"

"I don't know what's gotten into you," I said. "But fine. For one night."

"Every night."

"*No.* Maybe we can…I don't know. Trade off. Every other night, someone's on the air mattress. But I'm not evicting you from your bed permanently. Okay?"

We stared each other down.

"Say yes, Beckett, or I'll sleep on the damn floor too."

"Fine," he snapped back after a silence, and climbed onto the air mattress. His feet stuck out unless he pulled them in, and he tried to conceal this with the blue blanket.

"I told you," I said. "You're too tall."

He pulled the blue blanket over his head. "Your prejudice against tall people is duly noted."

I stared in silence, not sure whether to laugh at his joke or curse him out. I was completely adrift, the old walls and protections around my heart crumbling and my brain working like mad to mortar them back up.

My legs moved slowly to Beckett's bed. I lay down and pulled the covers up to my chin.

Oh God help me…

The pillow, the blanket and the sheets were all suffused with Beckett's clean, masculine scent—a mix of cologne and soap, aftershave and skin. With every breath I inhaled him.

"Happy now?" I demanded.

"Getting my way always makes me happy," he said.

I had to bite the inside of my cheek to keep from laughing, and sank into sleep almost at once, surrounded by everything that was him.

12

Beckett
December 16th

I woke to the scent of coffee permeating the air. Zelda was at the desk, hunched over her work with one knee drawn up to her chin. Her long black hair tied up on her head, glasses on, her small frame bundled against the cold. The radiator was close to her feet, wheezing and clanking softly. The Christmas lights were on, pushing back the gray haze of the winter morning.

Those lights. And the rug. Such small changes to the grim drabness of this place, but they'd had the strangest effect on me.

Over the last ten days, I'd been doing my best to stay casual with Zelda. To be friendly and professional as we collaborated on *Mother, May I?* And nothing more.

But for the first time in a long time, I felt hopeful. For so many things. Maybe Zelda and I were building something incredible on the foundation she'd laid. Maybe this novel would take off and pay well. My life could take a different path.

Until now, thoughts of my future were limited to an endless stretch of days riding my bike around New York. Being a messenger until I was too old or until I got injured. Maybe Zelda was changing my destiny. Already she was an artistic partner—something I never saw coming.

I gazed at her beneath a garland of twinkling lights. She was something I never saw coming.

I threw off the blue comforter and hauled myself off the air mattress.

Zelda turned and gave me one of her sarcastic glances I'd come to love. "How was that? Sucked ass, didn't it? Because you're too big."

I refrained from rubbing the stiffness in my lower back and gave her an innocent smile. "I have no idea what you're talking about."

She narrowed her eyes at me through those damn glasses, then sniffed and went back to her work.

I poured myself some coffee. "Do you want to work on *MMI?* today?"

"It's your day off," Zelda said, not looking up.

"Which means we can get a lot of time in."

She toyed with her pen, and then finally turned to face me. "I want to go out," she said. "Into Manhattan, I mean. I've lived here for weeks and I haven't seen anything but the restaurants where we work and a Target."

"Some people would kill to see the Atlantic Terminal Target," I said. "You don't know how lucky you are."

She rolled her eyes at me. "It's the eighth Wonder of the World, I'm sure. But I'm serious. *MMI?* is in good shape. Let's *go* somewhere."

I leaned on the counter, thinking for a second. My eyes landed on the little Christmas tree on the desk.

"I have an idea."

The N train into Manhattan was packed with baby strollers and Christmas shoppers. We switched to the F at Herald Square and got off at 47th Street.

"Rockefeller Plaza?" Zelda asked. She wore a gray knit beanie pulled over her ears. Her hair spilled down her pea coat, and white knit gloves with a quaint, flowery pattern covered the ink stains on her fingers.

"Have you ever been?"

"Never. Only seen the tree-lighting on TV. The size of it always..."

She trailed off as we rounded the corner and the plaza spread out below us.

"Holy shit," she finished.

The rectangle of the ice rink spread like a white carpet at the feet of the gold Prometheus statue. Above his shoulders, the Rockefeller tree rose up, ninety feet tall and strung with lights of every color.

"I never thought it was so…tall." Her gaze slowly descended from the top of the tree to the people gliding around the ice rink.

"You want to skate?" I asked.

"Can we? You want to?" Now her eyes looked up at me, and they were so fucking brilliant, I had to wrench my gaze away.

"Yeah. I do," I said. "It's the best way to see the tree up close."

We went to the rental area and had to wait a good hour for a turn, as the rink only let in 150 people at a time. Finally we were allowed to take to the ice. I'd never been skating in my life, but how hard could it be?

I found out in the first nanosecond my skate touched the ice and nearly slid out from under me. I made a frantic grab at the low wall to keep from falling on my ass.

Smooth, Copeland. Real fucking smooth.

Zelda laughed but that laugh turned into a squeal as she did the exact same thing. Her arms pin-wheeled at her sides, and her skates slid back and forth beneath her. I reached one hand out to grab her. She flailed and clutched at my hand, and I pulled her in to me.

Slowly, like two people battling their way against hurricane-level winds, we made our way along the wall.

"Oh my God, this is a nightmare," Zelda said, though her smile stretched across both cheeks that were brushed pink with cold.

"No, wait. We can do this." I moved around to her left, off the wall, with choppy, marching steps. I took her hand. "Okay, now let go of the wall."

"Like hell," she said.

"I got you."

"Oh really?"

"No, not really," I said, nearly losing my balance. "But it sounded confident, right? This is all your fault."

"Mine?" she shrieked, laughing.

"You were supposed to secretly be a figure-skating prodigy to help me around on the ice."

"You were supposed to be a weekend hockey player to help *me* around the ice. We both suck."

As if to prove her point, my skate slipped out from under me and I went down, taking Zelda down with me. We both landed on our asses in a tangle of legs and skates and painful laughter.

"You okay?" I asked her.

"I bruised my ass and my pride. Otherwise, I'm just peachy."

"Okay, good." I lay down on the ice, on my back. "I'm going to stay like this for awhile."

Zelda laughed. "Safer down here."

I looked upwards and the smile slid from my face as my mouth fell open in awe. My chest tightened as I blindly reached for her arm. "Zelda. You have to see this."

I thought she'd make a joke or tell me I was crazy, but she lay on the ice beside me, her hair almost touching my cheek.

We stared upward, at the sky that was deepening to a dark blue, and the Christmas tree that towered above the rink. A glittering, glowing cone of green, wreathed in thousands of colored lights. The city was alive with light. In the tree and the towering high rises. Glinting off the white ice and the gold statue of Prometheus.

The world was beautiful. Even more with Zelda beside me, shoulder to shoulder, warming me when the cold should have been seeping into me from the ice below.

"Are you seeing this?" I asked.

I felt her nod. "So beautiful."

We remained there for only a few minutes before an ice rink official skated over to remind us it wasn't exactly smart to lie down on the ice while one hundred and forty-eight other people with blades on their feet whizzed past our heads. But it was worth it. My jacket was damp but it was worth it.

Seeing the city light reflected in Zelda's eyes was worth it.

We returned our skates, and I bought us two hot chocolates. We sat under a heat lamp at a little table next to the rink, sipping our drinks. I looked at Zelda. My emotions were a tangle, but maybe if I just let my words come as they wanted, a new story would unravel in the cold, night air between us.

But Zelda spoke first, her voice hesitant. Almost shy.

"I wanted to ask you something," she said. Her gloved hands clutched her hot chocolate, her teeth grazed her bottom lip.

"Sure," I said. "Ask away."

She glanced down at her drink. "So you know I get these panic attacks about seeing my family. Or even if I think about them too much."

I nodded.

"And because of that, I hardly ever see them. Maybe once or twice a year. And that sucks. I miss them. A lot. But it's just…too hard." She shook her head. "I know it sounds cowardly as hell…"

"It doesn't," I said.

She gave me a grateful smile, then gone again. "It *feels* cowardly. I know it hurts my mom, but… Anyway, now that I'm only a few hours away from Philly, I can't *not* visit them for Christmas. It may be a huge mistake but I need to try." Her gaze had been fixed on her cup, but now she raised her eyes to meet mine.

"So I was wondering if maybe you'd like to come with me."

I sat back in my chair. "You want me to spend Christmas with your family?"

She nodded. "Because… I know this sounds crazy, but I feel safe when I'm with you."

My heart began to pound a steady, heavy pulse against my ribs. "Zelda… I don't know what to say."

"It's weird, right? I don't know why, but ever since I first met you…" She shook her head. "Remember at the burger joint? You knew exactly what to do. I never had a panic attack vanish that fast. You didn't just help it. You *stopped* it. And when I told you the story of what happened to Rosemary, the actual story…" She shrugged, looked away. "It was okay. Somehow you made it okay for me to say the words that had always burned me like poison."

I stared, and Zelda must've mistaken my silence for discomfort, because she buried her face in her hands. "Oh God, I'm sorry," she said between her fingers. "I'm really not trying to pity you into coming with me. If you don't want to, you don't have to. But I—"

"I want to," I said, and in the short second of her raising her head, her expression full of hope—and maybe even happiness—the shitty reality of my situation sucked all the warm possibility out of the air.

"But I can't," I said.

Her face fell. "You can't?"

"I can't leave the state without written permission from the Parole Board," I said, hating every syllable that came out of my mouth. Hating that I'd forgotten the hard limits on my life. Hating how the city lights now turned into a barbed-wire wall keeping me inside. Most of all, hating those few magical moments when I lay on the ice and felt normal. I didn't feel like a felon. My future didn't feel ruined.

The moments laughed in my face now and I hated it.

"Can you get permission?" Zelda asked.

"The process takes thirty days."

"Maybe Roy can do something—"

"He can't." I chucked my hot chocolate into a trashcan even though it was still nearly full, and got to my feet. "Ready to go? It's getting fucking cold out here."

"Beckett…"

"I'm sorry, Zelda. It was nice of you to offer, but I can't do it."

Because I'm a felon. And fuck me for forgetting that.

13

Zelda
December 22nd

Over the next week, Beckett was a different person. He was hardly around the apartment, barely spoke when he was, and twice texted me to eat dinner without him because he was hanging with friends after work. He retreated from working on the graphic novel, and I gave him his space about it. I could hardly concentrate on it myself. I'd shared it with him, and it hurt like mad to think he was giving it back.

Whatever, it's fine, I told myself. *I can manage. I always do.*

My heart whispered it was anything but fine.

Thursday afternoon, Annabelle's was busy with holiday traffic, and I left my shift an hour later than usual. I had a fat wad of tips stuffed in my bag, and a gourmet tuna sandwich on sourdough in a plastic bag on my wrist. Someone had called in a to-go order and never picked up.

I stopped in at the Halal grocery down the street from us. I'd become something of a regular, searching for fresh produce three times a week. The wife, a middle-aged woman with striking brown eyes, knew me well.

"Hey, Afsheen," I said, laying a gourd of butternut squash and a bunch of arugula on the counter. "How are you today?"

"Quite well, darling. This will make a beautiful salad, no?" she asked, bagging my purchases.

I smiled. "That's the plan. If I don't mess it up. New recipe."

"I have faith in you," she said with a wink. "Oh, and if I don't see you before the 25th…" She bent to pick up something from behind the register and stood holding a small houseplant in a ceramic bowl. It had waxy green leaves and brilliant clusters of little orange, red, and yellow flowers.

Afsheen set the plant on the counter and smoothed back her multi-colored hijab that had fallen over one shoulder. “Something to brighten a room in the cold gray of winter.”

“For me?” Tears jumped to my eyes and I had to blink hard. *Come on, Rossi, you’re tougher than that.* I cleared my throat. “You didn’t have to do this.”

“It is the holidays,” Afsheen said, and wagged a finger at me. “I won’t take no for an answer.”

“Thank you, Afsheen. It’s beautiful.”

We said our goodbyes and I left the store with two bags of food on one arm and a houseplant tucked under the other. Such a small thing—a houseplant—but I loved it already. The flowers were little bursts of color, like fireworks.

I walked the rest of the way home, and made it to my place just as the rain started up again. I stopped at 2C. My arms were full, but I managed to knock on the door. Mrs. Santino opened it and peered through the crack left by the chain.

I held up the to-go bag from Annabelle’s. “Do you like tuna?”

The door shut again and I wondered if she’d only take food from Beckett. But it opened three seconds later and she snatched the bag from me and shut the door.

I grinned in triumph. “I’ll take that as a yes.”

I walked down to 2E and wrestled the key out of my bag. I turned it, pushed the door open, and nearly dropped my bag and the houseplant.

Darlene was on the couch, facing the door. Topless, her small breasts bounced as she straddled a man, riding him hard. Her head was thrown back, her mouth open. She pressed the guy’s hand to one of her breasts with hers. Her other was tangled in his hair.

His blond hair.

I sucked in a breath.

Darlene was fucking some guy in my apartment.

A blond guy.

Beckett.

Darlene was fucking Beckett in my apartment.

The entire reaction couldn’t have taken more than three seconds, but it felt like three years before I could shut the door again. I stood in the hallway, my breath trapped in my throat, trying to process what I’d just seen. My embarrassed shock curled and blackened into something ugly, and my heart beat slow and heavy in my chest.

You only saw a flash of blond hair, I reasoned. *That doesn't mean anything.*

But it was Beckett's apartment, not mine. He and Darlene had been friends for a year. *Close* friends, to use his words. She'd told me herself she'd been trying to sleep with him for ages.

She's been lonely. He's been distant...

The details were solidifying, sketching out the scene in vivid Technicolor. It was Beckett. Beckett was fucking Darlene on the couch.

You don't know that.

And yet I couldn't make my hand open the door to see for sure, because if it was…

"So what?" I whispered. "It's fine. It's nothing."

I swallowed the jagged lump of *nothing* and felt the pain slide into my chest. I put my hand on the closed door and leaned my forehead there, listening to muffled voices on the other side.

"What's going on?"

I jumped and spun around, my breath catching in my throat.

Beckett stood there, his bike beside him, his face flushed red with the cold.

"Beckett…?"

"Last I checked." He gave me small, perplexed smile. "You okay?"

He's here. Not in there, screwing another girl.

Relief as profound and surprising as the pain washed over me, warming me from the inside out. "Fine," I said, with a nervous laugh. "Great. Couldn't be better, actually."

My eyes ate him up, devouring tiny details. The light mist of rain sparkling on his jacket, the redness of his cheeks, the deep, concerned blue of his eyes.

"Why are you out here?" he asked. "Lose your key?"

"No, I…" Now the laughter was bursting out of me. "Darlene is in there. With a guy."

A guy who's not you. Because you're here. With me.

"What is she doing?" he asked with a frown. "Or do I even want to know?"

"It involves nudity and strong sexual situations. Viewer discretion is advised."

Beckett's expression darkened. "Are you serious? I've told her a hundred times…"

I stepped aside to watch Beckett pound on the door, feeling almost lightheaded, like I'd just taken a hit off the world's strongest joint. Everything was funny and bright and perfect.

"Darlene?" Beckett called, his voice hard. "You have ten seconds and then we're coming in." He shook his head at me. "I'm sorry about this. I gave her a key for emergencies, but I warned her: no drugs, no parties, and no using my place like an hourly motel."

"It's fine," I said, still beaming like an idiot. "Totally fine."

Beckett gave me a final scrutinizing look and then shouted at the door. "Darlene? Time's up."

He opened the door and I stuck close behind him, squinting my eyes in case Darlene and lover-who-was-not-Beckett were still in flagrante delicto. They were both standing, both smoothing rumpled clothes and hair and looking sheepish.

"I'm sorry, Becks," Darlene said, tugging on her boots. "We were in the neighborhood to say hi. I wanted Kyle to meet Zel, and it was raining and no one was home. One thing led to another…"

The guy—Kyle—tucked his shirt into his jeans. "Yeah, sorry, man. We got carried away."

Beckett ignored him. "On my *couch*, Darlene?"

"Well, it's better than in your *bed*," she said petulantly. She looked to me. "Hey, Zel. Sorry about all this."

"It's perfectly okay, Dar," I said. "Perfectly. Okay."

A sudden, crazy urge to tell her she could fuck any non-Beckett guy she wanted, any time she wanted, rose up in me. I bit the inside of my cheek to keep it in.

"So this is Kyle Hayes," Darlene said. "That's Zelda, and the guy being super pissy right now is Beckett."

Kyle half-smiled. Waved. His fly was unzipped. "Hey."

"Hey, *Kyle*," Beckett said slowly, still obviously annoyed.

"Hi, Kyle," I said loudly. "It's *great* to meet you."

Beckett shot me another look—each one was more laden with concern for my mental health than the last—and then turned back to Darlene. "Now's not a good time to hang out."

"Gotcha," Darlene said, and grabbed Kyle by the hand and dragged him to the door. "We're gone. C'mon, Kyle."

"And don't do it again, Dar," Beckett added, slowly setting his bike against the wall.

She stuck her tongue out at him, then glanced at me with a 'call me' motion of hand.

"*Come* again, any time," I called, and a cackle escaped me.

Beckett shut the door and crossed his arms over his chest. He rubbed his right elbow. "What's with you?"

"What do you mean? It was funny. *Three's Company*-style shenanigans, except…pornographic."

"When I first saw you in the hallway I thought you were…"

"Thought I was what?"

"Crying."

My smile faltered but I managed to keep my eyes on his. "Not even close. I have the sensibilities of a fifteen-year old boy. The whole situation was hilarious."

He nodded slowly, his brows still furrowed. "Yeah, okay." He looked to the closed door as if he could still see Darlene and Kyle through it, his expression cloudy, his lips turned down.

My high crashed further as I wondered if maybe I had it backwards. Maybe it hurt him that *Darlene* was fucking someone else.

"You don't look happy," I began slowly. "Not a fan of Kyle? Do you know him?"

"No, and that's what bothers me," Beckett said. "I worry about her. She hooks up with random guys and God knows if they're on something. If they are, it's only a matter of time before she'll get lured back in."

Beckett pushed off the door, limping. It occurred to me—finally—that he was home four hours early.

"Wait, what happened?" I said. "Why are you walking like that?"

He winced as he hobbled to the couch and sat down, heavily.

"I was run off the road," he said.

"You were *what*?" I gasped, followed by a whispered, "Oh shit," as he eased up the bottom of his torn pant leg. His sock was bloodied and a swath of road rash ran along the outer side of his calf. Ankle to knee, a scraped mess of striated blood streaked with grime.

"Goddamn." He finished rolling up his pant leg, then winced and flexed his right arm.

"And your arm?" I asked, alarm growing.

"Just bruised. I skidded on the street and landed hard on my elbow, but I think it's okay."

"What the hell happened?"

"Some guy made a sudden right in front of me. I think he almost missed his turn. Missed me too, but not by much."

"What an asshole," I said through gritted teeth. I knelt by the couch and examined Beckett's leg. "It's not deep but you've got a bunch of dirt in there."

"I need to rinse it off in the shower," he said, taking off his shoe and bloody sock. "Would you mind turning the water on? Lukewarm."

"Yeah, of course."

I did as he said, then helped him over to the bathroom. Beckett gritted his teeth and stuck his leg in the water. I watched as a good amount of blood and dirt fell away but some small bits of gravel and dirt were visible, streaked through the scratches closest to his ankle.

"Damn. All that grime has to be scraped out," Beckett said.

"Scraped out?" I made a face. "You've done this before?"

"Once or twice." He smiled wanly. He looked worn out.

Nearly getting hit by a car will do that to a guy.

"Go lay down on your bed," I said. "Where's your first aid? Bathroom?"

"I can do it myself."

But I was already on my way. Under the sink, behind my boxes of tampons, I found a small box with a bottle of hydrogen peroxide, a wad of gauze, and some anti-bacterial ointment. At the bottom was a round, silver brillo pad, still in its package.

"Shit, this *does* happen a lot," I muttered.

I grabbed the box and came out to see Beckett gingerly settling himself against his pillow on the bed.

"Maybe you should go the hospital."

"I'm fine," he said. "I've had worse."

I remembered what Darlene said about his lack of health insurance. Still, the ER couldn't turn him away.

He saw me gnawing my lip. "Zel, it's fine. My elbow's bruised and I've got some gnarly road rash. I don't need a doctor for this."

"Did you hit your head? Do you have a headache?"

"I wear a helmet."

I gave him another scrutinizing look as I set the box of first aid stuff next to the bed, then grabbed a spare towel from the closet. I put the towel on the bed and carefully lifted his leg onto it. He settled back on his pillow.

"This isn't too deep," I said, inspecting the wound. "But it's going to hurt like a bastard. You want me to run out and get you some hard liquor?"

He cocked his head.

"In movies, they're always giving the guy a swig of whiskey or moonshine to help dull the pain before some gruesome medical procedure."

"Are you going to saw my leg off?"

"I probably should. Before you turn."

He chuckled for the first time in days since his shut down. "I'm okay," he said. "I can't get wasted, anyway. I have to work tomorrow."

My eyes flared. "You are *not* going back out tomorrow."

"I have to, Zel. Can't afford not to."

I sniffed. "We'll see." I tore the plastic wrap off the Brillo pad and doused it in hydrogen peroxide. "Are you ready?"

"Are *you*?"

"I got this. I think." I put my hand on his ankle to steady myself, noting absently that Beckett—by some miracle of nature—didn't have ugly feet. He had nice feet, and the muscle of his calf was lean and well defined. But now that I was this close, I noted a few other small scars around his knee. I thought about what Darlene said: how it was only a matter of time before he got hit.

"*Wait*," Beckett said just as I touched the pad to his skin.

I flinched back with a little cry. "Jesus, what?"

"You didn't give me a stick to bite down on."

"Goddamn you." I swatted the bottom of his foot. "You're not making me want to take it easy on you."

He smiled and laid back, his eyes closed. "That's the idea."

I snorted and got to work. Gingerly, and with the barest minimum of pressure needed, I cleaned out the tiny bits of pebble that were lodged in the wound. Beckett's foot twitched a few times and his calf muscle tensed under my touch, but he made no sound.

When I was done, the wound was raw and red, but the angry scratches were free of dirt. I slathered antibiotic gel over it and started to bandage it but Beckett waved a hand.

"It needs to breathe for the rest of the night. Bandage tomorrow."

"How many times has this happened?" I asked. "For real?"

He looked at me through heavy-lidded eyes. "I don't know," he said softly. "Enough."

I sat for a moment with him, wondering what to say or do next. The light at the window was fading.

"I'm going to make dinner," I said. "You rest up, but *do not* fall asleep on me or I swear to God, I'll call an ambulance."

"I didn't whack my head," he said. "I've been riding long enough, Zel. I know how to fall."

"Oh, that makes me feel *so* much better."

He laughed, and said, "Fine, I promise I won't sleep. But maybe put on a record, yeah?"

"Yes. Something loud."

I perused his collection and found *Paul's Boutique,* by the Beastie Boys. In moments, I had "Hey Ladies" filling the studio.

"No chance I could fall asleep to that," Beckett said.

"Exactly."

I made a squash and arugula salad, tomato soup and heated a loaf of French bread as the Beastie Boys rapped against seventies disco. As I cooked, the combined shock of catching Darlene and Beckett's accident wore off, which freed me to ponder my profound sense of loss when I thought Beckett was screwing another girl, and the even more extraordinary happiness when it turned out he wasn't.

I moved the coffee table over to Beckett's bed and we ate, and when the album finished, we watched the news; to keep the silence between us away. I felt as if I were holding my breath, holding in words I didn't know how to say. I cleaned up and went to the bathroom to change into comfy clothes.

I splashed some cold water on my face, and remembered how I'd once admonished my friend Theo, in Vegas, to stop denying his feelings and tell the girl he loved he wanted to be with her. I remembered how freely and confidently the advice flowed. So easy to be the one sitting on the sidelines, prodding and teasing and not risking anything. It was a million times easier to give advice than live it, especially when the advice was to trust someone else with your heart.

"Thank you for cleaning me up," Beckett said when I came out of the bathroom.

"No problem. It's exactly how I envisioned spending my Thursday night."

He didn't smile. "I'm sorry for being a dick to you lately."

"You haven't—"

"I have." He stared at the ceiling. "At the ice rink I forgot, for a little bit, what I'd done. It was like being on vacation somewhere warm and bright. And remembering again was like coming home to a dank, cold place and knowing it's where you live."

I nodded. "I know what you mean. My home isn't what it was. It's not home anymore. It will never be home ever again."

"And I'm sorry for that too, Zel."

"For what?"

"For not being able to go with you to Philly."

"Oh." I busied myself with tying up my hair for the night. "Don't be sorry. I should have considered your whole parole situation."

"Are you still going to go?"

"It would hurt my mom too much if I didn't." I forced a smile. "I'll survive. It's what we do, right?"

He nodded, watching me fluff out the blue comforter on the air mattress. Technically, it was his turn to sleep on it, but if he even tried to argue with me about it, I was ready to give him an earful.

A silence fell and then he said, "I think I'll take tomorrow off."

"Oh?" I said. "I guess you weren't knocked on your head after all."

He smiled. "Would you mind handing me my laptop and headphones? I'm going to watch a movie. Today was shit. I need a laugh."

"Sure." I brought him both. "What are you going to watch?"

"*Dumb and Dumber*."

"Ah. A classic."

"You want to watch it with me?"

I hesitated. Watching on his laptop meant lying in bed next to him. Before my brain had a chance to formulate a response, my head bobbed and I heard myself say, "Sure."

I climbed into bed—on top of the covers—on the other side of Beckett and lay next to him on the pillows, shoulder to shoulder. We watched the hilariously stupid antics of Harry and Lloyd, laughing at all the same places, until I my body felt heavy and my eyes started to droop.

"You falling asleep on me?" Beckett asked, his voice a low rumble.

"Maybe," I murmured. "Was this your grand plan all along? To get me off the air mattress?"

"I have no idea what you're talking about."

I glanced up at Beckett lying so close to me, his beautiful face in profile, and my thoughts were pulled back to the moment when I'd thought he was having sex with Darlene. Five seconds that had shaken me to the bone. It felt like I'd lost something I didn't know I wanted.

And I realized you could get used to anything—even being alone for years—right until the moment you touched something better than what you had.

14

Beckett
December 23rd

I woke with Zelda lying curled next to me. Carefully, to keep the bed still, I rolled to my side, facing her. Her hair fanned out on the pillow, and her face, in sleep, was free of the hard edges that pulled at her mouth, or that furrowed her dark brows. She looked peaceful without the shadows of the past hanging over her. She wasn't touching me but it would've taken me no effort to shift toward her and pull her against my chest. I could wrap my arms around her and feel the heat between us grow stronger against the cold.

And then what? You kiss her? Or more? Then let her leave for Philly tomorrow? Wave as she marches off to face her fears alone?

I got out of bed and gingerly hobbled toward the kitchen. The skin on my lower right leg felt tight. It stung like a bitch when I flexed my ankle, but a quick inspection showed it was already improved from last night. Zelda did a good job. I glanced at her, still asleep in my bed, and it was so easy to imagine it as a permanent arrangement.

Go to Philly. Be brave. I'll be here when you get back. It's not much but it's all I can do.

I had been on a course to make coffee, but I veered to the small desk instead where Zelda worked. I grabbed the first pen I could find and a blank sheet of paper and began to write.

Dec 23rd
Dear Mrs. J,

I dream of the robbery a lot. I'm sure you do too. It gets me at least once a week, almost always the same.

Most of it is blurry, or runs at a crazy speed, like a movie on fast forward. I see myself and three accomplices ransacking a living room, tossing valuables—your family heirlooms?—haphazardly into our bags. I can feel the gun tucked into the waistband of my jeans, pressing against my lower back.

And then the reel slows down, narrows its focus. It's the moment that will stay with me forever. The key turns in a lock that was already broken, the door opens, you and your husband come home. I reach for the gun just like my buddy Nash—our ringleader—told me to. To scare you.

And I did.

I don't know why I'm writing this. I'm sure it hurts you more than it does me, and I'm sorry for that. But I wonder, Mrs. J., if you feel as trapped in that moment as I do. Do you relive that instant where Mr. J starts to fall, over and over? Are you stuck there too? Or have you been able to move on?

Move on. People are always telling me to move on and I don't know what it means. How anyone can really move on from tragedy? I think we just find a way to live with it, because time <u>*is*</u> *going to move on, dragging us through the days like a conveyer belt under our feet, whether we like it or not. Whether we're ready or not.*

My path leads to a future of riding my bike, bussing tables, and wishing like fucking mad I could run the reel backward and stop what happened. Because no matter how much time passes between that moment and now, it will never be far enough. I can always turn my head and see that terrible day behind me. Right there, hanging over my shoulder. But when I look forward, I see nothing but gray.

At least, that's how it's been until Zelda.

Do you remember her? I told you about her last month. She became my roommate. She needed a place to live while she worked on a project and I needed the money. Now I feel like her being here is breaking some vow I made to you. The gray future I see in front of me now still isn't defined. It isn't concrete. But I swear I can hear a whisper in the fog. A hint of brilliant green light, luring me toward something else.

I'm not asking you to forgive me, Mrs. J. I never have and I never will, no matter how pathetic my letters might seem. No matter how I whine and bitch about my future, because your husband has none.

But I don't know what to do. I'm lost in this gray haze, and I wonder if maybe you are too.

I'm sorry,

Beckett Copeland

I stared at what I'd written, on Zelda's art paper with one of her special pens. Quietly, I tore the paper off the pad and folded it several times to get it down to a letter size. My hands were shaking. My thoughts scattered. The peace of waking up with Zelda beside me twined in my heart with that terrible day of the robbery. Her vibrant life and warmth a sharp and unforgiving contrast to the memory of watching a man die.

I tucked the letter in an envelope, and wrote Mrs. J's name on it. Then I grabbed my phone and shot Roy a text.

I'm not working today. Good time to have our monthly sit-down, if convenient for you.

The reply came a few moments later. **Works for me. Ten o'clock good?**

Fine. CU then.

I set the phone down and toyed with the letter. A crazy, desperate need to get it into Mrs. J's hands as fast as possible was making my skin itch.

Zelda stirred, sat up, her eyes going to the envelope in my hand.

"Some early morning correspondence?" she asked with a smile. "Need a stamp?"

"Yeah." I turned the letter over and over in my hand. "It's for…Never mind. Listen, I don't want to sound like a dick, but I asked Roy if he can come over today for our monthly meeting. I'm not going to work, so I figured it would be a good time."

Zelda smiled a perplexed smile. "Okay. Why does that make you a dick?"

"Because I don't want you here when he shows up." She flinched a little. I knew she would. "I'm sorry," I said, running a hand through my hair. "It's just fucking humiliating enough as it is."

Zelda moved to the edge of my bed. "What is? That you meet with Roy? It's not—"

"Yes it is, Zelda. It's embarrassing I have a fucking parole officer who will dig around my place—*our* place—searching for contraband items and asking personal fucking questions about my life."

Zelda moved off the bed, hugging her elbows. "I already knew that about you, Beckett," she said, her voice dancing on the edge of hurt and hardness. "This isn't a big newsflash to me. I know and I…" She shrugged, struggled to meet my eye. "And I don't care."

Oh Christ, she was too beautiful. I don't think she'd ever looked more beautiful, having just climbed out of my bed, telling me in a soft voice that she could look beyond what I was.

Because she can't see what I see when I look backward.

The anger and frustration drained out of me, leaving me with nothing but that sick feeling of regret. "I do," I said in a low voice. "I care. And I don't want you to see it."

She held my eye a moment more, then gave her head a shake. "It's not an issue, anyway," she said. "I'm at Annabelle's all day until two, at least." She grabbed her work clothes in a pile and headed for the bathroom. "Going to shower. Tell the coffee fairy to get going, would you?"

The false levity in her voice was almost worse than if she'd cursed me out.

After coffee and some painfully stilted talk, Zelda left for work and I limped a nervous circuit around the apartment until Roy arrived. Before he'd even finished saying good morning, I flapped the letter in the air between us.

"Tell me the truth," I said. "Do you give these to her?"

Roy's surprised expression melted down to a sad smile. "Yes, I do. Every one."

"But you mail them, right? You don't put them in her hand?"

"I mail them."

I nodded, continued my limp-pacing. I had my pant leg rolled up to my knee to keep it off the wound.

"My God, Beckett, what happened?"

I ignored that, my thoughts were speeding along their own train. "So you have no idea if she reads them? You mail them off and that's it. She could be throwing them out, every month, right?"

"Well, I…"

"She probably does. She probably sees who they're from and files them right in the circular bin, right?"

"You don't know that."

"What I *don't know* is why I even fucking bother." I limped to the trashcan in the kitchen and tossed the letter in it. Roy stared at me as I moved to sit on the couch. "Go ahead," I said. "Start your search. Let's get this over with."

Roy was silent for a moment, then sat on the chair next to me. He set his clipboard on the table.

"Tell me what happened," he said.

"Asshole turned in front of me. I skidded out. I'm fine."

He leaned over his knees, inspecting my leg. "It looks clean."

"Zelda took care of it."

Roy caught my eye and I tried to turn away. My chest tightened and I crossed my arms over it, swallowed the jagged lump in my throat but it wouldn't go down.

"I'm a fucking idiot," I said, my voice a croak. "I never should have let her stay. I knew that from the second she asked. No, from before that. When I first met her. I knew it would be a mistake."

"Why a mistake?" Roy asked gently. "Did something happen?"

"No," I said. "And nothing will, because I'm fucking *trapped* by a stupid fucking decision I made three years ago."

"You're not—"

"No?" I snapped at Roy. The anger was boiling out of me and I was going to explode if I didn't direct it somewhere else. "I need to go to Philadelphia, Roy," I said with sarcasm dripping form every word. "I'm putting in my request to go out of state from the twenty-fourth to the twenty-sixth. Maybe longer. Sound good? Can you sign off on that?"

Roy's lips pressed into a thin line. "You need a thirty-day advance—"

"Yeah, I know. Thirty days' advance notice for an out-of-state travel request. But life doesn't work like that. Zelda needs me *now*, not in thirty days. So tell me again how I'm not fucking trapped."

Roy didn't deserve this tirade. It wasn't his fault I'd fucked up my life. But I didn't have the will to acknowledge that just then. Instead I sat like a stone, unmovable and seething.

Roy tucked his clipboard under his arm, quietly got up, went to the trashcan in the kitchen and pulled out my letter. He dusted off a few damp coffee grounds that had stained one corner, and tucked it into his jacket. At the front door, he stopped.

"I can't get you to Philly tomorrow, and as your parole officer, I strongly urge you not to do anything that would jeopardize your standing with the DOC." His expression softened. "But the invitation is still open if you want to spend Christmas with Mary and me. Both you and Zelda are welcome."

My hands clenched into fists so they wouldn't reach for him, so I wouldn't break down like a goddamn baby. He went out and I realized he hadn't read the letter to Mrs. J in front of me.

So what? He'll read it before he mails it. A waste of fucking postage, anyway.

I sat for a long while, letting my emotions drain out of me. I felt like shit for treating Roy like that. I'd text him an apology later. Right now I wallowed, feeling more scraped, raw and stinging than my leg. My eyes landed on a cluster of orange, red and yellow flowers on the desk. A houseplant I hadn't even noticed until then.

I hobbled over to the desk and sat at the chair, staring at the riot of color against the city's winter gray. Zelda had brought the plant in. And the Christmas lights. And the rug. Filling this crappy apartment with color and light.

My gaze fell to her work. A drawing of Ryder, bursting from the space-time ether to stop Kira from killing.

I blinked. "Ryder," I said.

Ryder.

Rider.

I looked at the speech bubble above Ryder's head. *There is another way.*

I'd made a silent promise to Zelda: to help her find a better way to carry the incredible pain of losing her sister. I couldn't go to Philadelphia with her…

…to keep her safe…

But maybe I could do something for her anyway. I had to try. I had no Butterfly Project to send me back in time. I'd be trapped in New York for two more years.

Still, maybe there was another way.

I SHOULD'VE KILLED THE SICK BASTARD. I SHOULDN'T HAVE LET YOU STOP ME. DON'T EVER FUCKING STOP ME.
IT'S MY JOB TO KILL HIM AND EVERY OTHER ABOMINATION LIKE HIM.
IT'S KILLING YOU.
I DON'T CARE.
IT WON'T BRING HER BACK.
I KNOW.
GIVE YOURSELF SOME PEACE, KIRA. LET HER GO.
I... I DON'T KNOW HOW.
I'LL HELP YOU.

15

Zelda
December 23rd

After my shift at Annabelle's, I didn't feel like taking the train back to Brooklyn. Instead I found a Starbucks, ordered a latte and a croissant, and called Darlene. She'd sent me a dozen apologetic texts I couldn't answer while I was at work.

She picked up on the first ring. "Oh my God, Zel, I'm so sorry about yesterday. It was so tacky. I'm mortified."

I smiled against the phone. "Don't be. It's not a big deal."

"You're too good to me," Darlene said. "Is Becks mad?"

"No, he's worried that Kyle might not be good for you."

Darlene made an incomprehensible sound and then said, "Zelda, I'm telling you, I've never been happier. For real."

"Really?" I picked at my croissant. "When did you meet this guy?"

"Oh my God, get this: he came into Giovanni's for a blind date but she never showed. We got to talking and… I don't know, we just clicked. He's so *nice,* Zelda. Nicer than any guy I've ever been with." Her voice dropped and quavered. "I'm actually a little scared."

"You're scared because you like him so much," I said, and began tearing long strips of buttery crust off the pastry.

"Yeah, but I slept with him too soon. I promised myself I wouldn't, but we can't keep our hands off each other."

"I noticed," I said with a faint smile. My croissant was shredded, a pastry dissection gone bad. "That's good though, Dar. I'm happy that you're happy."

"I'm more scared than happy. Or maybe I'm scared *because* I'm happy. I don't want to fuck this up, Zel. But I also… I don't know, I don't want to hold back either. I'm just going for it, you know?"

No, I don't know, I thought. *I'm not as brave as you.*

"He'd better be worthy of you," I said.

"Of me?" she asked, her voice loud with incredulity.

"*Yes,*" I said. "If he hurts you I'll kick his ass."

"Zel, you're the best. How are you? Am I going to see you before Christmas?"

The few sips of coffee I'd drunk churned in my gut.

"Probably not. I'm leaving tomorrow." I shifted in my seat and hunched over my table. "Hey, Dar, if Beckett doesn't visit Roy, would you check in on him?"

"I'll do better than that," Darlene said. "I can only take so much of my family, even on Christmas. After the morning festivities, a bunch of us will go out like we did last year." I could hear her smile over her words. "I really want Becks to meet Kyle. I mean officially meet him. And like him. I really want them to like each other."

"I'm sure they will," I said.

"I hope so. Okay, I gotta run. Merry Christmas, Zel. Love you!"

"I love you too."

I wandered SoHo to do some Christmas shopping. A music store lured me inside. It was mostly instruments, but one section along a back wall had a collection of vinyl. I perused, thinking it was hopeless I'd be able to find something Beckett might like out of so much music, until I hit the S section. Then a smile spread over my face and I plucked the album from the bin without glancing at the price.

Outside, back in the cold, my smile dimmed. I hadn't yet packed for my trip to Philly. The thought made my skin tingle, like the air tightening right before lightning strikes. My train left at noon the next day, and the closer I got to that time, the more fractured and scattered I became. Out of the tangle of feelings I had for Beckett, one screamed louder than all others: I wanted him to come with me.

But he can't. And he obviously feels like shit for it, so don't go home a fucking mess and make him feel worse.

Thanks to a puny budget, I finished my shopping quickly and was dismayed to see it was only seven. I headed to the nearest movie theater so I could stuff my face with popcorn and stuff my eyes with someone else's story. A story I forgot as soon as the credits rolled.

I headed out and walked around the stores of Times Square. I had an urge to go back to Rockefeller Center and see the tree, but the air was icy cold and threatened snow. Resigned, I headed for the subway and back to Brooklyn.

It was nearly eleven when I turned the key in the apartment door. Only the Christmas lights were on. Beckett was on the air mattress, buried under the blue comforter, even though it was my turn.

"Of course," I whispered, smiling. Already my jumpy nerves were settling, just from walking into the same room as him. Maybe I'd sleep tonight, too.

But an hour later, I was still tossing and turning.

I threw off the covers, crept over to the desk and flipped on the lamp, trying to be as quiet as possible. I took up a pen and paper, hoping to lose myself in the work. But my work was my past. It was Rosemary and me and my terrible failure.

I can't do this. I can't go to Philly...

"Hey," Beckett said softly.

I wiped my nose on my sleeve. "Hey, yourself," I said, not looking at him. "Did I wake you?"

"No. Can't sleep."

"Me neither," I said. "I was hoping to get some work done before I left but… It's all tied up in these stupid drawings."

"What is, Zel?"

"My family. Rosemary. All of this is for her. And for my mom…" The words poured out on a tide of shaky breaths. "Some days the work feels like punishment. Every time Kira kills someone, it's not *relief.* It just ties her more tightly to her loss."

Beckett's hand slipped to the back of the chair as he bent over my shoulder. I watched his eyes scan over the sketches. "So where are we?"

I shuffled some paper to find what I was looking for. "Ryder and Kira have come back from the jump, to their own time. She's pissed that he stopped her from killing her victim. The perv's in jail, but it doesn't feel like enough to her. She doesn't think he should live, but… Deep down she knows she can't go on like this. Not anymore."

I glanced up at him, damn tears in my throat again.

"What happens next?" I whispered. "He said there was another way. What is it, Beckett? I can't see it."

"He tells her it's killing her," Beckett said softly. "That the guilt will eat her alive until there's nothing left but hate." He looked at me. "Or nothing at all. Not even hope."

"How does he know?"

"Because he's been there." Beckett blinked and looked back to the pages of drawings. "He doesn't want what happened to him to happen to her."

"What happened to him? What's his backstory?"

Beckett's smile tightened. "Ryder killed an innocent man once. By accident. They sent him back but the data was wrong. The perv wasn't a perv at all. *Ryder* became the criminal and he wishes like hell someone could go back in time and stop *him*."

I drew in a breath to speak, but Beckett continued, his voice heavy.

"But they can't, so he wants to help her. Ryder tells Kira that it wasn't her fault," he said, his eyes finding mine in the dimness again. "Nothing that happened was her fault. Not one second of it."

"But she saw it happen," I whispered. "She was there and she couldn't stop it."

His hand reached up to lay his palm against my cheek, his thumb softly sliding over my skin.

"And he tells her he's so fucking sorry she has to carry that around with her for the rest of her life. He says he'd take it if he could."

For the first time in years, tears were escaping my eyes, sliding down my cheek. They slipped in between his skin and mine.

"He's taken enough," I whispered brokenly. "More than he should."

Beckett shook his head. "This isn't his story." He slowly let his hand slip from my face. "It's hers. And she deserves some peace."

I felt the knot of anxiety that was twisting me inside out begin to loosen. Enough so I felt like I could breathe a little after feeling suffocated for ten years.

Beckett started to move back to the air mattress.

"No," I said, wiping my eyes on my sleeve. I shut off the desk lamp and got up from the chair. "You're not sleeping on the floor. Not tonight."

Without waiting for an argument, I took his hand and guided him to the bed. We crawled in together and pulled up the covers. I lay beside him then. Not touching, but I could feel the heat of his body.

"Goodnight," I said.

He exhaled a long breath. "Fucking hell, Zelda…" Then he was pulling me toward him, wrapping his arms around me.

A sob rose to my throat but I choked it down, and held him tight. As tight as he held me, and wherever we touched became proof to one another that we were not alone.

16

Zelda
December 24th

I slept well, with no bad dreams, and woke the next morning in a sleepy hangover of warmth. When I blinked my eyes open, I saw Beckett's half of the bed was empty. I remembered he said he had to work on Christmas Eve. Last-minute shoppers kept messengers busy all day and into the night.

I hugged his pillow closer, inhaling his scent, as if I could fill my bones with his peace. Store it in my cells for the trip to Philly.

The coffee in the pot was cold. I turned it back on to heat while I showered and dressed.

How do you feel? I asked myself.

My therapist in high school would ask me constantly, and I always lied and said, "Okay."

"I feel okay," I said to the green tiles of the shower. This morning, it was the truth. And not a bad truth, either. Compared to the alternative of free-falling anxiety, feeling merely *okay* was…fine.

"I'm fine," I murmured, as I dressed and packed and puttered around until it was time to head to Manhattan.

I'm doing all right, I thought on the subway ride to Penn Station. *I'm okay,* as I lugged my rolling suitcase to the upper level and the Amtrack concourse. I was early, so I bought a couple magazines and a latte from Starbucks. I found a bench and settled down to wait, my feet on my suitcase.

Everything is perfectly okay.

My phone rang. It was Beckett.

"Hi," I said.

"Hey, Zel." I could hear the din of city streets behind him. "I just finished a job and I'm a block from Penn Station. Are you there now?"

"I just got here."

"Where are you?"

"In the Amtrack waiting area. I'm sitting on a bench across from Starbucks."

"Don't move. Be there in ten minutes."

"Is something wrong?"

"No, I just want to talk to you." The call ended.

I let my phone hand drop to my lap, wondering what this meant. For a second, a shooting star of hope shot across my heart that he'd been able to get around the thirty-day notice for a leave, maybe with Roy's help. But even if he hadn't, I could stand seeing Beckett one last time before I left for Philly. I needed him. His safety. Even if it only meant his arms around me once more.

Beckett came off the escalator, looked around the concourse to locate the green and white signage of Starbucks, then came walking over. He carried his helmet by the chin strap. His hair was sweaty and flattened. Above his beard growth, his cheeks were pink with cold.

He's beautiful.

"Hey," he said as he got closer.

"Hey, yourself. You're hardly limping," I said, because telling him he was beautiful was out of the question.

"I know," he said. "You did a good job cleaning it up."

"Takes a lot to gross me out. I read a lot of horror comics." I pulled my jacket closer to make room for him to sit.

"I don't have a lot of time," he said. "Your train's coming and I have to get to another job." He shot me a quick look then, traced a whorl of wood on the bench with his finger. "Okay, so there's no good way to segue into an anecdote from my prison years, so I'm just going to launch straight in."

"Okay."

He leaned back on the bench. "Prison sucks, as you can imagine," he said, his eyes straight ahead. "Or maybe you can't. The worst of it isn't the obvious. It isn't the small cells, the lack of privacy and dignity, or the dangerous guys you're locked up with. That's all pretty fucking awful, don't get me wrong. But the real punishment is what prison does to you on the inside."

His voice sounded scratchy, as if this subject was rusty.

"The boredom is pretty bad. You live with stretches of mind-numbing monotony interrupted by bursts of violence. If you're lucky and keep your head down, the boredom is the best you can hope for. I read a lot. As much as I could, and that's the closest I found to escape. There's no joy in your life. No happiness." He smirked. "I mean, it's *prison*, not a vacation."

I smiled gently. "Go on."

"You have a lot of downtime to sit around and ponder your life choices," he said with a dry smile. "Most guys lived in their memories. Some guys—like my first cellmate—never shut up. He told stories all day long. I kept mine in my head, watching them over and over like home movies. And when I came to a good memory—a good moment—I did my best to go back there. Not just to remember it, but to *live* it again. Recall what I smelled, the textures of what I touched. And feel how I felt. When I came to a happy memory—like Gramps taking me to Coney Island when I was twelve—I held on, dug deep and lived it over and over."

"And it worked?" I asked.

"It's how I survived." His eyes looked at me, heavy with regret. "When you go back to Philly, to your house, and the bad shit starts starts to get you, grab a good memory, Zel. Grab it, hold on to it, and live in it. It might help." He shook his head, freed his arms from their tight cross and held up his palms. "I know it's not much but it's all I got."

The PA system announced my train then.

"That's me," I said.

"C'mon," he said. "I'll walk you."

We were quiet down the length of the platform to the waiting train. Beckett's eyes were narrowed, watching the rush of travelers coming and going, boarding and disembarking trains.

"Text me when you get there, okay?" he said.

"I will."

Beckett rubbed the stubble along his jaw. He seemed about to go, then he hesitated, his eyes flicking to the end of the train and back. "Zelda…"

"Don't even think about it," I said. "If you get caught breaking parole they'll send you back to prison, right?"

His jaw clenched.

I pressed him. "Won't they?"

He looked away. "Yeah, probably. For a few months, anyway."

"A few months is too long. And I'd never forgive myself." I put my fist on his shoulder and gave a push. "I'll be fine. You stay put. For me. Okay?"

His shoulders dropped with a tremendous exhale. "Okay," he said finally.

"Promise me."

"I promise," he said. "But only because the fucking State of New York says I have to."

I laughed a little as I touched his shoulder again. "Now hold still so I can store you up."

He didn't laugh or move. He held still. I didn't do any more than run my hand from his shoulder down his arm, but it was a collection. His jokes, his smile, his blue eyes and the gold in his hair. That he'd considered breaking parole for me. Stupid as all hell, yet it made me want to die that he'd take such a risk for me. All I had to do was ask.

No chance, I'd never risk his freedom. This heroine has to save herself.

"Miss you, Zel," he said.

I threw my arms around his neck. His arms wrapped around my back and we hugged tight. My eyes fell closed as I melted against him, inhaling, holding on to him as long as I could before it was too long.

"I'll be back in a few days," I said, finding the will to pull away. "Have fun with Darlene and don't give Kyle a hard time. She really likes him. But if he's an asshole then kick his teeth in."

Beckett laughed a little. "Call me when you get there. Call me anytime. If it ever gets to be too much. *Especially* then. Okay?"

I nodded quickly. "I will."

"Promise me," he said.

"I promise," I said. "But only because you're so goddamn good-looking."

He raised his eyebrows and he coughed a small laugh. "Is that so?"

"Yeah, you're pretty easy on the eyes, Copeland. No one's told you that before?"

His smile slipped, his eyes held mine in their sapphire depths. "No one who mattered."

My heart pounded as the moment stretched out, full of electricity, then cracked apart as the conductor made a final call for boarding.

"I gotta go," I said. "I'll talk to you soon."

"Yeah, Zel. I hope so."

I headed for the entrance of the train. I didn't look back, but I knew he was watching me go. I knew he'd stay until the train pulled out of the station. I found my seat and closed my eyes, safe in the knowledge that when I came back, Beckett would be there.

17

Zelda
December 24th

I took a cab to my Rittenhouse neighborhood, my hands balled into fists in my coat pocket. My breath kept trying to stop in my throat but I forced it down, exhaled it back out slowly.

I can do this.

I took in the townhouses standing shoulder to shoulder on either side of the narrow cobblestone street. The trees were skeletons, their black bony hands spread against the gray sky. In fall they would've been dressed in yellow and orange, littering the streets with a carpet of gold.

When we were younger, Rosemary and I would pile the leaves up high and fall into them, moving our arms and legs to make leaf angels…

That's a good memory, I heard Beckett say. *Hold onto it. Keep it there.*

With the sound of remembered laughter in my head, I took the steps to my house, a red brick townhome with dark gray trim over the door and windows. I set down my suitcase, raised a trembling hand and knocked.

The door opened and my mother was there. Her eyes, the same green as mine, all lit up and shining with joy.

"Hi, Mom," I said.

Without a word, she pulled me into her arms. I leaned into my mother's perfume, the softness of her sweater, the strength of her embrace. I closed my eyes and let the moment be my home. Dad was there too, and I did the same thing, clinging to his sweater.

"So good to see you," he said into my hair.

Inside, Dad took my rolling luggage and headed for the upper floor where the bedrooms were.

"Wait, I want to sleep in the den, on the couch," I told him.

He hesitated. "Couch is pretty lumpy, kiddo. I would know—your mom sends me there when I've been bad."

"Which is a lot," Mom said. She smiled at me but her eyebrows furrowed. "You sure, honey?"

"I'm sure," I said. My room was too full of memories. Rosie sitting on my bed as I braided her hair. A pillow fight that ended with me knocking her to the floor…

I blinked, and made fists in the pockets of my jacket again. I hadn't taken any meds but wondered if I should.

Or else I'm not going to make it…

Dad studied my face a moment. "The den it is."

"Are you hungry?" Mom asked, linking her arm in mine. "Everyone's in the kitchen, as usual. Let's get a snack."

"Everything looks so nice," I said as we walked through the living room. The tree stood tall by the windows and the mantel was festooned with a lighted garland and candlesticks.

After Rosemary disappeared, I expected my parents to move from this house, at best, or divorce, at worst. I'd read that, statistically, the loss of a child drove married couples apart. Not Lydia and Paul Rossi. My parents loved each other, and the house they'd bought when they first married. They didn't want to give up either one.

Mom was an interior designer, and the house became her canvas. She redid all three floors—but for Rosie's room, which would forever remain untouched—and even that wasn't enough. She never stopped changing things or adding details. I think it was how my parents survived.

To me, the house was the same, just dressed differently. The memories were still there under the fresh paint. Like Clark Kent putting on glasses and a suit and suddenly no one could tell he was Superman.

I could tell.

"You painted again," I said to my mom. "This gray is new. I like it."

"Isn't it pretty?" Mom said, collecting some empty plates from the coffee table. "Your father picked it," she added. Her smile slipped a little. "It was time for a change."

From the kitchen, I could hear the din of Rossi-De Luca

relations, a dozen voices raised above the rattle of pots and pans. My two Grandmothers jostled each other at the stove, talking and bickering in Italian as they cooked and spiced and stirred simmering pots like Macbeth's witches. They took turns slapping Uncle Mike's fingers away from the prime rib.

"Look who's here," Mom said.

Like a switch, the room froze and the chatter ceased. A crystal moment of silence, then they descended on me. All at once, I was surrounded by voices and scents and embraces, all threatening to drive me off a cliff into a sea of wonderful memories tainted black with guilt and grief.

I inhaled, and remembered Beckett holding me last night, and hugging me tight on the train platform.

Just be here.

I exhaled and found my smile. "Hi, everyone. Merry Christmas."

But I knew before I even sat down to dinner that it was too much.

The dining room table was laden with bowls and platters of food, and glittered with Mom's best silverware. Dishes were passed up and down, from grandmothers and grandfathers, Uncle Mike, Aunt Stella and Uncle Louie, to my eighty-three year old Auntie Lucille.

On the surface, we looked whole and healthy. No empty chairs at the table. But I could see the gaping hole left by Rosemary's absence. It was as if my loud, Italian family was on a dimmer switch, turned a little lower. Sad looks and silences fell into the cracks of conversation when people were too afraid to talk about kids or Christmas or school, or anything else that touched too close to what Rosemary should have been experiencing right then.

Only Auntie Lucille seemed oblivious. She sat to my right, reeking of Shalimar and mentholated cough drops. She reminded me of a crane—tall and skinny, with knobby knees under her floral dresses, and bottle glasses behind which she regarded us all with large eyes. Her eyes were green too—it was a De Luca trait—and were miles deep. They looked as though they contained the wisdom of the universe, a huge contrast to the unhinged ramblings that often fell out of her mouth.

"There was once a movie theater… What was it called? Phantasus. Yes, I remember." A smile spread over her lips, crookedly painted with red lipstick. She leaned to me. "It was called Phantasus.

But it did more than show movies. It was a land where all of your dreams came true."

"Phantasus?" Uncle Mike said from her right. "Sounds like Phantasos, from Ovid's epic poem *Metamorphoses,* if I remember my classics from the old college days. A spirit who appeared in dreams?" He smiled broadly at Lucille, humoring her. "Is that where it comes from, Luce?"

She stared at him as if he were a child and patted his cheek. "Ssssh," she said. "The movie is starting."

Uncle Mike laughed and gave up. Auntie Lucille babbled on. Talk went back and forth around me, over me. The voices were too loud, the lights too bright. I sat carefully, moved slowly, afraid the slightest bump would shatter me. I could feel the memories swirl around me like ghosts, and I shrunk deeper into my chair, into myself. If I made myself small enough, the panic wouldn't find me.

"Zelda, it's too bad your friend couldn't come," Mom said, passing me a bowl of garlic-and-butter green beans. "Is he with his family?"

"Tomorrow he will be," I said, my voice sounding disengaged from my head. "He's working tonight."

"What does he do?"

He keeps me safe.

"He's a bike messenger," I managed. The table was blurring and wavering, like a flashback in one of those old TV shows. Beside me, Auntie Lucille prattled on about her mythical movie theatre.

"Phantasus. Isn't that a wonderful name?"

Now the voices were blurring. First pressing against my eardrums, then fading far away. I struggled to do what Beckett told me. I reached back in time for piles of golden leaves under an autumn-blue sky. I tried to grasp my mother's hug, her scent and softness. I looked for Beckett's hand on my cheek. His long, sleeping breaths in the dark. The strength and safety of his hug.

It all slipped through my fingers like water.

Someone touched my arm and it was like the starting gun of a race. The panic sprinted through me, forcing me to my feet. My chair fell over behind me and every head turned.

"I…I'm sorry," I said. "Sorry… Excuse me…"

Blind with tears, I fled down the hall, to the den, and curled up on the couch, shaking into pieces.

Rosie, I'm sorry. I'm so sorry...

Mentholatum and Shalimar filled my nose, then Aunt Lucille's thin, bony arms slid around me. I was sure my shaking sobs would be too much for her, but the strength of her embrace surprised me, as did the soothing comfort of her hand along my hair.

"Phantasus is where children go to watch any movie they want," she said, her voice steady and calm. "Only one screen, but it plays each child's favorite. They eat ice cream and candy, and each one gets a balloon tied to their wrist. Their favorite color."

She bent her lips toward my ear. "Can you see her there, darling?"

"Red," I whispered. "Her…f-favorite color was red."

"Her balloon is red at the Phantasus. And she laughs with other little angels and eats as much candy as she wants, and she'll never get sick, and she'll never be scared, and she'll only be happy. Forever."

My chest, which seemed about to detonate, slowly imploded. I caved in with it, and I cried against my Auntie Lucille. I wept until I was dry.

Then I slept.

18

Beckett
December 24th

I got home from work and took a hot shower to defrost. After twelve hours of riding, the cold settled in the marrow of my bones and it took a solid twenty minutes under the spray to get warm.

Toweling off, I checked my phone. I got dressed and checked it again. I warmed up some leftovers and popped a beer. Then checked my phone. I put on Blondie's *Parallel Lines.* I ate and sipped and listened, my eyes either full of the strings of light Zelda had put up, or glancing toward the phone.

By midnight, she still hadn't called. I didn't know whether to be disappointed or relieved. I told her to call me if shit got too hard. No call meant she was doing okay.

Or it could mean shit's really bad and she can't call at all.

"Fuck it," I said. I started to shoot her a text when the phone rang in my hands. It was her.

"Are you okay?" I blurted.

"Greetings and salutations to you too," she said, her voice hoarse.

"Zelda?"

"I'm okay." A ragged inhale. "Sort of. Not really."

I stood up. "What happened?"

"I lost it," she said, "And it was…bad. Real bad."

I covered my eyes with my hand, rubbing the bridge of my nose. "Shit, Zel. I'm so sorry."

"But crazy Auntie Lucille… She's not crazy after all. She's kind of a damned genius. And my parents… God, they're so good. I missed them."

"I know," I said. "How are you now?"

"Tired," she said. "It was a pretty bad attack. But it finally let up and I slept a little. Or maybe I just passed out. But I can't sleep now. I've been trying to do what you said. Hold on to a moment, you know? But it's so hard…"

Her voice was breathy and shaking and I hated that I wasn't with her. My chest constricted at the sound of her soft crying.

"Zelda…"

"I don't cry," she said. "Because once I start, I can't stop."

"Zelda, listen to me. Are you listening?"

"Yes," she whispered.

"Remember the tree."

"The tree…?"

"The tree at Rockefeller Plaza. Can you see it?"

A pause. A sniff. "Yes." She inhaled raggedly, exhaled smoothly. "I see it."

"Lie down with me on the ice again. Look up at the tree. All the lights in the branches, straight up over your head. Be there."

"You're there, too?"

"Right here."

A long, breathing silence. "How do you do that, Beckett?"

"Do what?"

"I called you feeling so goddamn lost, but your voice… It's like a searchlight in the fog."

"I'm right here," I said. "But fucking hell, I wish I was there."

"Don't you dare."

"I won't," I said. "I just wish it."

"I'll be okay. This whole trip… You know, as shitty as I feel, it's actually better than it's ever been before. Thanks to you. And my crazy Auntie Lucille."

"You'll have to tell me about her sometime."

"Or you could meet her," Zelda said. "I'd like that."

"Me too."

"Beckett?"

"Yeah?"

"Will you…stay on the phone with me? I think I'll be able to fall asleep if you keep talking to me."

"I'm that boring, huh?"

"Better than Xanax," she said, laughing softly.

"I'll stay with you," I said. "All night if you want."

"Thank you, Beckett," she said softly. "I'm so worn out but when I close my eyes…" I heard the click of her swallowing hard. "Tell me about your work. Tell me something funny. Tell me anything."

I settled myself on my bed and talked to Zelda for an hour or more. I told all my funny delivery stories, like the business executive who accidentally delivered his wife's Christmas gift to his mistress and vice-versa.

Zelda mostly listened, and laughed softly now and then. At a little after one in the morning she said, "I'm so tired."

"You should get some sleep if you can."

"I'll try but…" An inhale. "What happens next? What do we do when I get back?"

A thousand hopeful possibilities rose in my heart, but I let them all go. Too much hope was sometimes as bad as none at all.

"We finish the graphic novel," I said. "I want to see that done. For you. I want that more than anything."

"We're almost finished," she said.

"Yeah, we are." I closed my eyes and lay back on the pillow. "Let's see it through. If I fuck that up for you, I will never forgive myself."

Zelda was quiet for a minute, then she said, "I used to be scared of that too. Not that you'd fuck it up, but that I would. And living together in a shoebox—"

"We won't screw it up," I said.

"Promise?"

"I promise, Zel."

"I believe you. That's a nice feeling." She made a tired sound and her voice was heavy with exhaustion. "I'll see you soon."

I nodded against the phone.

Come home to me…

"See you soon."

19

Beckett
December 25th

Darlene buzzed the door the next morning. I stood at the kitchen counter, chugging coffee, barely functional on two hours of sleep. Moving like a sloth, I set my cup down to let her in but apparently she got sick of waiting and used her key to let herself up.

"Merry Christmas, Becks," she cried, barreling into my place like a hurricane. She threw her arms around my neck, squished a kiss on my face, then pulled away to study me at arm's length.

"What are you doing?" I asked after a good ten seconds passed.

"I'm trying to see how smitten you are so I know where to take you to buy Zelda's gift." She frowned. "We're still going shopping, right? God, you look like shit. Hangover?"

"Insomnia." I pulled away and grabbed my coat. "And is smitten still a word?"

"It's not a guy's word," she admitted, following me to the hallway. "How about, I want to see how bad you want to bone down with her."

"Jesus, Dar."

She cackled laughter. "That's exactly what Zel said when I told her the same thing."

I froze, stared. "You said… Wait, what?"

She laughed harder and slugged me in the shoulder. "Oh my God, you should see your face. Actually, I'm not kidding. You should." She rummaged in her bag. "Let me take a picture…"

"Stop," I said. "Not today, okay? I don't need relationship advice, I need help picking out something for Zelda. Some decent art supplies. That's all."

Darlene snorted. "Borrrring. Zel can pick out her own art

supplies. You need to give her something special."

I'd had the exact thought myself, about a thousand times, but kept steering away from it.

"Okay, like what?" I asked as we walked in the cold, slushy morning to the bus stop.

She shrugged. "I don't know. Maybe not something you plan for, but something you see and just know she has to have."

I nodded. "Yeah. Good idea." I felt Darlene stare up at me. "What?"

"You're smiling."

"I'm not smiling."

"You're smiling on the inside."

"That's not a thing."

"Yes it is. I can see it in your eyes, Becks, and it makes me so happy to see you *on the verge* of being happy."

"Zelda and I are just friends. We're staying friends until the graphic novel is done."

"How practical," Darlene said, rolling her eyes.

"We have to be," I said. "I can't let anything hurt the chances of getting her work out."

She frowned. "Isn't it your work too, now?"

"A small part," I said. "But it's her story. It'll always be her story."

"I'd think you'd see this as a way out, Becks."

"A way out of what?"

"Messengering. Bussing tables. There's so much more to you than that stuff."

"I never thought of myself as a graphic novelist."

"Do you like it?"

"I guess so. I like watching the story come together." I jammed my hands deeper in my coat pockets. "But it'll always be hers."

Darlene *hmmphed.* It steamed out of her nose.

"What's that?" I asked. "Didn't catch it."

She looked up at me with a serious expression I'd hardly ever seen her wear. "When are you ever going to take a little piece of happiness for yourself?"

I stiffened against her question, and looked over her head, away from her eyes.

"I know what you're looking at," she said quietly. "And you

have to forgive yourself, Becks. You *have* to."

"You weren't there, Dar," I said.

"Maybe not, but I'm watching it eat you up, day by day, and I hate it."

She turned away, her lower lip quivering and I knew I had 3.2 seconds to salvage the day.

"Well, shit, this shopping excursion is starting out on a downer note." I nudged Darlene in the side. "Come on, Dar. Cheer up. Aren't you dying to tell me about Kyle? Aren't we all hanging out tonight? Somewhere besides my couch?"

She snorted a laugh at the same time her face brightened. "Don't change the subject."

But it worked. She prattled about Kyle all through the short bus ride to Montague Street in Brooklyn Heights. We walked along the little shops that were open, my eyes roving for something for Zelda and striking out. We stopped for lunch, and I bought a small loaf of cinnamon bread for Mrs. Santino, then continued the hunt.

I was ready to give up when Darlene led me into a little gift shop that sold artsy knick-knacks, specialized stationary, candles and incense. Tourists filled the aisles, which is why I suspected it was open at all. I glanced around doubtfully.

"This isn't Zelda's style," I told Darlene.

"It's kind of girly for her, but she *is* a girl. I'm sure you've noticed."

Once or twice…or a billion times.

Then my eyes fell on a table covered in snow globes. Some were cheap plastic, with the Empire State Building standing tall in a drift of snow that looked like white fish food. Others were ceramic with chubby angels sitting on rocks playing harps. The one that drew my eye, however, was mounted on a music box stand. The base was heavy pewter, and the glass sphere enclosed a tall Christmas tree. It was carved out of something heavy but delicate—I could see the detailing on the branches. Hundreds of little dots in all colors covered the boughs, painted in a way that made them seem to glow. I dipped it upside down, then turned it right again. A small hurricane of iridescent snow swirled around the tree.

"That's pretty," Darlene said. "What does it play?"

I twisted the little knob at the bottom, and set the snow globe back on the table. It spun slowly while the music box played a tinny version of "Have Yourself a Merry Little Christmas."

"I like that," Darlene said.

"Me too."

It's perfect.

I took the snow globe to the cashier and Darlene gave a nervous squeak when the woman told me it was sixty-three dollars after tax.

"Fine," I said without hesitation. "And could you gift wrap it, please?"

"That'll be another eight dollars," the woman said.

"No problem."

Darlene's elbow whacked mine. "*Just friends* my ass."

We parted ways so we could get ready to go out with Kyle and my work buddies. My heart wasn't in it. The idea of laughing it up with friends while Zelda was suffering down in Philly made me feel like shit.

I stopped at 2C to deliver the cinnamon bread. Santino took it with her usual sniff and a slam.

"Merry Christmas," I said, and started to turn away when the door opened again.

Mrs. Santino held a sweater by the shoulders. A heavy knit turtleneck sweater in blinding lime green.

I blinked. "Is that…for me?"

She pressed its shoulders against mine to gauge the size, then nodded once, satisfied. She tossed the sweater over my shoulder, and then took my face in her hands.

"Che bravo ragazzo che sei, che ti prendi cura di Signora Santino. Tieniti questo per non prendere freddo. È verde come gli occhi del la tua ragazza. Magari lei che ti scalda invece, eh?"

She kissed me loudly on both cheeks, then retreated to her apartment and shut the door. Quietly.

I stood there, staring in shock for a solid minute.

"So that just happened…"

The sweater slid off my shoulder and I grabbed it before it hit the ground and rolled my bike down the hall.

I put Zelda's gift by our little Christmas tree, then showered and dressed. Over jeans and a T-shirt, I pulled on Mrs. Santino's sweater. I studied myself in the bathroom mirror.

"I'm ready for a debate tournament," I muttered, grinning. I'd hear no end of shit from my friends for wearing it, but there was no way I *wasn't* going to wear it.

I heard a key turn in the lock and the front door opened.

"Darlene, can you knock for once in your—?" I peeked my head out and nearly dropped dead.

Zelda. In her coat. A fine dusting of snow on her shoulders and beanie hat. Her long dark hair spilled over her shoulders.

"Hey," I said.

"Hey, yourself," she said. She eyed my sweater with a small smile. "Chess tournament?"

"Debate," I said. "You're not supposed to be here until tomorrow. Are you okay?"

"Not really." She set aside her rolling suitcase and shut the door behind her. "I couldn't stay. I felt like I was going to shatter into a million pieces. Your magic was wearing off."

"My magic?" I asked, my voice dropping backward into my throat.

Zelda smiled sadly, her eyes heavy and shadowed, and rimmed in red. "Yeah, Copeland," she said softly. "Magic." She took off her knit hat and spun it around in her hand. "But I don't really want to talk about it anymore, okay? The visit, I mean. I'm just happy to be back."

"Me too," I said.

A silence fell and then her eyes went to the Christmas tree and the gift beside it. "Santa came," she said. "Did he bring us a new radiator?"

I blinked. "No, that's…for you. From me."

Zelda went to the closet and retrieved a flat, square present, wrapped in solid red and tied with a black bow.

"You'll never guess what this is," she said, moving to the desk. "Not in a million years will you guess what this album-shaped present could possibly be."

She put the gift next to mine, then sank down on the couch. "Are you going out?"

"Yeah. Darlene and a bunch of us are going to a bar. You want to come? You should come. If you're up for it."

"I'm not up for it." A little light came back in her eyes. "But let me clarify: are you going out *in that sweater*?"

I sat beside her on the chair. "You'll never guess who gave it to me."

"Urkel? No…Sheldon Cooper."

"For shame, Rossi. You're going to feel so bad when I tell you it was Mrs. Santino."

"Shut up." She reached over and socked my arm. "For real?"

"She spoke to me too."

"She *speaks*?"

"A bunch of Italian I didn't follow, but yeah."

"Mine is rusty. Can you recall anything? She might've been spilling the secrets of the universe."

I held up my hands. "I took two years of Spanish and all I remember is ¿Dónde está el baño?"

"Wow," she said. "A gal leaves for one day and everything changes."

No shit, I thought.

"So," Zelda said. "What time do the festivities start?"

I glanced at my phone. "Darlene and Kyle should be here in about twenty. Meeting the rest at the bar. But I don't have to go."

"Yes, you do. But you have a little time." She got up and handed me the rectangular gift. "Merry Christmas." She curled back on the couch, feet drawn up and arms crossed tight.

I unwrapped the paper and *The Sinatra Christmas Album* slipped into my hands. I sat with it in my lap for a minute. "How did you know?"

"Know what?"

"My grandfather had this album," I said, trailing my fingers over the cover as memories swirled around my head. "We played it every year. It was lost or sold somewhere down the line. It wasn't in his collection when I got out of prison." I looked up at her, into her green eyed-gaze. "Thank you."

"You're welcome."

I took up her gift and set it in her lap.

"Gee, Copeland, you shouldn't have," she said. She pulled the champagne-colored bow off the beige box and opened it.

"Oh my God," she whispered, and withdrew the snow globe from a nest of tissue paper. I watched her turn it around in her hands and give it a small shake. Snow flurries surrounded the tree and then settled.

I rubbed the back of my neck. "It's a music box too."

Zelda found the little knob on the bottom and turned it. The tiny apartment filled with "Have Yourself a Merry Little Christmas."

"I am, Zel," I said. "Are you?"

Her green eyes found mine over the glass sphere. "I am now."

The door buzzed, shattering the small moment.

"Give Darlene a big hug for me," Zelda said, getting to her feet.

"Wait."

"I'm fine, Beckett," she said with a tight smile. "As much as I'd love to drink yesterday away, I'm not going to be any good in public. I'm going to take a shower, maybe order some takeout and watch *Love Actually*."

"Zelda..."

"Go be with your friends," she said, giving my shoulder a little push. "The world is waiting to see you in that sweater."

She went to the bathroom and shut the door. I stared for a moment, frozen with inaction until the intercom buzzed again, jolting me. I grabbed my wallet, keys, and jacket and headed downstairs.

20

Zelda
December 25th

The shower water couldn't get hot enough to wash off the worst parts of my trip. I could still feel the panic, like a sleeping monster. Restless and snorting, getting ready to wake and tear me apart.

I let the water fall over me and remembered Auntie Lucille's words. They'd saved me back in Philly, but I did my thinking in drawings. I needed to get out of my head for a little while.

I hurried out of the shower, dressed in baggy flannel sleep pants, socks, a T-shirt, and a sweatshirt. I went to the couch and picked up the snow globe, watched the little snow flurries swirling around inside but the silence in the apartment was so loud. I didn't want to be alone.

So why didn't you tell him?

Some habits, like doing everything for myself, were so instinctual, I hardly stopped to think about them anymore. Even when they left me lonely as hell.

Then get dressed and text him. Find out where the bar is and go.

But the thought of getting dressed in appropriate clothes and putting on makeup, then taking trains or busses in freezing weather, *then* sitting in a crowded bar to make conversation with Beckett's friends… Each seemed like a monumental task.

I carefully set the snow globe down and rose to find my laptop. Ordering food and a bottle of wine or two would help. Watching the movie would help.

I'd taken two steps toward my suitcase when a key turned in the door.

Beckett came in, dressed in that horrendous lime-green turtleneck under his jacket, his arms laden with bags. The smell of beef with broccoli, fried noodles and orange chicken came with him.

My heart crashed against my chest, like a colossal egg being cracked, and warmth flooded me.

I put my hands on my hips, trying to muster a stern tone. "You're supposed to be somewhere else."

"Were you going to throw a party while I was out?" he asked, setting the bags on the kitchen counter. "Busted."

My smile hurt my cheeks. "What's all this?"

Beckett unpacked the Chinese food. "Christmas dinner." He reached into another bag and pulled out a carton of eggnog and a bottle of Captain Morgan's rum. "And Christmas dessert."

"You are a sainted man," I said. "But what about your friends?"

"They're perfectly capable of getting drunk without me," he said.

"Weren't they pissed?"

"To not get to stare at this sweater all night? Hell yes. But they got over it." He spooned the rice, chicken, beef with broccoli and eggrolls onto two plates. He glanced at me staring at him. "Didn't you say there was a movie you wanted to watch?"

I blinked. "Uh, yes. Yeah, let's do it."

Beckett handled the food and I mixed eggnog and rum for us to drink. We settled carefully on the bed with our plates and *Love Actually* queued on my laptop.

"The single-greatest Christmas movie ever," I declared. "Ever."

"It's a chick-flick, isn't it?" Beckett said dubiously.

"How can you tell?"

"Hugh Grant is in it."

We ate and laughed and drank, watching the various romances in the movie play out. By the time we got to Hugh Grant—as the Prime Minister—kissing his former assistant at the school holiday show, I realized I'd drank several more glasses of eggnog than I'd planned. By the time the movie ended, I felt like I was underwater. The bed felt floaty. The corners of the room swam, and I had to blink hard to find my focus.

"How you doing over there?" Beckett asked, with the amused condescension of a sober person talking to a drunk person.

"I may have consumed a tad more alcohol than I initially intended," I said, forming each word perfectly.

Beckett's smile turned soft. "Feel better?"

"Yeah, I do." I squinted up at the ceiling. "But that light is killing me."

He got up and turned off the fluorescent, leaving the apartment bathed in the soft glow of the Christmas lights.

"You gonna crash?" Beckett asked.

"No crashing. Music. Frank, please."

He laughed as he slipped the Sinatra album out of its sleeve and set it carefully, reverently, on the player. He gently rested the needle until it found the perfect groove on the first track, "I'll Be Home For Christmas."

He leaned his tall form toward the window. "It's snowing. Not sleet or hail, or icy rain. Actual snow."

"Really?" I picked my way across the apartment to stand next to him. "It's pretty."

Beckett and I stood side by side, and I wished I hadn't drunk so much. My jumbled-up thoughts moved in slow motion, while my pulse sped up when Beckett looked down at me. He opened his mouth as if to speak, but then took my right hand in his and wrapped his arm around my waist.

"What are you doing?" I asked, as he moved my left arm up around his neck.

"I'm dancing with you."

I glanced up at him. "Aren't you supposed to ask me first?"

"Probably," he said, swaying us away from the window, toward the middle of the floor. "But asking means wondering and considerations and second-guessing, and I just wanted to…have the moment without all the mental noise." He looked down at me. "You want to stop?"

Not on your life…

"No, it's…nice."

Our eyes held, and I could see what I wanted reflected in his deep blue gaze. What both of us wanted, and what we thought we shouldn't have, with our promise to stay friends hanging in between.

"Stop thinking so much," Beckett said, pulling me closer. "I haven't forgotten our promise. But let's just have tonight."

"That sounds good."

It sounded perfect, actually. I was worn out from my trip and more than a little drunk. I sank into his arms and let all the old pain and fear and guilt recede.

Just be here now.

I rested my head against his chest, rubbing my cheek against soft, lime-green wool. "I love this sweater," I murmured. "It's the best sweater ever."

Beckett's chuckle rumbled against my ear. "Is it? Tell me more."

I shook my head, snuggled closer to him. We were hardly moving; small steps in a slow circle. "I'm not that kind of drunk."

"What kind?"

"The kind who gets wasted and throws all caution to the wind. I'm not going to say or do anything I'll regret tomorrow."

"Lucky me," Beckett said.

I laughed against his chest. "I didn't mean to get drunk. I really didn't. But here I am. Shitfaced. On Christmas."

His arm tightened around my waist. "I'm sure it's not a defense mechanism or anything."

"Ha ha."

Another small laugh, then Beckett's voice turned soft. "Be as drunk as you need to be, Zel. Take a break. I think you need it."

"Yeah." My arm around his neck was too heavy. I wrapped it around his waist instead. "I need it. I need this."

Frank Sinatra crooned he'd be home for Christmas, but only in our dreams. Beckett rested his chin against my head, and I fell deeper into the pleasant, heavy bliss of his presence. My body was conscious of every place we touched, and through the fog of rum and contentment, I wondered what would happen if I managed to lift my head off his chest and kiss him.

Just the thought sent a little jolt down my spine, potent and strong, and tinged with possibilities.

But the rum was stronger. I sank deeper against Beckett and listened to the pulse of his heartbeat in my ear. A steady count of life. All the seconds passing between us while we tried to keep from being hurt ever again.

There has to be another way…

The song ended and we stopped dancing. I could hardly move. Didn't want to.

"Are you awake?" Beckett asked.

"No."

He half-walked, half-carried me to the bed, and laid me down. I sank into the pillows immediately, feeling heavy…too heavy to move. It was so quiet.

"Is the song over?"

"Yeah, it's over."

"It was nice, Beckett," I said, trying to organize my feelings into words but my brain wouldn't cooperate. "Everything about this night was so good and warm and…good."

I felt Beckett lie down beside me, and I managed to open my eyes to see him propped on the pillow, head in hand.

"You falling asleep on me?" he asked softly.

"No," I said, struggling to keep my eyes open. To keep looking at him. He was so close, it would take nothing for him to kiss me… But I knew he wouldn't. Even drunk I knew Beckett wouldn't kiss me *because* I was drunk. But he was there, close to me, his eyes soft and heavy, and I struggled to hold on to this moment, to be in it when the rum kept trying to take me under.

"I'm going to remember everything tomorrow," I said.

He smiled. "You sure about that?"

"Mmhm. Keep talking. I like your voice. It's a searchlight in the dark…so I can always find my way back."

He shifted beside me. "What do you want me to say?"

I tried to focus again. *God, he's beautiful.* Without my permission, my hand lifted off the pillow and traced a sloppy line over the small break on his nose. "Tell me what happened."

"Prison. Got in a fight in the yard."

I furrowed my brows. My fingers were still touching him, trailing down his cheek now, feeling the small scratch of his stubble. "I hope you won."

"I lived," he said quietly. "In prison, that's a win."

My fingertips were on his lips now, and held there for a moment, feeling their softness… My hand dropped to the pillow. My eyes fell shut. Too heavy.

"Tell me something else. Something good, Beckett."

A silence, then, "You don't know how beautiful you are," he said softly, and I felt his fingers on my skin now, his thumb moving back and forth over my cheek. "That's something good. And I love that about you."

Oh god…Wake up. Remember this…

"Beckett…"

"I'm glad you're here, Zelda," he said softly. "Not in my bed—although I really don't mind that either. But here. In this apartment."

"You are?"

"I've never considered this a home," he said. "It's just a place to live. Sometimes, when the money gets tight, I'm sure I'll get evicted. And that would suck for obvious reasons, but an attachment to this crappy little apartment wouldn't be one of them. But now…this crappy little apartment feels like home, Zel."

His voice and his touch were my entire world. *Remember this. Remember all of it…*

I snuggled my cheek deeper into his palm. "It does?"

"Yeah." He brushed a lock of hair that had fallen over my neck. "But it's not just the stuff you added. Not just the lights or the tree or a plant. It's you. This place feels like home because you're in it."

I managed to open my eyes. "Beckett?" He was lying with his head on the pillow beside me.

"Shh." He traced the curve of my cheek and over my temple. "If you don't go to sleep, you might remember I said that. We're supposed to be friends."

"I want…" I whispered, and moved closer to him, curling my body against his. I sighed and sank deeper into this heavy bliss as he wrapped his arms around me and pulled me close. "I want…"

"What?" he whispered. "What do you want?"

I want you…

My thoughts were breaking apart now, as I fell deeper into that twilight space between sleep and awake, and Beckett's voice was there with me.

"Zelda?" he whispered against my hair. "I changed my mind. Are you listening?"

"Mm." *Yes. I'm here. I'm right here…*

"Good, because I want you to remember this part."

"'Kay…" *I will, Beckett. Tell me…*

"This is the best Christmas I've ever had."

I sighed and snuggled closer to him, fighting the pleasant slide into sleep. My lips brushed the warm skin of his neck, he held me so close.

"Me too, Beckett," I whispered. "I came home."

21

Zelda
December 30th

I sat at the desk and flipped through the new pages of *Mother, May I?* while outside, the rain came down in slanted bullets. After Christmas night, Beckett and I had thrown ourselves into the work. I kept my head down and the pace feverish, trying to distract from the memories of that night. The food, the dancing, the words he'd whispered to me.

He thinks I'm beautiful.

This is home because of me.

This was his best Christmas.

It was mine too. His words were the best gift I could've received. Beckett was the best thing to happen to me in a long time.

Oh God, what am I doing?

I was a pro at denial, but this deep, raw desire refused to be ignored. We'd touched too many times for my body to forget, and now I suffered the pleasant agony of wanting what I couldn't have. That sublime ache when the person you want is in the same space. The charge in the air, the tension that can snap with one look or one word…

I gave myself a shake.

Jesus, get a grip. Focus.

I bent over my work. *Mother, May I?* was nearly finished, which brought its own thrill. Half elation and half terror.

What if they don't like it?

What if they do?

A gust of wind tossed rain at the window like a handful of pebbles, and I bit the end of my pen. Beckett was out there, in that mess, but due home any minute now. I got up to stir the chili that burbled in the pot, and exhaled a sigh of relief when I heard the key in the door.

"Hey," Beckett said.

"Hey, yourself," I said. "Jesus, you're drenched."

And gorgeous. You're fucking gorgeous, damn you, Copeland.

His weather-proof jacket was shiny with water that ran off in rivulets, dripping onto the floor. He stripped off his gloves and blew on his hands, his cheeks ruddy, his hair glistening.

"What's that?" he asked, slightly breathless with cold. "Chili? Smells amazing. Let me warm up, then we can eat and work."

"Sounds like a plan."

Beckett showered and changed into dry clothes. We ate chili and the corn bread I'd bought at Afsheen's, then crammed ourselves around the little desk to work. The silence was loud and filled with our rum-soaked dance on Christmas and all the words that came after…

"You care if I put on some music?" I asked. "Something not a hundred years old?"

Beckett smiled a little. "Knock yourself out."

I set up my phone to play an alternative radio app. Oasis' "Wonderwall" came out sounding a little tinny. We didn't have a speaker deck, but it would do.

"I finished the text for the last two panels. What's next?" Beckett asked, leaning over the drawings.

I pulled out the most recent mock-ups, the rough sketches that served as guidelines for the finished drawings.

"So Kira and Ryder have jumped to 1983. She's caught a perv staking out a playground at night, readying to make his move the next morning. She's got her weapon aimed, ready to blow his brains out, but…" I bit my lip and then blew out my cheeks. "It's the moment of truth. Does she listen to Ryder's advice and spare the guy? Or not?"

He looked at me, then at the drawing of a scared-looking man on the ground at Kira's feet. He drew the rough sketch toward him and wrote, *P-Please, Mother…m-may I l-live…?* in a dialogue bubble above the perv's head.

"Kira always say no," I said. "What happens if she says yes? What happens to avenging her daughter? She's a vigilante who kills to stop the pain. That's all she knows. What happens when it's all gone?"

Beckett smiled softly. "We don't know. That's the finale of the book. The repercussions of her saying no, yet again. Or yes. And letting him live."

"I don't know what will happen to her."

He smiled gently. "Only one way to find out."

I met Beckett's eyes. I fell into the sapphire depths, like a warm, deep blue infusion where I was always safe. The music filled the quiet between us.

Because maybe, you're going to be the one that saves me...

I swallowed hard. "She says, yes."

Beckett's smile was brilliant. He lettered the dialogue and set the pen down.

"It looks good, Zel," he said. "Really good."

I blew out a shaky breath. "It's a start. Not sure what comes next." I looked up at him. "For her."

He slowly sipped his beer. "Maybe she thinks about what she didn't do and finds a little comfort in that. How she spared herself from seeing the life in the guy's eyes drain out."

I didn't miss the knowing look in his eye, or the fact he wasn't talking about my comic book heroine anymore.

"Is this your subtle way of telling me you're against the death penalty?" I asked tightly. "Specifically, you're against *me* going to watch the asshole who killed my sister put to death?"

"Yes."

I wasn't expecting a straight, simple answer. It knocked the wind out of me and I slumped in my chair. "It's what I've been waiting for, for ten years. Ten years, Beckett."

"I know," he said quietly. "And I know it's not my place or my business. But I've *been* there, Zel. I've seen a man die. It changes you. Forever."

I looked to the window where night had fallen and the rain was silver streaks against the glass. "It's not the same," I said. "Your guy was an accident. He wasn't a sick, depraved monster."

"No, he wasn't," Beckett said, his own words tightening. "But seeing it happen, Zel, no matter how or why..." He shook his head. "I don't know. Don't listen to me. It might bring you the peace you want and the last thing I want to do is stand in the way of that."

I looked at him straight on. "What about your peace, Beckett?"

He sat back in his chair. "It's not the same situation. At all."

"You're right," I said. "Yours was an accident."

"Same result. The guy is dead. But you have a choice, Zel. You still have it. I made mine. I made it when I decided to rob that fucking house."

He got up to throw his empty beer can away and remained in the kitchen, his hands on his hips, his head down. My heart ached for him. I wanted to give him one fraction of the comfort—the relief—he'd given me. Somehow.

"I know about your letters to Mrs. J," I said quietly.

Beckett jerked his head up. "What? How?"

"Darlene," I said. "Don't be mad at her," I added when his expression turned murderous. "You know how she is. Words flow in and out of her like a tide. She can't help it. And besides, she only mentioned it because she cares about you."

His hard look remained but I saw his eyes soften just enough to give me the courage to go on.

"The only reason *I'm* mentioning it," I said slowly, "is because I care about you."

He held my gaze for a moment more, his eyes full of thoughts and I knew every one was of me. But he shook his head as if to clear it and said in a measured tone, "The letters are nothing. Pointless. I'm sure she doesn't even read them."

"Does she send them back?"

"No."

"Then maybe she reads them."

"She hasn't replied," he said. "I've written her thirty-nine letters, Zelda. If she's read them all, why hasn't she replied?"

His voice was hard like a stone, but frayed at the ends. If I had to sketch him at that moment, I'd make him a heavy boulder. But streaked with veins of hope that could break the solid pain apart.

"Beckett—"

"There's nothing left to talk about," he said in a low voice.

"But you have plenty to say to Mrs. J," I said, hugging myself. "You need her to give you permission to live again, right? And if she doesn't, then what? What happens after we finish the graphic novel?"

What happens to us?

He was quiet for a moment, and then said, "I have nothing to offer you, Zelda."

"That's not true."

"I'm a felon. That's going to follow me around for the rest of my life. Every job application, every *rental* application. Do you know how hard it was to get into this place? If it wasn't for Roy, I'd be fucked, because not many people want to rent to criminals. I can't even open a fucking checking account until I clear it with him first."

"I told you I don't care." I looked away, tucked a lock of hair behind my ear and hugged myself tighter. "I don't care about any of it."

"I do," Beckett said. "I care. I care that when I close my eyes, I see Mr. J dying. I see the light in his eyes snuffed out, and all the shit I'll have to go through for the rest of my life seems so *goddamned easy* compared to that moment. That one fucking moment..."

He ran a hand through his hair, shaking his head. "I fucked up my future," he said finally. "The last thing I want to do is fuck up yours."

I fought for something to say but he was moving to pull the air mattress down.

"Today was rough in that weather," he said. "I'm tired. Let's just call it a night, okay?"

I watched him fold his six foot-two inch frame onto that stupid air mattress, and reluctantly climbed into his bed. The apartment was quiet but for the soft, half-hearted clank of the radiator.

I stared at the ceiling. "Mrs. J might write you back someday," I said softly into the dark. "Or she might not. You could write her every day for a long time, ten years, maybe, and never hear back. That doesn't mean you don't deserve some peace too."

Beckett didn't reply and the silence drew long and kept going, into a sleepless night where I felt Beckett lying three feet from me but trapped in a past he couldn't change. I was too—our pain was of the same fabric, even if the patterns were different, but he was helping me.

And I can't help him. I failed

I buried my face in Beckett's pillow, and drifted toward a restless sleep. Sometime in the early gray of morning, I heard him climb off the air mattress and go to the desk. He drew a paper and pen, and under the illumination given by the strings of lights hanging above, he began to write.

And when he was done, he dressed for work, tucked the letter into his pocket and went out.

22

Beckett
December 31

Dear Mrs. J,

I am haunted by words.

I started writing to you, stringing together words of regret for what I did to you and your family. Your life. The punishment was prison, parole and a lifetime of labels. I wear the words like chains around my neck. Felon. Criminal. Prisoner. I'm all those things, and remain them, even after time served. A freed prisoner with a life sentence.

Now I have a woman in my life who's turned everything that was cold and gray into warmth and color. She's inked new words onto my heart.

Us. Together. Peace. Home.

Remember I told you about a light in the fog? It's emerald green and it's showing me another way. Every day it feels less like something I shouldn't be allowed to have, and more like something precious I can't throw away.

I can't throw this away. I know I'll forever walk a tight rope, careful to never make even the smallest of mistakes. I know I'll never be free of the guilt for what I did.

But I met a girl.

She's woven herself into my life, so tightly that if I cut those threads, I'll unravel. The warmth will seep out, the light will dim until I'm nothing but dark.

I don't know what I deserve or what I don't, but I'm helping her. I make her feel safe. The words to tell her she does the same for me, a million times over, remain locked behind my gritted teeth. I can't keep telling Zelda how to find her peace while shutting her out of mine. I don't want to shut her out. I don't want to close that door. I want to say yes.

I'm sorry,
Beckett Copeland

23

Zelda
December 31st

Beckett returned from work around five, saying the day was cut short by the New Year's Eve prep in Times Square. He had plenty of time to relax and eat before we headed out to a party.

After the night before, I expected him to withdraw from me again. But his smile was light and conversation easy as we ate dinner. More than once, I caught him glancing at me then looking away, and every time it set my pulse racing. Nothing had changed between us, still, even the smallest look or smile had the power to fill me with hope.

We layered ourselves in hats and scarves and jackets. Outside, the New Year was being heralded with sleet and frigid temperatures. Beckett was wearing Mrs. Santino's turtleneck sweater, claiming it hadn't gotten enough exposure on Christmas Day.

"Whose party is this again?" I asked.

"Friend of a friend," Beckett said, pulling on his hat. "I don't know them but Darlene and Kyle will be there. And my buddy Wes and his girlfriend Heidi. My friend Nigel and…whoever he's currently sleeping with."

I glanced down at my leggings, ankle boots and oversized sweater. "Am I dressed okay? Wait, what am I saying? You're wearing that sweater. I could dress as a giant taco and you'd get more stares."

The buzzer went off. Beckett pressed the button. "Be right down." He grinned at me. "You reek of jealousy, Rossi."

He toted two bottles of champagne I assumed were for the party, but he stopped at 2C and knocked on the door. Mrs. Santino opened and peered at us between the length of chain. Beckett held up one bottle of champagne.

"Happy New Year, Mrs. S."

The door slammed, the chain rattled and then opened again. Mrs. Santino stared past the bottle of champagne, her eyes widening from under their nest of wrinkles at the lime green peeking from under Beckett's jacket.

She clutched her hands over her heart. "La tua gentilezza mi lascia senza parole," she said, then took the bottle, retreated back into her apartment. The door slammed.

I smiled up at Beckett. "And now she knows you're wearing it. Your gift to her."

He shrugged that off. "What did she say?" he asked as we headed for the stairs.

"I think something like, *Your kindness leaves me speechless*."

Beckett's smile tilted a little. "Okay," he said, and jerked his chin at the window in the front foyer. "Darlene's got a cab."

"Happy New Year," Darlene shrieked, hurling herself at me. She hugged me tight, her gold hoop earrings cold against my cheek. She wore tight jeans, a short-waisted faux fur jacket and boots. She released me to hug Beckett.

"Oh my God, that sweater," she said on a burst of high-pitched laughter. "You look like you should be painting happy little trees. Are you ready to go? Let's go."

"Where's Kyle?" I asked, as we climbed into the cab.

Darlene flapped a hand. "Oh, we broke up. Shit timing right? But what can you do? I'm ready to start the New Year off right. Fresh start and all."

I sat wedged in the middle of them in the back of the cab. I glanced up and exchanged looks with Beckett.

"Dar," he said slowly, his brows furrowed. "You okay?"

"I'm totally fine," she said, and told the cabbie the address. "It didn't work out, but that's men for you, right?" She nudged my elbow. "But I'm over it. Over him. Ready to party."

Darlene's eyes were heavily shadowed in smoky makeup but looked clear, as far as I could tell. I shot Beckett another look and a small shrug.

The party was at a loft in the Meatpacking District—a huge, converted industrial space. Exposed pipes and brick, loud with the laughing conversations of what looked like more than a hundred people.

"Beckett, my brother." A tall, athletic-looking guy with sandy-blond hair and an Australian accent approached, a petite brunette girl on his arm. "So glad you could make it this time after so rudely flaking out on Christmas." He squinted and held up a hand over his eyes, as Beckett took off his jacket and threw it in the pile by the door, revealing the sweater in all its glory. "On second thought, I'm going to have to ask you to leave. I'm going blind."

"If you go blind, Nigel, I think we can all guess why," said another guy, shorter with dark hair. He fist bumped Beckett and gave me an approving look. "I'm Wes. You must be Zelda, the comic book artist."

"Graphic novelist," I said automatically, shaking his hand. "Nice to meet you."

Nigel, the Aussie, gave Beckett an approving grin he must've thought I was too short to see, and introduced the brunette as Jackie. I met Wes's girlfriend, Heidi, a pale-skinned, freckle-face woman about my age with blonde dreadlocks down to her shoulders. Wes, Heidi, and Nigel greeted Darlene with cheek-kisses and questions about Kyle that she brushed off with a laugh. She waved at someone she knew in the crowd and took off.

"What happened to Kyle?" Heidi asked Beckett.

"Not sure. She says they broke up," Beckett said, his gaze following Darlene into the party.

"Maybe we should keep an eye on her," Heidi said.

"Yeah, probably. She shouldn't be drinking," Beckett said. "It's too easy for her to overdo it. Especially when she's upset."

"I, on the other hand, am not leaving until I get wasted enough that I can't remember how I had to spend the holidays with my family," Wes said.

We headed away from the front door, and Wes took my arm and slowed me down so that the others could get ahead. "Thank you."

"For what?"

He jerked his chin at Beckett in front of us, talking to Heidi. "I've never seen him like this," he said in a low voice. "Happy."

A little thrill surged through me, even as I said, "We're not together. Just friends."

Wes snorted. "Someone needs to knock that stubborn fucker on his ass." He winked at me. "I think you're just the gal for the job."

I tried to play it cool, but Wes's words sank pleasant teeth into me and wouldn't let go.

We moved further into the loft and were absorbed into the party. At the far end, a DJ with a small turntable played techno for a small crush of dancers. The loft's slanted windows were lined in Christmas lights on the inside, and dusted with snow flurries on the outside. By the open kitchen, two tables of food, bottles of booze and Solo cups were set up for the guests.

Darlene bounded back to me, and took my hand. "I need you to meet, like, everyone."

She dragged me all around the loft, introducing me to people whose names flew out of my mind a nano-second after I heard them. She talked and laughed easily with friends, nursing a single light beer.

Eventually I showed her my empty cup and left her caught up in conversation with two guys. I made my way back to Nigel, Wes and Beckett, who were standing by the window.

"It's official," I said over the pulsing music. "Darlene knows everyone here and I've met all of them."

Beckett handed me a cup of beer. "How's she doing?"

"She seems fine. Good spirits."

"Are you responsible for this sweater?" Nigel asked me, jerking his thumb at Beckett. "I've been trying to come up with the appropriate joke but too many are clouding my brain."

"He must've lost a bet," Wes said. "I don't think even Crayola has a name for that color."

"They do, mate," Nigel said. "It's called Holy Fuck My Eyes!"

Beckett just smiled and shrugged and sipped from his cup, the jokes bouncing off of him. I felt a strange swell of pride rise in me.

I'm here with him.

The four of us talked easily. Nigel had an arsenal of filthy "Guy walks into a bar" jokes which left us howling with laughter. Jackie scolded Nigel for his vulgar language. He apologized, which immediately prompted Wes to rag on him for being whipped. Jackie blushed while Nigel stared daggers at his friend over her head.

I looked up at Beckett. "I like your friends."

"They're assholes," he said loudly. Wes heard and scratched an itch on his eye with his middle finger.

"Nigel might be a lost cause," I said in a low voice, "but that one..." I inclined my head toward Wes. "He's good people."

"He's all right," Beckett said, but I didn't miss the fond look he shot his friend.

"You're good people, too," I said.

"Why? My taste in sweaters?"

Before I could answer, one of the party's hostesses came by with a tray full of champagne. "It's almost time," she said. "Three minutes to countdown."

Beckett took two glasses and handed one to me.

"You're good for lots of reasons," I said. "La tua gentilezza mi lascia senza parole." My accent was nowhere near as fluid as Mrs. Santino's and Beckett just stared at me.

"Your kindness leaves me speechless, Copeland," I said. I couldn't quite lift my eyes to meet his.

"You leave me speechless, Zelda."

Heat swept across my cheeks, and I glanced up quickly to see him watching me intently. "That's a pretty romantic thing to say. The Copeland I know would never say such a thing to his roommate in public. Too much to drink?"

"I'm stone cold sober." His eyes were intent on mine. "And reckless."

"You're…" My voice trailed off. Because all I could think was *beautiful.*

Kind.

Good.

Sexy as all hell…

The crowd began to count down from ten.

"What am I?" His lips shaped the words over the noise. His gaze widened and the blue of his eyes deepened.

Mine, I thought.

"Five…four…three…two…one…Happy New Year!"

The crowd cheered and sloshed cheap champagne or cocktails onto the floor as they paired off to kiss. Nigel picked up Jackie, turning in a circle and kissing her as she wrapped her arms and legs around him. I stared, fascinated and envious. I looked up at Beckett then. His eyes were full of heat.

"I guess it's you and me," I said, moving a little closer to him.

"Guess so," he said, moving closer.

"Happy New Year, friend."

"Happy New Year."

We stared.

"You don't have to kiss me if you don't want to," I said. "It's a stupid tradition."

"Is it?" His gaze was steady, but the breaths he was taking looked shallow. At the base of his throat, his pulse was fast.

"I don't know," I said, my own heartbeat thrashing my eardrums, drowning out the party, drowning out everything but Beckett. "I just thought—"

"Zelda?"

"What?"

"Stop talking."

I lifted my chin a little. "Make me."

Beckett's eyes widened. His smile flared, brilliant and wicked, then it softened into something beautiful. In a room of a hundred people, he saw only me. His hand came up to cup my face, his thumb brushing my cheek.

"Happy New Year, Zel."

Beckett laid his lips to mine. A soft touch and then a retreat, before he moved in deeper. His tongue sliding softly, his mouth gentle and hesitant but wanting.

I was utterly unprepared for his kiss. It turned my bones to sand and stole my breath. My legs trembled and I clutched his arm with my free hand to keep upright. I could feel his muscles contracting. His body hummed with electricity and mine answered. We'd possessed the kind of magnetic tension that pushes the other away until right then, that that moment, where we finally crashed together.

And this crash…

From far away I heard the party guests cheer as the dance music kicked up. Beckett held my face in both hands now, angling his head to kiss me harder, his tongue sweeping deep into my mouth. I could taste champagne, a rush of sweetness chased by a bite of alcohol. Sweet and strong. Just like him.

I imagined he'd taste like this without the champagne, always, every minute of the day, and I had a sudden, fierce desire to know if that were true. To kiss him in the hottest, darkest part of the night, in the sleepy warmth of morning, or even after ten hours of biking across the city in the summertime, where the salt of his sweat would mingle into this intoxicating concoction that was him.

This is you.

Beckett's mouth moved over mine and a hundred doors opened. I was out of my head and in the moment. I was *being here.* Letting it happen, warning bells silenced, shields down. This beautiful man was kissing me and all I ever wanted to do for the rest of my life was kiss him back.

"*Get a room,*" Nigel bellowed.

Beckett and I broke apart, breathing hard, the warm perfection of the kiss shattered. We stared at each other. A thousand unspoken thoughts danced behind Beckett's eyes. He wrenched his gaze from me to glare at his friend.

"Not cool, man." He looked ready to punch Nigel.

Nigel held up his hands. "Just playing, mate."

Wes stepped in, clapped Nigel on the shoulder. "I'm cutting you off, buddy. You've done enough damage for one night." Wes winked and manhandled Nigel back to Jackie.

"Jesus," Beckett muttered.

Wes turned back to us. "Nigel's a dick," he said to me. "He's better when he's sober. No, come to think of it, he's pretty much a dick then too."

I laughed a little, unable to look at Beckett. The party was in full swing, the crowd amped up by the DJ playing "HandClap" by Fitz and the Tantrums. My nerve endings were lit up and my lips tingled from Beckett's kiss. My entire body was clamoring for him now—more touches, more kisses. I wanted his hands to roam my bare skin instead of layers of winter clothing. I wondered if he felt the same. If we could slip out and go somewhere. Anywhere. I'd taken a hit from the most potent, euphoric of drugs and I needed more.

But some people whom Wes knew joined us, and new introductions were made. I smiled and said hello. Attempts at conversation fell out of my mouth. All I wanted was Beckett. All my senses were tuned into him. He could go hide in the crowd of guests and I'd be able to feel where he was. My body hummed with tension, and when Beckett slipped his hand into mine, I clutched him tight, like a reflex.

He bent to put his mouth near my ear. "Can I talk to you for a minute?"

I nodded and mumbled some excuse to the group at large. Beckett led me toward the kitchen. It was crowded with people talking and mixing cocktails from a dozen bottles on the counter. Off the kitchen was a T-shaped hallway. A bathroom must've been at the end, as there was a line of impatient people—mostly women—waiting to get in and complaining loudly about the wait.

Beckett tried the first door on his left. It opened on a dim, cluttered office. I caught an impression of rolled up posters, a graphic design desk, and huge poster prints. Then the door closed, cutting the noise of the party in half, and Beckett had me up against the wall. He pressed against me, tall and strong in the dark, and crushed his lips to mine.

With no audience and no drink in my hand, I kissed him back ferociously, my hands surging into his hair and down the broad muscles of his back. He pinned me against the wall, kissed me hard and deep. I clung to him, took his kiss and gave it back with a desperate intensity. He was all muscle and tightly coiled need, and it stole my breath to think of what he was capable of if we were home, in bed and naked. What he could do to me if the power I felt thrumming beneath my hands and pressed against my body was unleashed.

His hands skimmed along the sides of my body until they landed on my hips then he pulled me close to him, ground his hips against mine.

"Please," I begged him against his mouth. "Touch me. Put your hands on me, Beckett..."

My fingernails dug into his skin through his sweater as both of his hands slipped under my shirt.

"God, baby," he whispered, as he touched the bare skin of my stomach for the first time. "You're so warm. So soft..."

I'd never let a guy call me baby before. It always sounded silly or condescending. But *baby* coming out of Beckett's mouth made a wave of heat sweep over me. I arched my back, offering myself to his touch. He moved higher, my small breasts fit perfectly in his palms.

"Beckett...more..."

He pressed in harder, kissed me as if he were drowning and I was his air. His hands glided around my back, down to grip my ass and press me into his hips. Blindly, I slipped my own hand under the hem of his sweater, greedy for his bare skin. I found hard muscle, the ridges of a six-pack, all of him tight and defined everywhere my fingers trailed.

"Jesus, Zelda." His voice was a damp growl against my throat. He drew up my sweater, then sank to his knees. His mouth kissed below my breasts, then my stomach.

"Oh God, what are you doing?" I asked, breathless as his hands traveled down my body, his lips following with delicious, biting kisses.

His voice a rumble against my bare skin. "Something we can never take back."

When his fingers hooked in my waistband, my head fell back. "*Yes.*"

He tugged my leggings down, his tongue circling my navel. "Do you want this?" he asked, his voice strained with need. "I know it's fast, but *fuck*, Zelda, I need you. I need to make you feel good. I want to so bad. Please…"

"Yes," I breathed, then louder, "*Yes.* Anything. Everything."

He stripped my leggings off of one leg, taking my ankle boot with it, and moved my panties aside.

"I want this for you," he whispered, his breath hot against the inside of my thigh. "I want everything for you."

I bit back a cry as Beckett put his mouth between my legs. His tongue sent licks of fire up and down my body, and my hands flailed against the door behind me, searching for something to grab on to.

He hooked one of my legs over his shoulder so he could go deeper, his fingertips digging into my hips. My scrabbling hands found his hair, made fists and pulled his head to me. Now that he was touching me I couldn't get enough.

"You taste so good," he whispered. "Want to make you come…"

He brought me to a crashing climax within seconds and I wondered, even in the fever dream of ecstasy, how he could make me feel this desired but cherished at the same time. This was no stepping-stone to his own pleasure or an obligation. It was Beckett's pure desire to give me everything he had.

I came again with his name hissing out of my throat when I wanted to scream it. I wanted more skin, more nakedness, more of everything. I was desperate to give him a fraction of the searing pleasure that coursed through me. It left me shuddering and weak so I could hardly stand.

"I can't," I whispered, my head lolling against the door, my legs feeling like jelly. "I can't again…"

Still on his knees, Beckett put my underwear back in place and helped me step back into my leggings. I slid down the door, utterly spent. Beckett sat across from me, and even in the dimness I could see the satisfaction writ on his face, as if I'd been the one who'd given him two of the most intense orgasms of his life.

"So that happened," I said with a tired little laugh.

"Too much?" Beckett asked, uncertain.

I shook my head. "No, it felt right. And amazing and incredible and mind-blowing…" I laughed again, feeling more than a little tipsy and not from any champagne. "You're pretty good at that."

"I like doing it," he said.

"You do?"

"For you." Beckett said. "I like doing it for you."

"You know what this means don't you?" I asked, hauling myself off the door to sit in his lap, straddling him.

"This means a lot of things," Beckett said, his voice low. "You thinking of something in particular?"

I grazed my fingers on either side of his head, at his temple. "I'm talking about how as soon as we get home, I'm going to toss the air mattress out the nearest window."

"It won't fit out of our window."

"I'll find a way." I held his face in my hands and kissed him softly.

"Let's go home," he whispered against my mouth.

I nodded and moved to kiss him again, but stopped when I heard a frantic commotion outside the door. Footsteps thumped down the hallway. Then a woman cried out, "Someone call 911!"

Beckett's eyes widened in the dark.

"Darlene."

24

Beckett
January 1st

Zelda and I scrambled to our feet and yanked open the office door. A crowd gathered in the hall leading to the bathroom. I pushed through them, panic coursing through my veins, chatter coming at me from all directions.

"How long has she been in there?"

"Twenty minutes, at least."

Twenty minutes, with people pounding on the door, and I hadn't been one of them. A guy was fumbling with a screwdriver at the door to get the knob off. I shoved him aside.

Riding on pure adrenaline, I planted one foot and aimed the heel of the other just above the knob. The impact rocketed up my leg but the door banged open.

Darlene sat slumped like a ragdoll between the toilet and the sink, legs were splayed out. White foam bubbled out of her nose and mouth.

Jesus Christ, she's dead.

I sank to my knees just as Wes muscled his way into the bathroom and crouched down with me. "We called 911. Look for a pulse, does she have a pulse?"

Both our hands slid on either side of her jaw. I felt a flutter beneath my fingertips and pressed deeper. "I got it," I said. "I feel it."

"So do I. She's breathing."

"Dude, what did she take?" I demanded. "Who gave it to her?"

Wes only shook his head. The people crowded in the doorway stared.

"What do we do?" His voice was verging on frantic. "I don't know what to do. I only know what I saw in *Pulp Fiction*"

"Let's get her out of here," I snapped. *Off the bathroom floor and away from the goddamn toilet.*

We lifted Darlene out of the bathroom and laid her on the hallway carpet, her head in my lap. I used the sleeve of Mrs. Santino's sweater to wipe Darlene's face. Her lips had a bruised, bluish tint. Her shallow breaths stunk of something like vinegar. She moaned then, and her eyes fluttered open. The pupils were constricted to tiny black dots.

Heroin? I couldn't be sure. Darlene hadn't been a very loyal addict to any one drug, but dabbled in many. Too many.

"Darlene," I said, driving my voice through her fog. I slapped her cheek lightly. "*Darlene,* come on. Wake up."

Her head lolled toward me. "Becks."

"I'm here, sweetheart."

Her voice was a croak. "I can't hold on…to anything. I try. I try so hard…"

"Shh, you're going to be okay."

Zelda knelt beside me, handed me a wet washcloth. I brushed Darlene's hair back and gently wiped her face.

"Ambulance just turned down the street," someone yelled.

Darlene's head lolled on her chest. She dipped in and out of consciousness, crying softly in between.

Finally the EMTs bustled in, driving us out of the way. One shone a penlight in Darlene's eyes and spoke in a loud, clear voice, giving his name as Julio and asking her what she was on. But Darlene had fallen under again.

"Does anyone know?" Julio asked the room at large.

"No," Wes said. "We found her in here. We don't know what she took, how much or who gave it to her."

"Looks like heroin," the second EMT said, his gloved finger touching the small leak of yellowish white that dribbled out of her nose. "Easy to snort too much."

He let go of her arms. Her hands tumbled into her lap and rested there, turned up, palms facing the ceiling. My legs trembled and I stood over the scene, Zelda beside me, watching as the EMTs gave Darlene a shot of Naloxone. Her breathing evened a little and some color returned to her cheeks. Then they were strapping her on the gurney and wheeling her away.

I walked alongside, holding Darlene's hand. I saw Zelda and reached my free hand out. Her fingers slipped into mine and held on tight as we took the service elevator down.

"An addict?" Julio asked.

"Recovering," I said. I glanced down at Darlene, an oxygen mask over her mouth and smeared make-up streaking her cheeks like black tears. "Or relapsed."

"Is she going to be okay?" Zelda asked in a small voice.

"She's pretty stable," Julio said. "Vitals are good. We'll let the ER physicians make the call."

The elevator opened and we stepped outside just as two policemen were exiting their squad car. They talked with the EMTs as Darlene was loaded into the ambulance. I started to help Zelda climb in but Julio stopped us.

"Only one person rides with her."

Zelda hugged herself in the cold, worry etched into every delicate feature of her face.

"You go," she said. "Go with her. I'll see if I can help here and then meet you at the hospital. I saw Darlene talk to two guys earlier. Maybe they sold it to her? Or know something?"

"I'll text you from the hospital."

We exchanged a final look and then the ambulance door closed between us. Darlene was stabilized on the Naloxone, and the EMTs asked me for her personal information—full name, family to contact, and her drug history. I told them as much as I could, and felt like a traitor for it. But I couldn't lie or hide it. The officials would know soon enough and Darlene's parole might be extended or her restrictions would tighten.

Or she'll go back to jail.

I squeezed her hand.

Darlene couldn't do more time. She'd barely made it out of Bedford Hills after her last eighteen-month stint. She'd worked her ass off for a year to stay clean, and it'd all come crashing down in a single night.

Kyle, that fucker…

It wasn't his fault but that didn't stop me from wishing pain on him. I wished too, that Roy was Darlene's parole officer. Instead she had some strict asshole who didn't care whether she lived or died, only that she did as he said.

I wondered if I could call Roy anyway. For advice, or to see if he could make things easier for Darlene—help get her into a better rehab plan or something. My wallet was tucked in my back pocket, but no phone. Of course. My phone was in my jacket, which was back at the loft.

Fuck.

The ambulance pulled into New York-Presbyterian Hospital. Darlene was swiftly wheeled into the ER and into a curtained-off cubicle. Julio pointed to a line of chairs against a wall and I took one.

And waited.

Finally, a doctor with a bald head and kind eyes emerged from behind the curtains. "Your friend is in fair condition but needs rest and observation. There's nothing more you can do for her tonight."

I wanted to tell him I hadn't done anything for her. She'd fallen backward, hard, and I hadn't been there to catch her.

A nurse approached and laid her hand on my arm. "Go home and get some sleep. Visiting hours begin at eight in the morning. Come back then and see your friend."

I let her lead me away from the curtained partitions, and used the phone at the nurses' station to call an Uber. I struggled to recall Zelda's cell number but couldn't, so I called my own phone, hoping Zelda had it. The call went to voicemail. I left a quick message and hung up to wait for my ride.

Outside, it was snowing, the large flakes blown by an icy wind into swirls and eddies against the dark, starless sky.

25

Zelda
January 1st

I told the police about the two guys I'd seen talking with Darlene, but people had been filtering out of the loft and I didn't see them among the scattered few who remained. Darlene's episode had effectively ended the party.

Wes and Heidi, Nigel, Jackie, and I waited for a cab on the street outside. We huddled shivering in the cold. Nigel's laughter was gone, and Heidi wiped her tears against Wes's shoulder.

"I should've been watching her," she said.

My heart echoed the sentiments. I'd been too busy stealing a moment of bliss with Beckett. Drunk on euphoria while not twenty feet away, Darlene was suffering.

My phone showed no texts or missed calls from Beckett. I worried about him being out in this weather in only a sweater. I slung his jacket around my own shoulders and the pocket banged heavy against my side. I reached in and found his cell phone.

The display showed a voicemail message waiting from an unknown number. The call was ten minutes earlier, while I'd been talking to the police. I hit the button.

"*Hey, it's Beckett. Not sure if you can get this but I'm at New York-Pres. Darlene's going to be okay. They're kicking me out until morning. I'm getting an Uber home. I'll see you soon, okay? Bye.*"

I relayed the info to the others. "New York-Pres?"

"Presbyterian," Jackie said. "Should we head over anyway?"

"They won't let us in until morning," Wes said. "We're not family."

"Yes, we are," Nigel said, earning my affection for life.

"We'll go in the morning," Heidi said.

We piled into the Uber Nigel had called. Nobody said much on the ride. A road closure sign was up on Penn Street, and the driver had to let me out a block early.

I walked fast, head down and Beckett's jacket clutched around me. It was bitter out. The sleet-filled wind stung my cheeks and brought tears to my eyes.

The wind, and nothing more.

Inside, I went immediately to the radiator to give it a kick. It whined in protest, but a steady stream of warm air started leaking out. On the other side of the window, the wind was picking up and howling.

God, Beckett.

I changed out of my clothes and piled on sleep pants, shirt, sweatshirt. As I paced the studio, worry for Darlene began to morph into worry for Beckett.

He's okay. He called a car. He's on his way home.

Home…

I curled up in the bed and waited.

Next thing I knew, I was coming out of a doze to the scrape of a key in the lock. Beckett came in, bringing a draft of cold with him. He tossed his keys on the counter and blew on his hands. He looked tired. Broken and beat down.

"Hey," he said.

I sat up. "What happened? How is she?"

He leaned against the counter, his eyes on the window where the snow gusted and swirled on eddies of icy wind. "They knocked her out. Pumped her full of Naloxone. She's going to be okay, I guess. As okay as she'll ever be."

Beckett's voice sounded so heavy, his shoulders slumped. He blew on his hands again and then shook them as if they hurt. The Christmas lights showed his sweater was damp with melting snow, and his face and ears were ruddy.

"You had no jacket," I said. "And the road was closed a block away…"

He nodded. "I can't feel my hands."

"Oh my God, come here."

He took off his boots and pulled the sweater off to reveal a plain white undershirt.

"Those too," I said, indicating his pants that were damp with melted snow.

"Zelda…"

"Come *here*," I said again.

He took off his pants, revealing plaid boxers, and climbed into bed with me. We lay on our sides, facing each other, and I took his hands in mind.

"Jesus, they're like ice." I brought his fingers to my lips, to alternately breathe on them and rub warmth into his skin. "She's going to be okay?"

Beckett nodded against his pillow. This close, his eyes were the darkest blue, like the sky right before the sun rises.

"How are you?" I asked, still cupping his hands. I blew the warm air of my breath over his fingers, my eyes never leaving his.

"Better, now," he said softly.

A small smile played over his lips then faded. His entire expression caved in after it, leaving him stunned and staring. He lay next to me, his hands in mine, but the night was dragging him away. I clutched him tighter.

"Talk to me," I said. "What are you thinking?"

He stayed quiet for a moment, his eyes searching mine. "Do you ever wonder, Zelda, if you're allowed to be happy?"

Tears sprang to my eyes. "Yes," I whispered. "All the time. Every minute."

His brows furrowed and he brushed the backs of his fingers along my cheek. "I hate to hear you say that. I hate that I can't take that pain from you."

"Me too," I said. "For you. You carry too much."

"Maybe we both do," he said. "But I don't know what to do or what is too much to ask for. All I can think about is you and how you've taken my shitty life and made every single bit of it better."

A single tear escaped and slid down my cheek. He brushed it with is thumb, shaking his head, then rolled to his back, to stare at the cracks crawling along the plaster ceiling like black lightning. "Jesus, Zelda. You deserve so much more than this."

"What do you mean, *this*?" I asked, finding my voice.

"This." He gestured upward. "This cold apartment and talking to the police about drug dealers, and…"

"Don't," I said. "Don't pull away from me. I'm scared too."

He turned his head to look at me. "No, you're brave. You're

braver than anyone I know."

"I'm not. I'm scared shitless. I don't know what I'm doing or how to be good for anyone. I suck at relationships. What am I saying? I've never had one. Not a real one. I don't know what I'm doing and I'm scared I'll fuck it up. I'm scared of being happy. Or maybe it's exactly what Darlene said. I'm scared *because* I'm happy."

"Are you, Zel? Happy?"

A flame of hope flickered in his eyes.

Now. This moment. Take it.

I crawled over him, on top of him, straddling his waist. I bent down, rested my arms on his chest so our faces were inches apart. My hair fell down around us, blocking the rest of the world out.

"Let's just be you and me, and no one else," I said. "No past, no guilt, no Mrs. J or Rosemary. Just you and me. Let's stop thinking so much about the past or the future. Stop thinking or talking or wondering what we deserve. What do you *want*, Beckett? Do you want me?"

His hands came up under my hair to take my face in both of his hands. "God, baby, yes." His voice shook. "I want you so badly. I've never felt like this before and it scares the shit out of me too. I'm scared I can't give you everything you should have."

"You've already given me more than anyone else," I whispered my lips brushing his. "I don't want to mess this up. The graphic novel or me living here."

"You live here," he said fiercely. "This is your home too."

"And if something goes wrong?"

"We won't let it," he said. "There's too much to lose. Isn't there?"

I nodded, knowing he wasn't just talking about the book or the apartment. "There's so much between us," I whispered, pleaded, because it was scary for me to admit it. I needed to know he felt the same.

The smile that broke over his face was beautiful and told me everything.

"Yeah, Zel. There is. And I want more…"

He pulled me to him and kissed me. The softest, sweetest kiss of my life. More than a New Year's kiss, more than any kiss I'd ever known before. It was *more.* There were promises in our kiss. Unspoken vows to take care of what we had, of what we were creating in that very moment, because after tonight, there was no going back.

We kissed and breathed and kissed again. He pulled his shirt over his head and I sat up to take him in, my eyes raking over his body. A new flush of heat swept through me at the sight of him.

"Jesus, Beckett…"

His body was magnificent—sculpted and smooth and powerful with lean muscle. Matching tattoos I'd never known he had were inked onto each pec, small and precise: a diagonal arrow and a drop of blood. Immediately, I bent to kiss each arrow, as if I could heal the wound they represented.

Beckett reached for me again, pulling my mouth to his. We kissed, our hands roaming over skin. His touch was warm now, his mouth hot on mine. I felt his erection beneath me and my hips ground against him, rolling hard as our kiss turned dire. Biting, teeth grazing and nipping.

Beckett's hands surged into my hair and tightened into fists. He pulled gently, exposing my neck to his mouth. I gasped as he sucked and licked, all the while his hips bucked under mine. I tore at my shirt and stripped it off, leaving my naked breasts exposed.

"Oh God, baby," he said, his eyes drinking me in. "I knew you'd be beautiful, but Jesus, Zelda…"

His words sent another sweep of heat through me, the need to have him turning into a fever pitch. He rolled me onto my back and covered my body with his. I felt the hard length of him between my thighs, against my leggings. I arched my back, my hips rising, offering.

He acquainted himself with my breasts, holding one in the palm of his hand while his mouth worked over the other, biting and sucking the nipple. Mindless sounds of want fell from my open mouth, and my fingers tangled in his hair.

"Beckett," I breathed. "Please."

I didn't know what I was asking for. Anything. More kissing. More touching. His body on mine and inside me—God, I'd never wanted a man inside me as badly as I did at that moment.

"I want all of you," he said, his words infused with fire.

He rose up on his hands and knees and found my mouth with his. A kiss that was all tongue and teeth and a growl deep in his chest. His hands slipped down to my waist and tugged at my leggings. I pushed him aside and sat up to do it myself, while he slipped out of his boxers.

I stared.

"Holy God…"

I had no other words. The sight of him, hard and ready, emptied my mind, leaving nothing but intense desire. His own eyes roamed over my naked body, dark and hooded and greedy, and I'd never felt more beautiful.

We reached for each other at the same time, our mouths crashing together, his arm wrapping around me. I grabbed his shoulders, scratching at his skin desperate to have him and we tumbled down, me on my back and Beckett over me. He braced himself on both elbows kissing me again and again. I melted into the bed, dissolved under the weight of him, glorious and naked at last.

I reached for him, ringed my arms around his neck and brought my mouth to his ear. "Now, Beckett," I whispered. "God, now. I need you."

Out of my throat came a moan of relief and ecstasy as he slid inside me. He was huge and hard, and yet warm and gentle and everything *Beckett.* He pushed into my body until his hips touched mine and his face found my neck.

We held still for a half a breath. I pulled everything I had around him, feeling him inside me. Like nothing and no one before. A perfect heaviness. A completion. I knew I'd never want anyone else the way I wanted Beckett Copeland.

"Jesus, Zel." His breath was hot against my skin. "What are you doing to me?"

He lifted his head to look in my eyes. His hands cupped my cheeks. I was his. In every way. And he was mine. In that one heartbeat, I knew he felt it too, and the most beautiful smile flitted over his lips before he kissed me. Another vow. Another promise to keep me safe.

The kisses deepened, reignited our bodies. He moved in me, slowly at first, reveling in the tight heat that wouldn't let him go, before sliding back inside as deep as he could. My breath was his. He took it from my lungs and gave it back. Give and take. Hard and fast. I clung to his powerful body that was over me and inside me, taking me to the highest peak and keeping me there for one heartbeat.

Then another.

"Beckett," I whispered, a wisp of breath, all I had left as my body cinched tight, bound by an ecstasy I hadn't thought possible.

I cried out then. Called his name and hissed the word *yes*, because it was all I knew. This was all I wanted. To say yes to everything that was him, and us, and the life we were going to have when the sun rose that morning.

I shuddered as the orgasm ripped through me, but didn't let go of him. I held him tight, pulling his hips to mine. He reached one hand between us, held my hip to push himself deeper in me, his thrusts hard and relentless. His own release came moments later. His beautiful face contorted with something that looked closer to pain than pleasure. Then he crumpled down, his face buried in my neck again, groaning into my shoulder as he came. His body shuddered one last time, then went still.

"Zel," he whispered.

"I know," I said, keeping him wrapped in my arms and legs, heated skin to heated skin. Outside, the wind howled and beat at the glass but inside, we were together. And together, the cold couldn't touch us at all.

26

Zelda
January 1

I couldn't sleep.

My body had never felt so satiated and heavy and warm in my life, but my mind wouldn't shut down. Worry for Darlene kept floating to the top, mingled with the guilt that her night had been the polar opposite of mine.

I lifted my head from where it rested in the crook of Beckett's shoulder. Warmth permeated the bed, our skin, the space between us. He slept deeply, his handsome face unmarred by worry or pain. I started to smile and noticed a scarred pattern burned onto his left bicep—a crude circle with an X over it. A souvenir from prison, I guessed.

"My felon," I whispered, marveling again at how I always felt safe with him. But now that I was naked in his bed, I felt it even more acutely.

I've never had this before.

I never will again.

With the handful of guys I'd been with, sex had been a matter of course. I hung around a guy long enough to feel we should start doing it, and we eventually did. And every time, I hoped for a fraction of what I felt now with Beckett.

I had no idea sex could be like this. I never knew I could feel cherished and wanted at the same time. That sex could be rough and raw and yet also sublime. Beckett's lust and want were vibrant splashes of the most brilliant color, while the gentle intensity in his eyes revealed what was in his heart—written in solid ink across mine, and indelible.

Afterward, Beckett had held me as if he'd never let me go. He'd kissed me until his own weariness took him to sleep. Yet still he held me.

I laid my head back down, trying to find sleep again. No luck. I lay awake another hour or so, until Beckett stirred, woke, and gently extracted himself to use the bathroom.

The door clicked shut behind him. Seeing the coast was clear, my old defenses crept out of hiding. Did Beckett need to get away from me? Did he need space? Was he feeling pressured to come back and cuddle, which so many guys, in my experience, hated?

The bathroom door opened. Beckett climbed back into bed. He pulled me to him, wrapped me in his arms so my face was nestled against the crook of his neck. In ten seconds, my senses were suffused with him. The warm, clean smell of his skin, overlaid with a faint salty tinge of sweat. The sweetness of his breath wafted over my cheek.

It was then I stopped playing coy with my feelings. Stopped letting the ridiculous walls rise up and surround me every time I felt the slightest bit vulnerable.

Instead I wrapped my arms around him and held on. I hooked my leg around his hip so we were entwined like vines. Somehow, I felt him smile.

"You'll come with me this morning to the hospital?" he whispered.

"Of course. I love her."

His hand ran the length of my hair. "Thank you."

"For what?"

"For being here," he said. "For coming with me. For standing by my side while I face something ugly and hard. I know she's your friend too, but I've done this before and it never gets easier."

"I'll be there." I burrowed my forehead against his collarbone, slipped my hand into his and squeezed. "From now on, I'll be there."

When we arrived at New York-Presbyterian Hospital the next morning, Darlene's family was there. Her mother and sister had the same brown big hair, lots of makeup, and big jewelry. Her father was a solid-looking man with intense gray eyes. While the women stood together and talked, I noticed he sat apart from it, his hands clasped in his lap, his lips pursed.

Heidi, Wes and Nigel came out of Darlene's room together.

"How is she?" Beckett asked.

"Not good," Wes said. "She's physically okay, but her parole officer was here first thing in the morning. He's going to recommend a probation extension and rehab to the judge, but I didn't get the feeling he was going to talk anyone out of more jail time if it came down to it."

Beckett rubbed the stubble on his chin. "Shit."

"Yeah, she's taking it pretty hard," Nigel said. "And no sign of that arsehole, Kyle."

Beckett and I went into Darlene's room. She looked pale against the hospital sheets, and her right arm was punctured with needles and tubes that fed her from a clear plastic bag hanging over the bed.

She stared out the window and didn't look at us when we came in.

"Hey," Beckett said softly, moving to sit next to her on one side of the bed. She shook her head, as if it hurt to look at him.

I went around to the other and put my arms around her gently. She broke then clung to me weakly, her tears dampening my shoulder.

"I keep doing this to myself," she cried. "I keep fucking up my own life."

"It'll be okay, Dar," I said, perching on the edge of the mattress and letting her lean on me.

"It will?" Darlene said wiping her eyes. "I just don't know how else to cope, you know? When Kyle left, I felt the big emptiness come back and I had to fill it with something."

"You just described every single person on this planet," I said. "We all have to fill the voids with something." I brushed a lock of hair from her face. "You just happened to pick a highly addictive illegal substance."

Darlene sniffed a laugh and glanced over at Beckett for the first time. Her face fell and her eyes filled with tears again. "Oh, Becks," she said, reaching for his hand. "I'm so sorry."

"There's nothing to apologize for." Beckett said.

"No, I know but you've always been so good and so strong."

"I haven't," he said. "I've just been going through the motions. I may not have been doing drugs but I kept myself numb just the same." Beckett's eyes found mine across the bed. "Until recently. If you risk nothing, you have nothing. You are brave, Darlene. Never forget that."

Darlene cried a little more and then wiped her eyes. Her friends and family came and went, as the visiting hours drew to a close. The nurse came to kick everyone out but I waited behind. I gave Beckett's hand a squeeze and craned up to give him a kiss.

"I'll be right out. Give me a minute."

Darlene watched the exchange and a smile broke over her face, even as fresh tears filled her eyes. "You two…?"

I nodded and resumed my seat next to her bed.

"Oh my God, I'm so happy for you. For both of you. I've always hoped Becks could have something like this. It couldn't have been me. Even if I wasn't a hopeless drug addict."

"You aren't hopeless," I said. "And you may be addicted to drugs but that isn't all you are."

"Try telling that to my parole officer," Darlene said. "Or my dad. I disappoint him so badly. But how can I not? Look at me." She indicated the hospital room and the tubes trailing out of her arm.

"I've looked at you, Darlene," I said and pulled my bag onto my lap. "As an artist, it's my job to observe the human condition, and since I am an artist of the *highest* caliber, the way I see the world is the absolute truth."

A small smile found its way to Darlene's mouth. "Oh, is that so?"

"One hundred percent," I said, my voice wavering at the edges. I pulled out a piece of paper from my bag and handed it to her. "This is you, Darlene."

Darlene took the sketch I'd been working on, off and on, for weeks. She held it in both hands, as if it were something fragile. It was her on the subway, the day we went to shopping for Christmas lights. She laughed against her arm, her smile wide, her eyes bright and clear.

"Zel," she whispered.

My throat threatened to close. "That's you. Okay?"

Darlene nodded, wiped the tears off her cheeks and heaved a deep breath. "Okay," she said. "I love you."

"I love you too," I said, hugging her quickly, then busied myself with gathering my bag.

A knock at the door. It opened and a young blond man, tattoos creeping up his neck, poked his head in. He held a bouquet of pink roses.

Darlene's eyes widened. "Kyle?"

"I know I'm late," he said, stepping into the room. "The nurses are trying to kick me out but I had to come. Jesus, Darlene, are you okay? I didn't know where you were."

I rose to my feet and shouldered my bag. "I'll leave you two…"

"No. Stay," Darlene said, not taking her eyes off Kyle. "What are you doing here?"

His brows knit together. "I'm visiting you."

"But we broke up," Darlene said, her voice cracking.

"We did?" Kyle's face was twisted with perplexity. "Babe, we had a fight. An argument. It happens sometimes, right?"

"But you walked out," Darlene said. "I thought I wasn't going to see you again."

I backed away and Kyle took my seat. I wanted to give them this moment, but I didn't entirely trust Kyle or his version of the story yet. Still, the concern on his face looked genuine. He took her hand in both of his, pressed her fingers to his lips. "I got frustrated, babe. I walked out to get some air, I *told* you that."

Darlene looked away. "I know," she said in a small voice. "It's not the first time I've heard it, but… No one's ever come back."

Kyle inhaled raggedly and touched her face with his other hand. "I'm sorry, babe. I'm so sorry…"

I slipped out the door. Out in the hall, I leaned against Darlene's hospital door and exhaled.

"Did you kick his ass?" Nigel asked. "He got past me, the slippery little weasel, before I had a chance."

I laughed and wiped my eyes. "No, no ass kicking necessary. It's all good."

Beckett shot me a confused look as I moved to him and slipped my hand into his.

I smiled up at him. "I'll explain when we get home."

Part III

Those things that nature denied to human sight, she revealed to the eyes of the soul.
--Ovid

P-PLEASE, MOTHER... M-MAY I L-LIVE...?
KIRA... DON'T.
YES.
CHACK
HI! I AM A PEDOPHILE AND CHILD KILLER. PLEASE SEARCH MY VAN THANKS!
WELL, WELL, WELL, WHAT HAVE WE HERE...?

27

Beckett
January 12th

The winter morning sun slanted gold across our desk as we finalized the playground panel. In it, Kira and Ryder were sparing the life of her latest target. Zelda decided to add some humor and leave the guy wrapped up in swing set chains for the police to find. I took the humor in that as a good sign.

"Can I ask you a question?"

"You just did," Zelda said.

"Let me rephrase: can I ask you a question without you getting pissed at me?"

"Impossible to know." She narrowed her eyes through her glasses. "Why? Are you about to say something stupid only a guy would say?"

"Probably."

She laughed. "You're so goddamn cute, you could get away with it. Go ahead."

"Why is Kira's haircut so severe?" I tapped my finger on our heroine's razor-edged black bob. "It looks like she could cut glass with her bangs."

"Because it's badass. She has zero vanity. She doesn't need hair to hide behind and she definitely doesn't need it to get in the way while she's fighting the bad guys." She frowned. "You don't like it?"

I reached over and let a lock of Zelda's long silky hair slip through my fingers. "I like your hair better."

"Yes, but I'm not Kira, as we've established."

"Yes, we have."

"She's definitely not a proxy of me."

"Of course not."

"And Ryder is definitely not a love interest."

"Definitely not." I leaned over and kissed her.

I fucking loved that I could do that. That I could touch her, and kiss her, and sleep tangled in her. We donated the air mattress to Goodwill and now Zelda slept in my arms every night. Together, we staved off the cold—usually by creating our own heat that carried through till morning.

Zelda's mouth turned sweet, warm and wet, her tongue sliding along mine. I felt a pleasant pull in my groin as the kiss threatened to turn into sex, which happened frequently. But her phone rang from the corner of the desk. She frowned at the number on the screen.

"Don't recognize this one." She hit the green button. "Hello?" After a second she said slowly. "Oh, hi Iris."

I had no idea who Iris was. I went back to work, half-listening as Zelda explained some of the new concepts she'd been working into *Mother, May I?* The addition of Ryder, and Mother's conflicted struggle to reconcile her need for vengeance with her need for peace.

I bent my head and lettered the playground panel, carefully, as this was to be the final product. With a few pen strokes, a word appeared. For the first time, when one of her pervs asked, "Mother, may I live?" Kira answered, *Yes*. I smiled to myself and set the pen down just as Zelda clutched my arm, her eyes wide.

"A week from now?"

Her fingernails dug into my arm through my sweatshirt, hard enough to make me wince. She had a fiercely strong grip for having such small hands.

"It's not finished," she said into the phone. "It doesn't have an ending yet." Another pause then, "Okay. Okay. No, that sounds good. We'll see you then. Thank you. Thank you, so much."

She hung up the phone and stared at me. "Do you know who that was?"

"That was Iris," I said. "We'll see her in a week from now."

Zelda swatted my arm. "That was Iris from *Blackstar Publishing*. We'll see her in a week from now, along with two other editors and the acquisitions manager."

My eyes widened. "No shit?"

"Iris is the assistant who told me to make revisions and try again. She's been talking up the project to them ever since my first pitch back in November. She's got them excited about seeing revisions. Or maybe they're just hungry for fresh blood."

"Holy shit," I said. "This could be it, baby. Your big break."

"Our big break," she said. "*Mother, May I?* is ours now. Holy shit, look at me." She showed me her trembling hands. I took one and kissed it. Then kissed her.

"We need to celebrate."

"We can't celebrate," she said. "We have too much work to do. We don't have an ending."

"A non-celebratory celebration, then. I'm taking you out."

"Are you?" Her green eyes lit up. "You know we haven't actually been on a real date."

"That gets fixed today."

"Where are you taking me? Someplace warm I hope."

Good question.

I actually hadn't the first clue where to take her. While Zelda showered, I jumped on my laptop and Googled "warm," "romantic," and "New York in winter." I prayed for something remotely acceptable that didn't involve me taking out a small loan. The first search result blew my mind, and I started to doubt the existence of coincidences.

Zelda and I bundled up in our winter gear and took Fulton Street subway to Manhattan, then the C line to the Upper West Side. Central Park was frosted white, the trees bearded in snow under a heavy gray sky. We walked a few blocks in the early afternoon cold to 79th Street. Zelda eyed the hulking building in front us, its majestic pillars flanking a huge arched entrance.

"The American Museum of Natural History," she said.

"Not a fan?"

"No, no," she said. "I just…wasn't expecting a museum for our first date."

I bit the inside of my cheek, swallowing laughter. "You're going to love this. They have an exhibit going on right now: ancient Mayan dirt samples. I've been dying to check it out."

"Dirt samples."

I widened my eyes. "Uh, *yeah.* This dirt is hundreds of years old. All different shades of brown and everything."

She stared at me a moment more, then punched me in the arm. "You're so full of shit."

"Some of them probably have shit too," I said, as we climbed the steps. "Ancient shit dropped from ancient cows."

She rolled her eyes and let me lead her by the hand through the museum. I stopped outside a gallery and watched her eyes soften as she read the sign over the exhibit hall.

"The Butterfly Conservatory," she said, a small smile dancing over her lips.

"We'll have to visit the dirt some other time," I said, pulling her in.

We took off our jackets, scarves, and hats, and hung them on hooks. Then we stepped inside a tropical paradise.

"Oh my God," Zelda said. "It has to be eighty degrees in here."

We'd stepped through a portal, out of New York and into the Amazon. We walked among bright green ferns, broad-leafed plants, and trees dripping with colorful blooms.

And everywhere, butterflies.

The air was thick with them. Butterflies of every color, different sizes and shapes. They flitted from leaf to leaf, crammed and jostling around flowers or the little trays of sugar water hanging from tree branches.

"Hold still," Zelda said, tapping my shoulder. "Don't move, just turn your head."

I looked and a butterfly rested two inches from my chin, the brilliant blue of its wings rimmed in black. It opened and closed its wings, then took off to disappear into the greenery.

"Better than dirt?" I asked.

Zelda watched a monarch butterfly land on her wrist. "Best date ever," she said.

I bent to kiss her, and her mouth was sweet and warm. I kissed her there in the rain forest instead of surrounded by the winter cement of New York, and I felt as if I was free to go anywhere.

I can love her anywhere…

We stayed nearly an hour, then grabbed dinner at The Smith. We sat at a little wooden table, industrial lights glinting warmly off white subway tile. Zelda ate salmon and heirloom rice and I had marinated shrimp. Afterward I took her to a museum that was more her speed: (le) poisson rouge, in Midtown.

"Now *this* is what I'm talking about," she said, clutching my arm and craning up to plant a kiss on my cheek. "You did good, Copeland."

(le) poisson rouge was an eclectic multimedia museum and cocktail bar. We sipped gin and tonics in a dark room filled with electric lights and pounding techno music, then headed into the exhibit.

The current show was called "Juxtapose." The gallery was lined with huge black-and-white photographs of the city's homeless, caught sitting or sleeping or panhandling in front of garish advertising. The people were in black and white, while the ads were rendered in full Technicolor.

One photo revealed a bone-weary-looking mother holding a screaming child on her lap as she waited for the bus. Behind her, on the bus stop wall, was an impossibly fit female athlete leaping over a hurdle. On another, a blind man sold pencils out of a coffee mug, while behind him an advertisement exhorted users to upgrade their smart phone for the latest design.

"This is incredible," Zelda said, having to shout over the sounds from overhead speakers. Different commercials blared on one side. Crying children and people asking for spare change from the other.

"It's amazing, isn't it?" she said, as we left the exhibit. "How there's so much disparity in the world. So much that's beautiful and so much that's heartbreaking living side-by-side."

I touched her cheek. "Then there are those who take something ugly and cold and small, and make it beautiful." I bent close to her ear. "Do you remember what I told you on Christmas night?"

"I told you I would," she said. "You said the apartment felt like home because I made it that way. With lights, and the plant and the rug."

"That's what I said. But I was wrong."

"You were?"

"Yeah, baby, I was. You didn't make it home, Zelda. You are my home. Where you are is home."

I heard her breath catch, and her eyes fluttered like the wings of a butterfly. "You are turning me into the world's biggest sap, Copeland. Either that or you're just trying to get me into the sack."

"The second one." I said automatically. "Did it work?"

She grinned and stood on tiptoe to whisper hotly in my ear. "Hell, yes."

The subway ride took a hundred hours. Then it was a hundred miles more before we were finally at our front door. I could barely get the key in the lock. The door slammed behind us, and then I had Zelda in my arms.

I pressed her hard against the wall and then lifted her up to better kiss her. I couldn't get enough kissing her. She tasted sweet and spicy, this fiery woman with a heart miles deep.

Zelda wrapped her legs around my waist and arms around my neck and kissed me back, sexy little sounds of want escaping her in between each lick and bite of our mouths.

I carried her and set her down beside the bed, releasing her long enough to strip off my jacket and shirt. I kicked off my boots, while Zelda took of her soft black sweater. Her hair settled around the pale skin of her shoulders and over her bra-clad breasts like silk.

"Fuck, Zelda," I growled. I tore off her skirt and knelt to put my mouth over her panties.

"Beckett, oh my God…Wait." Her hands pulled at my shoulders. "No, I need you. I need you now…"

I stripped off her panties and lifted her again, carried her on my knees over the mattress so I could press her against the headboard. Her legs went around me again, drawing me inside. One smooth push and I sank into her tight heat.

"Jesus, Zel. You feel so good."

She locked her legs tight around my waist. "This," she breathed. "Nothing else. I only want this."

My body began to move in concert with hers. I gripped the headboard as I drove into her, kissing her in short, desperate touches until she bit down on my neck and screamed her orgasm into my skin.

The little bite of pain shot down my spine and ignited the pleasure that had been building. I came harder than I'd had in my life, giving her everything, shuddering with my release. I sank onto my knees, and held her there, still inside her, my hands sliding up the sweaty silk of her back to tangle in her hair.

This, I thought, my thoughts echoing hers.

Her. Her and no one else, ever again.

28

Zelda
January 15th

I bent over my work, carefully putting the last touches to the playground panel. I shaded in shadows, added little details. The note pinned to the chained-up perv's jacket. The fear twisting his face.

The work had been flowing beautifully these last few days. Beckett had a way of digging into the dynamics of the story and its characters. He said much with only a few words; something I could never do but was necessary, given the space constraints on a comic book.

It made me wonder about the letters he wrote to Mrs. J. I wondered what he talked about. I knew he'd never ask for her forgiveness, but I wondered if he wrote about his life. Or me.

I would never ask. The letters were intensely private. A piece of him I didn't get to share. Still, I wanted him to have the same peace he was giving me. With every finished drawing, with every decision Kira made, I felt closer to touching something I hadn't thought possible. Not peace, maybe. But a reckoning.

I wished terribly he could find the same.

Around ten in the morning I called Darlene. "I'm totally not checking in on you."

She laughed. "What's shaking?"

"Oh nothing. How you doing?"

"I'm doing great. Thanks to Roy Goodwin. I don't know what Beckett said to him, but he talked to my PO, and I think it's the only reason I'm not back in jail right now."

"Roy is a quality human being."

"Speaking of trying to be a quality human being, I can't talk long. I have to go to yet another meeting pretty soon. Two a day, Zel."

"Is it hard?"

"In the beginning I thought it was way too much, but I admit they really help."

"I'm happy to hear that, Dar."

"Kyle says hi. Well, not really," she added with a giggle. "He's at work, but I know he would if he were here. I just wanted you to know we're still together."

"Of course you are. He's smitten. All he wants to do all day is bone down with you."

"You are so bad."

I grinned. "Just giving you a taste of your own medicine."

"Speaking of boning down, how are you and Becks?"

"Walked into that one, didn't I?" I felt a ridiculous flush color my cheeks. "We're fine. He's at work. I have the day off since a friend needed me to switch shifts."

"Bummer. Too bad he couldn't play hooky too."

"Yeah," I said, thinking of last night, and how Beckett used his fingers, lips and tongue to make me come three times.

"Okay, I have to go. If I'm late to the meeting, my PO will kill me."

"I'll talk to you later, Dar."

I went to the kitchen and cooked up a quick lunch of a grilled cheese sandwich and tomato soup. I was about to resume work on the book when my cell phone buzzed a text.

I smiled. It was *him.* The words traveled from my eyes to my chest, where they settled warmly in my heart.

I miss you.

I was too happy to be a smartass about it.

I miss you too, I typed back. **How's work?**

Slow. Too cold to be sitting around, waiting for a job.

A pause and then another text popped up: **Actually I lied. I don't just miss you. I want you. Badly.**

My heart stuttered within my ribs as I typed out my reply. **Yeah?**

Almost took wrong turns twice today. Can't stop thinking about you. And last night.

I bit my lip, hesitant and inhibited. Beckett was my boyfriend now, wasn't he? I hadn't had a real boyfriend in years, if ever. I'd had guys I hung around with, and sometimes engaged in sexual activities. But nothing I'd ever had cause to use the words *boyfriend* or *relationship.* Until now.

I wasn't good at this girlfriend stuff. But I wanted to give it a try. Badly.

Come home, I texted.

I watched the rolling dots that indicated he was typing.

I've never ditched work before.

My thumbs flew, my heart pounding harder. **I'll make it worth your while.**

Don't toy with my emotions, woman.

The old me would've felt self-conscious about sexting in any form. Beckett's girlfriend, however, felt exhilarated.

Want to know what I'm wearing right now?

The reply was almost instant. **YES.**

I laughed. *Such a guy.* I glanced down at my bulky sweater, leggings, and socks. My hair was piled up on my head in a messy bun. Tendrils were falling out, but not in the sexy, disheveled way. Just sloppy. The radiator was behaving itself but it was still too cold to parade around half-naked.

But for Beckett…

I'm wearing one of your t-shirts and nothing else.

I cringed as I hit send, but truth was, I was more turned on than embarrassed. I waited for his reply, sure he was going to tease me for being so cliché.

You're making me hard.

Holy shit. A white-hot thrill shot through me. My fingers flew. **Come home. I'm waiting for you.**

Will u be wearing ur glasses?

It didn't escape me his texts were becoming short. **Maybe. Why?**

B/cuz when u wear ur glasses, u look so fucking sexy I can hardly control myself.

I wasn't having the easiest time, myself. My fingers didn't want to cooperate as I tapped out my reply.

I don't want you to control yourself.

There were no texts after that. Beckett was racing back to me. I had at least forty minutes before he'd make it from Manhattan, but I rushed to change anyway, my own need fueling me. What started out as a little game had turned to heavy, desperate warmth between my thighs.

I went to the bathroom to freshen up and brush my teeth, then hurried to Beckett's dresser and rummaged around until I found a plain black t-shirt of his. I stripped naked but for my socks, and drew his shirt on over my head. It smelled so strongly of him—wind and cologne, his soap and his skin. I held the collar to my nose and inhaled deeply, thinking of what would happen when Beckett came home.

Come home, I'd told him. Because I knew he loved those words. Because I was his home.

My hair fell out of its messy bun and I brushed it out so that it fell around my shoulders and down my back in soft waves, and then I had to wait. My skin shivered but not from the cold this time. I hardly felt it. My blood ran hot as I waited for my boyfriend to come home to me.

Finally, I heard footsteps on the landing. I put on my glasses, grabbed a magazine, and lounged against the kitchen counter, my back to the front door. As the key turned in the lock, I willed myself to appear calm. Cool. Casual as hell. I kicked my hips back and lazily flipped through the pages, letting Beckett's t-shirt ride up my thighs.

The articles and glossy photos blurred into a collage of color and text as Beckett slammed the door shut behind me. I turned my head over my shoulder and gave him a cool glance over the top of my glasses.

Holy shit…

He looked like a fucking god. Or a rock star fresh off the stage. His hair was windblown, his cheeks ruddy from cold. And his eyes… God, the look in his eyes as they raked me up and down set my skin on fire. I'd never seen such hunger in a man. Not directed at me. I fought to keep my voice as smooth as I could.

"It's about time," I said, and turned back to my magazine, barely recognizing myself like this. I bent slightly more.

The t-shirt rode up higher.

I felt the cool air on the backs of my bare thighs and between my legs.

Behind me, the sound of Beckett's gloves hitting the floor, the unzipping of his jacket, then his footsteps as he strode toward me. I cried out when his hands touched me. His arms slid around my waist, his mouth finding the bare skin of my neck.

"Your pants are cold." I managed to still sound indifferent. "Take them off."

He did, then slid his mouth along my neck again. I moaned, my charade falling to pieces under the onslaught of kisses along my throat and the hands that explored my body beneath his t-shirt.

He roughly spun me around and brought his mouth to mine in a crushing kiss. I could smell and taste the icy crispness of winter on him, but the cool skin of his cheeks warmed instantly as I kissed him back, my mouth just as demanding as his. I was starving. I needed to consume him, take him into my body in any way possible. In every way.

I dropped to my knees and unzipped his pants. He groaned, his fingers tangling in my hair, as I took him into my mouth.

"Oh fuck," he said. "You're so warm…"

I heard his breath catch and I knew he was watching me. I couldn't quite bring myself to meet his eye, but felt a rush of satisfaction as his hand in my hair tightened.

"You doing that," he said through gritted teeth. "In those glasses…"

I wanted to finish him off, but I was too greedy. I stroked him a final time and then rose to my feet. He pulled me up and kissed me roughly, his mouth mauling mine with delicious need. Then he turned me around again, his chest to my back, pinning my body to the counter with his.

"Yes," I whispered, almost a whimper, as Beckett moved one hand under my chin. He turned my head into his kiss while his other hand slipped down to my hip, pulling me against him.

"You want this," he said. It wasn't a question.

"Yes," I said again, begging. My back arched toward him. "Please…"

His breath was hot against my ear. "Spread your legs for me, baby."

His body was hard against mine, his hands demanding and rough, and his command sent licks of fire down my skin. Surrendering all control to him only made me feel more empowered.

I did as he said—eagerly, brazenly—and Beckett grunted against my neck as he entered me. A little cry escaped my throat at the heavy thickness and the heat. I pushed back on him, taking him as deeply as I could. Beckett bit down on my skin. The perfect balance of pleasure and pain sending electric jolts down my spine, through my chest to my breasts. My nipples ached until his hands slipped under the shirt to cup them. To knead and pinch and caress while he moved in and out of me.

"Oh my God, Beckett…"

His hips ground against mine harder, faster. His need was a wild energy I could feel wrapping around me and growing inside me, stoking my own into a frenzy. I was sure he wasn't going to last long. I didn't care. His lust fulfilled me. I thrilled in the desperate want and greed for my body. I felt it in every touch, every pounding thrust. His hands slipped down to my hips, his movements intensifying, even as he kept his chest pressed tight to my back. I gripped the edge of the counter at the force of him and held on.

"Come, Beckett," I said, closing my eyes, feeling my own climax nearing but certain his release was closer. "I know you need to. Oh God, I want you to come so hard…"

His reply was almost a growl. "You first."

Beckett released one hand from my hip and slipped it around, between my legs. His fingers found my most sensitive flesh, and rolled in gentle circles without breaking the punishing rhythm of his thrusts.

I cried out as my orgasm flared up immediately, shocking me with its sudden intensity. I clenched around Beckett, shuddering as the currents tore through me, tensing every muscle and stealing my breath. I held onto the counter, eyes squeezed shut, reveling in the sensation as it crested and crashed and washed over me.

Beckett's deep sounds of release came seconds later, his thrusts growing erratic, slowing, and then stopped. He collapsed against me, propping an elbow on the counter on either side of me. I was enveloped by him. Shielded by him. His strong body was between me and the rest of the world and I wanted to stay there forever.

His heart pounded against my back, his breath hot against my cheek as we shuddered together, sucked in air together. I turned my face to nuzzle the stubble along his chin and his mouth found mine.

"You have to be the sexiest woman alive," he said, breathing hard.

"I can live with that."

He slipped out of me, and I went to the bathroom for a moment. When I came out, he had his pants low-slung off his hips, and hadn't put a shirt back on.

"Are you heading back out?" I asked.

"Oh, I see how it is," he said. "You got what you want out of me—no pun intended— now you're kicking me to the curb."

I slapped his ass. “Damn straight.”

I started past him but he grabbed me and pulled me back to rest his hands on my hips. “I thought I’d play hooky for the rest of the day,” he said, moving me toward the bed. “Since I’m already here.”

“Shame to waste you.” I gave a little squeal as Beckett lifted me straight off the ground and set me on the bed. I knelt on it and he went to remove his pants.

“Stop,” I said. “Let me objectify you for a minute, if I may. You’ve got a lot going on in this area…” I waved my hand to encompass his broad chest, the cut of his abs, and those ridiculous inverted Vs that started at his hips and disappeared in his pants.

I scooted on the bed towards him and placed a kiss on his heart.

I was trying for sexy, but the warmth of skin drew me in, and I rested my cheek on his chest, wrapped my arms around him. He stroked my hair then brought both hands to my chin to tilt me up to look at him.

“Zelda,” he whispered, as if my name was an answer to a question he’d been asking for a long time. He kissed me, his mouth sweet and deep, and I lay back, taking him with me.

Every touch was soft and slow. He took his time, and by the time he was done he left no doubt in my mind—or on any part of my body—that I was sexy and beautiful and precious to him.

29

Beckett
January 18th

Roy came over that Saturday for our monthly parole visit. Zelda had gone out to brunch with some friends from Annabelle's and probably wouldn't be back before I had to leave for Giovanni's.

Roy searched the bathroom and under the bed while I made coffee. The fact he was now rooting through Zelda's belongings too, took a little shine off of me. Another reminder she'd be affected by the decisions I made for at least another two years, if not longer.

Roy must've sensed my discomfort because he made it quick, and after only a few minutes we sat together, him on the couch, me on the chair sipping coffee.

"You're looking good, Beckett," Roy said, smiling into his mug. "How's the leg?"

"It's fine. Healed up."

"Got a birthday coming up too, don't you? The big two-five?"

I shrugged. "Happens once a year."

He laughed. "And you and Zelda…?"

"Yeah, me and Zelda," I said.

Roy's grin widened and he slapped his hand on his knee. "Fantastic," he said. "I couldn't be happier."

"Oh yeah? What's so great about it?" I asked. I knew how fucking wonderful Zelda was, but I figured it wouldn't suck to hear it from someone else.

Roy obliged. "She's beautiful, she's smart, she's got a sense of humor." He waggled his eyebrows. "She's got no priors."

"Yeah, she's the whole package," I said. The teasing tone fell out of my voice. "I just hope I can do right by her, Roy."

"What makes you think you can't?"

I shot him a look. "Says my parole officer."

"You've hidden nothing from her," Roy said. "She knows the score."

"She doesn't know all of it," I said. "*I* don't know all of it. I don't know what it's going to do to my future. What I can or can't do." I set my mug on the table. "Any word from Mrs. J?"

"No," Roy said. "But I'm wondering, Beckett, if maybe it's time you let that go."

"There's nothing to let go of, Roy," I said. "I carry it with me in my bones. I can't set it down. I have to learn to live with it. But if maybe she would talk to me…" I shook my head. "Fuck it, never mind. She doesn't owe me anything."

Roy looked like he had a thousand more things to say about the subject, but instead asked, "How's Darlene?"

"Thanks to you, she's great. You saved her life, to be honest."

Roy waved his hand as if to dispel the notion entirely. "I just said a few words to Carl."

"Those few words kept her out of jail. Which saved her life. I don't think she could've handled more time."

Roy's smile told me he was touched. "Mary says hi," he said suddenly. "She's clamoring for another dinner. Your birthday, maybe? Or Valentine's Day is coming up in a few weeks. I know you young folks would love nothing more than to double-date with a couple of old fogeys like us."

I laughed. "I'll run it by Zelda."

We shot the shit for a few minutes more, then Roy got up to go. At the door he stopped, and rubbed his chin in the way that he did right before he said something he knew I wasn't going to like.

"Beckett," he said slowly. "About Mrs. J…"

"Oh, Christ, I knew I couldn't get off that easy."

"She's moving to Australia."

I froze. "Okay," I said slowly. "When? Or am I not allowed to know?"

"In the next few weeks."

"So you've had contact with her."

"She called me not long after I mailed your last letter."

I nodded and looked away, ran a hand through my hair. "Okay, so what does this mean?"

"I don't know," he said. "I don't know why she contacted me.

She wouldn't say anything more than that she was moving."

"Did she give you her new address? In Australia?"

Roy's face told me the answer before he said the word. "No."

I nodded again, and tried to ignore how my stomach clenched. "Okay, well thanks for the meeting, Roy. I'll see you soon."

Roy smiled and I thought he was going to pat my cheek like usual, but he knew better this time. I shut the door after him and locked it, processing this information.

She contacted Roy shortly after my last letter.

She's leaving the country.

She's not leaving a forwarding address.

The message was clear: she didn't want any more of my letters. Whether she read them or not, she was done with them. And with me.

"Okay, good," I said. "That's good."

I told myself that as I readied for work at Giovanni's and all through my shift. It didn't stick. I felt as if a train were pulling out of the station and no matter how fast I raced to catch it, I'd never make it.

That night, Zelda and I passed the hours in sweaty, intense sex. We filled the apartment with her cries; the headboard banging against the wall made the neighbors bang back. We fell into an exhausted sleep, spent and entwined, keeping the cold away. I reveled in the nearness of this other human being in my space, sharing my breath, my bed, and home.

Sunday was my day off. I slept as late as I wanted, with Zelda wrapped in my arms. Around ten o'clock, she kissed me and said, "I'll make coffee."

I watched her get up and throw some clothes on, her hair a sexy, tangled mess from last night's activities. She stood in the kitchen for a moment, hands on her hips and shook her head.

"You want something else?" she asked. "Maybe a latte? Something nicer than just pot coffee?"

"Zel, it has to be twenty degrees out."

"You like stronger coffee don't you? Cappuccinos? And those blueberry muffins from the café around the corner?"

"Yeah, I do but you don't have to go out into the cold. I'll go."

"Stay put," she said, cutting me off. "I'll be right back."

I watched her bundle herself against the weather, putting on boots and a jacket. She blew me a kiss at the door and went out. Twenty minutes later, she returned with muffins and two small cappuccinos.

"Thanks, babe."

"You're welcome," she said and bent down to kiss me. "Isn't there a football game on today?"

"Playoffs," I said. "The Falcons are playing the Eagles. That's your team."

She shot me a sly smile. "I don't have a team. Football is barbaric. I'd rather draw pictures of vengeance-seeking women blowing guys away with futuristic laser weapons. But that's just me."

She curled herself on the chair at the desk and shuffled through her papers.

"Do you need help today?" I asked

"No, I'm just brainstorming for the ending. Besides, today is your day off. No working for you."

"I can help if you need me to."

She gave me a dry look, one I had grown to love. "Day. Off."

"You're the boss." I settled myself on the couch with the remote, and turned the game on. I watched Atlanta destroy the Eagles, then answered a few texts from Wes. I was starting to feel pretty lazy, thinking about nodding off when Zelda closed up her portfolio and came to sit next to me on the couch.

"Not feeling it today," she said and curled up against my shoulder.

"I like this better," I said.

"Me too."

Zelda watched the last of the game with me, but whenever I glanced down at her, her eyes were on anything but the television.

I gave her a squeeze. "You okay?

"I'm fine," she said. "Really fine, actually," she added after a moment. Her fingers trailed along my jaw.

"Really, really, fine?" I asked.

"Mmhm." She crawled onto my lap and kissed me in a such a way that my body responded immediately, as if we hadn't spent last night bringing each other to one mind-blowing orgasm after another.

"Zel," I managed, as she ground her hips down on me.

"Beck," she mimicked, and stripped her shirt off.

I don't remember much after that.

"You're going to put me in a sex coma," I said thirty minutes later, when I'd regained the strength to speak. I lay stretched out on the couch, my legs hanging off the side because it was so damn small. Zelda lay over me, her small, perfect breasts pressed against my chest.

She smacked a kiss on my chest and got up. "I'm going to make us some lunch," she said, throwing her clothes back on.

I frowned and sat up, drew up my pants. "You don't have to, babe," I said. "I think there's leftover pizza from the other night."

She acted as if she hadn't heard me. "You like pastrami right?"

"*Like* is too weak a word."

She hardly cracked a smile, but rummaged in the fridge. "I think I have what it takes to make a hot pastrami with melted Swiss on rye, and maybe some vinegar chips? I bought some last week."

"Um, yeah that sounds fucking amazing. But also a lot of work."

"I don't mind."

I frowned. "Zel, what are you doing?"

"Isn't there another football game coming up?" she asked. "Aren't these games kind of like a big deal?"

"Yeah. Playoffs. But—"

"So it's kind of a special occasion, right?" she asked.

"Not really," I said.

She stood up from where she was rummaging under the sink and planted her hands on her hips. "You want pastrami or not?"

I laughed and held out my hands. "Okay, okay if you're willing."

Zelda cooked and within a few minutes the apartment was filled with the heavenly scents of hot pastrami and Swiss cheese. She brought me a heaping sandwich—the pastrami thick as a deck of cards—cut in half, slices of cheese oozing between layers of pastrami. Pickles and vinegar potato chips on the side. She topped that off by handing me my favorite beer.

"Holy shit," I said. "This looks epic, Zel."

"Is it good? I wasn't sure about the mustard."

I had to squeeze the sandwich down to take a bite. My eyes rolled back in my head. "Fucking hell," I said around a mouthful. "This is insane."

She smiled with satisfaction but still seemed distracted as she sat back against the couch with the salad she'd made for herself. Twice, I caught her watching me, her gaze flickering away.

The third time it happened, I turned to face her. "Okay, what's going on?"

She shrugged, a jerky little movement. "What do you mean?"

"I mean what's with you today? The coffee, the epic sex, the epic sandwich…"

She tried for another of her patented Zelda-glares but if fell flat. "I just want…"

"What, baby?"

She picked up our empty plates. "Done? I'll throw these in the sink."

I wiped my mouth on the napkin and followed her into the kitchen. Her back was to me, her shoulders were rounded.

"Zelda, talk to me." I turned her around. "What is it?"

She shook her head, her hair falling to cover her face. "Nothing, okay?"

"Don't tell me it's nothing. C'mon."

"I don't know. I don't know what's wrong with me. Just…I care about you, and I want… I want you to…"

I lifted her chin and brushed the hair back from her face. I wiped away the two tears that had slipped down her cheeks. "You want to be nice to me?"

It was a flimsy word and I expected a smartass reply, but her eyes welled up again and she nodded. "I don't have much practice being a good girlfriend. And I woke up this morning with an overwhelming feeling… I don't know. I wanted to make you happy. Is that terrible? Am I a traitor to the women's movement?" Before I could answer, she wiped her eyes dry. "I don't know what's wrong with me. I'm just hormonal or something. Pay no attention."

"I can't not pay attention," I said. "And I get it."

"Do you?"

I knew she had a feeling in her chest, like a balloon expanding. The kind of feeling you got at the first hill of a rollercoaster, poised in the sky before the fall. The plunge. Terrifying and exhilarating. Lightning fast and slow as hell before gravity catches you.

I once read that you fell in love like how you fell asleep: slowly at first and then all at once.

Neither Zelda nor I were easy at giving a voice to our own feelings. She put them on paper, in pen and ink, and I put them down in words to send away, never to be heard from again. But speaking them out loud…

"I love what you do for me," I said.

I held Zelda close to me again that night, and felt in her small but powerful body everything she was feeling but couldn't say. Maybe that's why I held her so tightly every night too. So that what I felt for her seeped into her skin through some sort of osmosis. I lay awake listening to Zelda's breath and feeling the soft heat of it against my chest. I thought of Mrs. J moving to Australia, moving half a world away.

As gently as I could, I extracted myself from Zelda and went to the desk. To write one letter. One final letter.

Dear Mrs. J,

Roy told me you're moving to Australia. Part of me thinks you told him so that he'd tell me. Did you? Otherwise you could've just left. You don't owe him or me any explanation.

I know it's time to stop writing you. Maybe you've read all my letters. Or maybe you're tired of taking them from a good-natured man like Roy only to throw them in the trash or burn them.

Whatever your reason, I'll honor it. This will be our last letter. The most important letter.

I'm falling in love with Zelda Rossi and my imperfect heart wants to think she's falling for me too. I can't help myself. It's not a decision to be made, and even if it was, I wouldn't want to unmake it. I want her. For the rest of my life, if she'll have me.

And I want your blessing, Mrs. J.

I think I can be a better man for Zelda if I knew some part of you thought so too.

I'm sorry. I will always be sorry.

Beckett Copeland

30

Zelda
January 21st

"Holy shit, I'm nervous as hell," I said smoothing down my skirt. It was longer than I usually wore, down to mid calf, and I'd paired it with an oversized maroon sweater and black boots. My hair was braided down one side and I took it easy on the makeup.

"How do I look?" I asked Beckett. "Professional? Or like an imposter?"

"You look beautiful," Beckett said, and bent to kiss me. "What about me? I haven't dressed up like this since my parole hearing."

"You clean up good, Copeland," I said.

In truth he looked devastatingly handsome in dress pants, dress shirt and tie under his regular winter jacket.

I tucked my portfolio under my arm and held it with my other hand as if it were a briefcase filled with money, handcuffed to a security guard. Our future was in that portfolio. *Mother, May I?* didn't have an ending yet but Iris had said to bring what we had and we'd go from there.

We took the train into Manhattan and up to the 12th floor in a high-rise on 7th Avenue. The elevator opened on posh offices that looked like they might belong to an accounting firm, except for the poster-size graphic novel covers on the walls.

I pointed at the one above the receptionist desk and leaned into Beckett. "*Seventh Son*. I must've read it a hundred times, under my bed covers with a flashlight."

Beckett smiled down at me. "You're the sexiest geek I've ever met."

"Hush, you." I approached the front desk. "Hi. Zelda Rossi and Beckett Copeland. We have a one o'clock meeting."

"Yes, of course," the receptionist said. "Your conference room is second door on the right. They'll be joining you shortly."

The door was already open on a smallish conference table, laden with pastries, water pitchers, and a pot of coffee.

Iris came in before we could even sit down, looking fiercely professional in a black pencil suit and white blouse. Her black hair was pulled from her face in a sleek, high ponytail, and black-frame glasses like mine perched on her nose above a mouth painted with red lipstick.

"Nice to see you again," she said shaking my hand. She turned to Beckett. "You must be Beckett Copeland, letterer and partner? I'm Iris Hannover, assistant to the managing editors."

"Good to meet you," Beckett said.

Iris moved in close to us, speaking rapidly and in a low voice. "So here's the deal. I haven't been able to stop thinking about *Mother, May I?* since our meeting back in November. I think I told you then I love the concept, the art is amazing but it needed more…" She gestured with her hands.

"Heart," I said. "You said it needed more heart."

It amazed me how wounded I'd been to first hear that all those months ago and how easily I said it now. She'd been right. As a professional, I had to take the criticism, but I hadn't known what to do with it. But Beckett had.

I glanced up to my handsome boyfriend and partner. "Beckett added so much," I said. "I think you'll like the revisions."

"I'm super excited," Iris said. "I loved what you told me on the phone. Can I take a peek?"

I handed her the portfolio and she quickly flipped through it, muttering to herself. "Yes. Yes, exactly." She snapped it shut. "I was worried I'd gone to bat for you too hard without seeing this. Now I feel vindicated. This story has legs."

My heart crashed against my chest. "It isn't finished," I said. "It doesn't have an ending."

"We can worry about that later," Iris said. "First let's impress the shit out of my editors."

Two men and one woman came into the room, all of them middle-aged, all of them dressed in business casual. The youngest was pushing forty, and when he shook hands, I saw tattoos creeping up his sleeve. "Mark Jamison," he said. "Acquisitions."

Rick Winslow, one of the editors, shook hands next. "Nice to see you again, Miss Rossi." He was the hard ass, I remembered from our meeting back in November, with hair that swept dramatically away from his face.

Eleanor Marshall still looked far too prim and proper to be working at a graphic novel publishing house, but I ignored those thoughts. Stereotypes, I knew, never did anyone any good.

I calmed my nerves and greeted them all politely and professionally. Beckett and I sat across from the three of them with my portfolio in the middle. Iris sat to the left of us, like an intermediary.

"Well," Rick said, folding his hands on the table. "What do you have for us today?"

I gave them a brief synopsis of the new plot, and slid my portfolio across the table. I chewed my thumb while they perused the work, until Beckett took my hand and gave it a squeeze. From the waist up he didn't look nervous at all, but under the table, his leg was bouncing up and down.

The two editors and Mark from acquisitions pored over the story, asking occasional questions but mostly focusing on the art, discussing its flaws and merits. I felt I'd handed over my firstborn child to a bunch of critical strangers.

"I remember your work from our first meeting," Rick said. "Lots of potential here. The revisions are a huge improvement."

"But what do you envision happening at the end?" Eleanor asked. "What finally becomes of Mother after her decision to spare the lives of her targets? Jail them, as opposed to killing them?"

"I don't know yet," I said, taking a breath. "It's something Beckett and I are working out. This story is personal to me, and what happens next for Mother needs to feel authentic and real. At the moment, she's still sorting out her feelings."

Eleanor and Mark smiled, while Rick made a face.

"If you'll please wait outside a few moments," he said. "I'd like to discuss some things with my colleagues…"

Iris gave me a small nod, and Beckett and I went outside in the hallway next to a half-dozen cubicles.

"He hates it," I said. "That Rick guy. He hates it this time just like he hated it last time."

Beckett shook his head. "Nobody hates it, babe. It's just business. To you it's your heart and soul, blood and guts. To him it's potential profit or not."

"What about the artistry?" I asked. "What about the quality? Does that count for anything?"

"Of course it does." Beckett said. "Breathe, baby, breathe."

"I know, I'm sorry I'm freaking out. It's just… What if I fail again? Even after all these changes you helped me to find in Mother—and me, what if they still don't like it? I can't fail Rosie again. I can't."

Beckett put his arms around me and held me in the middle of the office.

"If they don't like it, Zel, try again. Somewhere else. You keep trying and don't give up. If you'd given up and gone back to Vegas, we wouldn't be standing here right now. You and I wouldn't be here right now." He held my face in his hands. "If they don't like it, we'll take it to someone else."

The door to the conference room opened and Iris peeked her head out. Her eyes were lit up behind her glasses, and a smile spread over her sharp features.

"Would you mind rejoining us?" she said, and shot me a knowing, triumphant look that sent my heart into rapid fits.

Oh my God, is it happening…?

"Ms. Rossi, Mr. Copeland," Rick said. "We'd like to offer you both staff contracts to bring *Mother, May I?* to publication. We'll finish with this storyline and then continue in the sequel, following the life of Ryder. Possibly there could be a third volume featuring a spinoff character, depending on how the first two fare."

My hand clutched Beckett's so hard my knuckles ached.

"As employees, you'll be required to work here with our staff of formatters and colorists, and you'll be meeting regularly with Iris, to keep us apprised of progress and editorial suggestions. How does that sound so far?"

My head bobbed up and down. "Yes. Fine. Good." I stared blankly at Beckett. "Sound good?"

Becket had sat back in his chair and covered his mouth with his hand unable to conceal the smile. "Yeah, that sounds pretty fucking good, Mr. Winslow."

Rick smiled thinly. "Wonderful," he said. "I'll have Mark draw up a contract. Our standard advance is $3000 for each of you. Royalties are industry-standard and payable after the advances have been earned. And of course you'll be compensated for any time you spend here in the process of putting the book together. Also good so far?"

My head nodded again. "Sounds good."

"Excellent. If you'd fill out our standard information forms now, we can take them back and put together the contracts." He rose and offered his hand stiffly. We shook hands with him, Eleanor and Mark. They left and we were alone with Iris.

"I knew it," she said. "I fucking knew they would love it. Congratulations."

"Thank you," I said, feeling bewildered.

Rosie. For you, honey...

Iris pulled some forms from her own portfolio and handed them to us.

"The contracts will take some time to put together, but these will get us started. I'll be back in a second to grab them. Help yourself to water or coffee. Champagne is in order but we'll have to save that for when the contracts are signed."

She left us and Beckett and I threw our arms around each other.

"I'm so fucking proud of you, baby," Beckett said. "You fucking did it."

"Oh my God I can't believe it. It's happening. It's really happening for my mom for Rosie..."

"For you, Zelda," Beckett said. "This is all for you."

"And for you, Beckett," I said. "This wouldn't be happening if it weren't for you and your brilliant writing. How you looked straight into the story and saw what it needed." I gave him a last hard squeeze. "Come on. Let's fill this out and get out of this building and go somewhere I can scream."

We sat down to fill out the forms. Standard stuff: name, address, social security numbers, past employment. Beckett sat back in his chair, his jaw tight as he gazed at the paper.

"What is it?" I said.

"What do you think?"

I scanned the form and found it at the bottom:

Have you ever been convicted of a felony? If yes, please, explain:

"Oh." My stomach tightened. "Well. So what? Fill it out. They won't care. We're drawing pictures, not working in customer service."

He said nothing.

"They're not going to care about it," I said. "They can't. What difference could it make to them?"

"It's on their form so it makes a difference," Beckett said. "It makes all the difference." He hitched forward, slowly put the pen to paper and filled out the form.

Iris came to collect the paperwork a few minutes later. "Be back in ten," she said and breezed back out.

"I'm sorry, Zelda," Beckett said.

"Why? Nothing's happened. Nothing has changed."

He went quiet again, his arms crossed as if bracing himself.

Time began to stretch. Ten minutes came and went. More minutes added up and still no one came back. It was a full forty-five minutes later when Iris finally returned, and the expression on her face said everything. My heart cracked and then sank somewhere below my stomach.

She cleared her throat. "I'm sorry, but Eleanor doesn't feel comfortable with this situation," she said. "It's your felony conviction and how recent it is," she said to Beckett. "She once had an incident with her stepson, a few years ago. I shouldn't be telling you this, but she's overly cautious when it comes to these sorts of things."

"Overly cautious," I said, feeling sick. "What does this mean, Iris?"

"It means that they love the graphic novel, and they don't want to walk away," she said to me. "They feel that since you're the creator of the concept and its characters, they're willing to keep you on, as per what we discussed."

"What about Beckett?"

"They're willing to buy out his stake in the book with the $3000 advance. He would effectively be giving up any copyright or ownership claims you two may have established during your collaboration."

"No," I said the exact same time Beckett said, "Fine."

I whipped my head to stare at him. He looked back at me, shaking his head slowly.

I felt cold all over. My thoughts were racing in a hundred different directions at once.

"Do we have to give a final decision right now?" I asked. "Can I think about it for a few days?"

I didn't need to think about anything. I didn't want to do this without Beckett, but I had to get out of that office to talk with him, to get through this.

"Sure," Iris said slowly, "but maybe best not to wait too long." She slipped me her card. "Call me as soon as you come to a decision." She looked to Beckett. "I'm so sorry."

Beckett and I were silent as we left the conference room and walked stiffly through the office. We stayed silent in the elevator down to the street. No sooner had we stepped onto the sidewalk when Beckett said, "You have to take it. You have to sign that contract."

"And what will you do?" It was no more than thirty degrees outside but I felt feverish with panic. Someone had just offered us everything we could possibly desire and snatched it away a second later. "This is your book too, Beckett."

"It's not mine," he said, his voice turning stony. "It was never mine, Zelda. It's yours. I was just helping you out. It's not a big deal."

"Not a big deal?" I jammed my finger in his chest. "I'm not stupid, you know. I know what you're trying to do and it's not going to work."

"What am I trying to do?" Beckett said. "This is a no-brainer, Zelda. It's everything you wanted. You get a contract and I get three grand. Fine by me. This is your thing anyway."

"My thing." My eyes widened and the cold wind stung them making them tear up. That was the only reason. "Maybe it was *my* thing once, but not anymore. I can't do this without you. I don't want to do this without you." I hugged myself, no longer hot or cold. Just numb. "Don't you want this?"

Beckett's face softened, then fell into an anguished grimace. "I want this for *you.* More than anything. It's what you've been dreaming of. You have to take it."

I shook my head. "We'll talk about this later. We'll go home and eat some dinner and talk this out."

Beckett shook his head. "There's nothing to talk about, Zelda. I'll take the money, you sign the contract. End of story."

End of story.

Mother, May I? didn't have an ending yet but this wasn't it. This couldn't be the end of the story.

31

Beckett
January 22nd

I was up at five the next morning. I showered and dressed and when I came out of the bathroom, the coffee pot was cold. Zelda was curled in the bed facing the wall. Last night she'd tried to convince me we could take the book somewhere else, to a different publisher that didn't give a shit about criminal records. Or where we could work as freelancers, not employees.

I refused. It was possible another publisher would fall in love with the graphic novel as much as BlackStar had, but I couldn't take that chance. Zelda had a slam-dunk. A definite yes. The contract ready and a pen held out to her. All she had to do was sign. This wasn't just about her book being published. It was about her sister. It was about telling her story the only way she knew how. It was about giving herself some peace. There was no way in hell I'd jeopardize that.

She stopped talking to me and went to bed. I could practically feel the anger vibrating off of her but I could handle her being pissed at me if it meant her book could see the light of day.

I dressed in my Gor-Tex jacket, weatherproof pants. I put on my helmet, took my bike and went out.

The streets were slushy but the snow had stopped. The sky was clear. In Manhattan, I rode up Lexington to my first delivery, wondering if Zelda would turn down the contract on my behalf. It seemed impossible but, fuck, what if she did? I couldn't let her do that. I couldn't let her throw away her dream…

Lost in thought, I didn't see the sedan run a red light until it was a few feet away from me, and of course, by then it was too late.

32

Zelda
January 22nd

I listened to Beckett get ready for work and leave. I hadn't slept all night. I lay with my back to him, fighting the urge to roll over and hold him. Beg him to reconsider. But I couldn't do it. Part of me wanted to force him into trying again somewhere else, but the look of humiliation on his face when Iris told him they wouldn't hire a felon stabbed my heart. I felt trapped. I wanted nothing more than to see *Mother, May I?* published and shared with the world, but I didn't want to do it without Beckett.

I got dressed and went to work at Annabelle's, so upset and distracted, I brought the wrong orders to two tables and spilled orange juice all over another, forcing its occupants to sit elsewhere with a promise the restaurant would foot their dry cleaning bill.

Maxine sent me home early with a warning. Beckett was still at work, racing around Manhattan on his bike in terrible rain and cold. What BlackStar had offered might not be enough to let us quit our day jobs, but it might lead to him doing something else. It was a door opening, and I felt I was doing my best to keep it open while gale-force winds tried to slam it shut.

I needed to sort out my feelings because going over and over them in my mind just tangled them up tighter. Darlene was a sweet friend, but she was too close to Beckett. I needed someone neutral.

I picked up my phone and scrolled through the contacts until I came to one name, my friend in Vegas. A real friend. I hit 'call.'

"Theo Fletcher."

"Theo, it's Zelda."

His gruff voice brightened at once. "Hey, Z. Long time no hear. What's up? How's New York treating you?"

"It's going great," I said, suddenly feeling like an ass for calling up an old friend and just to immediately dump my problems in his lap. "Listen, I'm not going to keep you, but can I ask you a…business-related question?"

"Of course. Shoot."

"When you bought your tattoo shop, how did you feel right before? I mean, were you scared shitless or were you sure it was the right thing to do, or what?"

He chuckled. "All of the above."

"So what made you do it?" I asked.

"I wanted it bad enough," he said. "But that's the bitch about following a dream, I guess. You have to go for it despite the risk. The risk is what makes it rewarding in the end anyway."

I nodded against the phone.

"Are you thinking about buying a business?"

"No, I have a big decision to make and I don't know what's right."

"Shit, a client just came in. I'm really sorry, Z. I wish I could be more help but I've got to run."

"Yeah, for sure."

"Oh, but I can say one thing about big decisions that might help."

"What's that?"

God, anything please tell me anything…

"All the risk and reward is great but it doesn't mean shit unless you feel in your heart you're doing the right thing. So that would be my advice: go with your gut. How would you feel if you said no? How would you feel if you said yes?"

"Thanks T," I said. "That helps a lot, actually."

"Anytime. Call again soon so we can catch up."

"I will."

No sooner had I set the phone on the table when it vibrated again, with a New York number I didn't recognize.

"Hello?"

"Zelda? It's Wes."

His voice was tense and my heart began to pound. "What is it?"

"I'm at our old hang-out, New York-Presbyterian Hospital, with Beckett. He's fine, he's okay—"

"The hospital?" My stomach dropped to my knees and I went cold all over. "What happened?"

"The story of our lives. Some asshole ran a red light."

"Oh, my god, was he hit?"

"Yes and no," Wes said. "Beckett saw the dude and hit the brakes. From what I heard, he hit the ground and his bike slid another three feet and took the worst of it. He won't say much, but one witness said if Beckett had reacted one second slower, it would've been his legs under the car's front tires, not the bike."

A strangled sound escaped me. "Oh god…"

"Shit, sorry, Zel. I'm not trying to scare you. He's okay. But can you come down here and see if you can't get this knucklehead to stay overnight? They want to keep him here for observation."

I was already heading for the door, fumbling for my jacket. "I'll be right there."

I ran in the general direction of the hospital until I flagged down a cab. Ten excruciating minutes later, I raced into the hospital. The reception desk directed me to the ER. Wes met me there and showed me to the curtained cubicle where Beckett was lying, his right leg elevated and his ankle wrapped. A scrape of dried blood marred his cheek and a nurse was tending to more abrasions on his elbows.

His face was stony until he saw me, then it grimaced and he looked away. I went to his side, arms crossed tight.

"Are you okay?" I asked my voice much more fluttery than I intended. "Tell me the truth."

"I'm fine," he said. "Staying here is stupid and it's costing me a fucking fortune."

I stared. "You were hit by car."

Beckett glared at Wes. "I wasn't hit, it's my fucking bike that's trashed."

"And your ankle?"

"Not broken," he said. "Which I knew before they X-rayed but that didn't stop them."

"He has a second degree soft tissue sprain of the ATF ligament," the nurse said.

"What does that mean?" I asked.

"It means he tore some shit up in his foot," Wes said.

"*Partial* tear and it doesn't fucking matter anyway," Beckett said.

The ER doc came around and said they'd prefer to keep Becket overnight for observation, but because his concussion tests were negative, they were reluctantly willing to release him.

They put his ankle in a boot and gave him a pair of crutches. Because he'd re-injured his right elbow, he couldn't use them. Jaw clenched, he sat in a wheelchair and let himself be pushed to the front doors of the hospital where I'd called the cab. Wes, Beckett, I piled in the back and went back to our apartment.

"You take care, man," Wes said.

Beckett gave no reply but lay in bed with his eyes closed.

Wes sighed. "He's all yours. The doc told me he needs to keep ice on it for the next 48 hours and keep it elevated as much as possible. I got to get back to work."

"Where's his bike?" I asked at the door.

Wes shook his head. "Trashed. Repairing it would cost almost as much as getting a new one.

"How much is a new one?"

"For a decent one? Twelve hundred bucks, minimum." He shook his head. "Yeah, I don't know. But don't get bogged down in that shit. He can't ride anyway until the ankle heals up. Two weeks and not a minute sooner." He kissed my cheek. "Call me if you need anything."

Wes left. I put my back to the door and let out a shaky breath.

He's okay. The bike is trashed, but he's okay.

I went to the kitchen and made an ice pack out of a dishtowel and a bag of frozen peas. I sat on the edge of the bed and gently removed the boot. I laid the bag over Beckett's wrapped ankle.

"Can you feel that?"

He shrugged. "It's fine, thanks."

"Do you need anything else?" I asked softly.

He opened his eyes slowly, as if they weighed a hundred pounds. "Yeah, Zel, I do. I need that $3000. For a new bike and to pay off that fucking ER visit. And you need to sign that contract."

I sat for a minute, my anger bubbling up and then fading out. I was suddenly exhausted. I carefully climbed into bed with him, mindful of his elbow. He winced and then put his arm around me.

"I don't want to do this without you," I said. "There has to be another way. That's our thing, right?

"Not this time, Zel," Beckett said. "I need the money, it's my decision."

"What about doing this together? We can take it somewhere else, just like you said. Keep trying, again and again. We can work freelance. We can find someone who doesn't give a shit about your background."

"I have to work in the meanwhile, Zel. And I need a new bike for that."

"I could work double shifts. I could get a second job, just until you're better. We can save up."

"I'm not letting you give up your dream," he said slowly and deliberately. "It's right there hanging in front of you, Zel. You have to take it. If you don't..."

He shook his head, his expression stony, but Beckett's eyes gave everything away. I knew what he was going to say. If I didn't sign the contract, he would never forgive himself and it would eat away at him. Maybe eat away us.

I thought of Theo's advice. To go with my gut, and my gut was telling me that despite all of Beckett's arguments, despite my desire to see *Mother, May I?* in print for Rosemary, doing it without him wasn't the way.

My phone rang. I climbed off the bed with an irritated sigh and grabbed it off the kitchen counter. "What fresh hell is this?" I muttered.

I glanced at the screen and my heart stopped and then started again, like a startled horse. Slowly, I hit the green answer button.

"Hi, Mom," I said. "What's up?"

"Hi, sweetheart," she said, and I heard something like excitement and fear twining in her voice, making it vibrate across the line. "We got the call, honey. It's happening. It's finally happening. This Friday."

"What is?"

"Gordon James is going to be put to death."

33

Zelda
January 24th

My rolling suitcase was open on the bed and I threw random clothes into it. *How does one dress to witness a man die? Is that business casual or come-as-you-are?*

A hysterical laugh bubbled up but I swallowed it down.

"I called Nigel," I said to Beckett. "He'll come by later today to help you out. Darlene said she'd come tomorrow."

"Zelda…"

"Keep your ankle iced and elevated. Don't try walking around on it. It needs two weeks of rest."

"Zelda, look at me."

I stopped packing and looked. He sat on the couch, his leg propped on the coffee table. His expression was imploring, twisted with guilt.

"What are you going to do?" he asked in a low voice.

"I don't know yet," I said. "I think so. I mean, I'm going. I have to go. Even if I fall apart from a panic attack, I have to be with my family. Maybe it'll be the last panic attack. Maybe this is it. Maybe if I watch that fucker die, I'll have the closure I need. I won't have any more attacks. I don't know."

I was babbling, my thoughts flying in every direction, fueled by the adrenaline in my veins. I couldn't catch my breath. My nerves were lit up like a switchboard.

"Nigel will be here pretty soon," I said, turning back to my suitcase.

"You said that already. I don't need the help."

"Yeah, well, I need peace of mind that you're not going to do anything crazy." I stopped packing, a bra in one hand, a scarf in the other. “Promise me you won’t do anything crazy.”

Beckett crutched slowly to the window. He winced as he threw it open, as his elbows were still bruised. He sat on the sill and lit a cigarette, his booted ankle dangling.

“When is your train?” he asked.

“In an hour.” I went to the window and took the cigarette from his fingers. The first drag sent me coughing but the second inhale was smoother. I handed it back to him. “I’ll be back in two days.”

He nodded. “And then you tell BlackStar yes.”

“I can’t even think about that right now, Beckett. I can hardly see three feet past my nose.”

What I could see, within his soft expression, was the conflicted guilt in his eyes. The same self-blame and self-loathing for not being able to go with me.

“I’ll be okay,” I said. “I’ll survive this. And I’ll be better knowing you’re here.”

Beckett looked away. “You don’t want to miss your train.”

The intercom buzzed and I went to let Nigel in.

“Nurse Nigel is here,” he said, his booming voice filling the apartment. “I hope you weren’t expecting a little white uniform.” He stopped and rubbed his arms. “Bloody hell, it’s cold in here.” He spotted Beckett at the window. “Hey, there’s our own little Evil Knievel. Heard you pulled off some serious acrobatics, my friend.”

“Thanks for coming, Nigel,” I said and gave him a hug. I put my mouth on his ear and whispered, “Do *not* let him leave.”

Nigel gave me a brief nod and a wink. “So Becks, how about a sponge bath?”

Beckett ignored him.

“All right, time to go.” I went back the window. Beckett’s jaw was clenched tight, but then it melted into my palm as I kissed him.

“God, Zel.”

“It’s the end,” I said. “For better or worse, this is the end of the story.”

BLAM!

We took one car. My parents, Auntie Lucille and I, with Uncle Mike at the wheel, driving the three hours from Philly to Benner Township, and the State Correctional Institute at Rockview. Uncle Mike told me Gordon James was concurrently being transported from the supermax prison in Greene to the death house.

"That's actually what it's called," he said. "The death house."

Sounds like a good title for a comic book.

We arrived in Benner a little before nine at night, and checked into the Holiday Inn. The rooms had been provided by the State. We congregated in my parents' suite, talking and crying and reminiscing about Rosemary. Memories reached for me with ghostly fingers, but because we weren't in my childhood home, it was easier to brush them aside.

I stuck close to Auntie Lucille. She seemed subdued, not her usual bubbly self. I sat beside her on one of the stiff chairs near the window and put my hand in hers.

"Are you okay, Auntie Lucille?"

She shook her head mournfully, a rosary wrapped tight around one hand. "Their sins and lawless acts I will remember no more."

"What's that from?"

"The Bible," Uncle Mike said. "Book of Hebrews. She's been saying it since we got the call. I finally had to look it up."

I frowned. Our entire family was Catholic though we weren't particularly stringent about it. As I kid I went to Mass on all the holidays, but no one had ever quoted a verse I could remember outside of church.

"Tomorrow, we can put this behind us," Uncle Mike said. "I think that's what the verse means. Isn't that right, Auntie?"

Lucille didn't answer. She didn't look comforted, she looked agitated. Her hands toyed with dark brown beads on her rosary, and I wondered if she had the same doubts as me. This was the man who shattered our lives with one senseless act. I desired to see vengeance, to have Gordon James' life snuffed out too. But could I watch?

I wondered, too, if Gordon James was scared tonight? Was he watching the clock tick down, knowing he had hours left to live? Had he achieved the peace I still sought?

All through the sleepless night, my thoughts went back and forth like a ping-pong ball.

I want to see him die.

There's no way I can actually watch it happen.

I want to go home to Beckett.

I want to stay here and see it through.

My mother called my room the next morning, waking me to say the prison van was waiting outside.

It was time.

The morning was cold and gray. Lucille stuck close to me, her hand clutching mine, birdlike and dry as paper. The other held her rosary, the silver crucifix dangling against the back of her hand. The same murmured litany under her breath:

"Their sins and lawless acts I will remember no more."

The van drove us to the Correctional Facility. We walked through the parking lot in silence and filed into the main office. Our IDs were checked and we were made to walk through metal detectors. My heart began to thump so loudly I couldn't hear anything else. Not a voice, or breath or echoing footstep. Through a locked gate, down a hallway, a right turn, a left, and finally we were there. The viewing chamber. Outside the door Lucille stopped.

"*His* sins and lawlessness I will remember no more," she said, and firmly planted herself on a bench in the hallway.

"Lucille?" Dad asked, but she would not be budged. "You'll be okay out here?"

She folded her hands in her lap and looked straight ahead, but as I passed her she took my hand.

"Remember the red balloon?" she said, her eyes watery. "I do. I can see it. I can see it tied to her wrist and she's smiling." Lucille shook her head. "That's what I see. A red balloon and a child's smile. Doesn't that sound nice?"

I nodded mutely, my blood still thrashing in my ears. My father took my hand from Lucille's and walked me into the viewing chamber.

The small room had twelve chairs. Two reporters from local newspapers were there. One asked me a question but I only stared at him blankly. I took a seat between my parents, front row, their hands clutched in each of mine. My mother gave me a closed-mouth smile, her eyes full of fear and fire.

I remembered at James's sentencing, none of my family pushed for him to die as opposed to a life sentence. They only wanted justice, however the State saw fit to give it. They wanted closure. To move on.

None of the words held any meaning for me right now.

On other side of the glass was a gurney and a curtained partition on wheels. Beside the gurney was a strange machine with three bags of clear liquid suspended above them, tubes trailing down.

Any second now Gordon James would be walked into this room and hooked up to that machine. We'd hear his last words. I was told he'd never shown any remorse or regret during the trial. Maybe we'd have to endure cruel laughter or cursing. Or maybe ten years in solitary confinement had eaten away at his sanity. Maybe he'd come to regret what he did. Maybe he'd beg forgiveness.

No matter what he did or said, we'd watch him die.

Forgiveness.

The word was a whisper in my mind. If I were drawing it on the page, it would be written in small letters but contained in a large thought bubble. Eleven tiny letters floating in a sea of white. Like a balloon.

A red balloon and a child's smile...

The grief began to roar. I felt it coil and gather strength, a hurricane churning in my heart and mind and soul.

Oh God...I can't. I can't forgive him. Is that what I'm supposed to do? Impossible...

Grief like I'd never known, layered and tangled. Grief for Rosemary, grief for my family, for the man about to die and for me.

For me...

For ten years, I'd blamed myself. For not being smart enough, quick enough, brave enough. For not screaming louder, even though my vocal chords had been left torn and bleeding. For not chasing faster, even though I ran so hard and fell so many times, the skin was scraped off both knees.

I was fourteen years old. Too young to stop a horrific tragedy, but old enough to believe I could have.

Forgiveness.

Not for him, whispered a thought. *Not for him, but for—*

The door in the room on the other side of the glass began to open. In the reflection of the one-way window, I saw another balloon. This one was yellow—my favorite color—tied to the wrist of a skinny girl with long dark hair and large green eyes. She held hands with Rosemary, who had a red balloon tied to her wrist.

I stared at the taller girl. Me. My fourteen-year old self, there, in Auntie Lucille's movie theater—Phantasus. A shy, self-conscious girl who liked to read comic books while her friends were reading fashion magazines. She was holding hands with her little sister, and she'd never let go.

I forgive you, I whispered to that girl.

She smiled back like the sun. *Thank you.*

A sob tore out of me, and I rose to my feet, shielding my eyes from the murderer who was being led into the room. Blindly, I pushed past the rows of seats, ignoring the concerned calls of my family. I shoved the door open and ran down the hall. Auntie Lucille's voice chased me but it was a whisper against my pounding heart.

I passed through the security gates, then pushed to the front door out into the bracing cold, and kept running, toward the parking lot. I had no plan. I could hardly see with the tears streaming down my cheeks. All I knew was I had to get far away from this place. Gordon James had nothing to do with me. He didn't deserve one more iota of my attention. He meant nothing. Rosemary was everything. I had no reason to be here.

I needed Beckett. I needed his arms around me. His voice to guide me through the grief that was, at long last, ready to break free.

Home. I need to go home.

I stumbled through the parking lot. A cab was pulling up and had to swerve to miss me. Tires screeched and a horn blared. I stopped short. The car's back door flew open before I could touch it.

"Zelda!"

Beckett...

A deep, sweet ache spread through my chest—my heart and soul crying out for him. I fell to my knees on the asphalt, next to the cab, sobs tearing out of me. I felt strong arms go around me, lifting me. Beckett carried me, limping, to a nearby bench, away from the cars, and sat down heavily. I collapsed against him, clung to him as the grief and rage and pain flooded out of me.

"It's okay," he said, his voice thick and blurry. "You're going to be okay, I swear to you. I swear it."

I cried hard against his chest, my fists clenched around his jacket. He stroked my hair, kissed the top of my head, blanketing me in safety.

"I didn't watch. I ran out. I couldn't..."

Beckett held me tighter but I felt his chest expand with a sigh. "I'm glad, baby," he said. "I don't know if it's the right way to feel, but I'm so glad."

"I think...I am too," I said. "You were right. No relief...only fresh nightmares. Rosemary… She's not here. Not in this ugly place. Not here. She's somewhere beautiful. That's what I want to remember."

He held me until my sobs drained to cries, then to hiccupping breaths. My relief to be in his arms slowly turned into sharp concern.

"How are you here?" I croaked, not letting him go but scared that I needed to. "You can't be here. If they find out…"

Beckett pulled away just enough to hold my face in his hands, to brush the strands of hair clinging to my wet cheeks. His eyes were brilliant blue, shining with his own emotion.

"Together, Zel. Everything we do in this life… We do it together. Don't we?"

I nodded, my eyes and throat aching.

"They wouldn't have let me in there anyway." He said, nodding at the facility entrance and smiling crookedly. "It would've been the first time a felon tried to break *into* prison. My only hope was to be here when you came out, and that I wasn't too late." The smile slipped away. "It killed me to watch you leave the other night."

"I know, but—"

"If they send me back, I'll do the time and it'll be the easiest time served. Because it was worth it to be here with you." He swallowed hard, his eyes never leaving mine. His hands held me tight, with all the gentle goodness that lived in him. "I love you, Zelda."

I raised my eyes, a flood of happiness wrapping around me, protecting me from the winter cold. "You do?"

"God, yes." He clenched his jaw for a moment, the muscles twitching, his eyes shining. "I'm in love with you. Even though I'm not supposed to be. Even though I don't know that I deserve this kind of happiness, I love you anyway. I love you and I know I will for the rest of my life."

A fresh swell of tears rose in me. I took in his words, inhaled them like the air I needed to breath. I'd been suffocating on my own fears and guilt, but now I was free.

I was free…

The tears spilled over my eyes, but nothing could keep me from seeing what was in front of me. Everything that was so beautiful and kind and good. My voice was whispery but not broken.

"I love you too, Beckett. I love you so much. I want to say it a million times to make up for not saying it before, when I was too afraid…." My words trailed off and I touched his face. "What is it?"

"Nothing, I…" His smile wavered but his eyes held mine. "I came here knowing I was going to tell you I loved you, and I had the hope you'd say the same. But to actually hear it…"

"I love you." I kissed him, breathed the words into the kiss. "I'm in love with you, Beckett, and I will be forever."

"Together," Beckett said hoarsely. "All of this life…I want it with you."

He brought my face to his, kissed me softly, gently. I tasted our tears, his and mine, and couldn't tell the difference.

34

Zelda
January 25th

I texted my mother to tell her where I was, then decided to go back to the hotel with Beckett. I wanted to be with them, but I felt if we didn't get Beckett back in New York quickly, our luck was going to run out. But he insisted I wait for my family.

"They need you too, baby."

The cab was still idling in the parking lot, Beckett's crutches inside. It wasn't until Beckett was gingerly limping on his booted foot that I realized he'd lifted me off the ground and carried me twenty feet away.

"God, your ankle," I asked as we drove away from the prison.

He shrugged. "I'll live."

I elbowed his side. "I'd roll my eyes at your excessive man-pride but they're too fat from crying."

"You look beautiful," he said fiercely, and bent to kiss me.

"So do you," I whispered against his lips. "I'm so happy you're here. I'm pissed at you and even more mad at Nigel, but I'm happy you're here."

Happy wasn't a strong enough word. I held his hand, palm to palm, our fingers twined. *That is how I feel,* I said, looking at our clasped hands. *There needs to be a word for this.*

I rested my head against his shoulder, drained. Exhausted, but calm. Partly from him being there and partly for what I had done. Or what I hadn't done.

"You were right," I said again, as the cab pulled into the Holiday Inn lot. "If I'd watched James die, I wouldn't be okay. But I hope my mom and dad and everyone else can find some relief."

My family returned an hour later, my mother's eyes were red-rimmed and my father's face slightly confused, as if he were trying to work out some great problem. Uncle Mike was subdued, and Auntie Lucille's hands fidgeted and her eyes darted behind her thick glasses until they met mine. Then she smiled wide, as if she'd been searching for something and now it was found. She took a chair by the window, humming softly to herself.

I went straight into Mom's arms and hugged her tight. "Are you all right?"

She held me away, her smile uncertain, tears rimming her eyes. "I keep waiting for the sigh of relief. It's not coming. I've been waiting ten years."

I hugged her again, trying to infuse her with my newly-found peace. "When you go home tonight, pull Auntie Lucille aside, alone, and ask her to tell you about the movie theater…and the balloons. Okay?"

Her smile was confused as she glanced at Lucille humming and smiling to herself at the window, but she nodded, and wiped her eyes. She held my face in her hands. "My beautiful girl."

Behind me, Beckett rose to his feet, holding the chair for balance. I moved to stand beside him, for him to lean on me. "Everyone, this is my boyfriend, Beckett Copeland."

I felt such a swell of pride watching him and my father shake hands. My mother kissed him on the cheek. "I'm so happy to meet you," she said. She took in his ankle and his crutches. "You came all this way for our girl?"

He spoke to my mother, but his words were for me. "I'd go to the end of the earth for her, Mrs. Rossi."

I drove the rental car, taking Beckett and me back to Philly. My eyes darted to the rearview every other second, expecting to see a squad car roll up behind us, to take Beckett away, and I struggled to keep to the speed limit.

"How in hell did you ditch Nigel?"

"Easy," Beckett said. "I pretended I was a wreck from being stuck in New York, and that my ankle was hurting like a bastard. The only solution was to get drunk. I sent him to the liquor store and slipped out while he was gone."

"Poor Nigel," I said. "He's probably worried sick."

"Nah, I texted him," Beckett said, chuckling. "Judging by the long, ranting voice mail on my phone, he drank all the booze himself. He cursed me to hell and back, so we're good."

We returned the rental and took a cab to 30th Street Station. Beckett sank down heavily on a bench, yawning. I sat beside him, thinking of our future, and what Theo had said about knowing in my heart what was right.

"I love you," I said.

Beckett looked up at me, a small smile of surprise—saying the words out loud was still so new between us. "I love you too, baby. So much."

"I love you, I love saying it…." I cupped his cheek, the bristles of his stubble rough under my palm. "I love you so much that I'm going to turn down BlackStar."

His brows came together. "Zelda…"

"It's our story now, yours and mine. When I think about publishing it without you, the regret is bigger than the thrill. But when I think of us doing it together, my heart tells me it's right. I know we need the money, but we'll figure it out somehow. We'll survive. It's what we do, right?"

"Yeah," he said. "We do, baby."

He leaned in to kiss me, then stopped, his eyes widening at something over my shoulder. I turned and followed his stare to a middle-aged woman with perfectly-coiffed silvery blonde hair, crisp suit, and a briefcase in her hand. Frozen. Like a statue, while the bustling crowd moved around her. She stared at Beckett, eyes wide and her lips parted in shock.

"Holy fuck…" he whispered.

"Who is that?" I asked.

Beckett swallowed hard. His eyes followed the woman as she ducked her head and quickly walked away.

"Mrs. J."

35

Beckett
January 25th

It was almost eight when we staggered into the apartment. Zelda whipped up a quick dinner of pasta and salad but I hardly tasted it. My eyes were glued to my cell phone, waiting for the call. Or maybe it would be a knock on the door. DOC coming to take me back to Rikers, then Otisville.

Zelda kept up a stream of chatter, trying to take my mind off the impending repercussions. “Maybe Mrs. J doesn’t know your situation,” she said as we lay in bed. “The conditions of your parole?”

“She knows everything about the four of us who robbed her.” I raked hands through my hair, pulling it. “I should call Roy. I should’ve called Roy the second I got back. I have to call him now.”

“No, don’t. He might not know. Mrs. J might not say anything. You’d be walking back to prison for no reason.”

“Not for no reason, Zel. I broke the law. Again. I don’t regret it, not for a second. Not going to you would’ve tortured me forever. But if there are consequences then I have to take them. I want to take them.”

I called Roy before I could think it to death and before Zelda could talk me out of it. The call went straight to voicemail.

“Hi, Roy,” I said, my voice suddenly drained of strength. “It’s Beckett. I need you to call me back as soon as you can. Thanks.”

“Would they really send you back to jail?” she said.

“I’m low-risk,” I said. “They might put me back, or I might just get an extension on my probation. God, there’s no worse feeling than waiting for the shit to hit the fan.”

I lay back down, and Zelda immediately curled up close.

“Do you think Roy will be mad?” she asked.

"I don't know. Disappointed, maybe, which is almost worse than any punishment for parole violation."

"You love him," she said softly. "And he loves you."

I cleared my throat, looked to the ceiling. "I never had a real dad. Mine was gone for months at a time and drunk whenever he came home. I hardly remember him or my mother. They both took off when I was eight. Gramps took care of me but when I got older, I took care of him more than the other way around. But Roy…"

Zelda's arm slid across my chest and she held me tight. "He's not going to let anything bad happen to you. I know it. It's the only reason I can sleep tonight."

Sleep eluded me. Roy Goodwin might've loved me, but he was by-the-book, with a solid sense of law and order, right and wrong.

But Zelda needed me today. That's all that fucking matters.

The thought finally let me fall asleep, and I woke to the sound of my phone ringing the next morning. It was Roy.

"Hey," I said, my voice tight. "Listen—"

"I need you to meet me at the Plaza Hotel in one hour," Roy said, his voice like a blade. "The Napoleon Lounge. Alone."

"The Plaza Hotel?"

"In one hour."

"Roy, listen. I'm sorry I didn't tell you…"

"We'll talk when you get here."

He hung up and I stared at the phone in my hand.

Zelda's eyes were wide, expectant. "Well? What happened?"

"He wants to meet me at the Plaza Hotel."

She frowned. "Isn't that one of the most expensive hotels in the city?"

I nodded and slowly moved to get dressed. "I have to leave now if I'm to make it on time."

"Well, wait a minute, what happens at the hotel?" Zelda said, sitting up in bed and brushing her hair out of her eyes. "Are you going to be arrested or you are you going to have high tea with the Queen?"

"I'll text you as soon as I know anything," I said and kissed her softly. She clung to my wrists.

"Wait, I'll come with you."

"You can't, baby. I'll talk to you soon. I promise." I kissed her again.

"Beckett, wait…"

"I love you, Zelda. I have to go."

She pressed her forehead to mine, eyes squeezed shut. "Come home soon."

I took the subway into Manhattan and then a cab to the Plaza Hotel. My elbow complained every time I put pressure on it to use the crutches, and my ankle throbbed like it had a second heartbeat. A heartbeat that was pounding a rapid pulse of fear and confusion.

The magnificent Plaza Hotel lobby opened before me in a display of elegance and wealth. I crutched to the front desk and asked the concierge the way to the Napoleon Lounge. He immediately called someone to escort me personally, up four floors to the conference level. The bellhop opened the door to a little tearoom with antique furniture and a chandelier that probably cost more than my entire apartment building.

Roy stood by the window overlooking the city, his hands clasped behind his back. Sitting in one of the chairs, sipping tea from a delicate cup and saucer was Evelyn Johannsen.

Mrs. J.

Roy turned when he saw me and his expression melted into one of shocking worry at my crutches and foot. "Beckett, what happened?"

"It's nothing I'm fine," I said. I stared at Mrs. J. I'd only seen her twice before—once during the robbery, the second time at my sentencing. She'd been shrouded in black, a netted black veil over half of her face.

The eyes regarding me now were clear blue, lined with a few wrinkles. Her pantsuit still impeccable, but the blouse beneath it was soft. Her hand trembled as she set her teacup down, making it rattle against the saucer.

"Hello, Beckett," she said.

My mouth tried to shape a reply but nothing came out.

Roy came around the table and took my crutches so I could sit. I went on staring, mute and stupid, while my brain screamed, *What does this mean? What the fuck does this mean?*

"I don't have a lot of time," Mrs. J said. Her voice was pitched low and refined. The voice of a natural hostess who'd thrown many dinner parties and organized charity fundraisers. "My plane leaves for Melbourne this evening."

She reached for a small briefcase next to her chair and set it on the table. The locks popped open, the lid raised and she pulled out a stack of envelopes.

My throat clenched. There they were. My letters. All forty-one of them. Most sent from the Otisville Correctional Facility, the rest from Brooklyn.

Every envelope's seal was broken.

"You read them?" I found my voice.

"Every one," she said. "Several of them more than once. The last few I must've read twenty times each at least." She smiled faintly her eyes shining. "The letters about Zelda."

I swallowed hard, blinked harder. "You did?"

She nodded, her fingers trailing over the letter on top of the pile. The most recent one, in which I'd asked for her blessing.

"I didn't intend to speak to you before I left," she said. "I intended to board the plane without a forwarding address and go halfway around the world. But I couldn't. Not without answering two of your questions."

She folded her hands on the table and held me with her steady gaze. "Yes."

"Yes…" My voice was a croak, choked with so much hope I could hardly breathe.

"You asked if I was trapped in the moment of my husband's death. The answer is yes. I've been replaying it over and over in my mind for three years, just as you have. It occupies my waking hours and haunts my dreams. But your face haunts me, too."

"Mine?"

"I'd never seen such a look of anguish before. It was like looking in a mirror," she said, and smiled tremulously. "As if a fifty-year-old woman could share the reflection of a handsome young man. But in your eyes I saw what I felt: this was all a horrible mistake. And if only we could rewind time a few minutes, go back and undo it all…we would."

I glanced at Roy. His face was tense, a dam holding back some tremendous emotion. His eyes shone as he looked at Mrs. J.

"Before I answer your second question," she said, "I need to know something."

I nodded. "Of course. Anything."

"In forty-one letters over three years, you never asked me for forgiveness. Why?"

"It didn't feel right," I said, the words scraping my throat. "I don't know that I deserve that."

"Do you love her?"

"Yes," I whispered. Then louder, "*Yes.* I'm in love with her."

"Is she the reason you broke your parole and went to Philadelphia yesterday?"

"Yes." I sat up straighter in my chair. "And if I could rewind time a few minutes and go back, I'd do it again."

Mrs. J nodded. "You never asked for my forgiveness, but in your last letter, you did ask for my blessing. Your second question that I came here to answer. You were asking me permission to feel happy, weren't you?"

I started to speak but she shook her head, once.

"It's not for me to determine. I can't create your happiness, but I can give you my blessing to try to find it. With Zelda." Her eyes shone and her voice quavered. "Yes, Beckett. That is my answer. You have my blessing, and even though you've never asked me for it—or maybe *because* you haven't—you have my forgiveness as well. I forgive you." The tears were flowing now, dripping on the lapel of her expensive suit. "I forgive you."

I felt weightless. I clutched the chair to keep me in it and watched, struck mute, as Mrs. J moved around the table to me. I stood upon shaking legs as she put her arms around me.

Time ceased, stretching into some surreal dimension consisting of me saying I was sorry, and Mrs. J saying she forgave me.

I said it again. *I'm sorry.*

She said it again. *I forgive you.*

Again and again, until I finally found two more words. "Thank you," I said.

"Oh my goodness, this feeling…" Mrs. J said against my shoulder. "If I'd known it would feel like this, I would've done it sooner."

I held her tight, afraid I might crush her, overcome. I felt as if I'd been waiting to breathe for three years and now I could. Breathe and live and love Zelda with every bit of my heart that was now free.

After a moment, Mrs. J let me go and rested her palm on my

cheek. “Be good,” she said. “Love your girl and be happy. I think we both have a chance now.”

I watched her gather the letters and put them back in her briefcase. She shook Roy’s hand wordlessly, gave us a final, parting smile, and went out.

I felt strength draining out of me and I slumped into the chair, my shoulders shaking. Roy’s arms went around me then, holding me for a long time.

36

Zelda
January 26th

I called in sick to Annabelle's and paced our small apartment like a caged animal. My phone clutched in a sweaty hand, waiting for a call or text from Beckett that would tell me I could breathe again, that I wasn't going to lose him. Ten times I contemplated going to the Plaza, and ten times I talked myself out of it. Roy told him to come alone and I worried I'd only fuck things up if I butted in.

I gave a little shriek as the phone rang, but it wasn't Beckett, it was Iris.

"Ms. Rossi, I've been dying to talk to you."

"Hey, Iris. I'm sorry I haven't gotten back to you or the other editors, but the answer is no. I'm not doing this without Beckett."

She laughed at my nervous string of words. "When I hadn't heard from you I figured that was the case. So I have another proposal for you. I think Eleanor is an idiot for letting you guys go, but her loss is my gain, right? BlackStar is absorbing another, smaller publishing house and they've tapped me to run it. It was already in the works but I think Rick accelerated it for us. He sees the potential in *Mother, May I?* and doesn't want to let it go, even if they can't work with you directly. But I can. You guys can freelance under me, and we will get *Mother, May I?* published."

I sank down onto the couch. "Are you serious?"

"I can't offer the big bucks like BlackStar, but I can give you guys a $3000 advance. Total, not each. I know it's not much but—"

"It's perfect," I said. "So generous of you. Oh my God." The words were falling out of my mouth as fast as my brain could churn them. "But wait, you don't care about Beckett's felony charge?"

"I don't give a shit about it. I care about the work. I care about the people doing the work. And I'm a big believer in second chances."

"Yes," I said, calmer now. "I know that about you. You're the reason I'm still in New York and why all of this has happened for me."

How Beckett happened for me.

"I'm no saint by any stretch," Iris said with a laugh. "I see potential for the three of us to make a kick-ass graphic novel, and maybe make some money in the process. Sound good?"

"Sounds fucking amazing."

"Awesome. I'll courier over the contracts for you to sign and send back, and we'll talk next week. Lunch, somewhere nice. And oh, when do you think you'll be finished with *Mother, May I?* You have an ending yet?"

I thought about where Beckett was right now and what might be happening to him. "Not yet," I said faintly. "But soon."

I got off the phone and a text came in from Beckett a second later. I half-laughed, half-sobbed to see the three words in solid black and white.

I'm coming home.

37

Zelda
January 29th

Three days later, we signed the contract with BlackStar's newest studio, Second Time Around. Iris said the name was a nod to an antique store in a comic book series she loved. *Mother May I?* was to be her first imprint, and since she was our boss, she'd given us a deadline of one week to finish the graphic novel.

Roy and Mary Goodwin took us to dinner that night at Gramercy Tavern, to celebrate both the contract and Beckett's birthday.

We sat at a table under gleaming lights, ordered filet mignon and expensive wine, because Roy and Mary insisted on it.

"It's a special occasion three times over," Roy said, exchanging a glance with Mary.

"Three times?" Beckett asked, taking a bite of his filet. "The contract is one."

"The blessed occasion of your birth is the second," I said giving his hand a squeeze. I looked to Roy. "What's the third?"

Roy took a deep breath as if to say something, then let it out again, flapping his hands. "Later, later. After dessert."

It was the richest, heaviest meal I'd had in years. Afterward, the wait staff placed a delicate square of cherry cheesecake in front of Beckett with a single candle, then embarrassed him by singing Happy Birthday.

"Make a wish," I said.

He looked around the table, at Roy and Mary smiling sweetly at him, and then at me. "I have everything I could possibly want right here at this table."

Mary nudged her husband and mouthed the word *now*.

Roy cleared his throat. "I'm happy to hear you say that," he said, his voice thick. He withdrew a fat envelope from inside his suit jacket pocket. He handed it to Beckett across the table, his hand shaking. "You don't have to say anything right now, but… It's something to think about."

Roy looked like he didn't know what to do with himself after that. He picked up a napkin, put it down, shifted in his chair and shook his head against whatever Mary whispered to him, unable to take his eyes off Beckett. She clutched his arm, her own eyes bright, as they both watched Beckett open the envelope.

Beckett pulled a small sheaf of documents from the envelope. His ocean blue eyes swept across the pages rapidly.

"What is it?"

Wordlessly, Beckett handed me the papers.

New York State, Family Court, Petition for Adoption request form…

"Oh, Beckett…" I reached for him and he squeezed my fingers hard.

"But I'm twenty-four years old," he said hoarsely.

"Twenty-five, as of today," Mary said, her smile a beautiful thing.

Roy cleared his throat. "We don't feel that age has much to do with how strongly people care about each other," he said. "Family is family."

He shifted in his seat again, and his wife rubbed his arm reassuringly. They both stared at Beckett, waiting. Hopeful.

"I…I don't know what to say," Beckett murmured.

"We tried to find your birth parents," Roy said, "and could not, so there are a few pieces of the process missing. But because you're no longer a minor, the decision is yours. If you give your consent, you would…" He cleared his throat again. "You'd be our son. We'd like you to be our son."

I had to bite the inside of my cheek to keep from bursting into tears. Beckett stared at Roy and Mary, his chin starting to rise and fall. "Yes," he said, hardly a whisper. Then cleared his throat and said louder, "Yes, I… I'd like that." He laughed, wiping his eyes. "I'd like that a lot."

"Good," Roy said, trying mightily to sound gruff, as if they'd just finalized a business deal. "It's settled, then."

Mary and I exchanged looks and both burst out laughing and

crying. Mary shot out of her seat and threw her arms around Beckett's neck, then turned to me and did the same. I clung to her, watching Roy shake Beckett's his hand, then pull him in for a tight hug. He squeezed his eyes shut over Beckett's shoulder, knowing he held something precious.

When we got home, Beckett slumped on the couch, and put his foot up. I curled up next to him.

"Well that was a pleasant dinner," I said. "I can't get over the filet. Cooked to perfection. Quite the highlight of the evening, wouldn't you agree?"

A low chuckle rumbled out of Beckett's chest, growing louder and louder until he threw his head back as laughter roared out of him. He pulled me onto his lap and kissed me. "Yeah, that was the highlight all right."

"I'm so happy for you, baby," I said. "And damn if that's not the understatement of the year. Did you have any idea?"

"None."

I let my fingertips trail along his lips. "I love it. I love you." I kissed him softy. "Happy Birthday." I laughed against his lips as a thought occurred to me. "Today was your birthday in more ways than one."

"Yeah, I guess it was." He shook his head as if to clear it. "Jesus, my brain. I need to focus on something else. And we need to finish *Mother, May I?*"

I sat up. "Right now? Tonight?

"Let's just knock it out, baby," he said, his hands sliding up and down my thighs. "It's hanging there, waiting for an end, right?"

"Yeah, I guess so."

We changed into sweatpants, sweatshirts and scarves. The radiator gave a petulant clank when I kicked it, and wheezed out just enough warm air to keep our hands from freezing. Together, at the small table, I pulled out the graphic novel.

"This is where we're at: Kira spared the man. Put him in jail instead of killing him. And now she's ready to jump to the year 2111." I glanced up at Beckett. "So what happens when she gets there?"

"Ryder is waiting for her. He sweeps her into his arms and they have hot, sweaty, futuristic sex all night."

I swatted his arm. "He is *not* a love interest."

"Poor guy. Do they have a cure for blue balls in the year 2111?"

"Will you be serious?" I said. "The ending…"

"Her ending, Zel," Beckett said, his voice turning soft. "She deserves a happy ending."

I thought of my life, and how one decision had changed it forever, in the best way. A chain reaction. A series of opening doors, one after another, all leading me to this moment. This happiness. With this man. I covered Beckett's hand with mine for a moment, then picked up a pen.

"Maybe jailing the guy instead of killing him created a kind of…cause and effect," I said, thinking out loud as my pen scratched the paper. "Maybe he sought to better himself in prison, to tell his story in the hopes others wouldn't take the same path. One decision sent out ripples, wider and wider. The tiny lessening of one man's pain spawned other kindnesses. Which spawned even more. It kept going, on and on through the years in small ways. Until they found their way across decades, to the man who murdered Kira's daughter."

"Chaos theory," Beckett said. "One decision…"

"Yes," I said, my hand gliding over the paper, now. "It didn't change the sickness in his mind. By the time kindness reached him, the change was a small thing—smaller than the flutter of a butterfly's wings. But it was enough. Maybe he missed a red light on his way, or someone detained him at work to tell him a funny story. The window closed. Kira's daughter was spared."

I stared at what I'd sketched. It was 2111 in the panel, the skies a little freer from pollution's darkness. Kira's hair fell softly around her shoulders as she hugged her daughter. Gone was the black suit of a vigilante. She wore a nurse's uniform now. Her job was to save lives, not end them.

Kira no longer remembered the Butterfly Project or even Ryder. The course of her life reset to the one she was always supposed to have, and Ryder was there to witness the moment. And he smiled to himself and walked away.

"How does it look?" I asked.

"It's perfect," he said. "You found her heart."

I lifted my hand to touch his chin, his jaw, his lips. "No, Beckett.

You did."

He leaned over and kissed me. Gently at first, then opening deeper. I kissed him with everything I had. Nothing held back. I felt his arms go around me, holding me, then moving to seek my bare skin, find warmth under the layers. We stripped off our clothes and created our own heat. Built our own defense against the chilling winter winds of black memories, our bodies touching and moving together. His strength made me safe. My arms around him dispelled his loneliness.

"I love you, Beckett," I whispered afterward, holding his body tight to mine, no space between us. "Only you. Always."

"Me too, baby." His mouth found mine in the dark, kissing and whispering his promise. "I'll never love anyone but you."

I'LL PICK YOU UP RIGHT HERE AT THREE, OKAY?
OKAY, MOMMY.

Epilogue

Zelda
December 25th one year later

I stood at the window of our new apartment in Brooklyn Heights. White walls still smelling of fresh paint. Hardwood floors, new appliances. We'd moved in three months ago, and I still wasn't used to the heat that flowed like a miracle from a central unit.

The Christmas lights came with us, of course. I strung them over the window that framed the East River and Manhattan beyond. On the wall next to the window hung an enlarged panel from *Mother, May I?* with a pop-out of text taken from *The Guardian:*

"A story of cause and effect. Of violence, vengeance and redemption, touched with shades of chaos theory. An unapologetic affirmation on the power of forgiveness."

We'd received tons of generous reviews—so many I sometimes had to remind myself this was my life, not a dream. But the review from *The Guardian* stood out. All it lacked was a reference to love.

In my mind, *Mother, May I?* had ultimately been about love. But wasn't love a kind of chaos theory? One small look, one smile or one word could alter the course of a life forever. Beckett and I were living proof.

Readers were clamoring for Ryder's story. In one corner of our spacious living area was a new desk, stylish lamp, and two chairs where we worked to bring *MMI? Volume II—Sins of the Father,* to life.

Beckett came up behind me, put his arms around my waist and kissed my neck.

"They're here. Are you ready?"

I picked up a small painting I had finished the day before. A complete contrast to the black-and-white of the graphic novel panels, a burst of yellow and red. I slipped it into my portfolio and shut off the overhead lights, leaving the string of white Christmas lights on. Fireflies dancing across the white walls in the dying afternoon light.

"Ready."

We put on our coats and hats, grabbed our rolling suitcases and headed downstairs. Roy and Mary Goodwin were waiting with a taxi van. Mrs. Santino was in the backseat, bundled in a musty-smelling faux fox coat. She wore it every week, when we took her out to dinner or a movie.

No more handshakes—Roy hugged his son, slapped his back and shoulders and ruffled his head. Mary took Beckett's face in her hands, kissed his cheeks, and nagged him affectionately to get a haircut.

One of these days I'd be able to watch this new little family without getting misty-eyed. For now, I blamed the wind and climbed into the van.

"How are you today, Mrs. Santino?" I asked in choppy Italian.

Mrs. Santino shrugged and rattled off a list of complaints—I caught something about achy joints, but most of it was too fast for me to decipher. She waved away my pathetic attempt at a reply, then took my hand and held it between hers. When Beckett climbed in, she burst out with more Italian, like a machine gun.

"Bel giovanotto, siediti accanto a me e dammi un bacio."

Beckett shot me a confused look.

This was easy to translate. I pointed to the other side of the woman. "You sit there, handsome, and give the lady a kiss."

He gave Mrs. Santino a peck, and she gushed more Italian. Beckett raised his brows but I only held up my hands, my smile ready to split my face.

The van took us to Penn Station for the two-hour train ride to Philadelphia, followed by another cab ride to my parents' house. Beckett gave my hand a squeeze as walked up the front steps.

"You okay?"

I smiled up at him. "Never better." It was a stock answer, but in this case, the absolute truth.

We congregated on the front steps, Beckett helping Mrs. Santino who clung to his arm. Mary looked nervous as she readjusted the pot of poinsettias in her arm, and Roy straightened his tie.

The door flung open.

"Sweetheart," Mom cried, laughing and enveloping me in a long, warm hug. Then she caught up Beckett for a hug and kiss. "Merry Christmas, honey."

"Merry Christmas, Mrs. Rossi," Beckett said. "I'd like you to meet my parents, Roy and Mary Goodwin."

The wind stung my eyes again. I used to never cry, afraid the pain would come flooding out. Now I cried at the damn drop of a hat. Pain could be suppressed, but happiness knew no such bonds. It came flooding out whether I wanted it to or not.

Might as well let it gush.

My entire family crowded the doorway and the front entry, absorbing the Goodwins into the house with hugs and handshakes. Mom made a fuss over the poinsettias, and Dad gaped at the label on the single-malt Scotch Roy offered.

"And this is Mrs. Santino," Beckett said, helping the little lady up the stairs.

My mother greeted her in Italian and Mrs. Santino responded with a string of words too fast for me to catch. But to Auntie Lucille and my grandmothers, it was the call of one of their own. They swooped in like chattering crows, and drew Mrs. Santino into their circle. More complaints about joints, the cold, and recipes trailed behind them as they went to the kitchen to make sure no one was messing up the sauce.

Christmas dinner that night was completely different than the one the year before. The absence of Rosemary in our lives didn't go unacknowledged, but we didn't shut her out either. We told stories and laughed, and a few tears were shed. I know that my parents—my mom especially—hadn't found any closure, but how could they ever? I watched my mother's smile ebb and flow as thoughts and memories tugged her in different directions, and she made a comment that she thought maybe it was time to redo the curtains.

When she excused herself to use the bathroom, I grabbed the portfolio that rested at my feet under the table. Beckett squeezed my hand and kissed me.

"Love you," he said.

"Love you back."

I waited for my mother in the hall outside the bathroom door. She came out dabbing her eyes, and smiled tremulously when she saw me.

"Holidays will never be easy," she said. "Only easier.

"I know."

My shaking hands opened the portfolio and withdrew the small painting of Rosemary and me. Little sisters bathed in gold light, holding balloons in our favorite colors. I'd made myself younger. A best friend for Rosemary, not just a sister.

Mom's hands shook too, as her eyes grazed over the little painting.

"It's how I think of her. Us. Together," I said. "And it helps. I was thinking maybe it would help you to think of her like this too."

Mom put a hand to her mouth. Above her fingers, her eyes filled with tears. "Zelda…"

"Merry Christmas, Mom."

She drew me to her and held me a long time. All the years I'd spent away from her arms, torn apart by guilt, were erased forever.

Dinner lasted two hours, with Grandma Stella's tiramisu as the finale. We traipsed into the living room, where a fire roared. Conversation, wine, and brandy flowed. I don't know if it was the heat of the fire, or the booze, but my face grew warmer and warmer, until I excused myself to get some air. I noticed Beckett was nowhere in sight. Neither was my father.

I went upstairs to the guestroom and stepped out to its little deck that overlooked the street.

The cold air felt good, snapping me out of my food coma. In a few minutes, the sliding glass door opened and Beckett came out to join me.

"Hey," he said, standing behind me and wrapping me in his arms.

"Hey, yourself. So beautiful out here, isn't it?"

The street was quiet, and yellow rectangles of warm light filled the windows on the townhouses opposite, colored light strung in garlands across their fronts. Above, the sky was black and backlit with stars.

"It is," Beckett said. "*You* are so beautiful."

He turned me to face him and kissed me.

"I just had a nice chat with your dad," he said.

"I wondered where you'd gotten off to," I said. "What did you talk about? Let me guess, football."

He shrugged, gazing over my shoulder. "This and that. Stuff. Life. The future."

I narrowed my eyes at him. "What's that look for?"

"What look?" His usual teasing tone had a nervous edge to it.

"You look like you have a secret."

"I'm an open book. Ask me anything."

"You might regret that, Goodwin," I said. "Where should I begin?"

"You could start by asking what's in my pocket."

"Sounds like the start of a dirty joke."

He shook his head. "In about eight seconds, you're going to feel so bad you said that, Rossi."

I laughed. "Oh yeah?"

His voice grew soft. "Yeah."

Beckett pulled from his coat pocket a small black velvet box and turned it over and over in his hand.

I heard a little sound escape me as a tingling spread across my chest. The cold, bracing air was nothing to the warmth that flooded me. "Beckett…"

"Don't say anything," he said. "If you say anything, I'm going to forget all the words I prepared, and something ridiculous like, 'Us marry, yes or no?' will pop out instead."

I clapped my hands over my mouth, stifling laughter or a sob, I didn't know which.

Beckett's rugged features softened, and he took my hand in his.

"Zelda," he began, and smiled in the most charmingly self-conscious way at how thick his voice sounded. He swallowed and tried again.

"Zelda, saying yes when you asked to live with me was the best decision I've made in my entire life. And I think about that a lot, how brave you were to ask. To try again after life knocked you down. And how you gave me a chance that night, to do the same. To try again, when I'd given up on myself."

"I'd given up too," I whispered. "I was lost in the dark without you, Beckett. You found me. You brought me home."

"You are my home, baby," he said. "I never want to be anywhere else."

Beckett kissed me fiercely, then opened the box. Inside was a white-gold ring with a square-shaped diamond. It was set between two small butterflies outlined in tiny beads of silver, with smaller diamonds in their wings.

Beckett sank to one knee, his voice trembling at the edges, and removed the ring from the box.

"You and me, Zel," he said hoarsely, slipping the ring on my finger. "What do you say? Will you marry me?"

In that instant, I saw the scene sketched out in black and white. The lonely busboy and the desperate girl with no place to go, sitting on a step in a cold alley, sharing a cigarette. I thought of the string of kindnesses that led to this moment, in this house full of love and joy. It began with Beckett saying yes to me, taking me in. It would end right here, with me saying yes as he asked me to be his wife.

I looked down into Beckett's deep blue eyes, bottomless in their love for me. Tears slipped out of mine that had nothing to do with the wind and everything to do with perfect happiness.

"Yes."

More From Emma Scott

Thank you for reading and if you'd like more information about upcoming releases, news, or just want to say hi, I'd love to connect with you!

Find me on Facebook at http://on.fb.me/1O70M7A

You can join my fan group (we'd love to have you!): http://bit.ly/2bp8nTI

Or follow me on Twitter @EmmaS_writes

Made in the USA
Las Vegas, NV
28 December 2020

14957937R00154